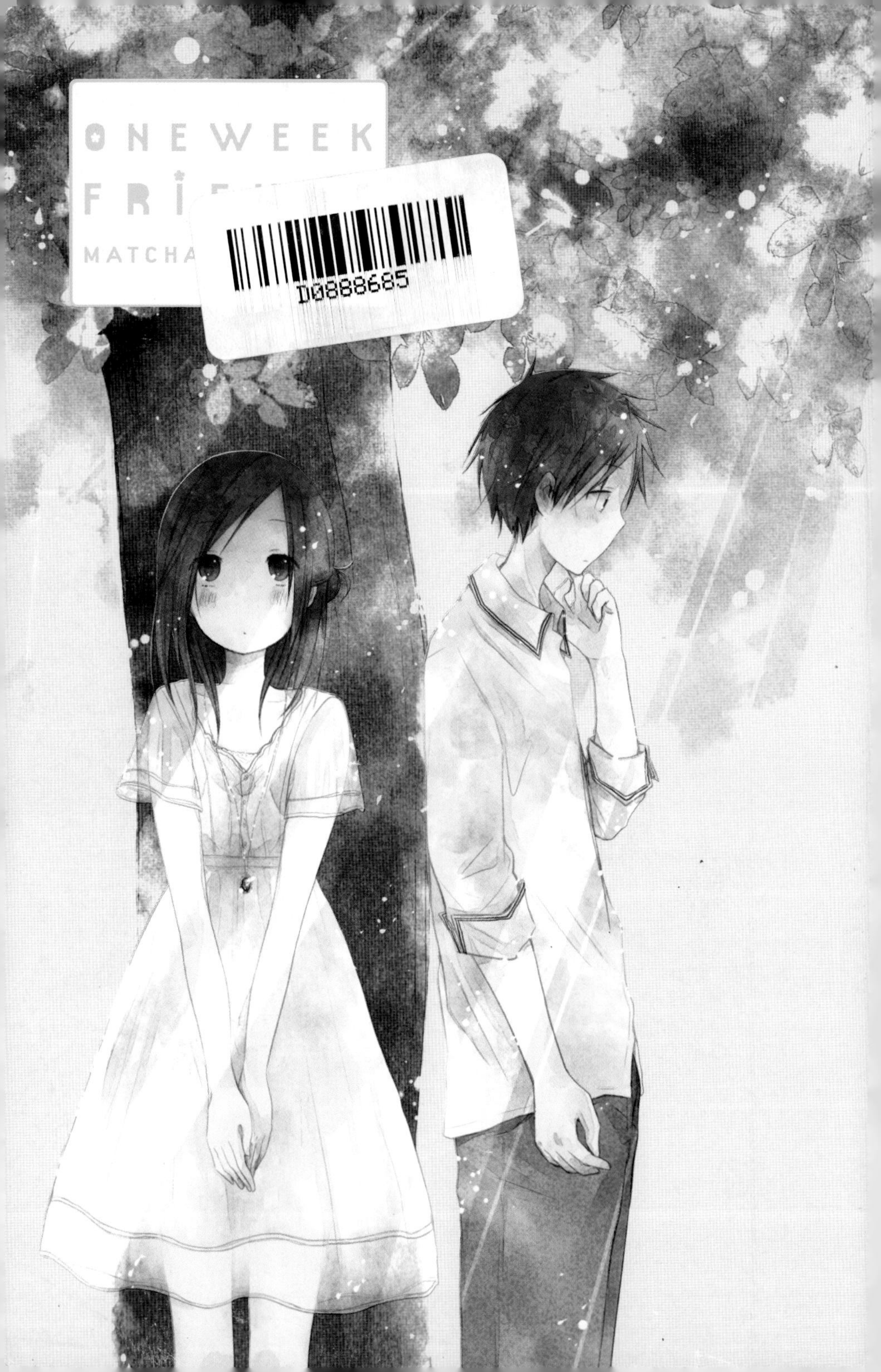
ONEWEEK
FRI
MATCHA

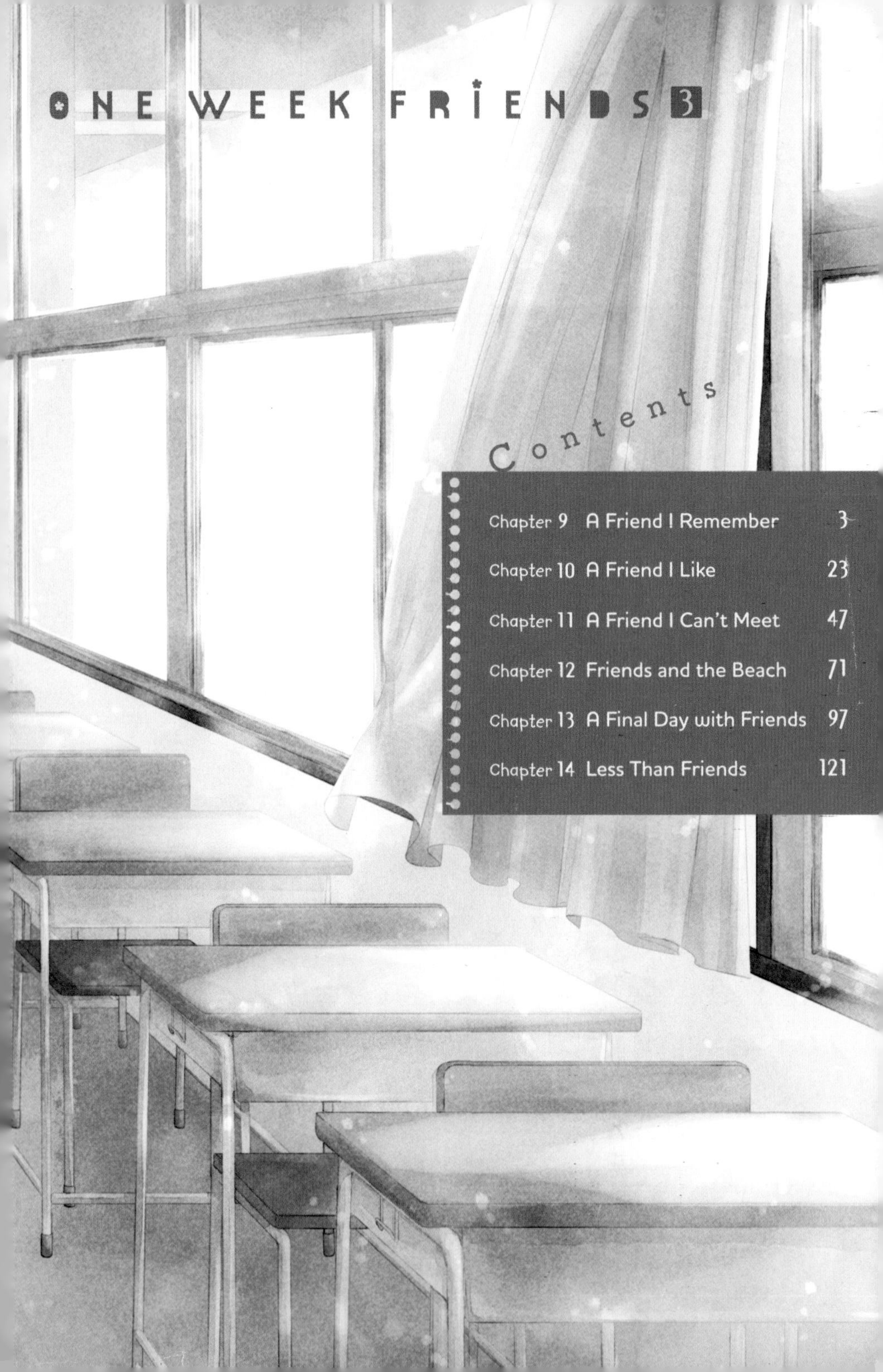

ONE WEEK FRIENDS 3

Contents

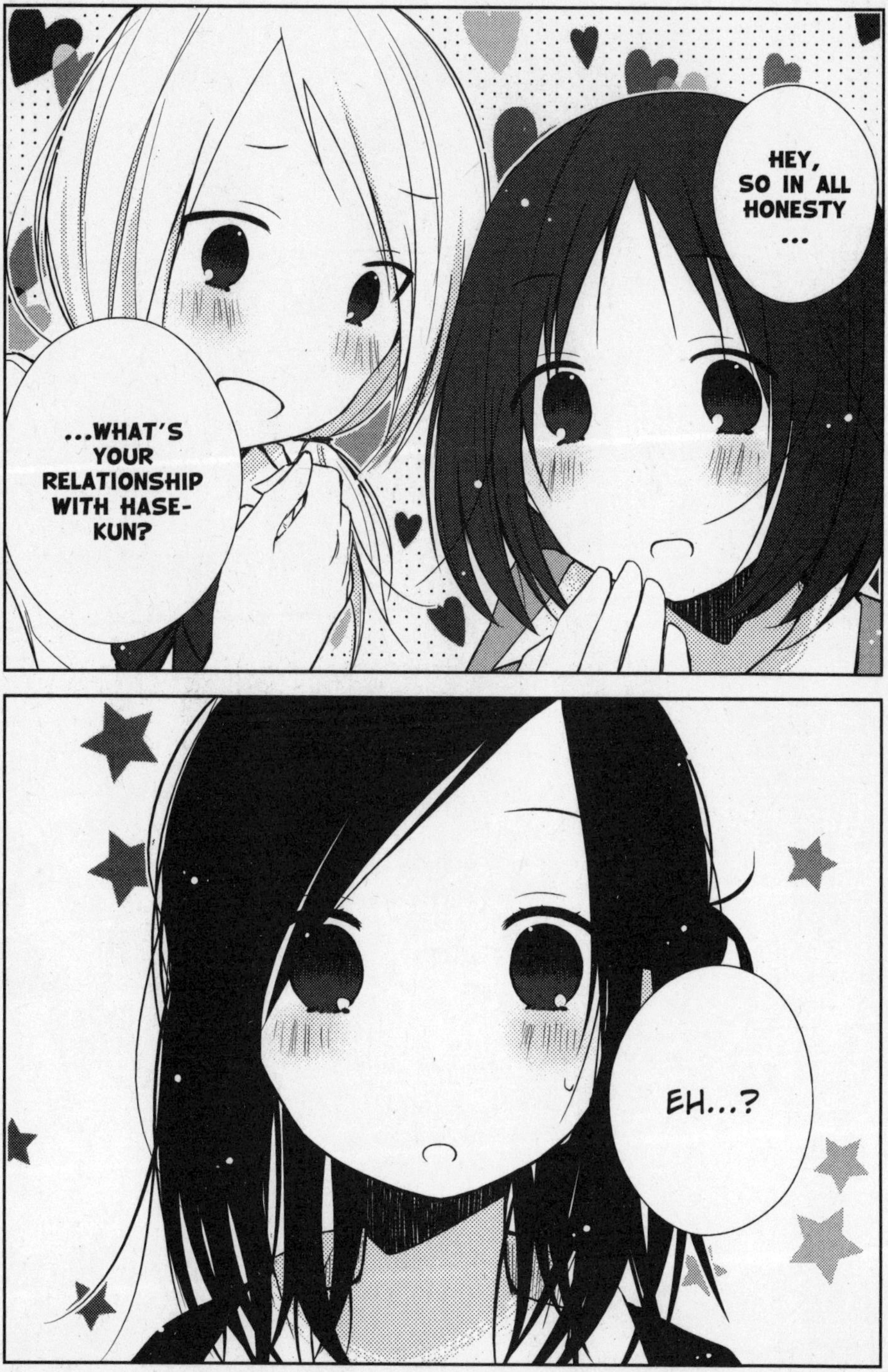
HEY, SO IN ALL HONESTY...
...WHAT'S YOUR RELATIONSHIP WITH HASE-KUN?
EH...?

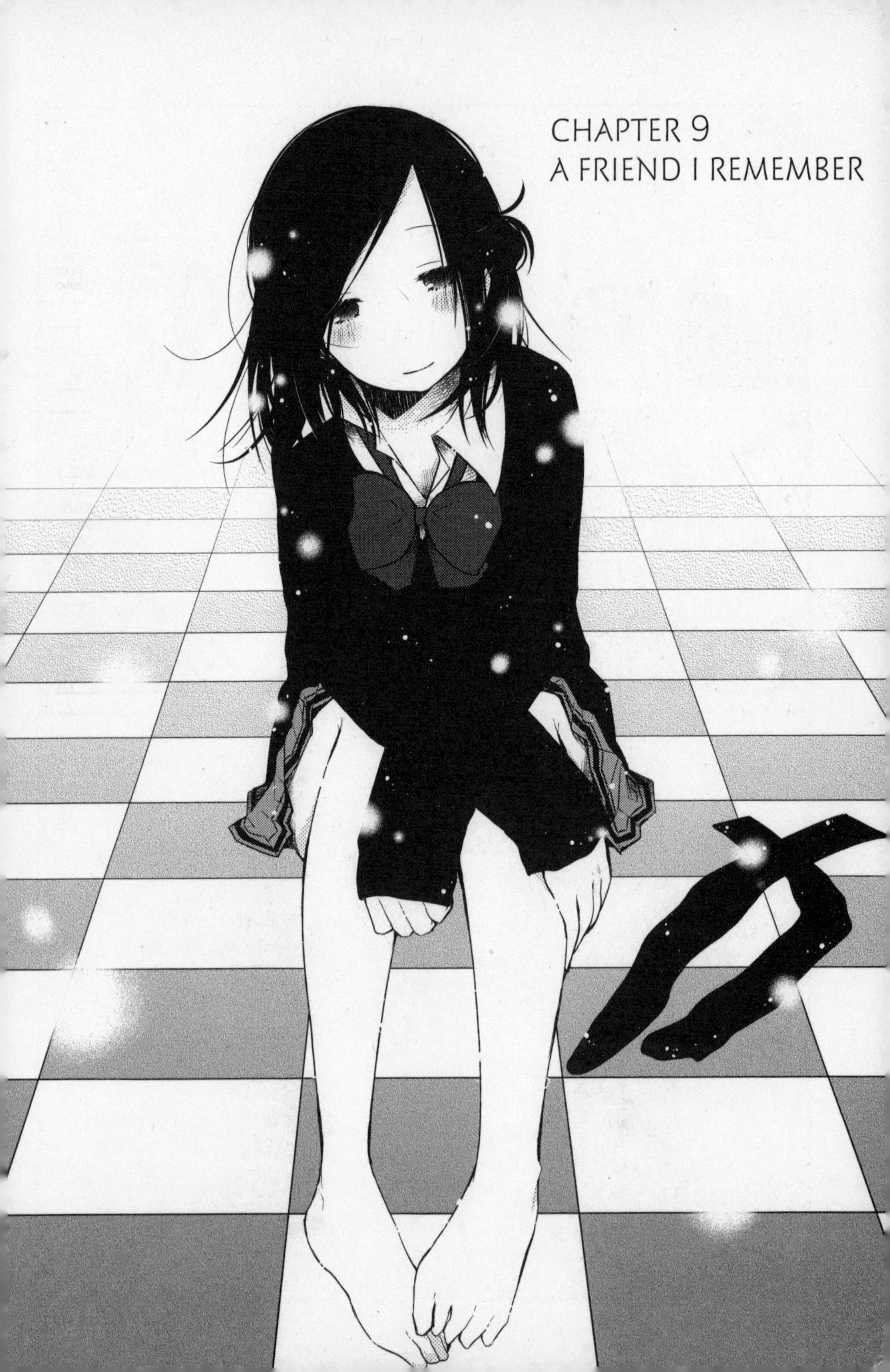
CHAPTER 9
A FRIEND I REMEMBER

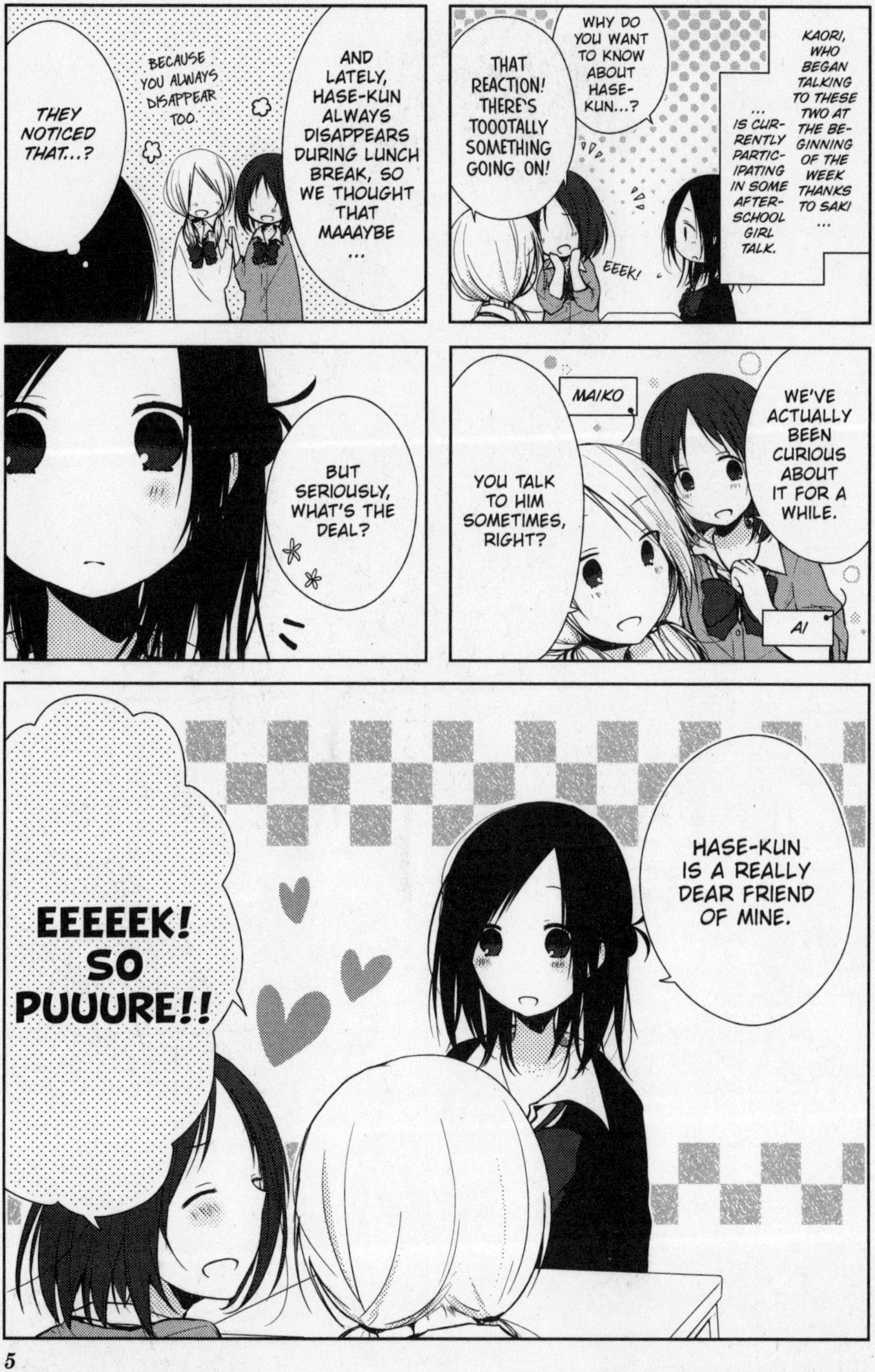
KAORI, WHO BEGAN TALKING TO THESE TWO AT THE BEGINNING OF THE WEEK THANKS TO SAKI ...
... IS CURRENTLY PARTICIPATING IN SOME AFTER-SCHOOL GIRL TALK.
WHY DO YOU WANT TO KNOW ABOUT HASE-KUN...?
THAT REACTION! THERE'S TOOOTALLY SOMETHING GOING ON!
EEEK!
AND LATELY, HASE-KUN ALWAYS DISAPPEARS DURING LUNCH BREAK, SO WE THOUGHT THAT MAAAYBE ...
BECAUSE YOU ALWAYS DISAPPEAR TOO.
THEY NOTICED THAT...?
WE'VE ACTUALLY BEEN CURIOUS ABOUT IT FOR A WHILE.
MAIKO
YOU TALK TO HIM SOMETIMES, RIGHT?
AI
BUT SERIOUSLY, WHAT'S THE DEAL?
HASE-KUN IS A REALLY DEAR FRIEND OF MINE.
EEEEEK! SO PUUURE!!

100% SINCERE

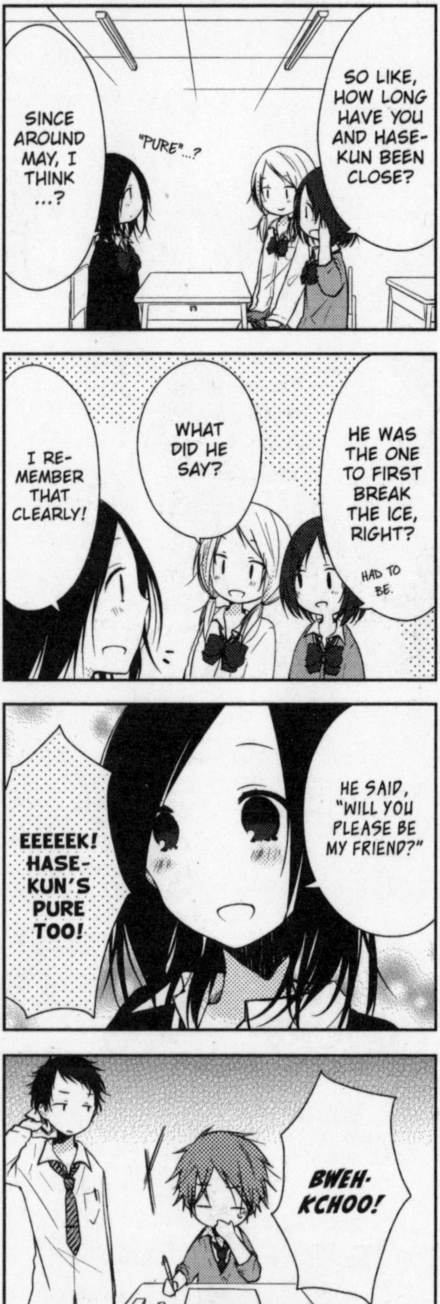

SO LIKE, HOW LONG HAVE YOU AND HASE-KUN BEEN CLOSE?
"PURE"...?
SINCE AROUND MAY, I THINK ...?
HE WAS THE ONE TO FIRST BREAK THE ICE, RIGHT?
HAD TO BE.
WHAT DID HE SAY?
I RE-MEMBER THAT CLEARLY!
HE SAID, "WILL YOU PLEASE BE MY FRIEND?"
EEEEEK! HASE-KUN'S PURE TOO!
BWEH-KCHOO!
TAKING A MAKEUP TEST IN ANOTHER ROOM

ALWAYS EARNEST

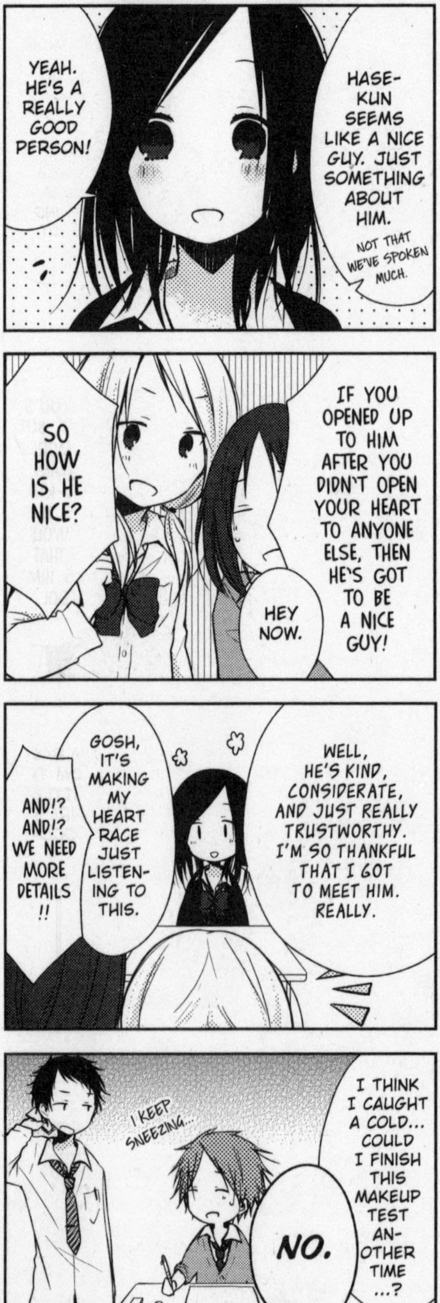

HASE-KUN SEEMS LIKE A NICE GUY. JUST SOMETHING ABOUT HIM.
NOT THAT WE'VE SPOKEN MUCH.
YEAH. HE'S A REALLY GOOD PERSON!
IF YOU OPENED UP TO HIM AFTER YOU DIDN'T OPEN YOUR HEART TO ANYONE ELSE, THEN HE'S GOT TO BE A NICE GUY!
HEY NOW.
SO HOW IS HE NICE?
WELL, HE'S KIND, CONSIDERATE, AND JUST REALLY TRUSTWORTHY. I'M SO THANKFUL THAT I GOT TO MEET HIM. REALLY.
GOSH, IT'S MAKING MY HEART RACE JUST LISTEN-ING TO THIS.
AND!? AND!? WE NEED MORE DETAILS !!
I THINK I CAUGHT A COLD... COULD I FINISH THIS MAKEUP TEST AN-OTHER TIME ...?
I KEEP SNEEZING...
NO.

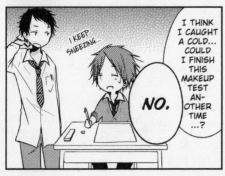

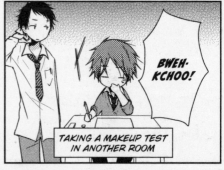

TOPIC: KIRYUU-KUN

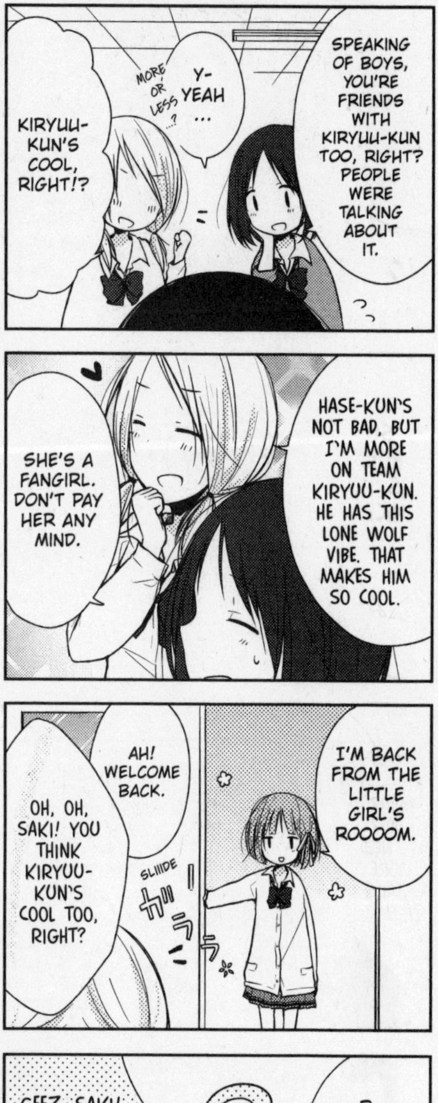
SPEAKING OF BOYS, YOU'RE FRIENDS WITH KIRYUU-KUN TOO, RIGHT? PEOPLE WERE TALKING ABOUT IT.
Y-YEAH ...
MORE OR LESS ...?
KIRYUU-KUN'S COOL, RIGHT!?
HASE-KUN'S NOT BAD, BUT I'M MORE ON TEAM KIRYUU-KUN. HE HAS THIS LONE WOLF VIBE. THAT MAKES HIM SO COOL.
SHE'S A FANGIRL. DON'T PAY HER ANY MIND.
I'M BACK FROM THE LITTLE GIRL'S ROOOOM.
AH! WELCOME BACK.
SLIIIDE
OH, OH, SAKI! YOU THINK KIRYUU-KUN'S COOL TOO, RIGHT?
? WHO'S THAT AGAIN? ONE OF THE TWO BOYS?
GEEZ, SAKI! YOU'RE SO CUTE, YOU LITTLE MISS FORGETFUL!

FRIENDS

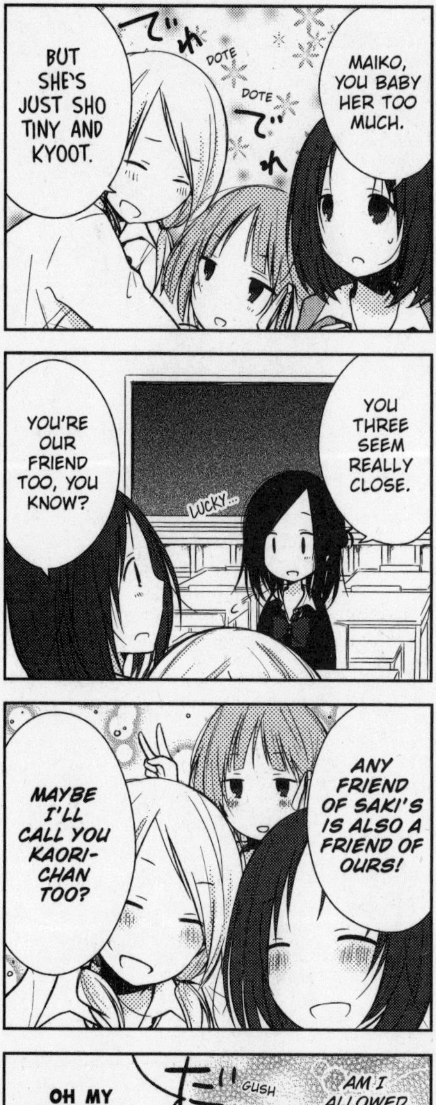
MAIKO, YOU BABY HER TOO MUCH.
DOTE
DOTE
BUT SHE'S JUST SHO TINY AND KYOOT.
YOU THREE SEEM REALLY CLOSE.
LUCKY...
YOU'RE OUR FRIEND TOO, YOU KNOW?
ANY FRIEND OF SAKI'S IS ALSO A FRIEND OF OURS!
MAYBE I'LL CALL YOU KAORI-CHAN TOO?
AM I ALLOWED TO BE THIS HAPPY...?
GUSH
OH MY GOD, SHE'S CRYING! SHE'S SO CUTE I COULD HAVE A HEART ATTACK!
HEY NOW.

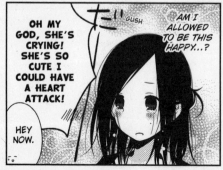

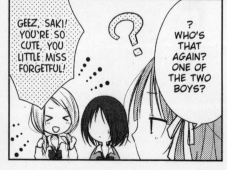

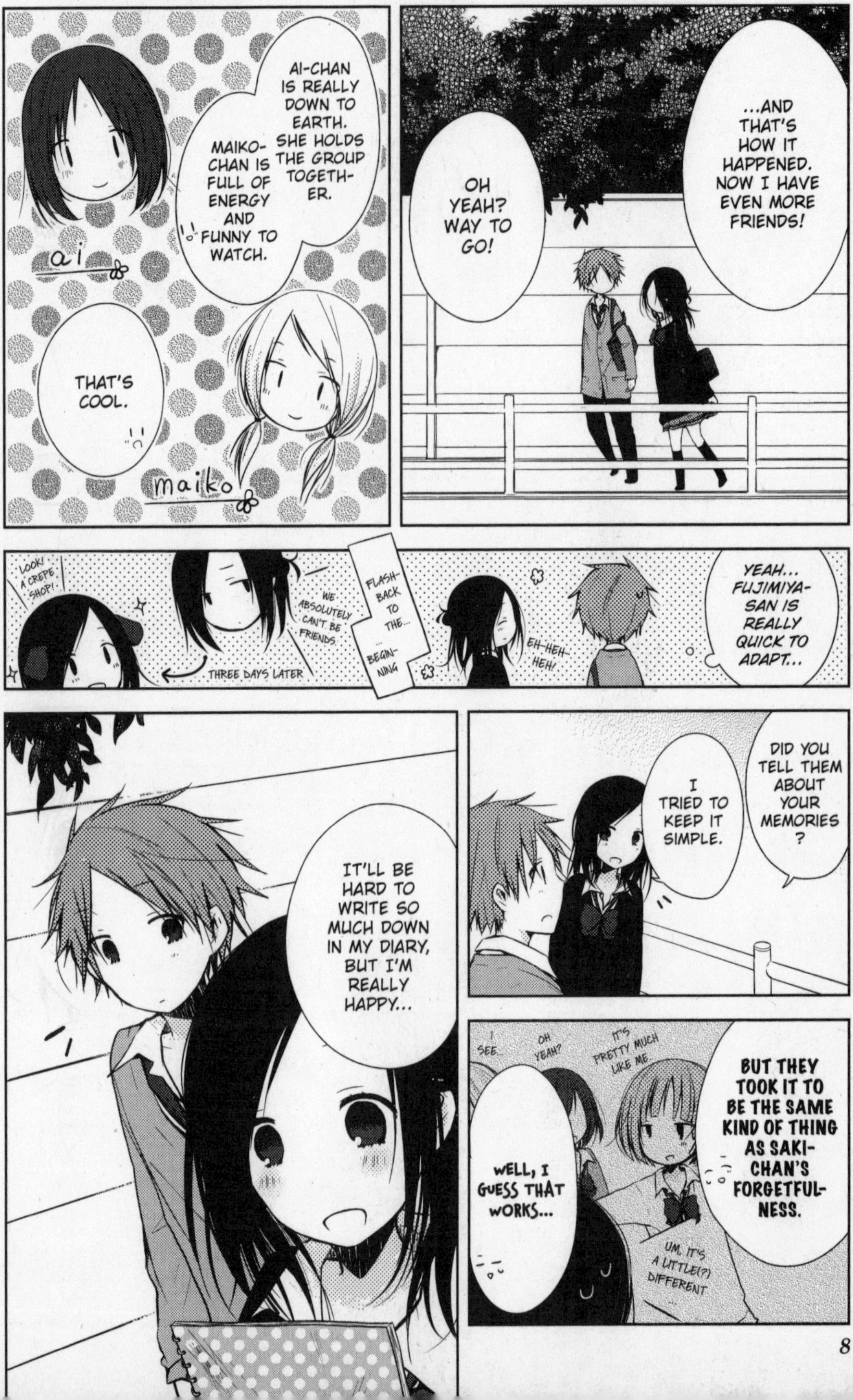
...AND THAT'S HOW IT HAPPENED. NOW I HAVE EVEN MORE FRIENDS!
OH YEAH? WAY TO GO!
AI-CHAN IS REALLY DOWN TO EARTH. SHE HOLDS THE GROUP TOGETHER.
MAIKO-CHAN IS FULL OF ENERGY AND FUNNY TO WATCH.
ai
THAT'S COOL.
maiko
YEAH... FUJIMIYA-SAN IS REALLY QUICK TO ADAPT...
EH-HEH-HEH!
FLASHBACK TO THE... BEGINNING
WE ABSOLUTELY CAN'T BE FRIENDS.
THREE DAYS LATER
LOOK! A CREPE SHOP!
DID YOU TELL THEM ABOUT YOUR MEMORIES?
I TRIED TO KEEP IT SIMPLE.
BUT THEY TOOK IT TO BE THE SAME KIND OF THING AS SAKI-CHAN'S FORGETFULNESS.
IT'S PRETTY MUCH LIKE ME
OH YEAH?
I SEE...
WELL, I GUESS THAT WORKS...
UM, IT'S A LITTLE(?) DIFFERENT
IT'LL BE HARD TO WRITE SO MUCH DOWN IN MY DIARY, BUT I'M REALLY HAPPY...

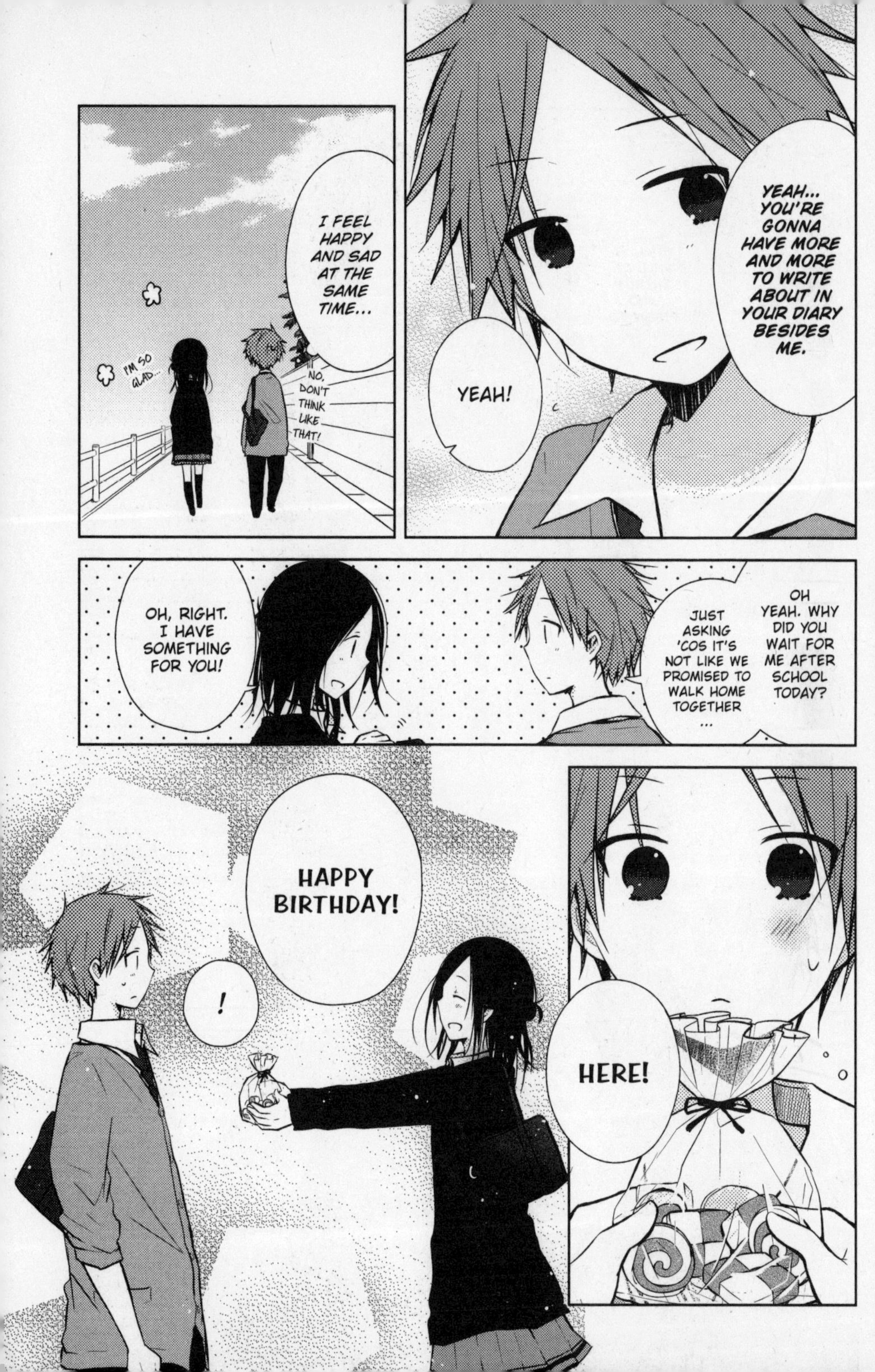
YEAH... YOU'RE GONNA HAVE MORE AND MORE TO WRITE ABOUT IN YOUR DIARY BESIDES ME.
YEAH!
I FEEL HAPPY AND SAD AT THE SAME TIME...
NO, DON'T THINK LIKE THAT!
I'M SO GLAD...
OH YEAH. WHY DID YOU WAIT FOR ME AFTER SCHOOL TODAY?
JUST ASKING 'COS IT'S NOT LIKE WE PROMISED TO WALK HOME TOGETHER ...
OH, RIGHT. I HAVE SOMETHING FOR YOU!
HERE!
HAPPY BIRTHDAY!
!

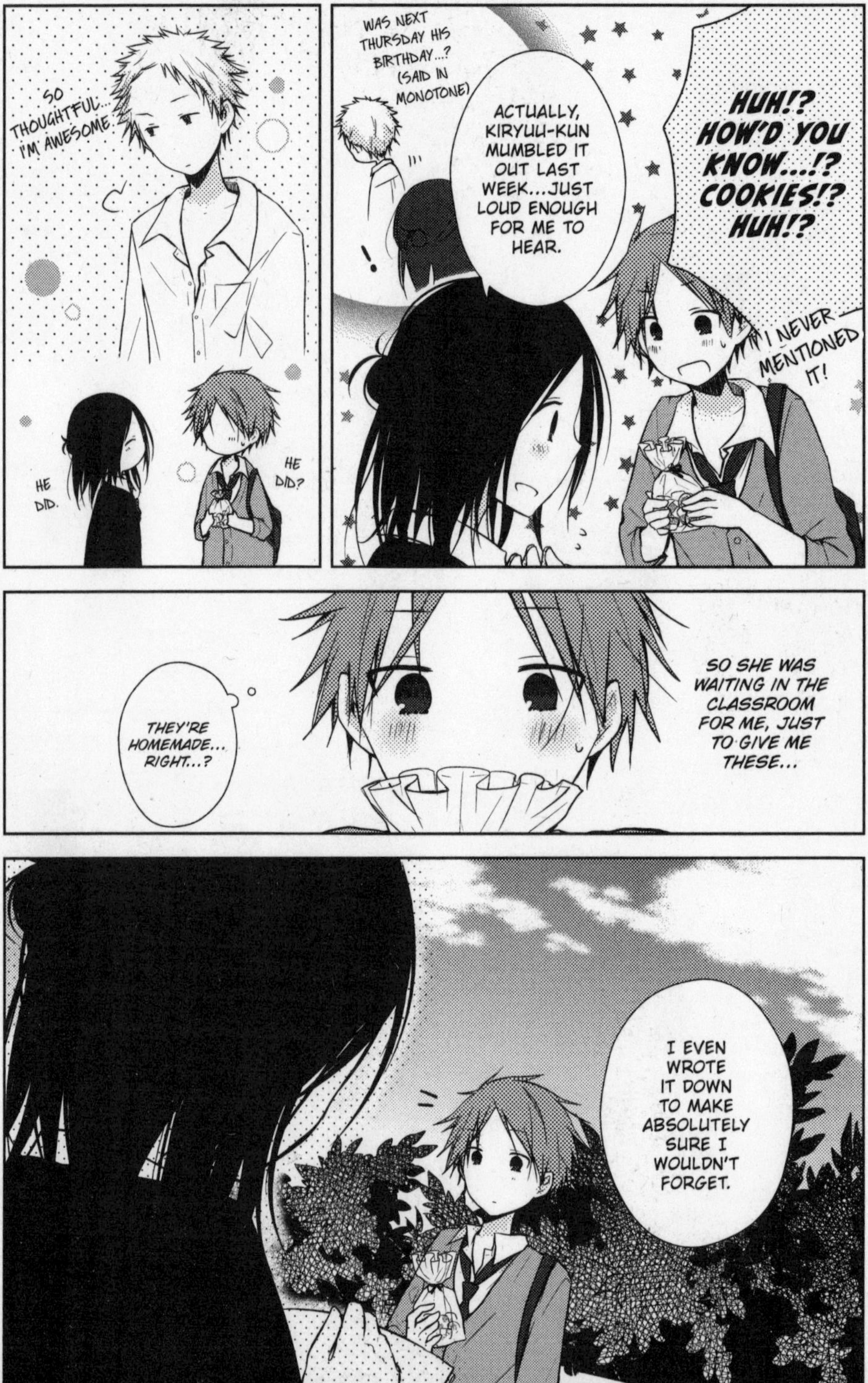
HUH!? HOW'D YOU KNOW...!? COOKIES!? HUH!?
I NEVER MENTIONED IT!
ACTUALLY, KIRYUU-KUN MUMBLED IT OUT LAST WEEK...JUST LOUD ENOUGH FOR ME TO HEAR.
WAS NEXT THURSDAY HIS BIRTHDAY...? (SAID IN MONOTONE)
SO THOUGHTFUL... I'M AWESOME.
HE DID?
HE DID.
SO SHE WAS WAITING IN THE CLASSROOM FOR ME, JUST TO GIVE ME THESE...
THEY'RE HOMEMADE... RIGHT...?
I EVEN WROTE IT DOWN TO MAKE ABSOLUTELY SURE I WOULDN'T FORGET.

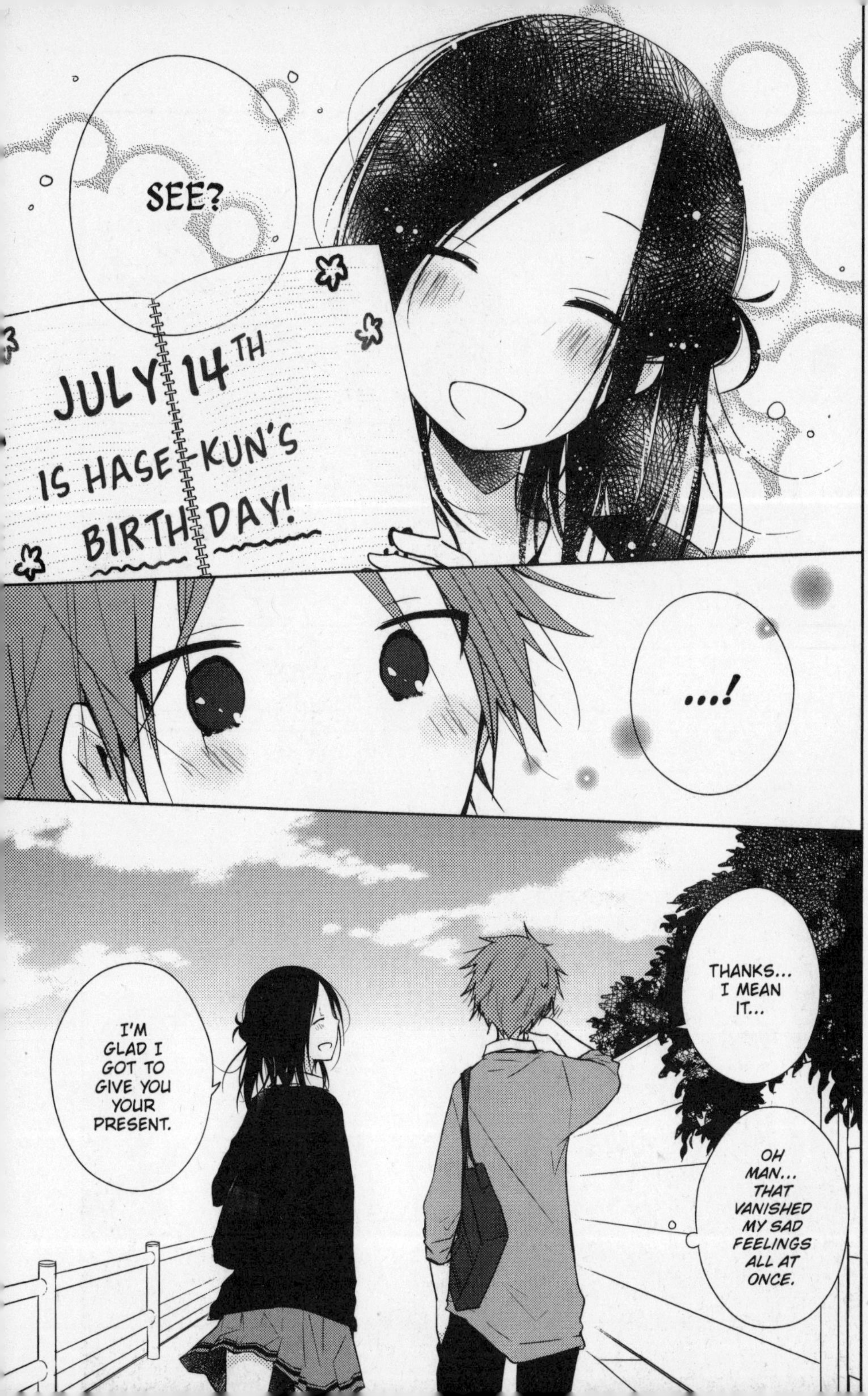
SEE?
JULY 14TH IS HASE-KUN'S BIRTHDAY!
...!
THANKS... I MEAN IT...
OH MAN... THAT VANISHED MY SAD FEELINGS ALL AT ONCE.
I'M GLAD I GOT TO GIVE YOU YOUR PRESENT.

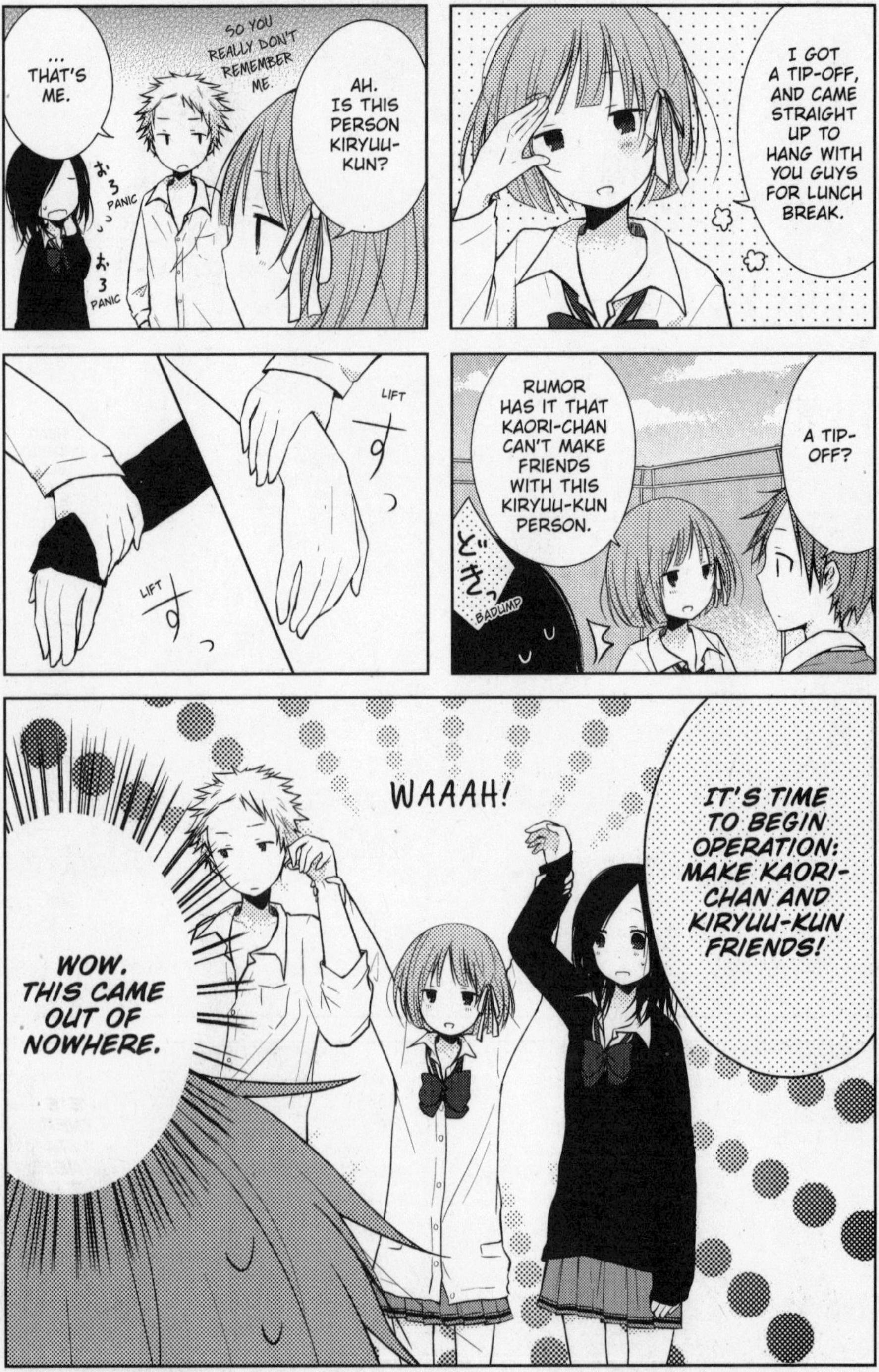
I GOT A TIP-OFF, AND CAME STRAIGHT UP TO HANG WITH YOU GUYS FOR LUNCH BREAK.
AH. IS THIS PERSON KIRYUU-KUN?
SO YOU REALLY DON'T REMEMBER ME.
... THAT'S ME.
おろ PANIC
おろ PANIC
A TIP-OFF?
RUMOR HAS IT THAT KAORI-CHAN CAN'T MAKE FRIENDS WITH THIS KIRYUU-KUN PERSON.
どきっ BADUMP
すっ LIFT
すっ LIFT
IT'S TIME TO BEGIN OPERATION: MAKE KAORI-CHAN AND KIRYUU-KUN FRIENDS!
WAAAH!
WOW. THIS CAME OUT OF NOWHERE.

POINT-BLANK

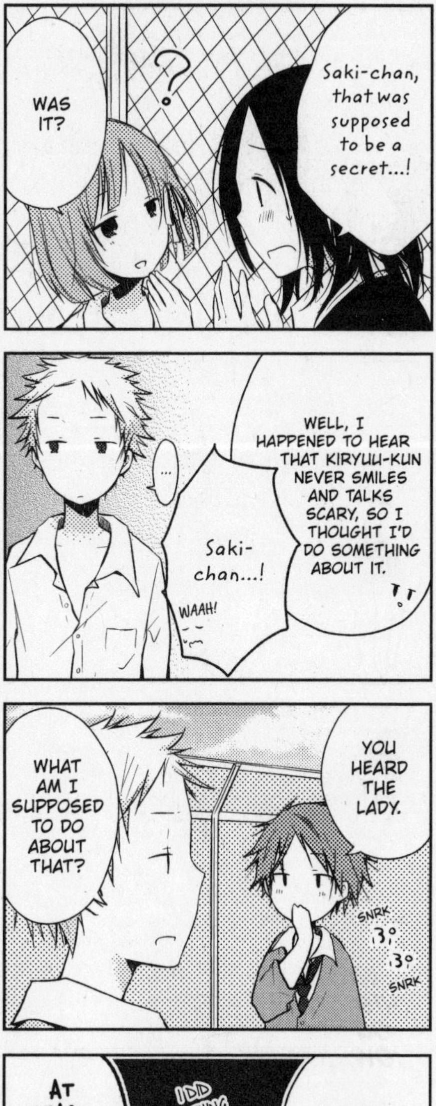

Saki-chan, that was supposed to be a secret...!
?
WAS IT?
WELL, I HAPPENED TO HEAR THAT KIRYUU-KUN NEVER SMILES AND TALKS SCARY, SO I THOUGHT I'D DO SOMETHING ABOUT IT.
Saki-chan...!
WAAH!
...
YOU HEARD THE LADY.
SNRK
SNRK
WHAT AM I SUPPOSED TO DO ABOUT THAT?
SHE'S EITHER GOTTA GET USED TO IT OR GIVE UP, RIGHT?
I DID NOTHING WRONG.
AT LEAST TRY TO MEET HER IN THE MIDDLE, MAN.

LET'S LAUGH

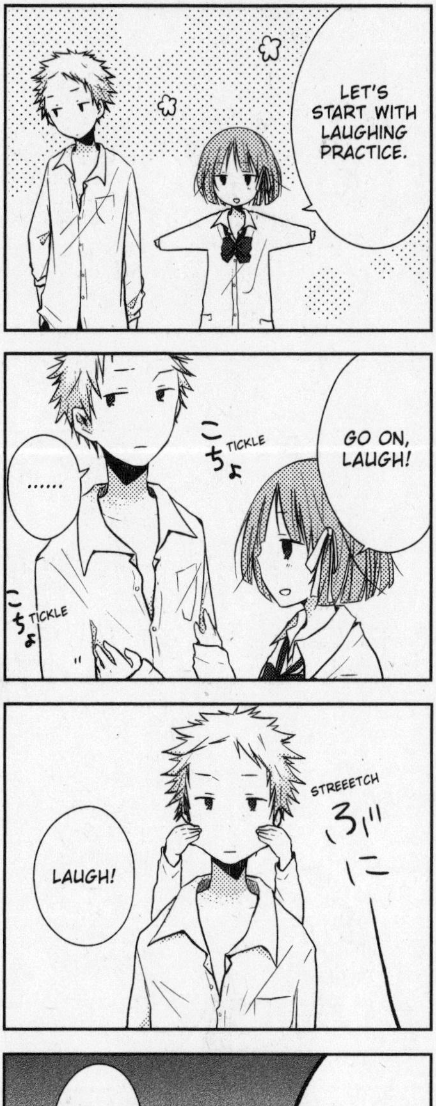

LET'S START WITH LAUGHING PRACTICE.
GO ON, LAUGH!
こちょ TICKLE
......
こちょ TICKLE
STREEETCH
LAUGH!
STOP LAUGHING.
SORRY ...

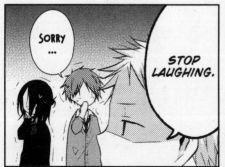

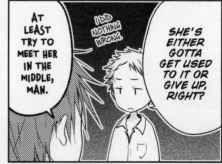

ABOUT THE PAST

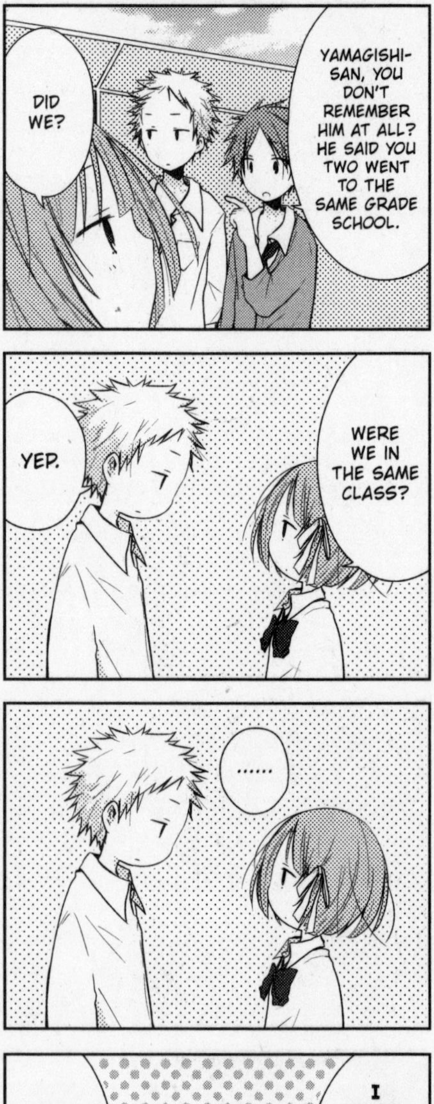
YAMAGISHI-SAN, YOU DON'T REMEMBER HIM AT ALL? HE SAID YOU TWO WENT TO THE SAME GRADE SCHOOL.
DID WE?
WERE WE IN THE SAME CLASS?
YEP.
......
I BELIEVE IN ONLY REMEMBERING FUN AND HAPPY THINGS.
OOPSIES!
HARD TO PLAY THE STRAIGHT MAN WITH A FUNNY MAN LIKE THIS...

IRRITATED

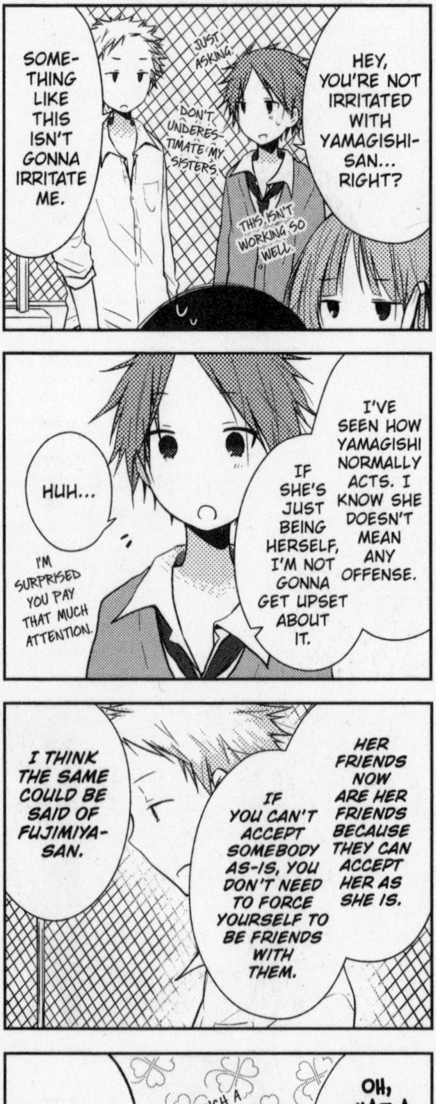
HEY, YOU'RE NOT IRRITATED WITH YAMAGISHI-SAN... RIGHT?
JUST ASKING.
SOMETHING LIKE THIS ISN'T GONNA IRRITATE ME.
DON'T UNDERESTIMATE MY SISTERS.
THIS ISN'T WORKING SO WELL.
I'VE SEEN HOW YAMAGISHI NORMALLY ACTS. I KNOW SHE DOESN'T MEAN ANY OFFENSE.
IF SHE'S JUST BEING HERSELF, I'M NOT GONNA GET UPSET ABOUT IT.
HUH...
I'M SURPRISED YOU PAY THAT MUCH ATTENTION.
HER FRIENDS NOW ARE HER FRIENDS BECAUSE THEY CAN ACCEPT HER AS SHE IS.
IF YOU CAN'T ACCEPT SOMEBODY AS-IS, YOU DON'T NEED TO FORCE YOURSELF TO BE FRIENDS WITH THEM.
I THINK THE SAME COULD BE SAID OF FUJIMIYA-SAN.
OH, WHAT A SMART LITTLE BOY YOU ARE...
SUCH A GOOD HEAD ON YOUR SHOULDERS.
YOU. YOU IRRITATE ME.
DON'T GET CARRIED AWAY.

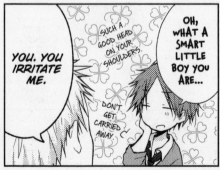

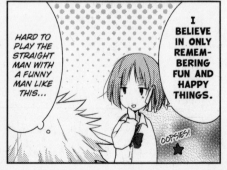

BREAK THROUGH BY FORCE

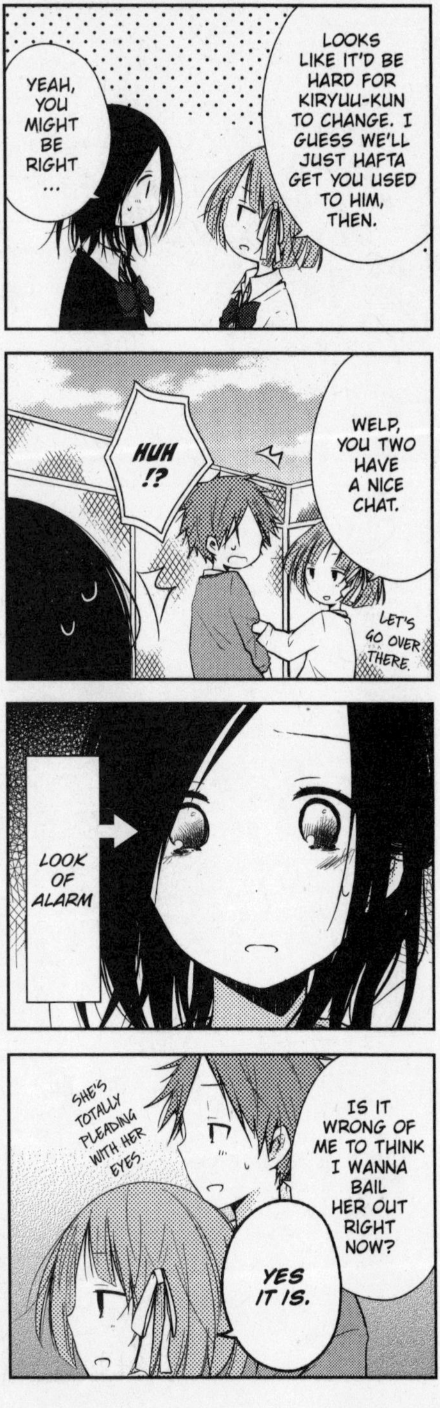

LOOKS LIKE IT'D BE HARD FOR KIRYUU-KUN TO CHANGE. I GUESS WE'LL JUST HAFTA GET YOU USED TO HIM, THEN.
YEAH, YOU MIGHT BE RIGHT …
WELP, YOU TWO HAVE A NICE CHAT.
LET'S GO OVER THERE.
HUH !?
LOOK OF ALARM
IS IT WRONG OF ME TO THINK I WANNA BAIL HER OUT RIGHT NOW?
SHE'S TOTALLY PLEADING WITH HER EYES.
YES IT IS.

SHE'S TRYING, AND YET...

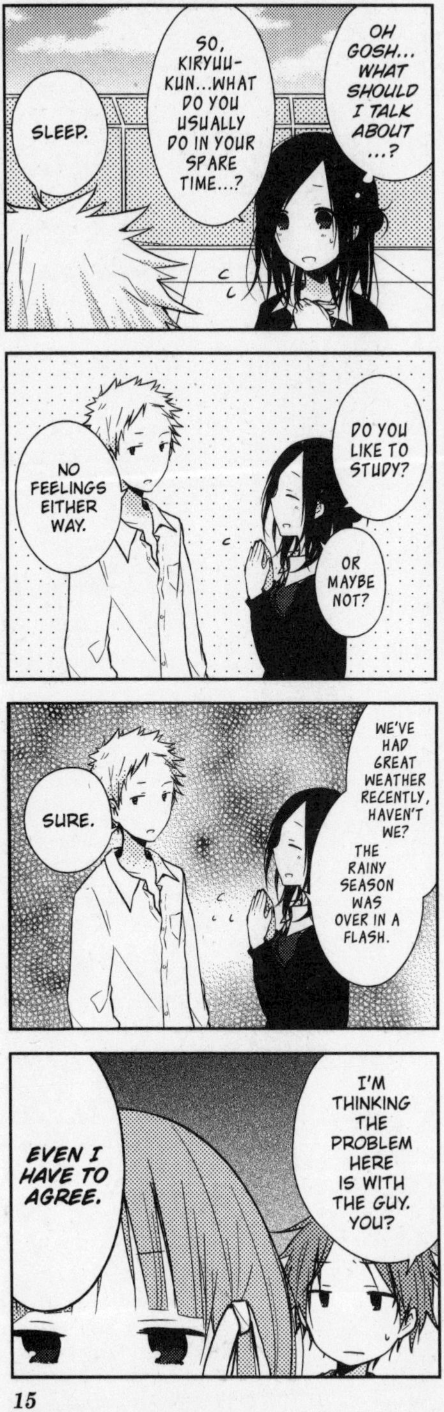

OH GOSH… WHAT SHOULD I TALK ABOUT …?
SO, KIRYUU-KUN…WHAT DO YOU USUALLY DO IN YOUR SPARE TIME…?
SLEEP.
DO YOU LIKE TO STUDY?
OR MAYBE NOT?
NO FEELINGS EITHER WAY.
WE'VE HAD GREAT WEATHER RECENTLY, HAVEN'T WE? THE RAINY SEASON WAS OVER IN A FLASH.
SURE.
I'M THINKING THE PROBLEM HERE IS WITH THE GUY. YOU?
EVEN I HAVE TO AGREE.

I'M CALLING OFF OPERATION: MAKE KAORI-CHAN AND KIRYUU-KUN FRIENDS!

I DON'T THINK YOU NEED TO BE FRIENDS!

BUT...!

I THINK THE REASON YOU ONLY REMEMBER HIM IS BECAUSE YOU TWO ARE JUST THAT INCOMPATIBLE!

ALSO, KIRYUU-KUN, YOU'RE BAD!

AM I THAT BAD...?

THAT'S PRETTY HARSH...

BUT YOU KNOW, I...

I FELT SO BAD WATCHING YOUUU. I DON'T THINK YOU NEED TO TRY SO HARRRD.

SAKI-CHAN...

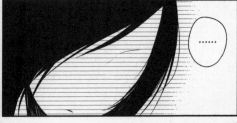

......

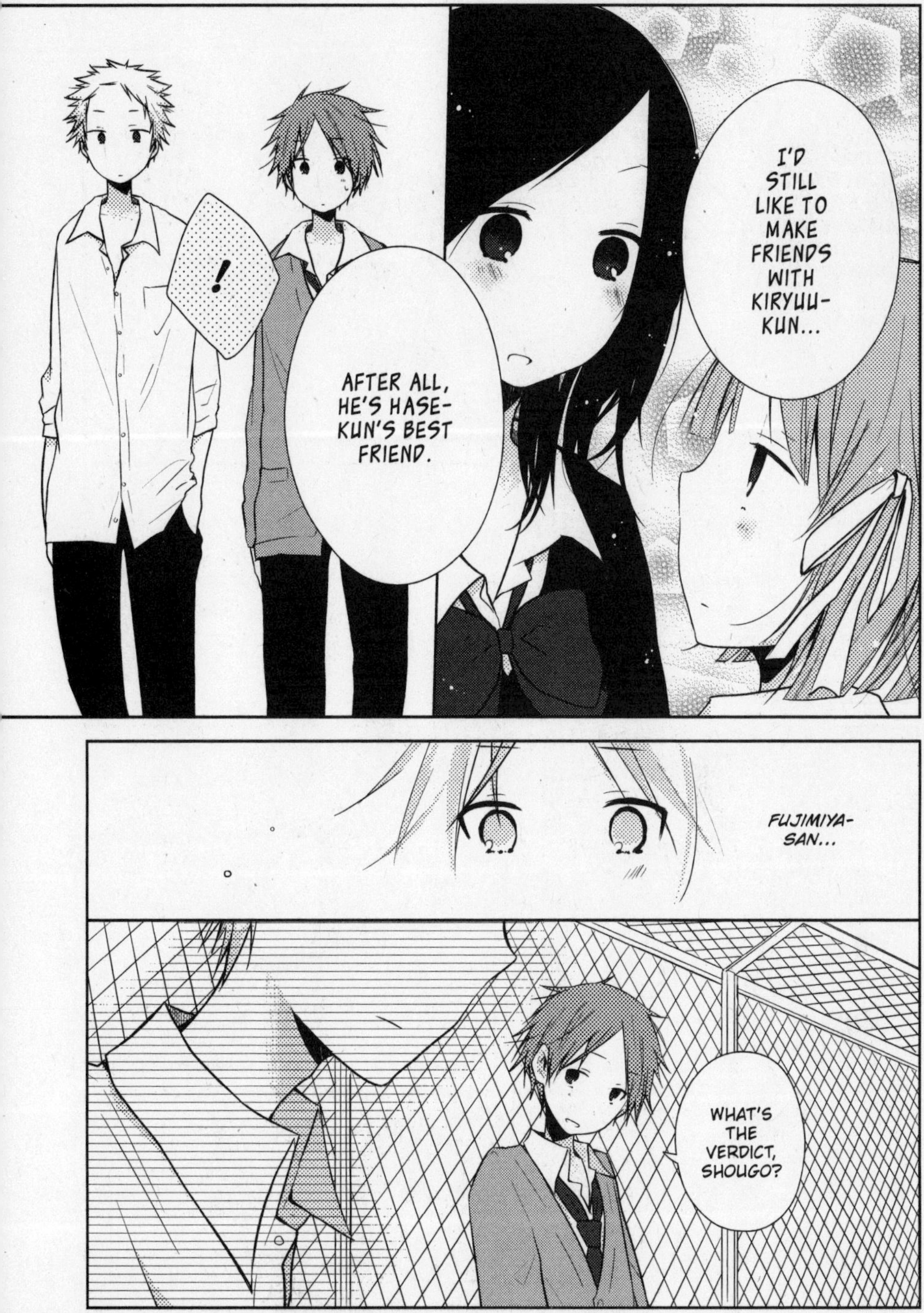
I'D STILL LIKE TO MAKE FRIENDS WITH KIRYUU-KUN...
AFTER ALL, HE'S HASE-KUN'S BEST FRIEND.
!
FUJIMIYA-SAN...
WHAT'S THE VERDICT, SHOUGO?

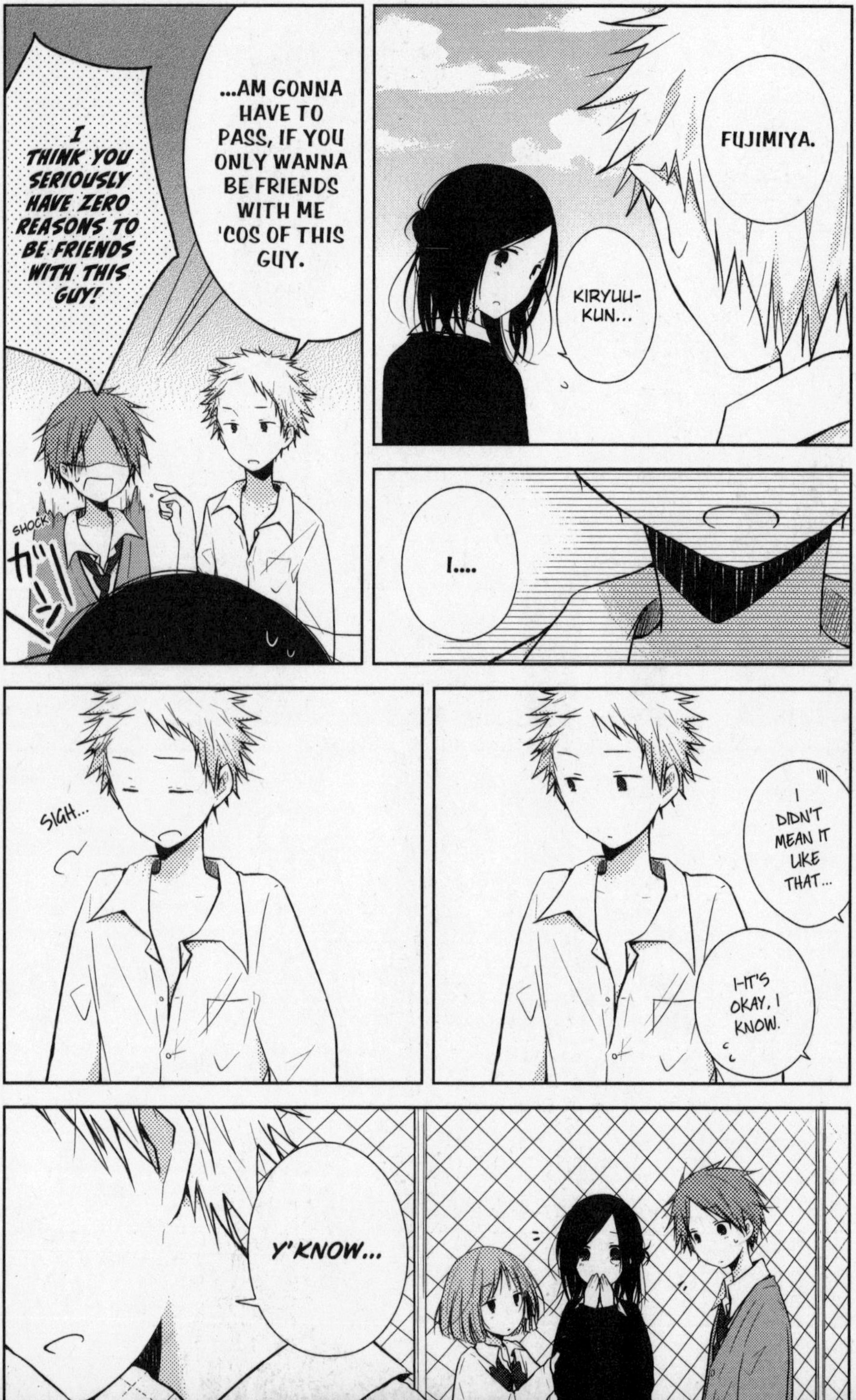
FUJIMIYA.
KIRYUU-KUN...
I....
...AM GONNA HAVE TO PASS, IF YOU ONLY WANNA BE FRIENDS WITH ME 'COS OF THIS GUY.
I THINK YOU SERIOUSLY HAVE ZERO REASONS TO BE FRIENDS WITH THIS GUY!
SHOCK
ガーン
I DIDN'T MEAN IT LIKE THAT...
I-IT'S OKAY, I KNOW.
SIGH...
Y'KNOW...

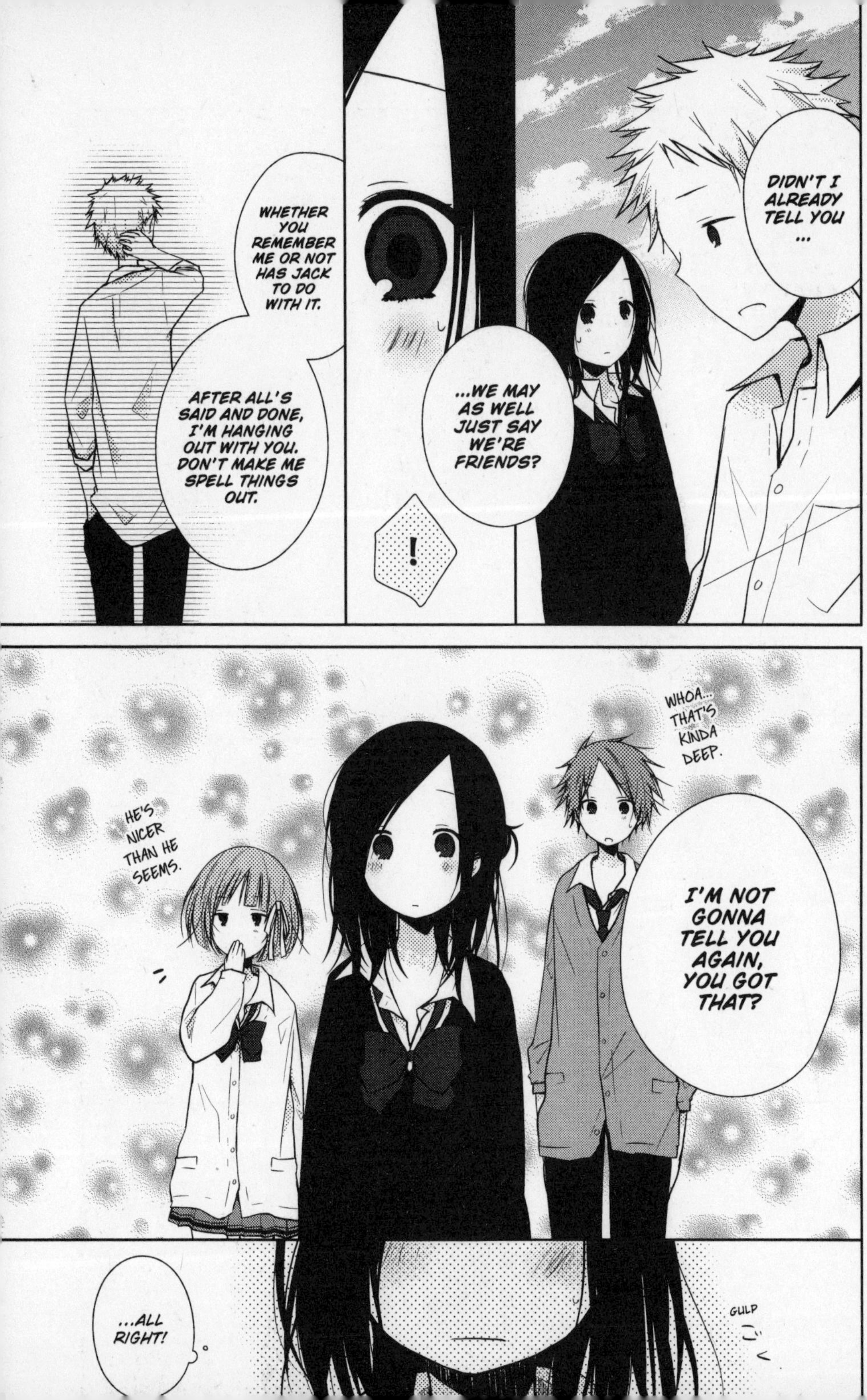
DIDN'T I ALREADY TELL YOU ...
...WE MAY AS WELL JUST SAY WE'RE FRIENDS?
!
WHETHER YOU REMEMBER ME OR NOT HAS JACK TO DO WITH IT.
AFTER ALL'S SAID AND DONE, I'M HANGING OUT WITH YOU. DON'T MAKE ME SPELL THINGS OUT.
I'M NOT GONNA TELL YOU AGAIN, YOU GOT THAT?
WHOA... THAT'S KINDA DEEP.
HE'S NICER THAN HE SEEMS.
GULP
...ALL RIGHT!

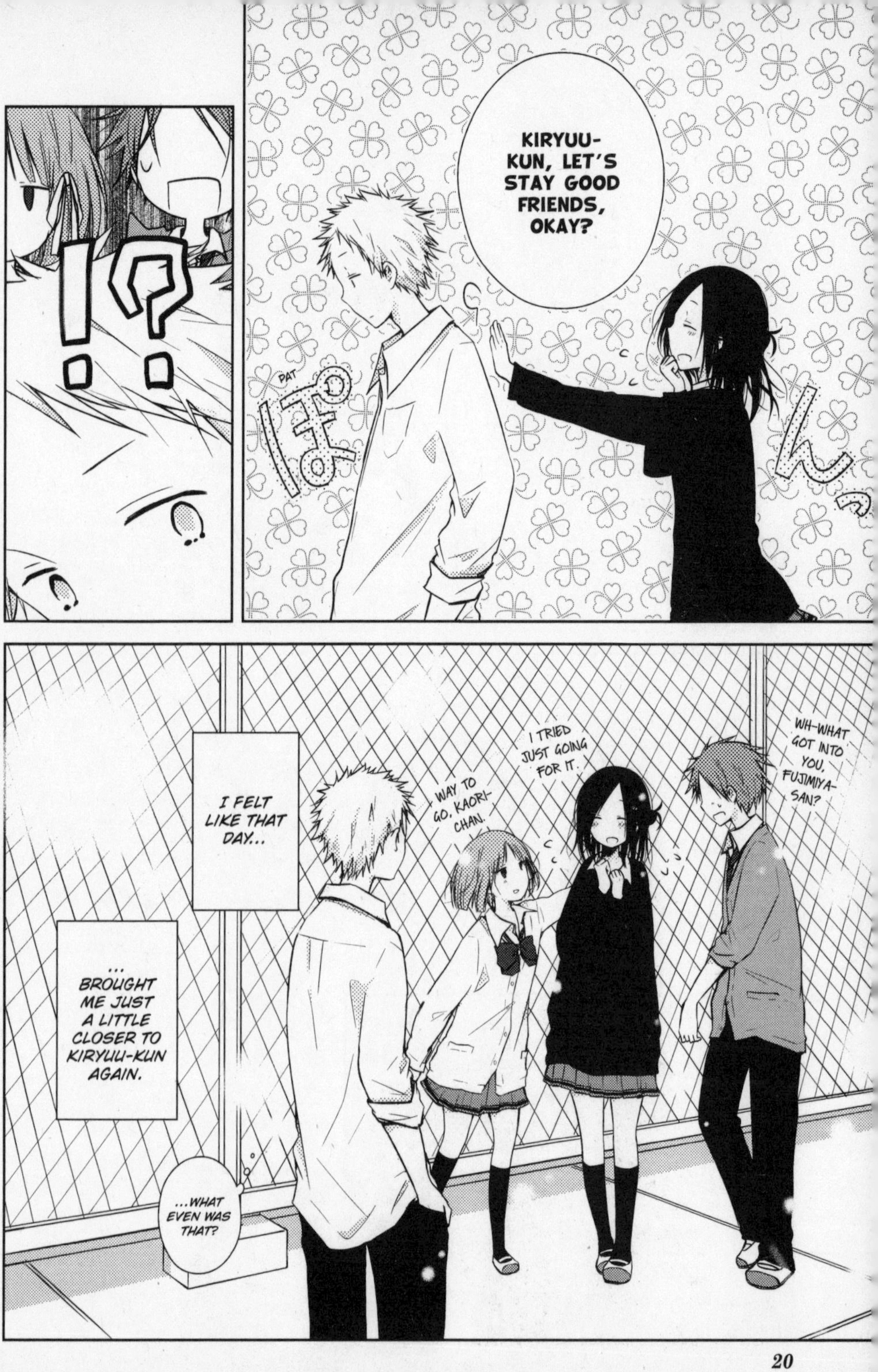
PAT
KIRYUU-KUN, LET'S STAY GOOD FRIENDS, OKAY?
!?
WH-WHAT GOT INTO YOU, FUJIMIYA-SAN?
I TRIED JUST GOING FOR IT.
WAY TO GO, KAORI-CHAN.
I FELT LIKE THAT DAY...
...BROUGHT ME JUST A LITTLE CLOSER TO KIRYUU-KUN AGAIN.
...WHAT EVEN WAS THAT?

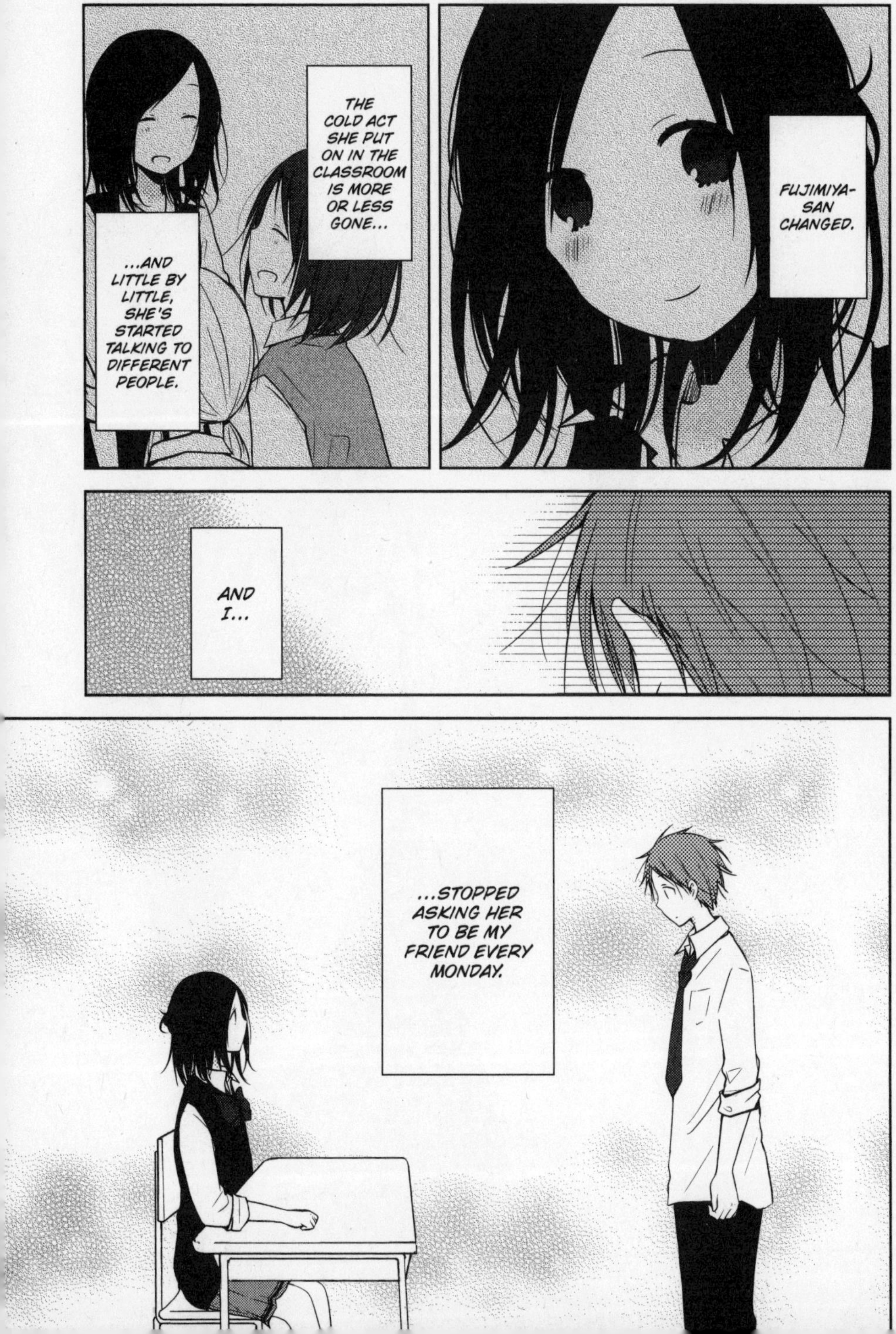
FUJIMIYA-SAN CHANGED.
THE COLD ACT SHE PUT ON IN THE CLASSROOM IS MORE OR LESS GONE...
...AND LITTLE BY LITTLE, SHE'S STARTED TALKING TO DIFFERENT PEOPLE.
AND I...
...STOPPED ASKING HER TO BE MY FRIEND EVERY MONDAY.

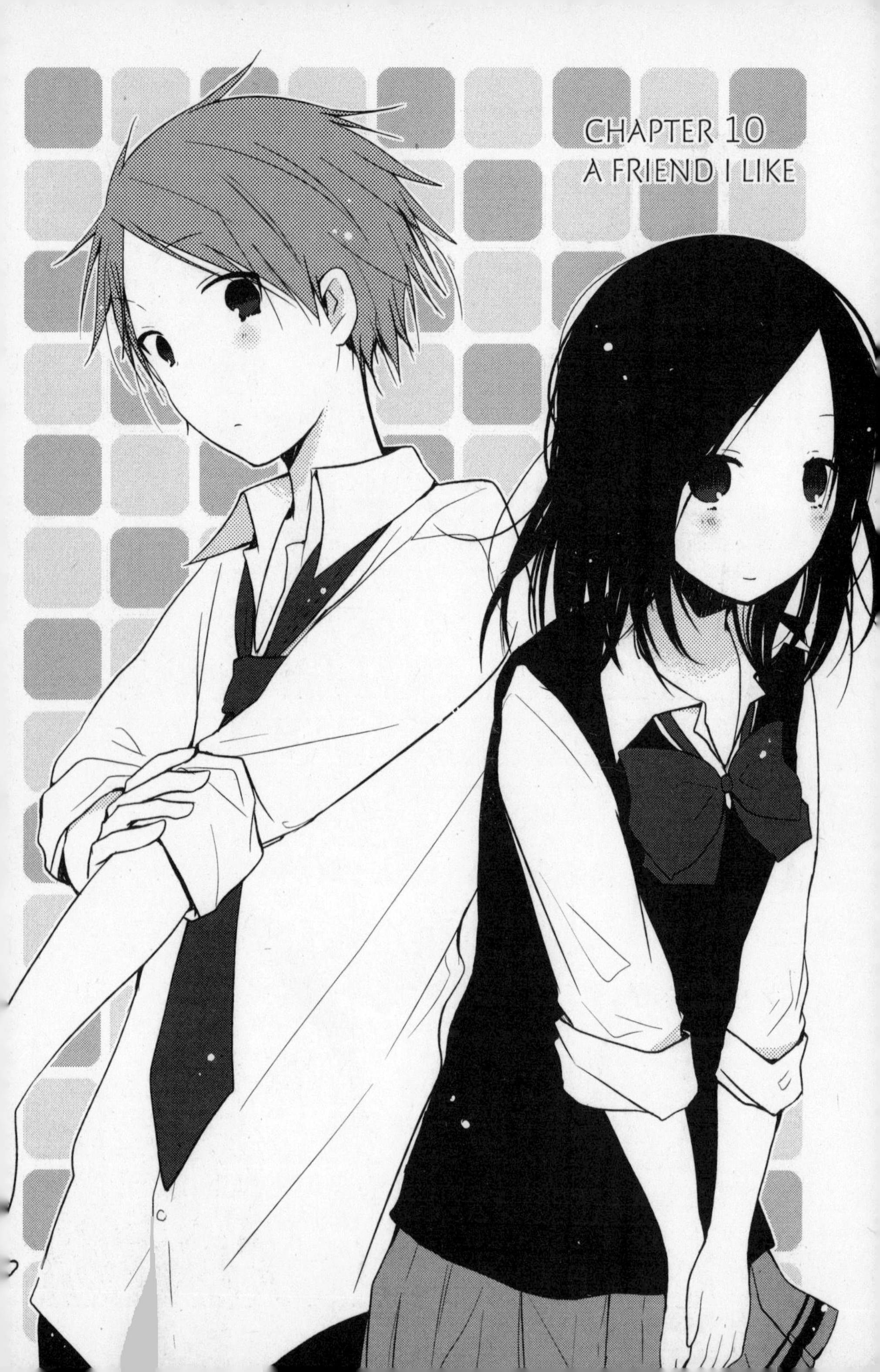
CHAPTER 10
A FRIEND I LIKE

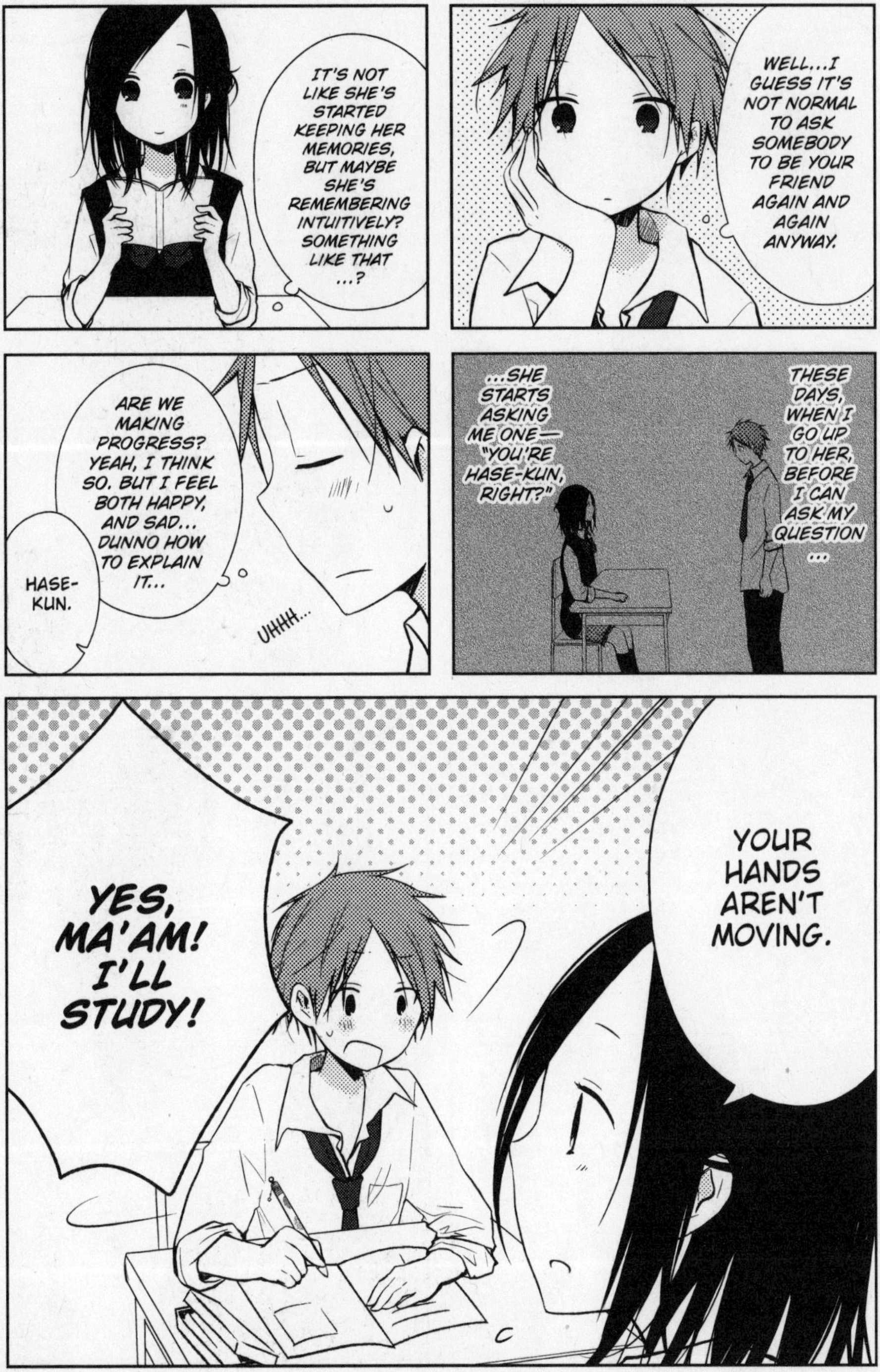
WELL...I GUESS IT'S NOT NORMAL TO ASK SOMEBODY TO BE YOUR FRIEND AGAIN AND AGAIN ANYWAY.
IT'S NOT LIKE SHE'S STARTED KEEPING HER MEMORIES, BUT MAYBE SHE'S REMEMBERING INTUITIVELY? SOMETHING LIKE THAT ...?
THESE DAYS, WHEN I GO UP TO HER, BEFORE I CAN ASK MY QUESTION ...
...SHE STARTS ASKING ME ONE— "YOU'RE HASE-KUN, RIGHT?"
ARE WE MAKING PROGRESS? YEAH, I THINK SO. BUT I FEEL BOTH HAPPY, AND SAD... DUNNO HOW TO EXPLAIN IT...
UHHH...
HASE-KUN.
YOUR HANDS AREN'T MOVING.
YES, MA'AM! I'LL STUDY!

STUDY DETENTION

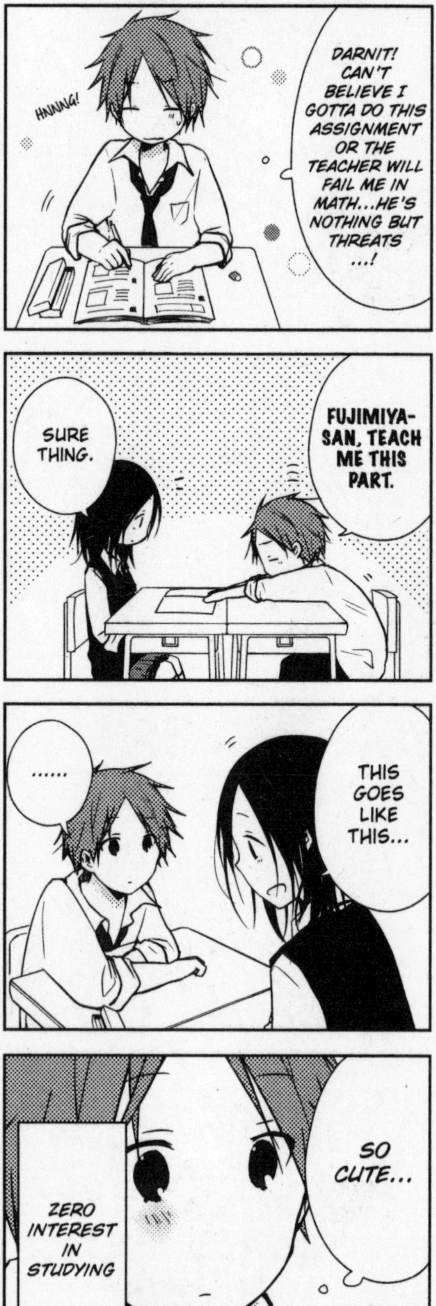
DARNIT! CAN'T BELIEVE I GOTTA DO THIS ASSIGNMENT OR THE TEACHER WILL FAIL ME IN MATH...HE'S NOTHING BUT THREATS ...!
HNNNG!
FUJIMIYA-SAN, TEACH ME THIS PART.
SURE THING.
THIS GOES LIKE THIS...
......
SO CUTE...
ZERO INTEREST IN STUDYING

WITH NO HESITATION

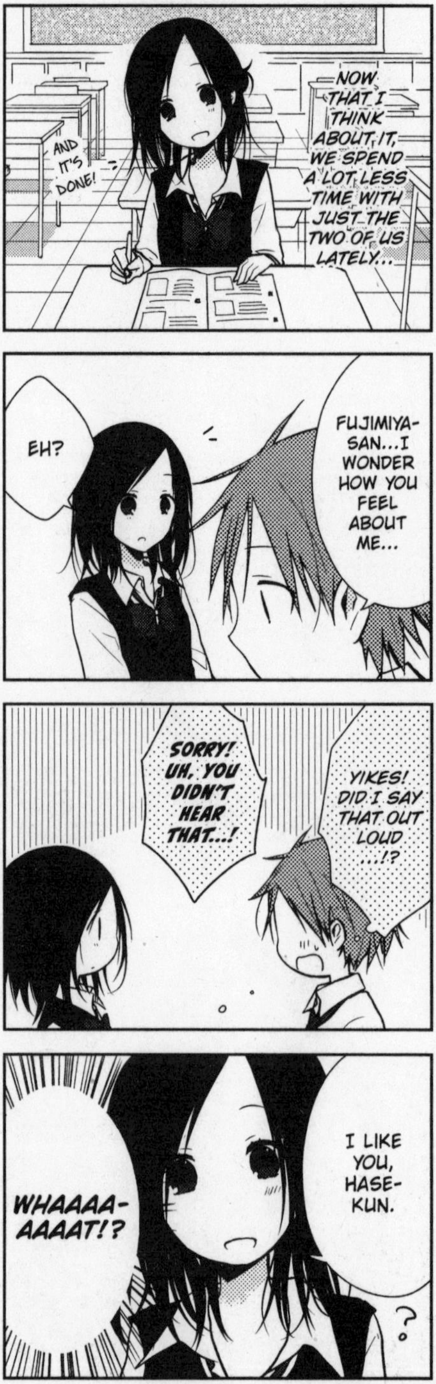
NOW THAT I THINK ABOUT IT, WE SPEND A LOT LESS TIME WITH JUST THE TWO OF US LATELY...
AND IT'S DONE!
FUJIMIYA-SAN...I WONDER HOW YOU FEEL ABOUT ME...
EH?
YIKES! DID I SAY THAT OUT LOUD ...!?
SORRY! UH, YOU DIDN'T HEAR THAT...!
I LIKE YOU, HASE-KUN.
WHAAAA-AAAAT!?

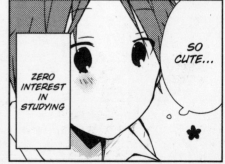

FUJIMIYA-SAN'S "LIKE"

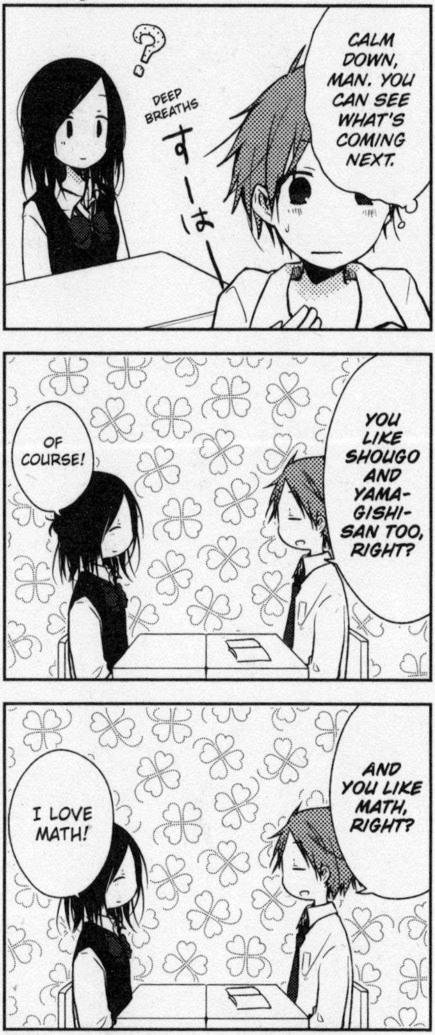
CALM DOWN, MAN. YOU CAN SEE WHAT'S COMING NEXT.
?
DEEP BREATHS
すーはー
YOU LIKE SHOUGO AND YAMAGISHI-SAN TOO, RIGHT?
OF COURSE!
AND YOU LIKE MATH, RIGHT?
I LOVE MATH!
WHEW ...
CALMED DOWN A LITTLE
?

WHAT YOU LIKE, PART 1

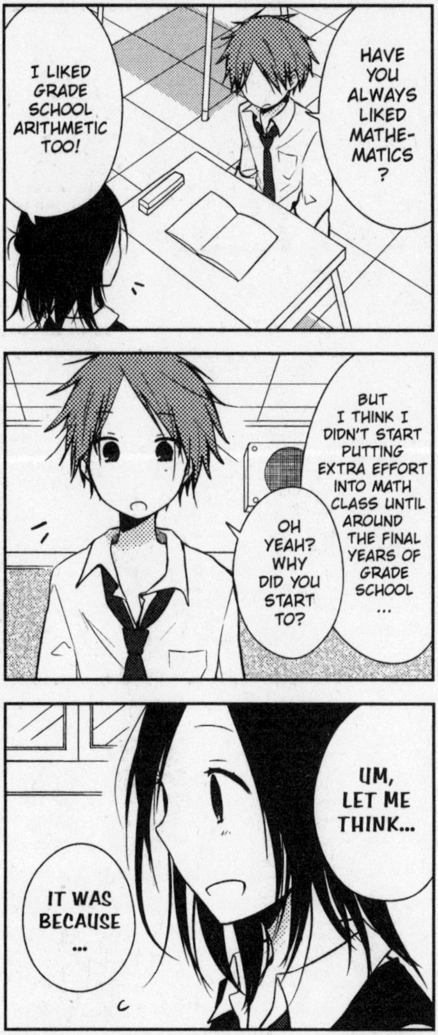
HAVE YOU ALWAYS LIKED MATHEMATICS?
I LIKED GRADE SCHOOL ARITHMETIC TOO!
BUT I THINK I DIDN'T START PUTTING EXTRA EFFORT INTO MATH CLASS UNTIL AROUND THE FINAL YEARS OF GRADE SCHOOL ...
OH YEAH? WHY DID YOU START TO?
UM, LET ME THINK...
IT WAS BECAUSE ...
... WHY WAS IT?
YOU'RE ASKING ME!?

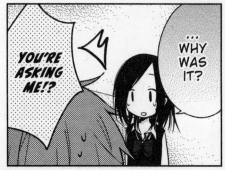

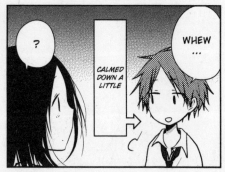

WHAT YOU LIKE, PART 2

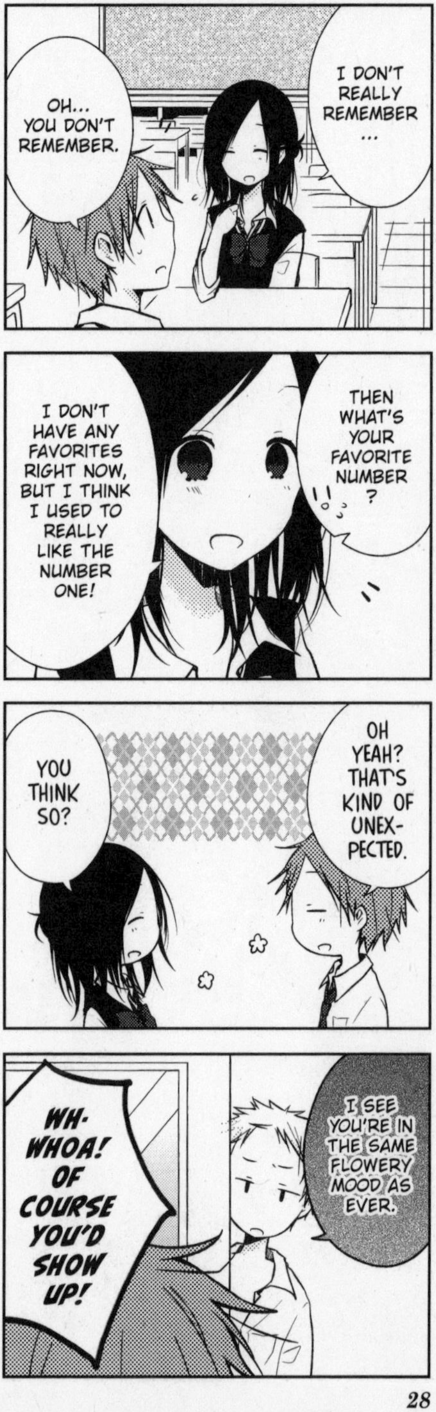
I DON'T REALLY REMEMBER...
OH... YOU DON'T REMEMBER.
THEN WHAT'S YOUR FAVORITE NUMBER?
I DON'T HAVE ANY FAVORITES RIGHT NOW, BUT I THINK I USED TO REALLY LIKE THE NUMBER ONE!
OH YEAH? THAT'S KIND OF UNEX-PECTED.
YOU THINK SO?
I SEE YOU'RE IN THE SAME FLOWERY MOOD AS EVER.
WH-WHOA! OF COURSE YOU'D SHOW UP!

TODAY'S THE DAY

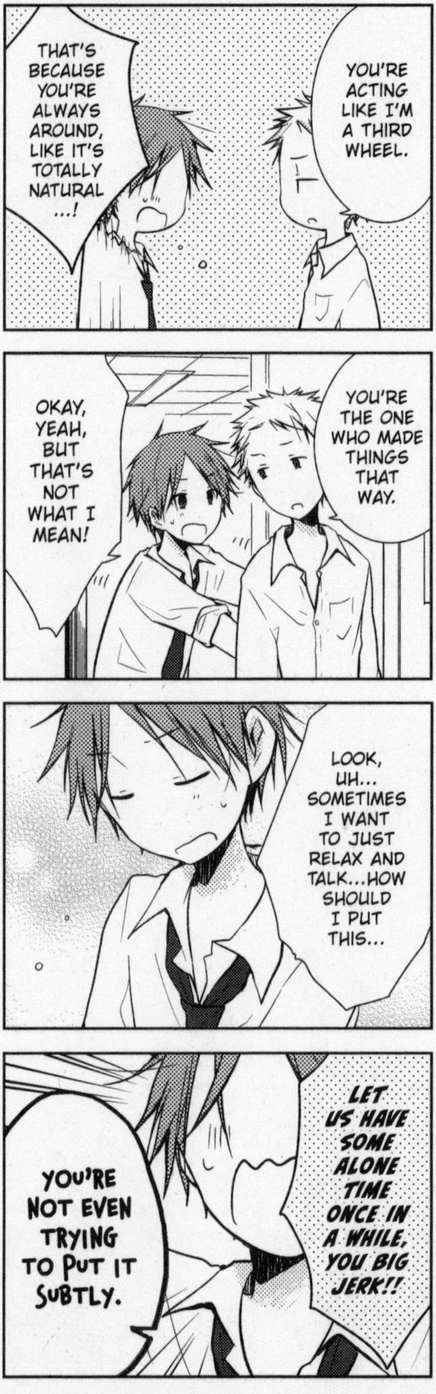
YOU'RE ACTING LIKE I'M A THIRD WHEEL.
THAT'S BECAUSE YOU'RE ALWAYS AROUND, LIKE IT'S TOTALLY NATURAL...!
YOU'RE THE ONE WHO MADE THINGS THAT WAY.
OKAY, YEAH, BUT THAT'S NOT WHAT I MEAN!
LOOK, UH... SOMETIMES I WANT TO JUST RELAX AND TALK...HOW SHOULD I PUT THIS...
LET US HAVE SOME ALONE TIME ONCE IN A WHILE, YOU BIG JERK!!
YOU'RE NOT EVEN TRYING TO PUT IT SUBTLY.

I HATE HALF-FINISHED THINGS

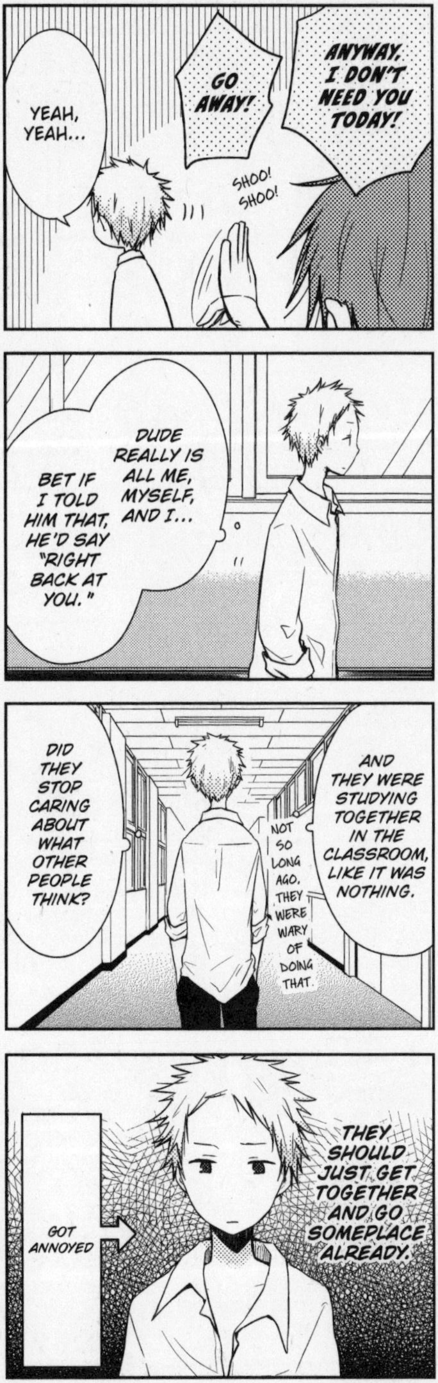

ANYWAY, I DON'T NEED YOU TODAY!
GO AWAY!
SHOO! SHOO!
YEAH, YEAH...
DUDE REALLY IS ALL ME, MYSELF, AND I...
BET IF I TOLD HIM THAT, HE'D SAY "RIGHT BACK AT YOU."
AND THEY WERE STUDYING TOGETHER IN THE CLASSROOM, LIKE IT WAS NOTHING.
NOT SO LONG AGO, THEY WERE WARY OF DOING THAT.
DID THEY STOP CARING ABOUT WHAT OTHER PEOPLE THINK?
THEY SHOULD JUST GET TOGETHER AND GO SOMEPLACE ALREADY.
GOT ANNOYED

TRIED IMAGINING IT

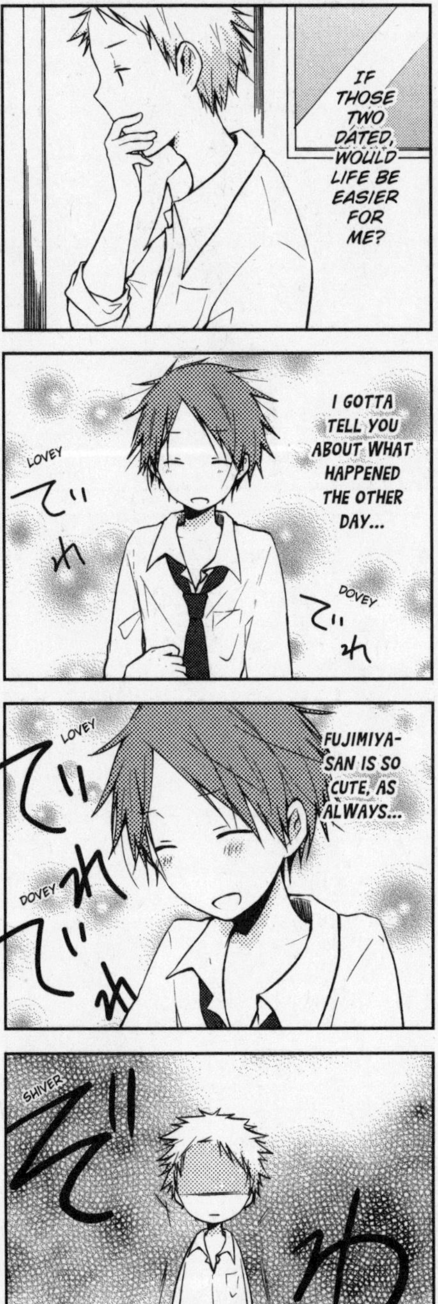

IF THOSE TWO DATED, WOULD LIFE BE EASIER FOR ME?
I GOTTA TELL YOU ABOUT WHAT HAPPENED THE OTHER DAY...
LOVEY
でれ
DOVEY
でれ
FUJIMIYA-SAN IS SO CUTE, AS ALWAYS...
LOVEY
でれ
DOVEY
でれ
SHIVER
ぞわっ

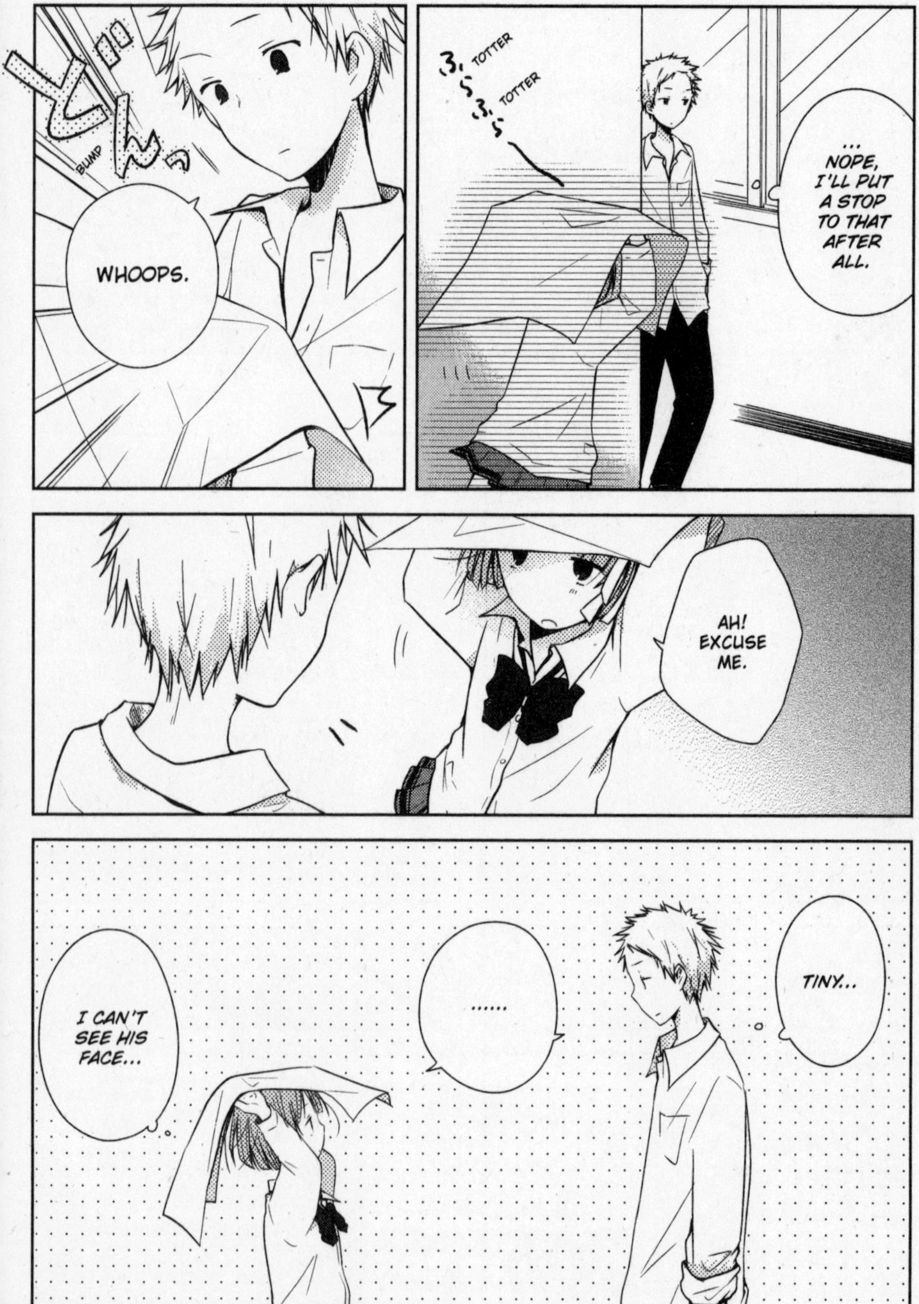
TOTTER
TOTTER
... NOPE, I'LL PUT A STOP TO THAT AFTER ALL.
BUMP
WHOOPS.
AH! EXCUSE ME.
TINY...
......
I CAN'T SEE HIS FACE...

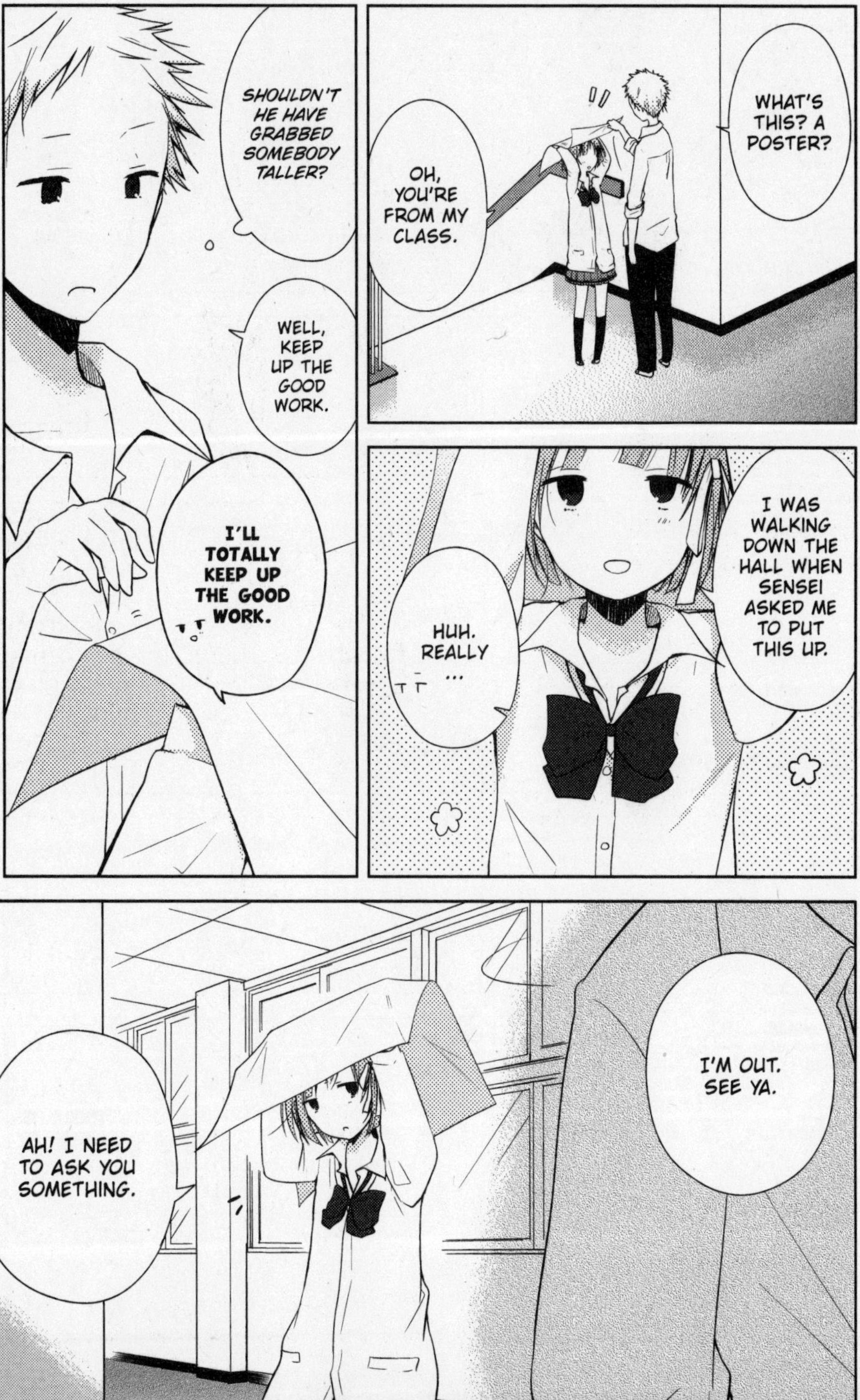
WHAT'S THIS? A POSTER?
OH, YOU'RE FROM MY CLASS.
I WAS WALKING DOWN THE HALL WHEN SENSEI ASKED ME TO PUT THIS UP.
HUH. REALLY ...
SHOULDN'T HE HAVE GRABBED SOMEBODY TALLER?
WELL, KEEP UP THE GOOD WORK.
I'LL TOTALLY KEEP UP THE GOOD WORK.
I'M OUT. SEE YA.
AH! I NEED TO ASK YOU SOMETHING.

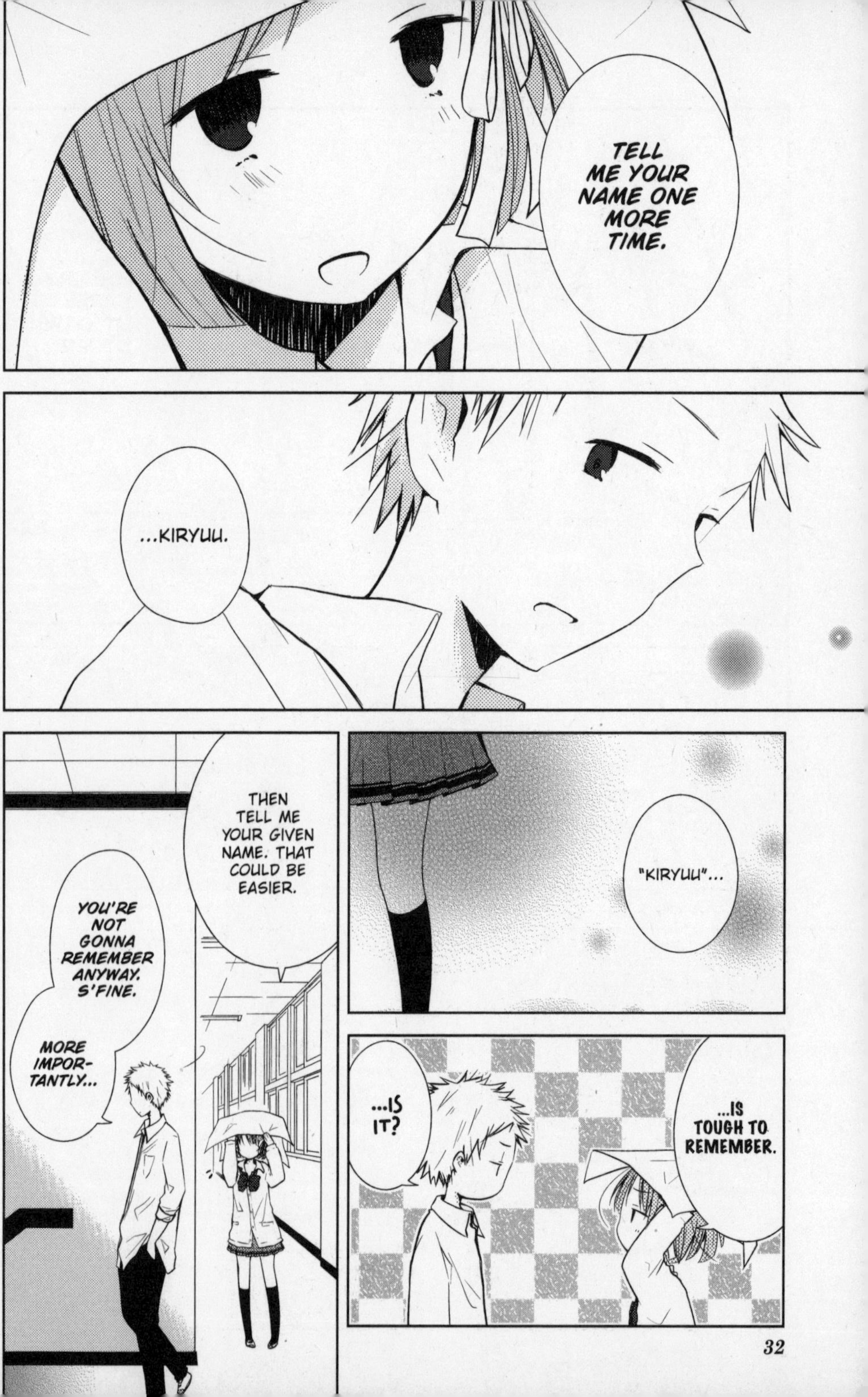
TELL ME YOUR NAME ONE MORE TIME.
...KIRYUU.
"KIRYUU"...
...IS TOUGH TO REMEMBER.
...IS IT?
THEN TELL ME YOUR GIVEN NAME. THAT COULD BE EASIER.
YOU'RE NOT GONNA REMEMBER ANYWAY. S'FINE.
MORE IMPOR-TANTLY...

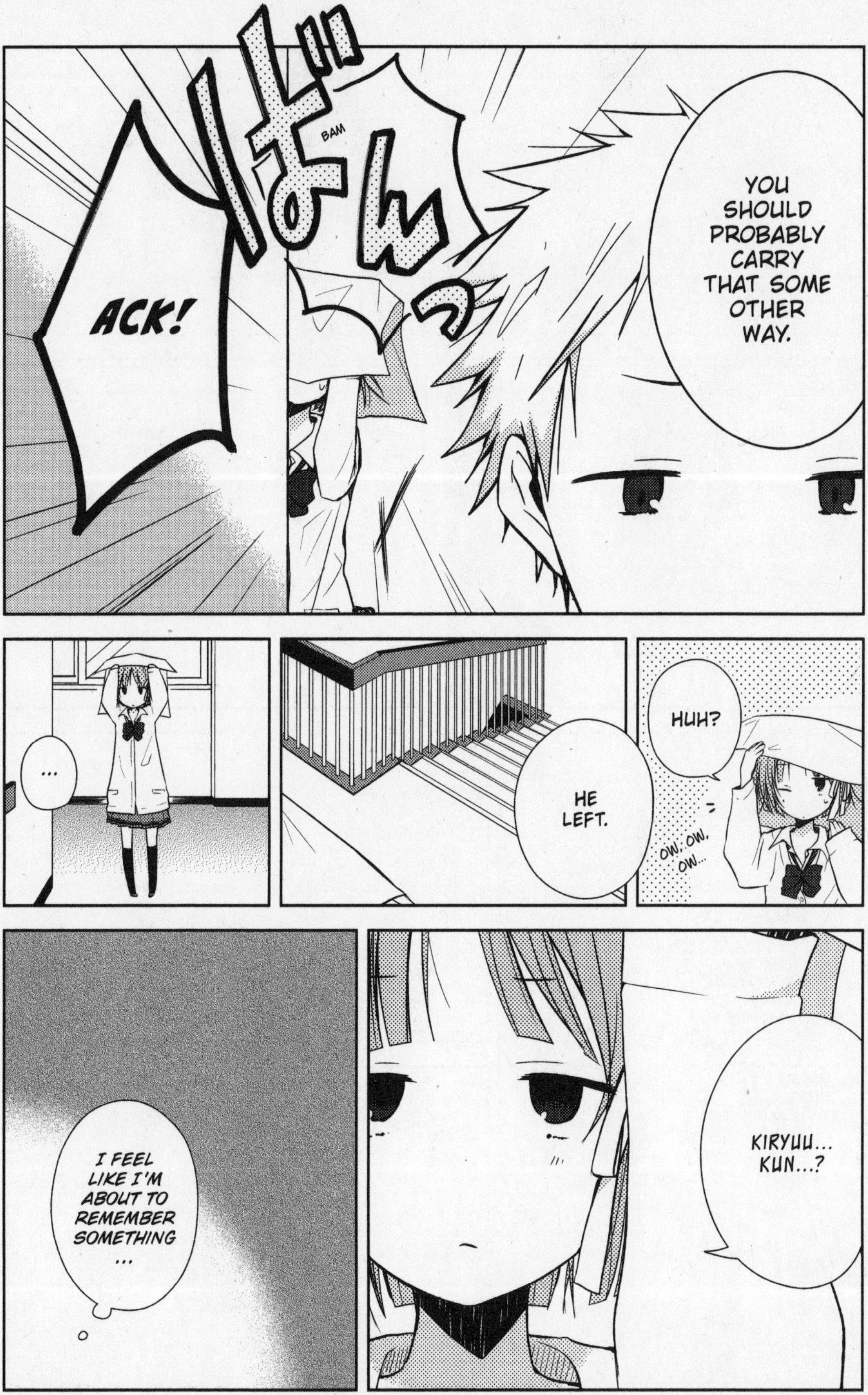
YOU SHOULD PROBABLY CARRY THAT SOME OTHER WAY.
ばんっ
BAM
ACK!
HUH?
OW, OW, OW...
HE LEFT.
...
KIRYUU... KUN...?
I FEEL LIKE I'M ABOUT TO REMEMBER SOMETHING...

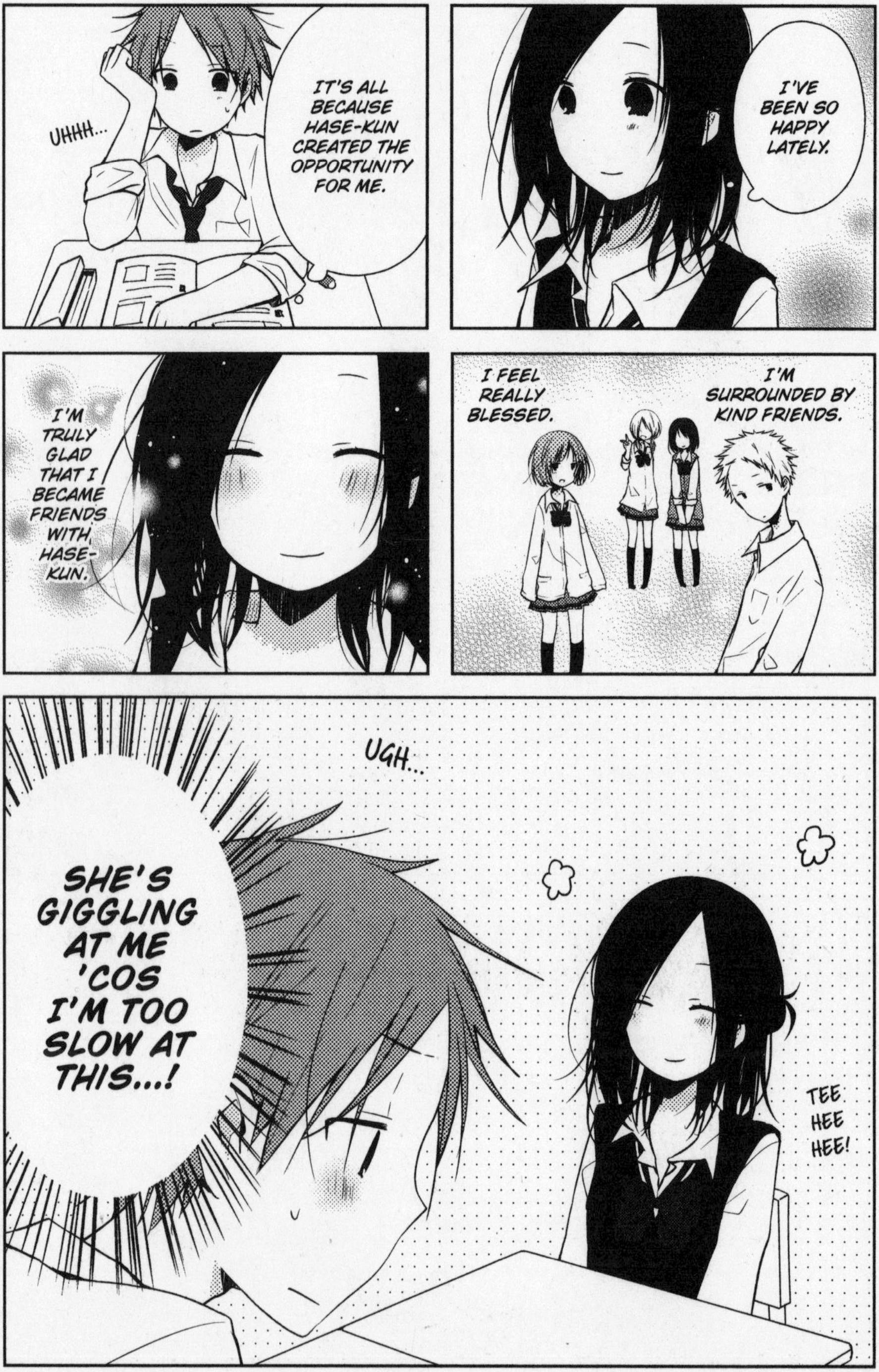
I'VE BEEN SO HAPPY LATELY.
IT'S ALL BECAUSE HASE-KUN CREATED THE OPPORTUNITY FOR ME.
UHHH...
I'M SURROUNDED BY KIND FRIENDS.
I FEEL REALLY BLESSED.
I'M TRULY GLAD THAT I BECAME FRIENDS WITH HASE-KUN.
UGH...
TEE HEE HEE!
SHE'S GIGGLING AT ME 'COS I'M TOO SLOW AT THIS...!

CAN'T LOOK STRAIGHT AT IT

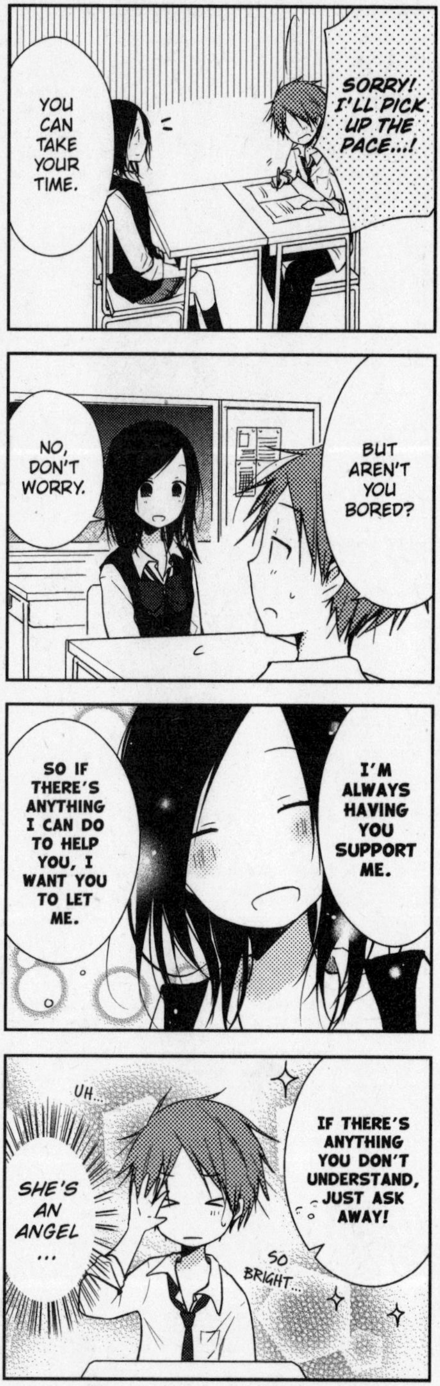
SORRY! I'LL PICK UP THE PACE...!
YOU CAN TAKE YOUR TIME.
BUT AREN'T YOU BORED?
NO, DON'T WORRY.
I'M ALWAYS HAVING YOU SUPPORT ME.
SO IF THERE'S ANYTHING I CAN DO TO HELP YOU, I WANT YOU TO LET ME.
IF THERE'S ANYTHING YOU DON'T UNDERSTAND, JUST ASK AWAY!
UH...
SHE'S AN ANGEL...
SO BRIGHT...

"FRIENDS"

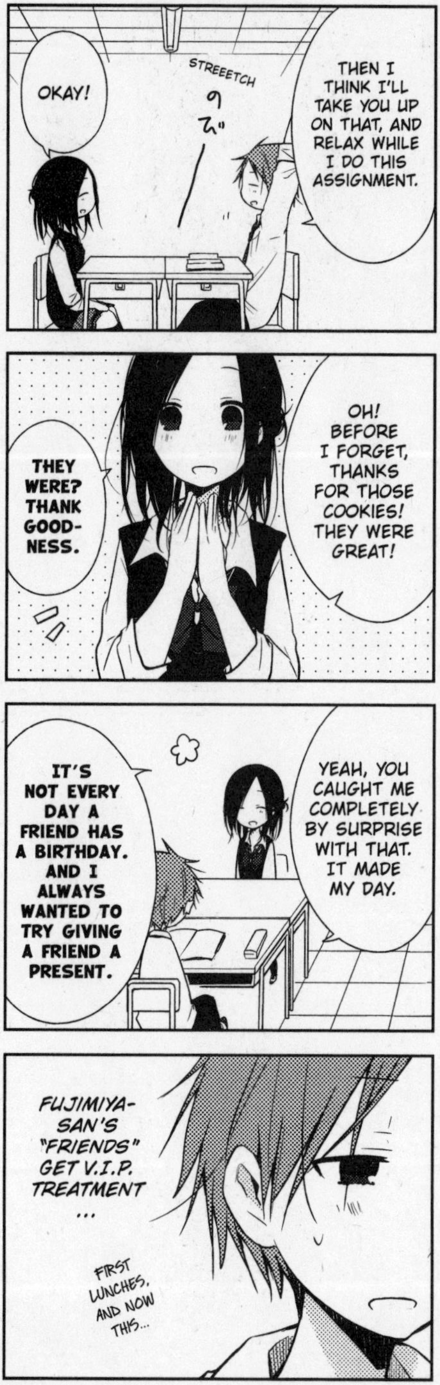
THEN I THINK I'LL TAKE YOU UP ON THAT, AND RELAX WHILE I DO THIS ASSIGNMENT.
STREEETCH
のび
OKAY!
OH! BEFORE I FORGET, THANKS FOR THOSE COOKIES! THEY WERE GREAT!
THEY WERE? THANK GOODNESS.
YEAH, YOU CAUGHT ME COMPLETELY BY SURPRISE WITH THAT. IT MADE MY DAY.
IT'S NOT EVERY DAY A FRIEND HAS A BIRTHDAY. AND I ALWAYS WANTED TO TRY GIVING A FRIEND A PRESENT.
FUJIMIYA-SAN'S "FRIENDS" GET V.I.P. TREATMENT...
FIRST LUNCHES, AND NOW THIS...

SELF-DESTRUCT **!!**

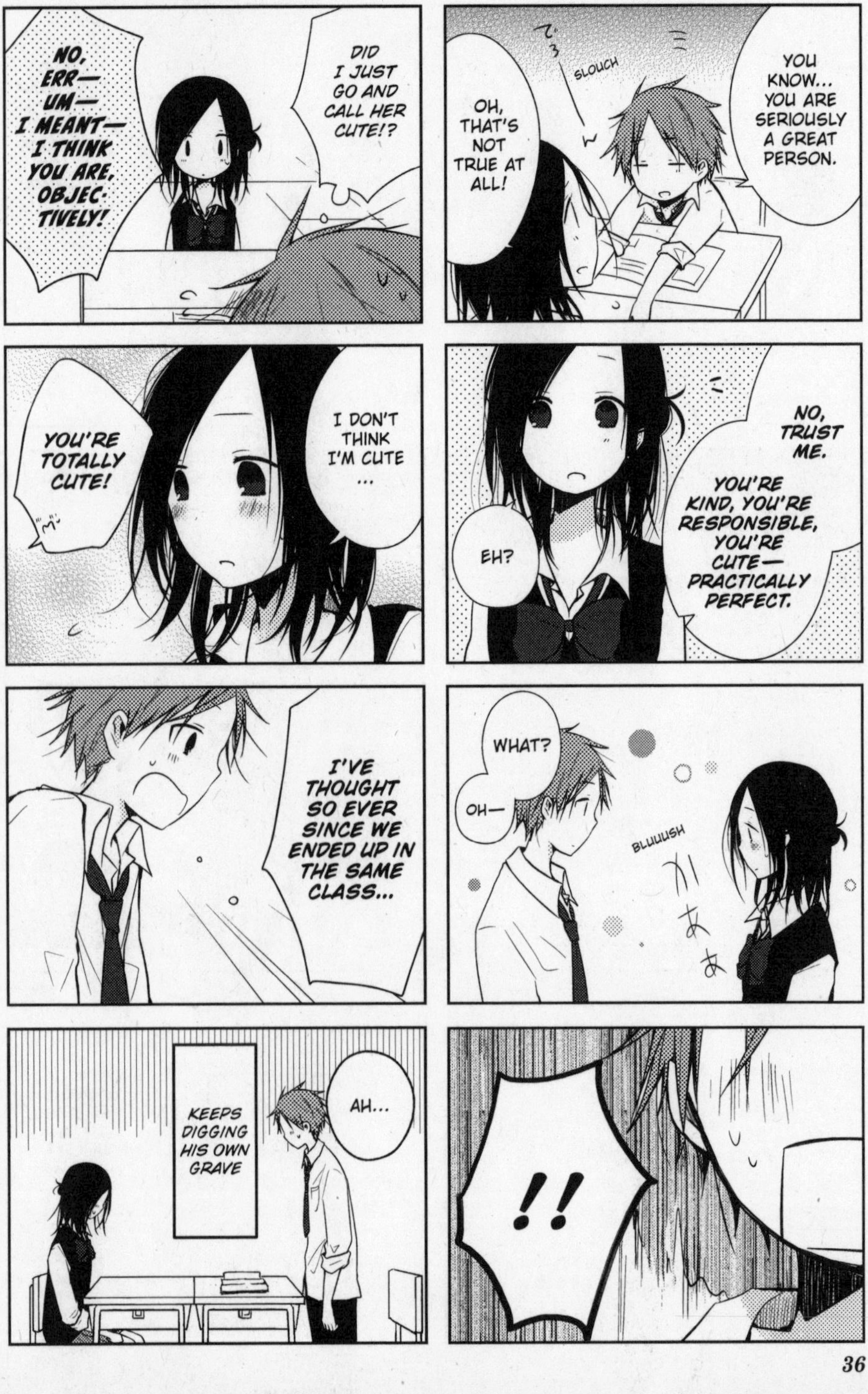

YOU KNOW... YOU ARE SERIOUSLY A GREAT PERSON.
SLOUCH
OH, THAT'S NOT TRUE AT ALL!
NO, TRUST ME.
YOU'RE KIND, YOU'RE RESPONSIBLE, YOU'RE CUTE— PRACTICALLY PERFECT.
EH?
WHAT?
OH—
BLUUUSH
!!
DID I JUST GO AND CALL HER CUTE!?
NO, ERR— UM— I MEANT— I THINK YOU ARE, OBJECTIVELY!
I DON'T THINK I'M CUTE ...
YOU'RE TOTALLY CUTE!
I'VE THOUGHT SO EVER SINCE WE ENDED UP IN THE SAME CLASS...
AH...
KEEPS DIGGING HIS OWN GRAVE

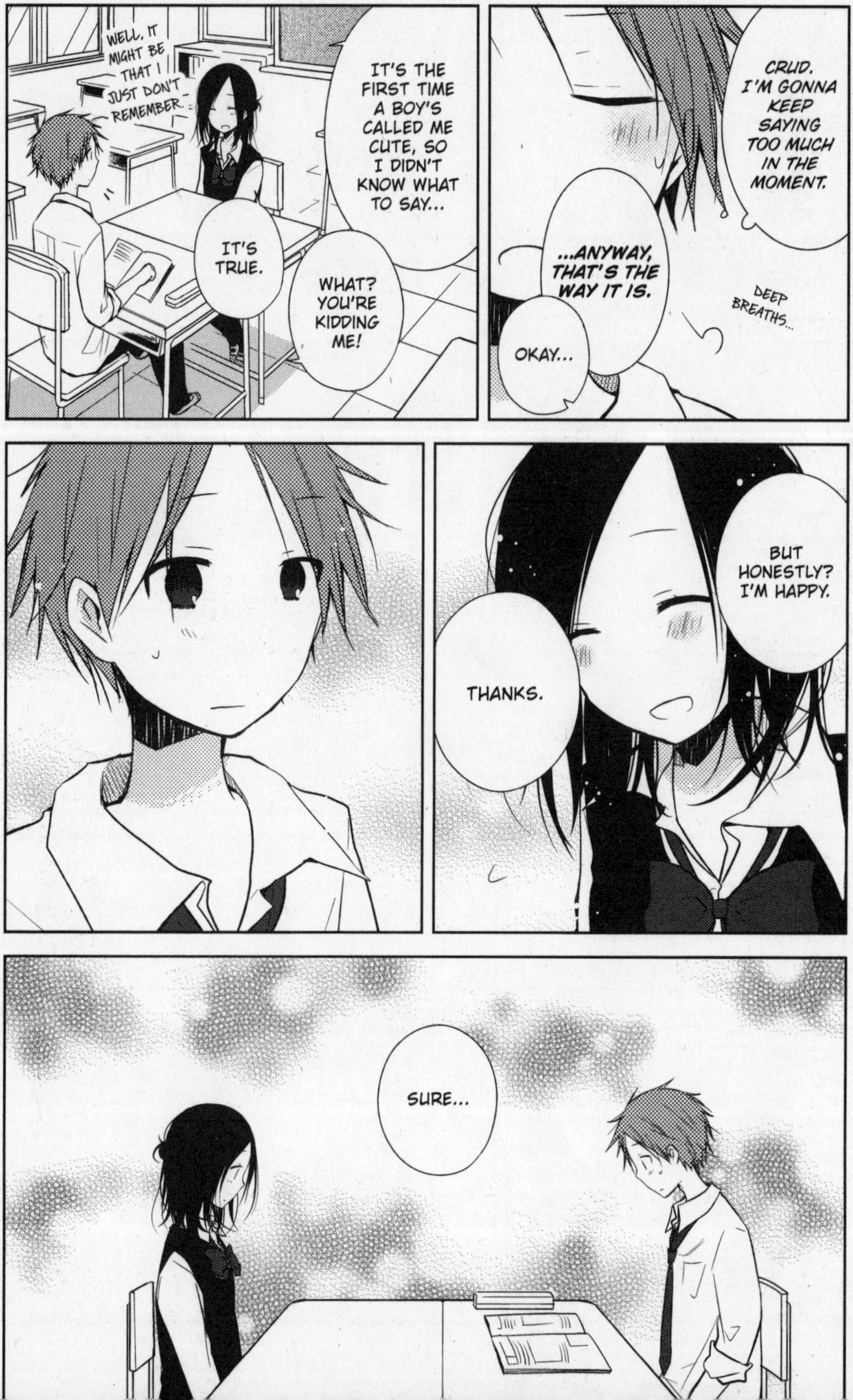
CRUD. I'M GONNA KEEP SAYING TOO MUCH IN THE MOMENT.
...ANYWAY, THAT'S THE WAY IT IS.
DEEP BREATHS...
OKAY...
IT'S THE FIRST TIME A BOY'S CALLED ME CUTE, SO I DIDN'T KNOW WHAT TO SAY...
WELL, IT MIGHT BE THAT I JUST DON'T REMEMBER.
WHAT? YOU'RE KIDDING ME!
IT'S TRUE.
BUT HONESTLY? I'M HAPPY.
THANKS.
SURE...

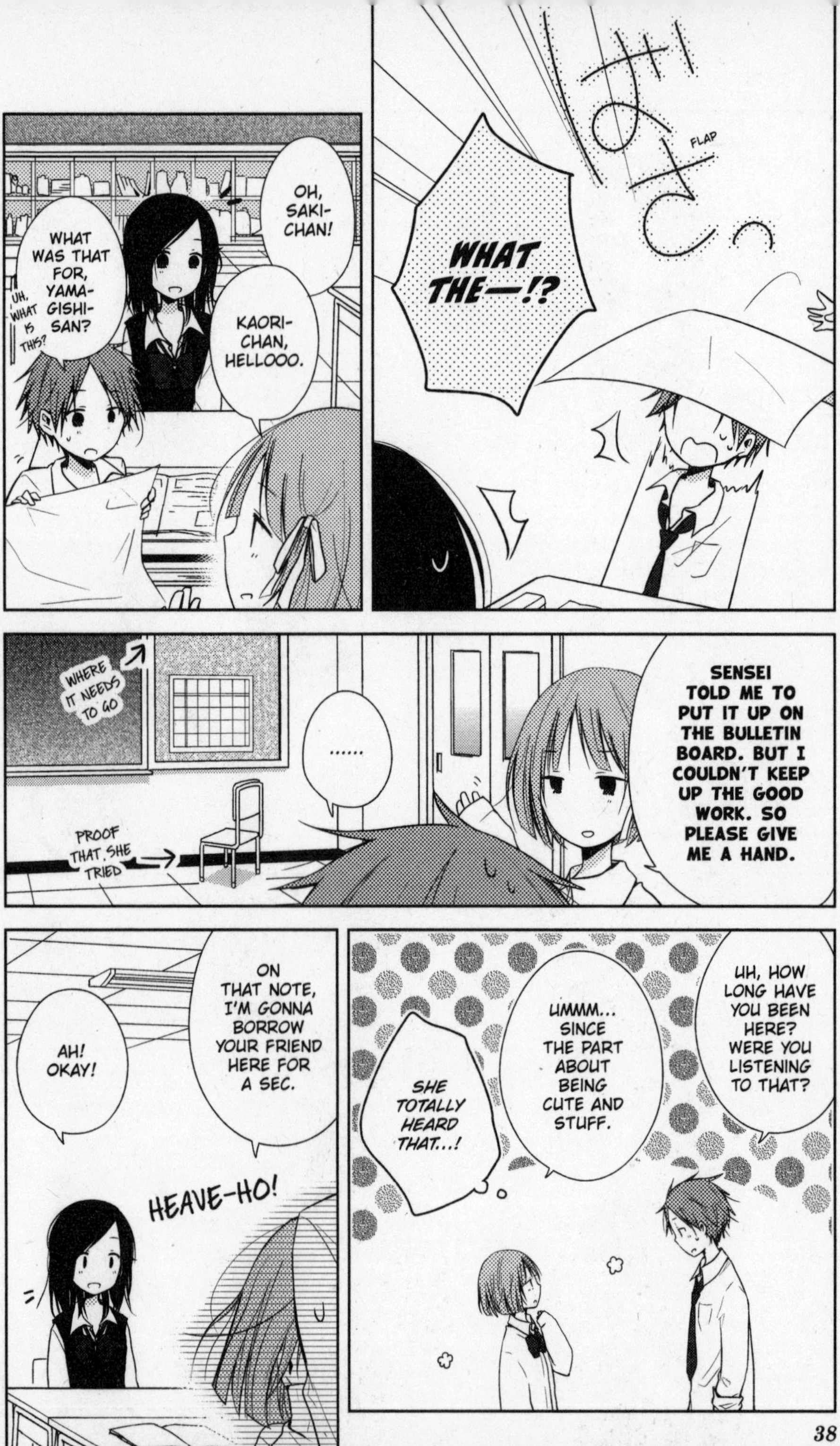
FLAP
WHAT THE—!?
OH, SAKI-CHAN!
KAORI-CHAN, HELLOOO.
WHAT WAS THAT FOR, YAMAGISHI-SAN?
UH, WHAT IS THIS?
SENSEI TOLD ME TO PUT IT UP ON THE BULLETIN BOARD. BUT I COULDN'T KEEP UP THE GOOD WORK. SO PLEASE GIVE ME A HAND.
......
WHERE IT NEEDS TO GO
PROOF THAT SHE TRIED
UH, HOW LONG HAVE YOU BEEN HERE? WERE YOU LISTENING TO THAT?
UMMM... SINCE THE PART ABOUT BEING CUTE AND STUFF.
SHE TOTALLY HEARD THAT...!
ON THAT NOTE, I'M GONNA BORROW YOUR FRIEND HERE FOR A SEC.
AH! OKAY!
HEAVE-HO!

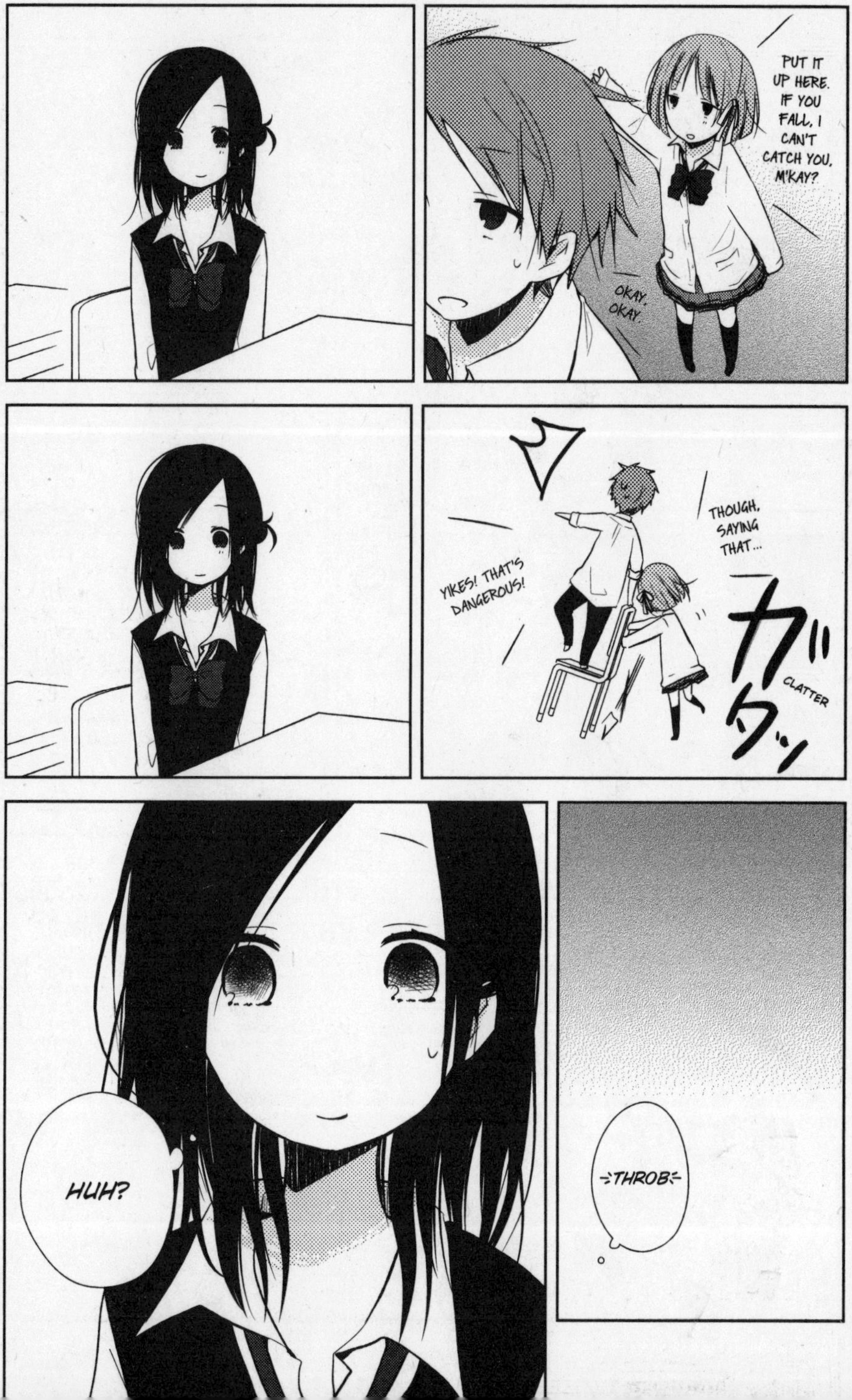
PUT IT UP HERE. IF YOU FALL, I CAN'T CATCH YOU, M'KAY?
OKAY, OKAY.
THOUGH, SAYING THAT...
ガタッ
CLATTER
YIKES! THAT'S DANGEROUS!
THROB
HUH?

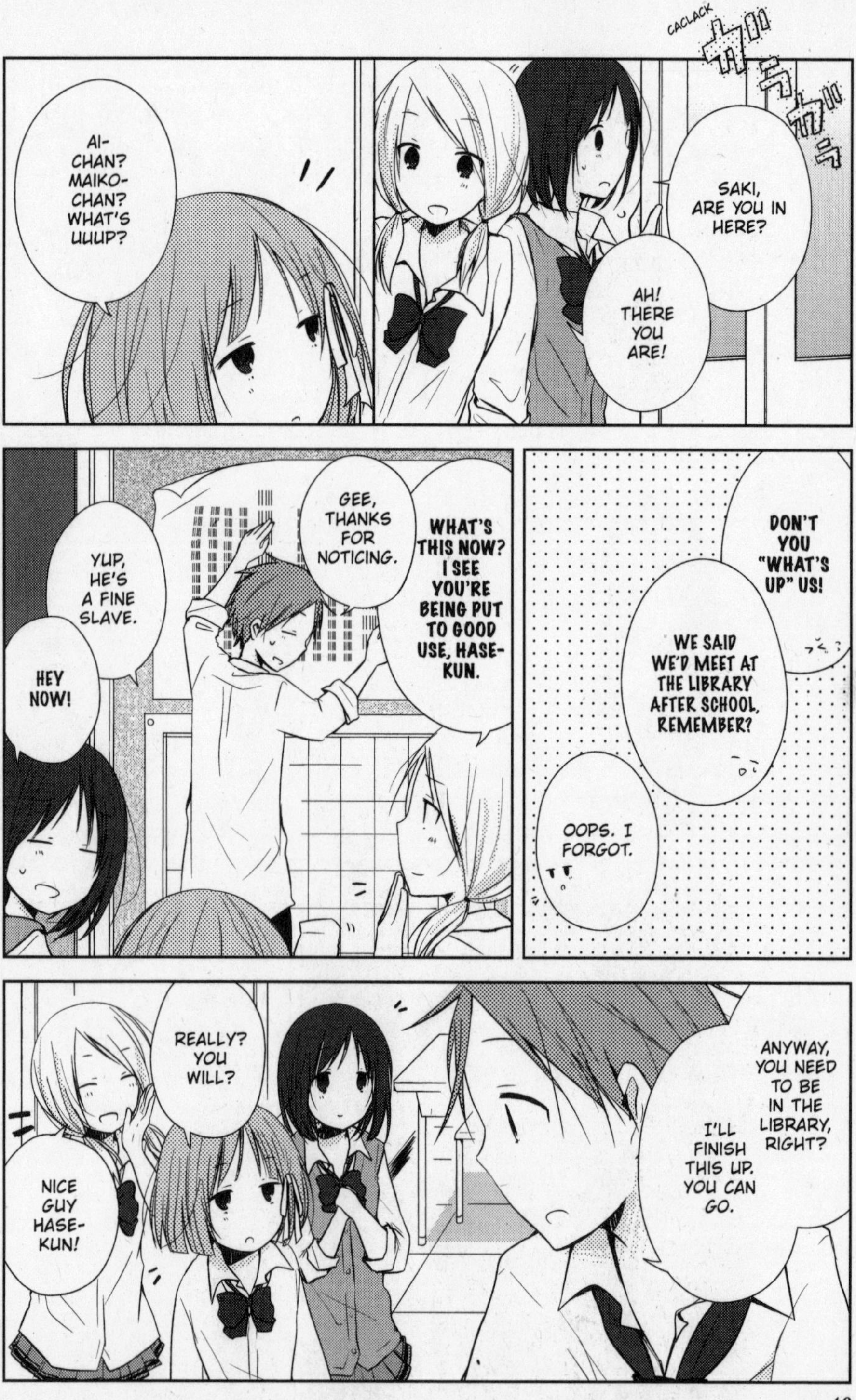
CACLACK
SAKI, ARE YOU IN HERE?
AH! THERE YOU ARE!
AI-CHAN? MAIKO-CHAN? WHAT'S UUUP?
DON'T YOU "WHAT'S UP" US!
WE SAID WE'D MEET AT THE LIBRARY AFTER SCHOOL, REMEMBER?
OOPS. I FORGOT.
WHAT'S THIS NOW? I SEE YOU'RE BEING PUT TO GOOD USE, HASE-KUN.
GEE, THANKS FOR NOTICING.
YUP, HE'S A FINE SLAVE.
HEY NOW!
ANYWAY, YOU NEED TO BE IN THE LIBRARY, RIGHT?
I'LL FINISH THIS UP. YOU CAN GO.
REALLY? YOU WILL?
NICE GUY HASE-KUN!

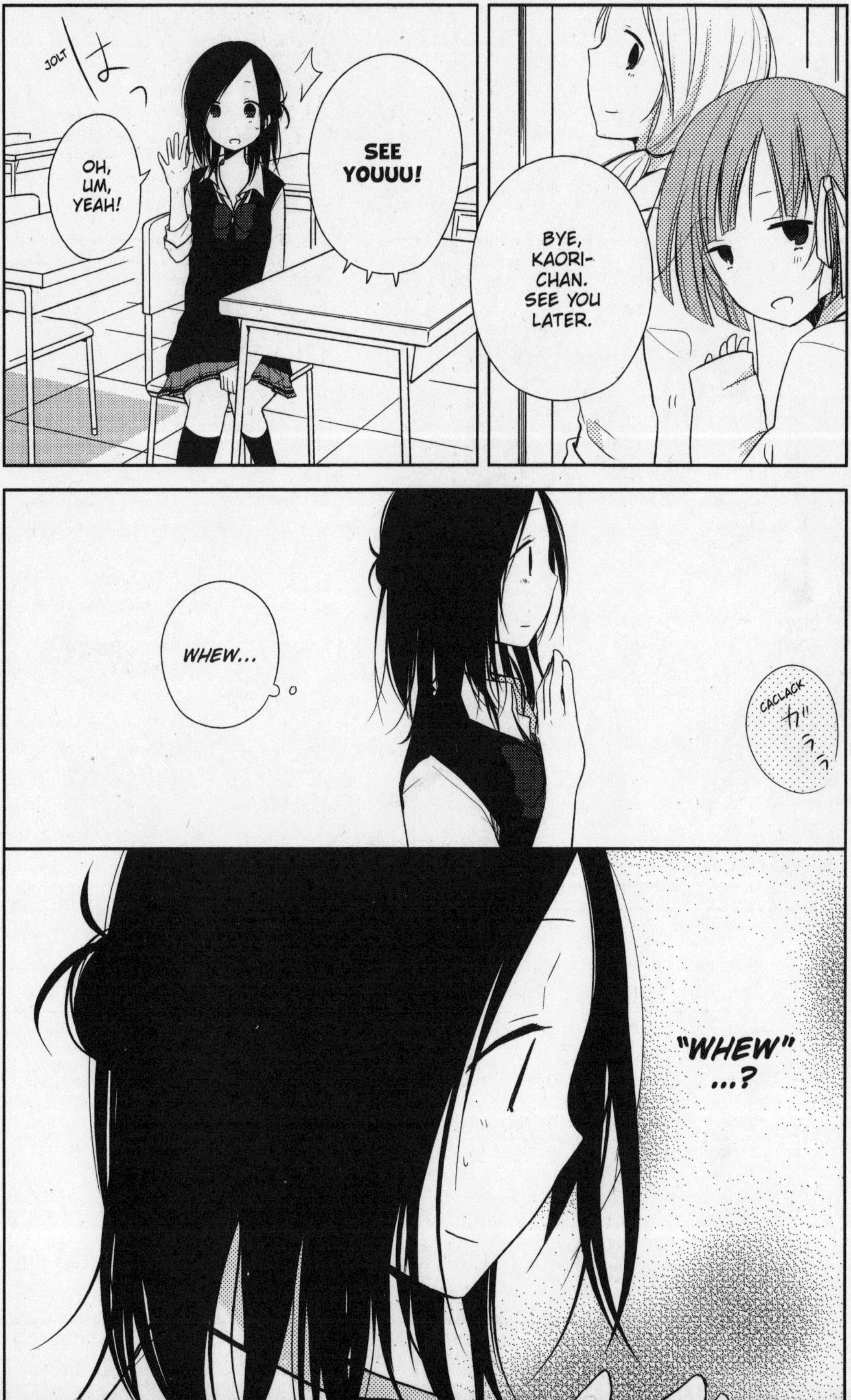
BYE, KAORI-CHAN. SEE YOU LATER.
SEE YOUUU!
JOLT
はっ
OH, UM, YEAH!
CACLACK
ガラララ
WHEW...
"WHEW" ...?

SORRY FOR HOLDING US UP.

MAYBE IT'S BECAUSE I COULDN'T HELP?

WHAT'S GOING ON WITH ME...?

MY CHEST FEELS STRANGE...

BETTER GET THIS ASSIGNMENT DONE AND OVER WITH.

HUH? THAT'S NO BIGGIE.

IT'S OKAY.

SORRY I DIDN'T HELP.

HEY, HASE-KUN?

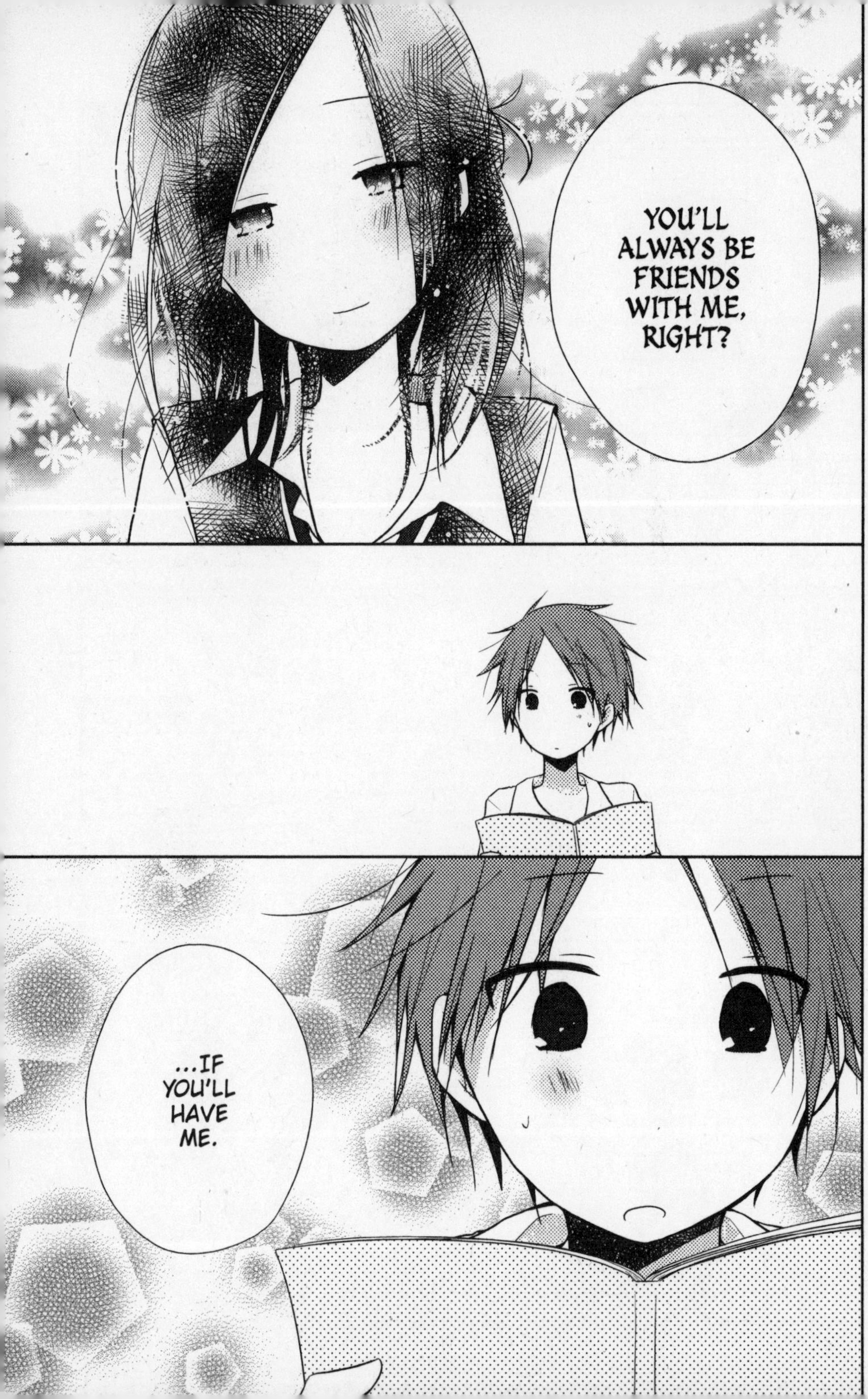
YOU'LL ALWAYS BE FRIENDS WITH ME, RIGHT?
...IF YOU'LL HAVE ME.

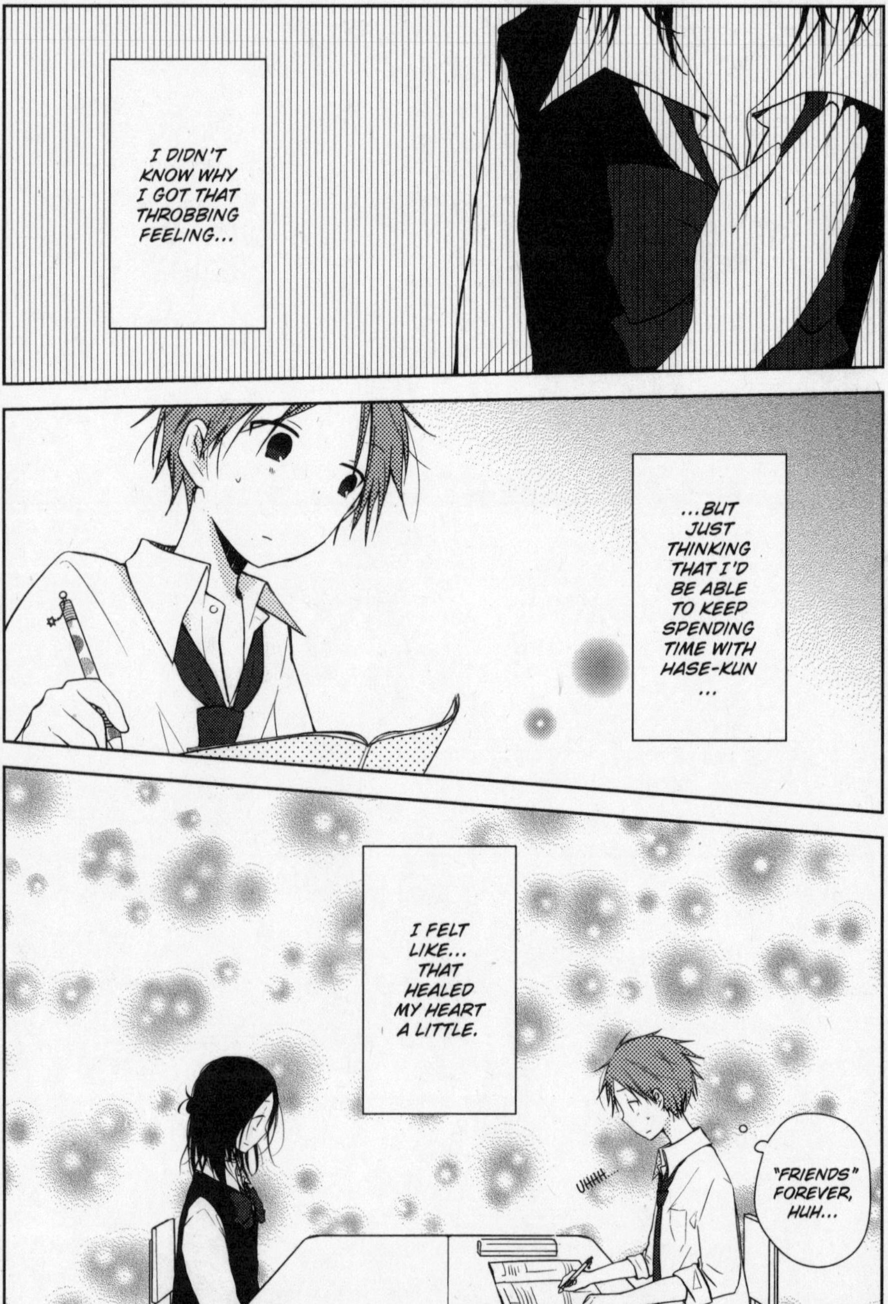
I DIDN'T KNOW WHY I GOT THAT THROBBING FEELING...
...BUT JUST THINKING THAT I'D BE ABLE TO KEEP SPENDING TIME WITH HASE-KUN...
I FELT LIKE... THAT HEALED MY HEART A LITTLE.
"FRIENDS" FOREVER, HUH...
UHHH...

CHAPTER 11 A FRIEND I CAN'T MEET

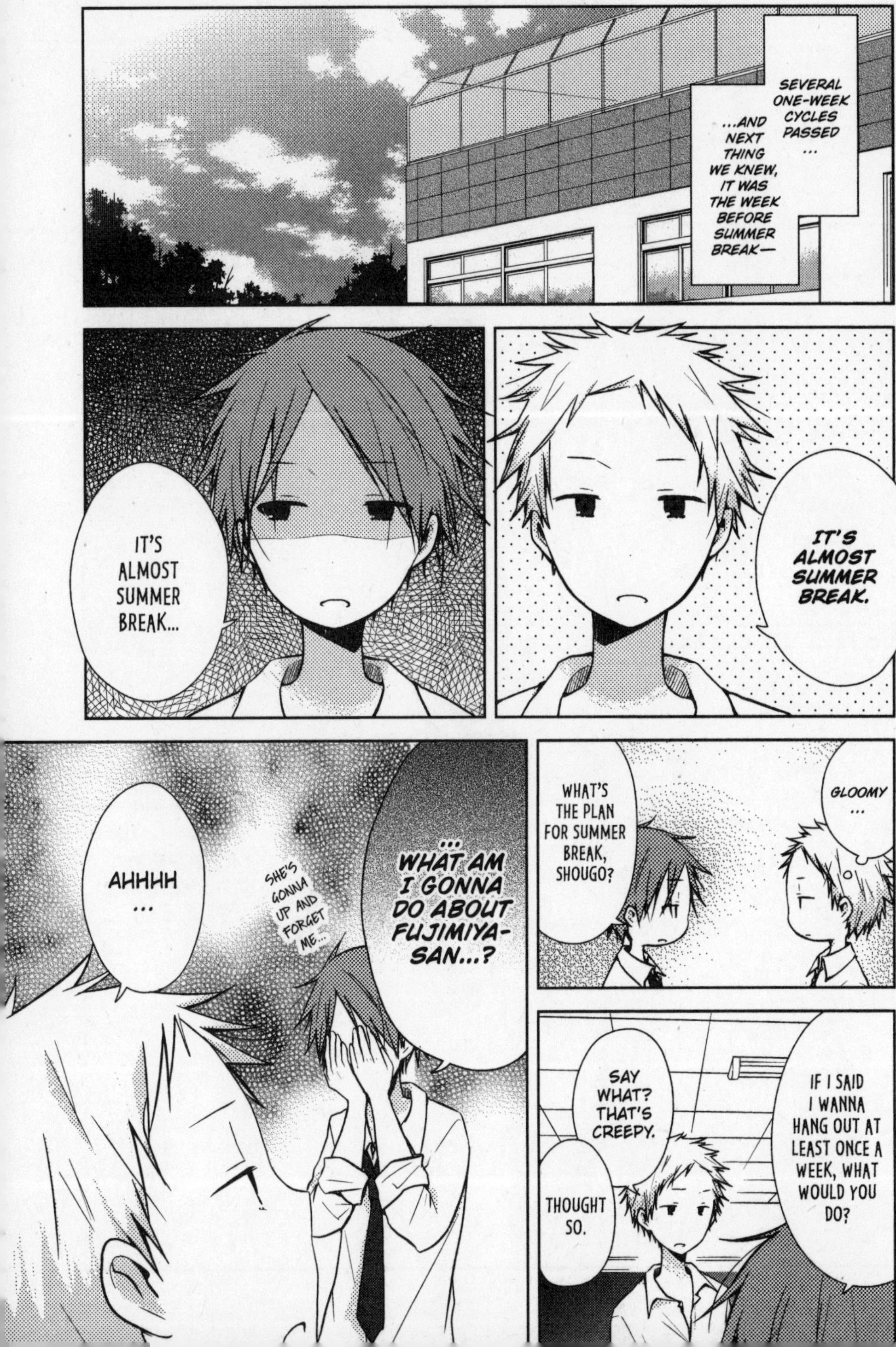
SEVERAL ONE-WEEK CYCLES PASSED ...
...AND NEXT THING WE KNEW, IT WAS THE WEEK BEFORE SUMMER BREAK—
IT'S ALMOST SUMMER BREAK.
IT'S ALMOST SUMMER BREAK...
GLOOMY ...
WHAT'S THE PLAN FOR SUMMER BREAK, SHOUGO?
IF I SAID I WANNA HANG OUT AT LEAST ONCE A WEEK, WHAT WOULD YOU DO?
SAY WHAT? THAT'S CREEPY.
THOUGHT SO.
...WHAT AM I GONNA DO ABOUT FUJIMIYA-SAN...?
SHE'S GONNA UP AND FORGET ME...
AHHHH ...

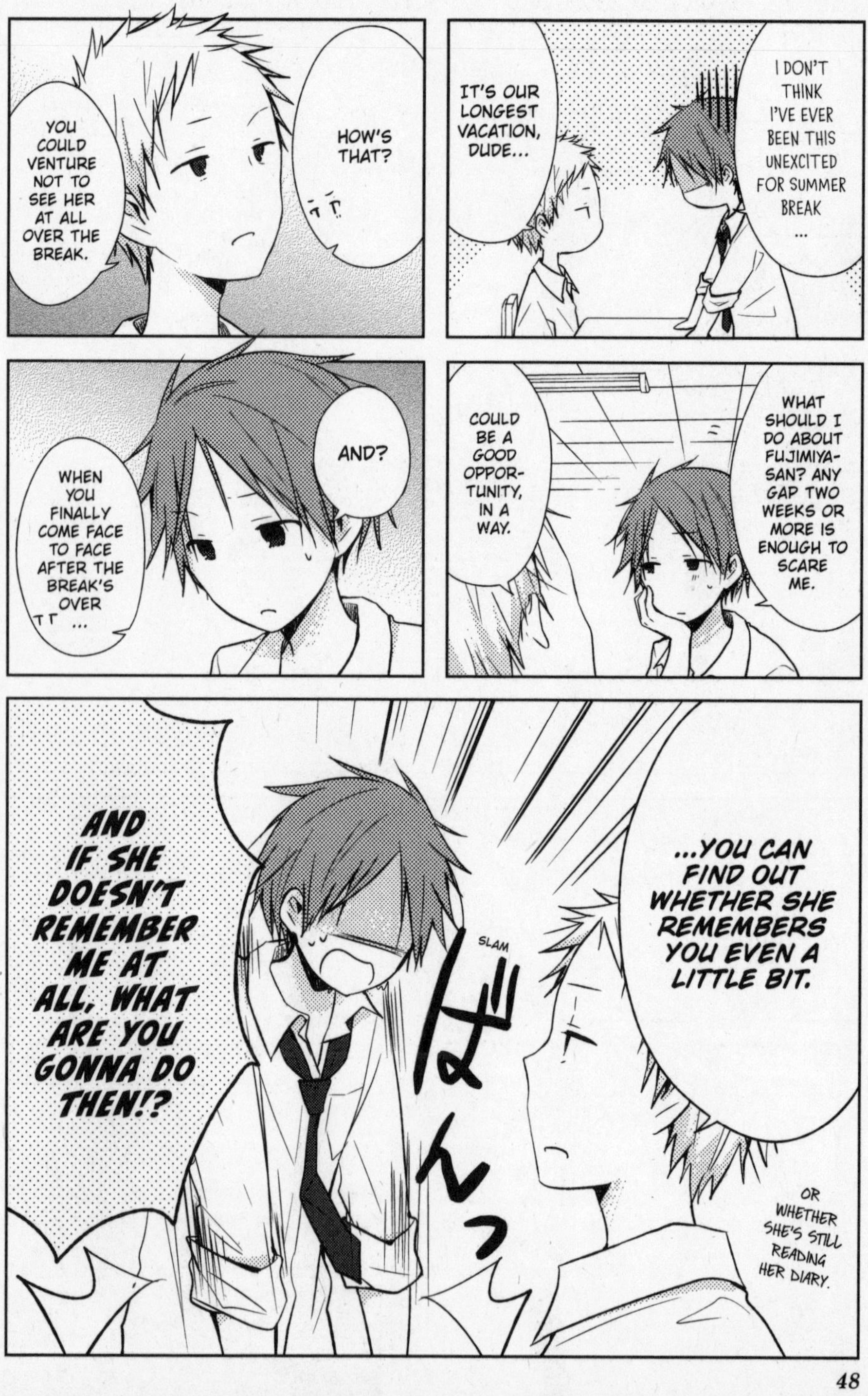
I DON'T THINK I'VE EVER BEEN THIS UNEXCITED FOR SUMMER BREAK ...
IT'S OUR LONGEST VACATION, DUDE...
HOW'S THAT?
YOU COULD VENTURE NOT TO SEE HER AT ALL OVER THE BREAK.
WHAT SHOULD I DO ABOUT FUJIMIYA-SAN? ANY GAP TWO WEEKS OR MORE IS ENOUGH TO SCARE ME.
COULD BE A GOOD OPPORTUNITY, IN A WAY.
AND?
WHEN YOU FINALLY COME FACE TO FACE AFTER THE BREAK'S OVER ...
...YOU CAN FIND OUT WHETHER SHE REMEMBERS YOU EVEN A LITTLE BIT.
OR WHETHER SHE'S STILL READING HER DIARY.
ばんっ
SLAM
AND IF SHE DOESN'T REMEMBER ME AT ALL, WHAT ARE YOU GONNA DO THEN!?

THAT'S WHAT YOU GOT OUT OF THIS?

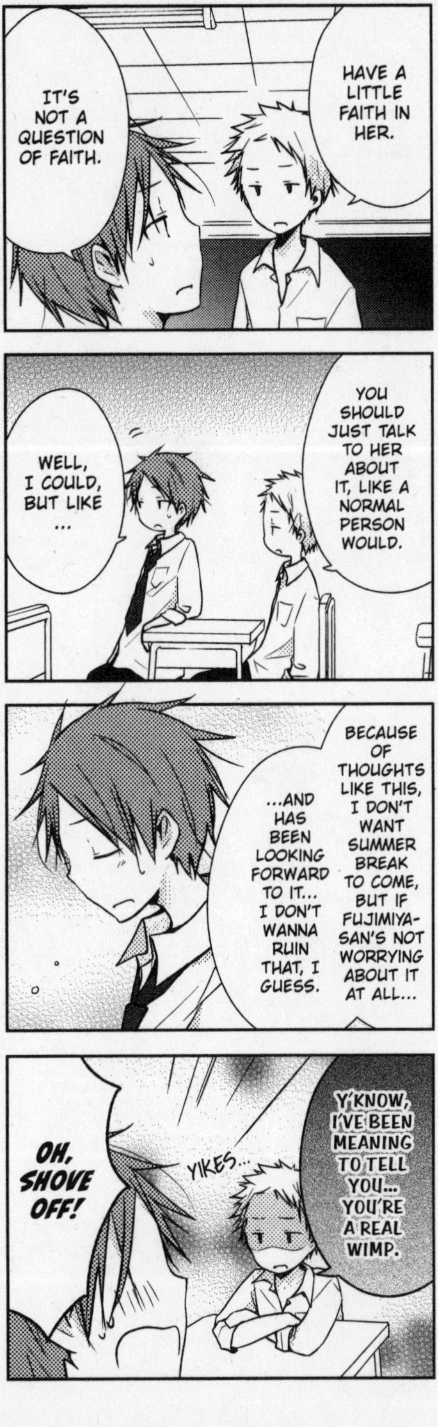
HAVE A LITTLE FAITH IN HER.
IT'S NOT A QUESTION OF FAITH.
YOU SHOULD JUST TALK TO HER ABOUT IT, LIKE A NORMAL PERSON WOULD.
WELL, I COULD, BUT LIKE ...
BECAUSE OF THOUGHTS LIKE THIS, I DON'T WANT SUMMER BREAK TO COME, BUT IF FUJIMIYA-SAN'S NOT WORRYING ABOUT IT AT ALL...
...AND HAS BEEN LOOKING FORWARD TO IT... I DON'T WANNA RUIN THAT, I GUESS.
Y'KNOW, I'VE BEEN MEANING TO TELL YOU... YOU'RE A REAL WIMP.
YIKES...
OH, SHOVE OFF!

BULL'S-EYE

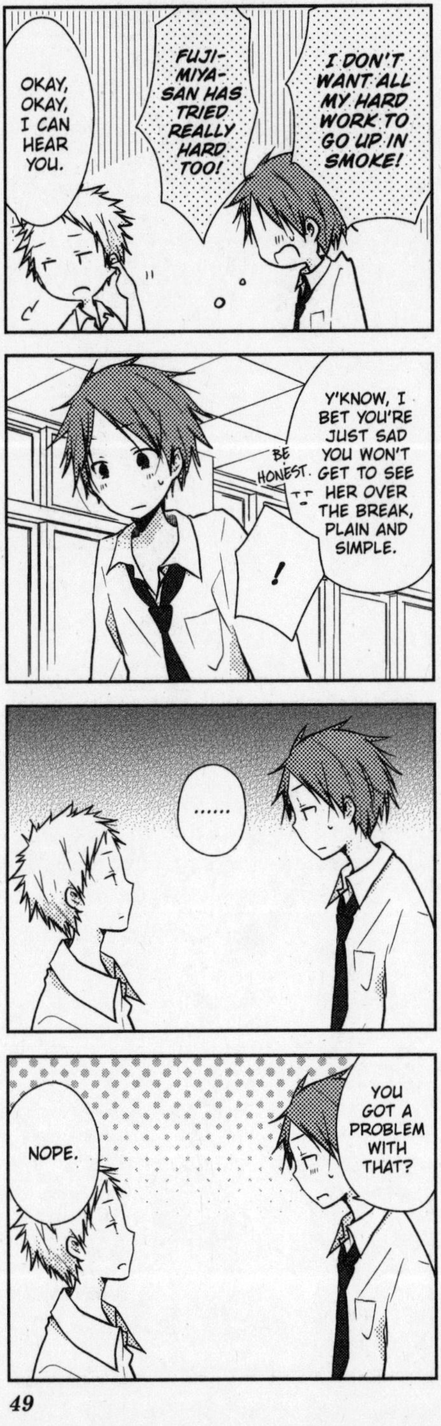
I DON'T WANT ALL MY HARD WORK TO GO UP IN SMOKE!
FUJI-MIYA-SAN HAS TRIED REALLY HARD TOO!
OKAY, OKAY, I CAN HEAR YOU.
Y'KNOW, I BET YOU'RE JUST SAD YOU WON'T GET TO SEE HER OVER THE BREAK, PLAIN AND SIMPLE.
BE HONEST.
!
......
YOU GOT A PROBLEM WITH THAT?
NOPE.

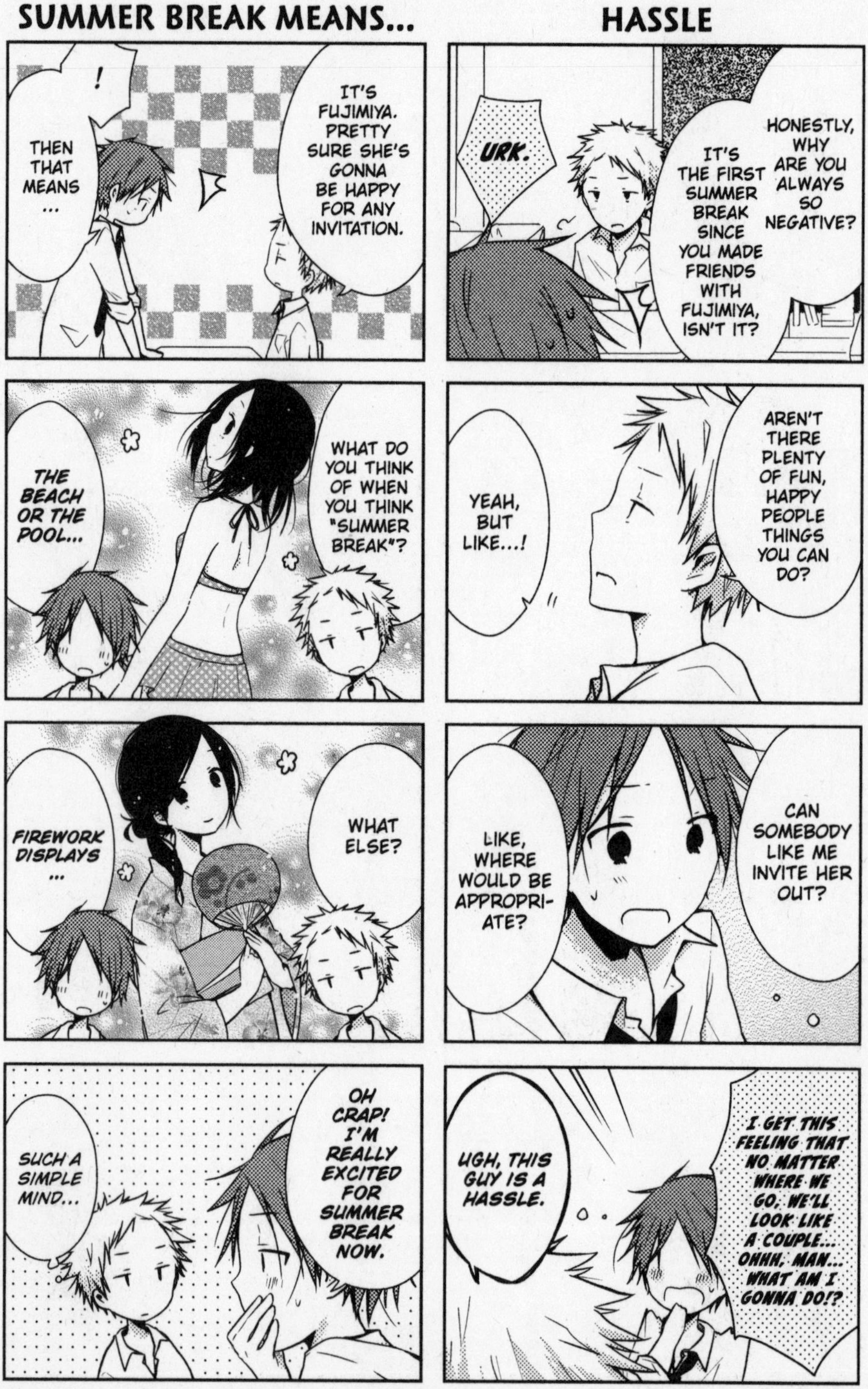
HASSLE
HONESTLY, WHY ARE YOU ALWAYS SO NEGATIVE?
IT'S THE FIRST SUMMER BREAK SINCE YOU MADE FRIENDS WITH FUJIMIYA, ISN'T IT?
URK.
AREN'T THERE PLENTY OF FUN, HAPPY PEOPLE THINGS YOU CAN DO?
YEAH, BUT LIKE...!
CAN SOMEBODY LIKE ME INVITE HER OUT?
LIKE, WHERE WOULD BE APPROPRI-ATE?
I GET THIS FEELING THAT NO MATTER WHERE WE GO, WE'LL LOOK LIKE A COUPLE... OHHH, MAN... WHAT AM I GONNA DO!?
UGH, THIS GUY IS A HASSLE.
SUMMER BREAK MEANS...
IT'S FUJIMIYA. PRETTY SURE SHE'S GONNA BE HAPPY FOR ANY INVITATION.
!
THEN THAT MEANS...
WHAT DO YOU THINK OF WHEN YOU THINK "SUMMER BREAK"?
THE BEACH OR THE POOL...
WHAT ELSE?
FIREWORK DISPLAYS...
OH CRAP! I'M REALLY EXCITED FOR SUMMER BREAK NOW.
SUCH A SIMPLE MIND...

MORE THAN EXPECTED

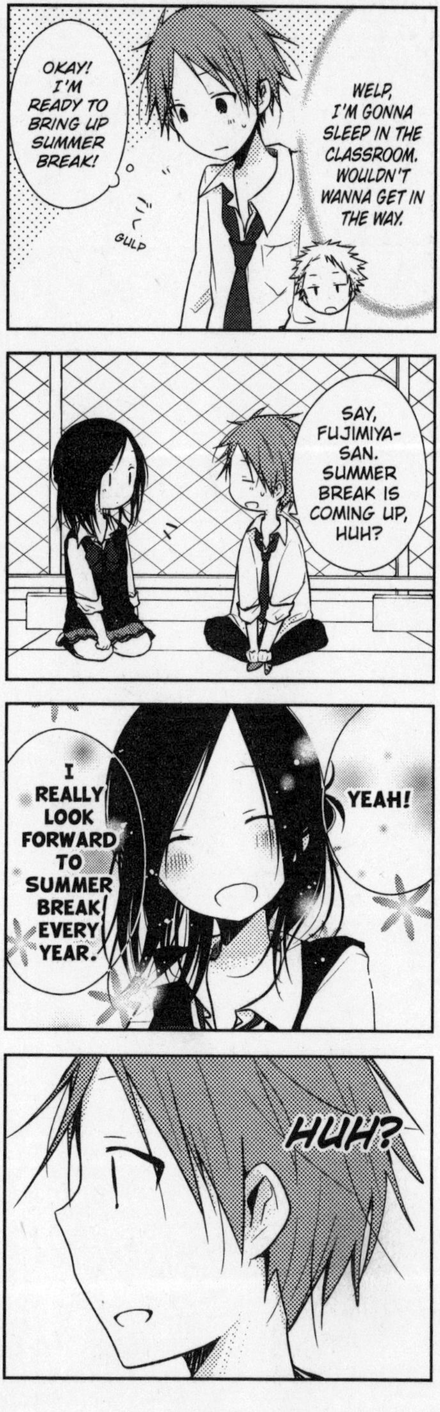
WELP, I'M GONNA SLEEP IN THE CLASSROOM. WOULDN'T WANNA GET IN THE WAY.
GULP
OKAY! I'M READY TO BRING UP SUMMER BREAK!
SAY, FUJIMIYA-SAN. SUMMER BREAK IS COMING UP, HUH?
YEAH!
I REALLY LOOK FORWARD TO SUMMER BREAK EVERY YEAR.
HUH?

TIMING

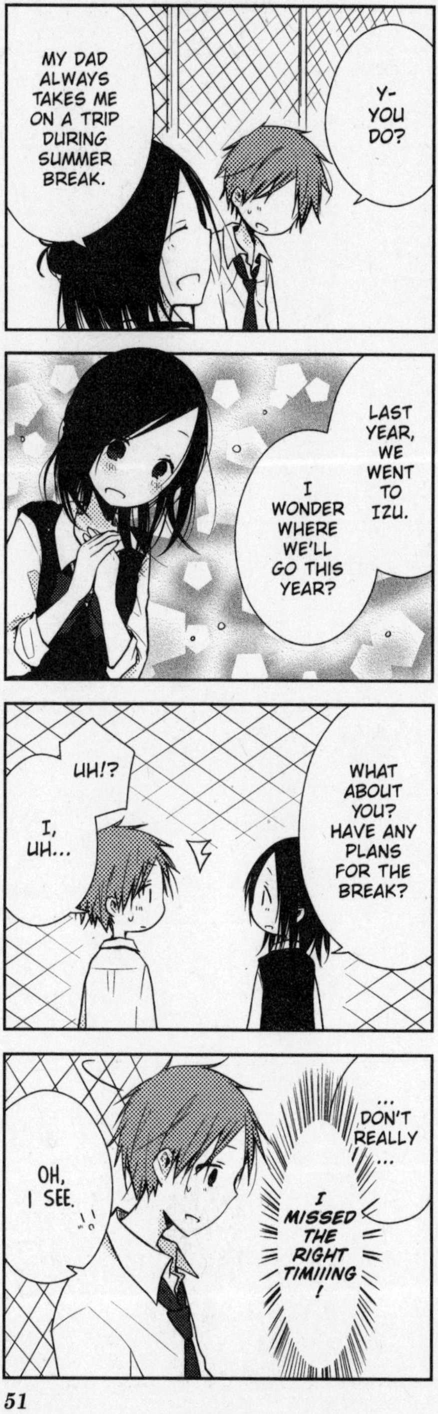
MY DAD ALWAYS TAKES ME ON A TRIP DURING SUMMER BREAK.
Y-YOU DO?
LAST YEAR, WE WENT TO IZU.
I WONDER WHERE WE'LL GO THIS YEAR?
WHAT ABOUT YOU? HAVE ANY PLANS FOR THE BREAK?
UH!?
I, UH...
...DON'T REALLY...
I MISSED THE RIGHT TIMIIING!
OH, I SEE.

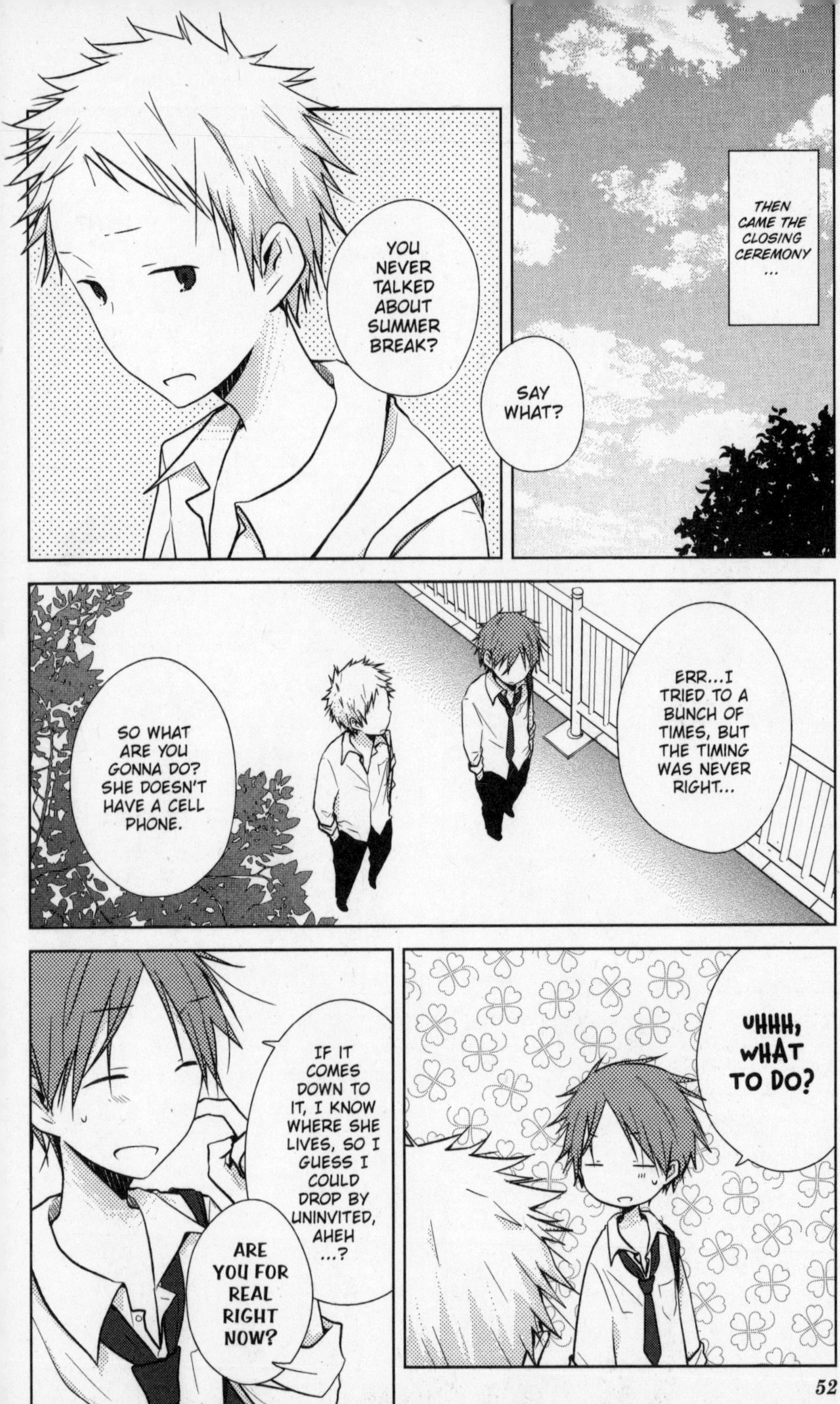
THEN CAME THE CLOSING CEREMONY ...
SAY WHAT?
YOU NEVER TALKED ABOUT SUMMER BREAK?
ERR...I TRIED TO A BUNCH OF TIMES, BUT THE TIMING WAS NEVER RIGHT...
SO WHAT ARE YOU GONNA DO? SHE DOESN'T HAVE A CELL PHONE.
UHHH, WHAT TO DO?
IF IT COMES DOWN TO IT, I KNOW WHERE SHE LIVES, SO I GUESS I COULD DROP BY UNINVITED, AHEH ...?
ARE YOU FOR REAL RIGHT NOW?

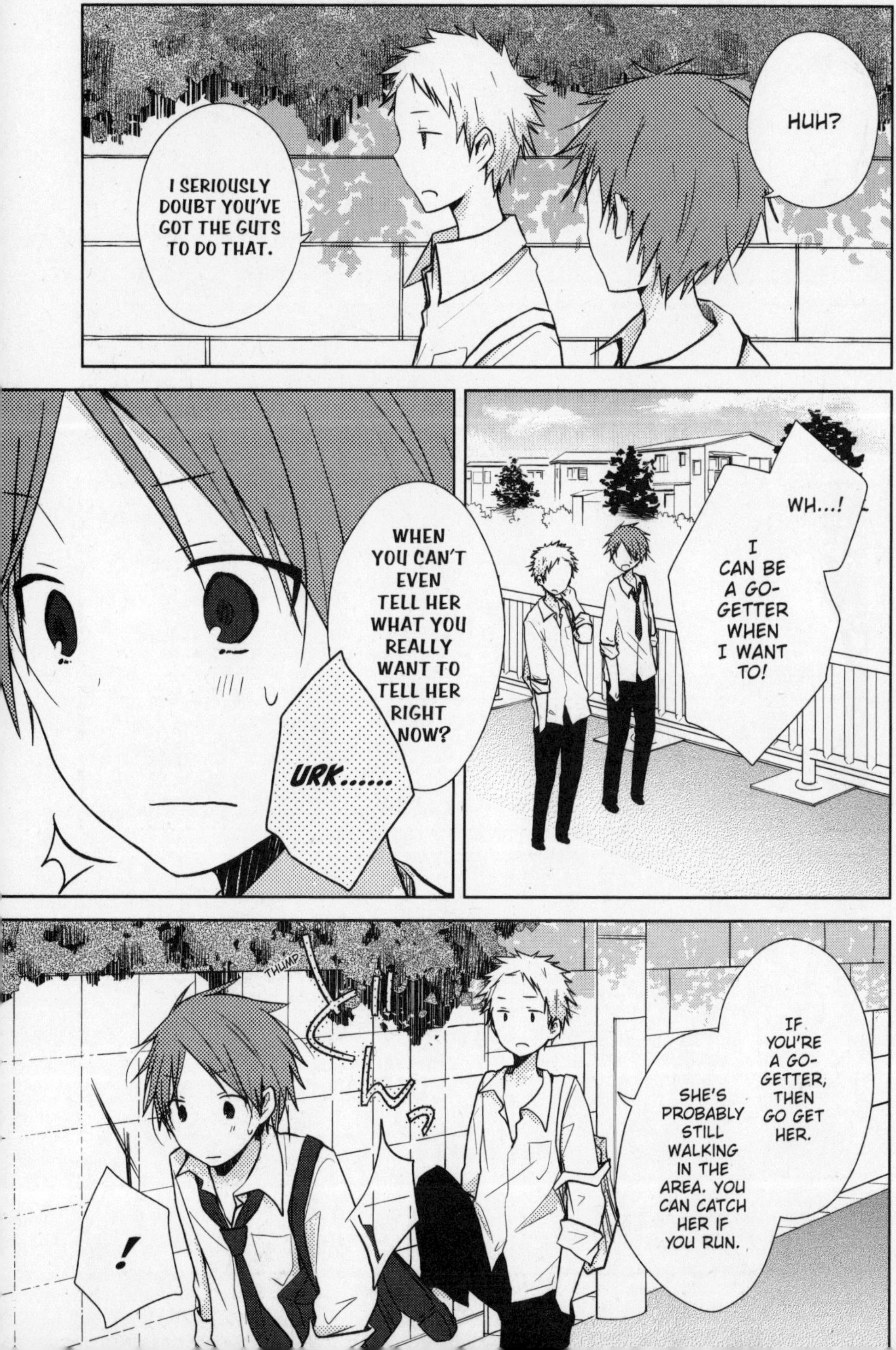
HUH?
I SERIOUSLY DOUBT YOU'VE GOT THE GUTS TO DO THAT.
WH...! I CAN BE A GO-GETTER WHEN I WANT TO!
WHEN YOU CAN'T EVEN TELL HER WHAT YOU REALLY WANT TO TELL HER RIGHT NOW?
URK......
IF YOU'RE A GO-GETTER, THEN GO GET HER.
SHE'S PROBABLY STILL WALKING IN THE AREA. YOU CAN CATCH HER IF YOU RUN.
THUMP
!

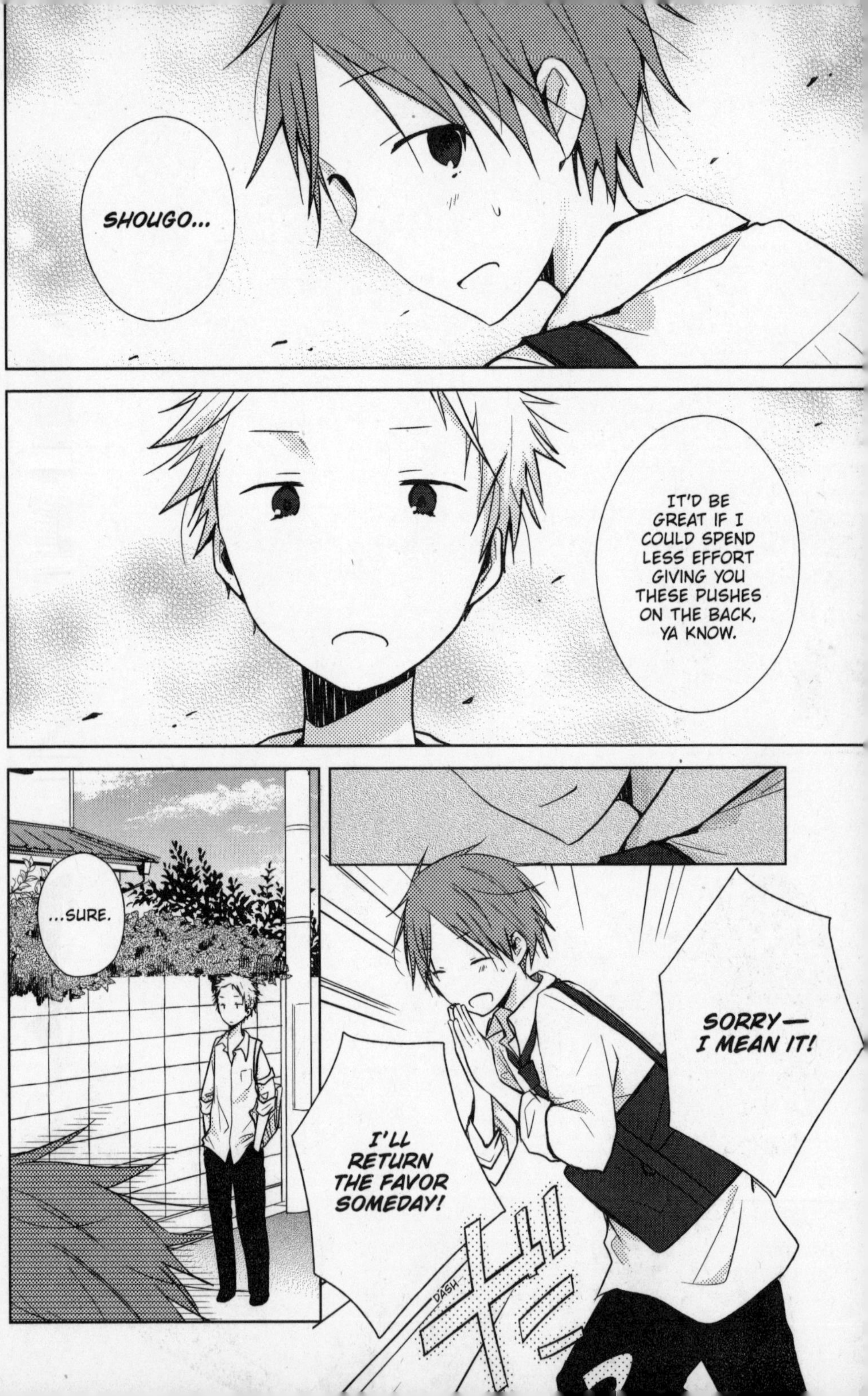
SHOUGO...
IT'D BE GREAT IF I COULD SPEND LESS EFFORT GIVING YOU THESE PUSHES ON THE BACK, YA KNOW.
SORRY— I MEAN IT!
I'LL RETURN THE FAVOR SOMEDAY!
DASH
...SURE.

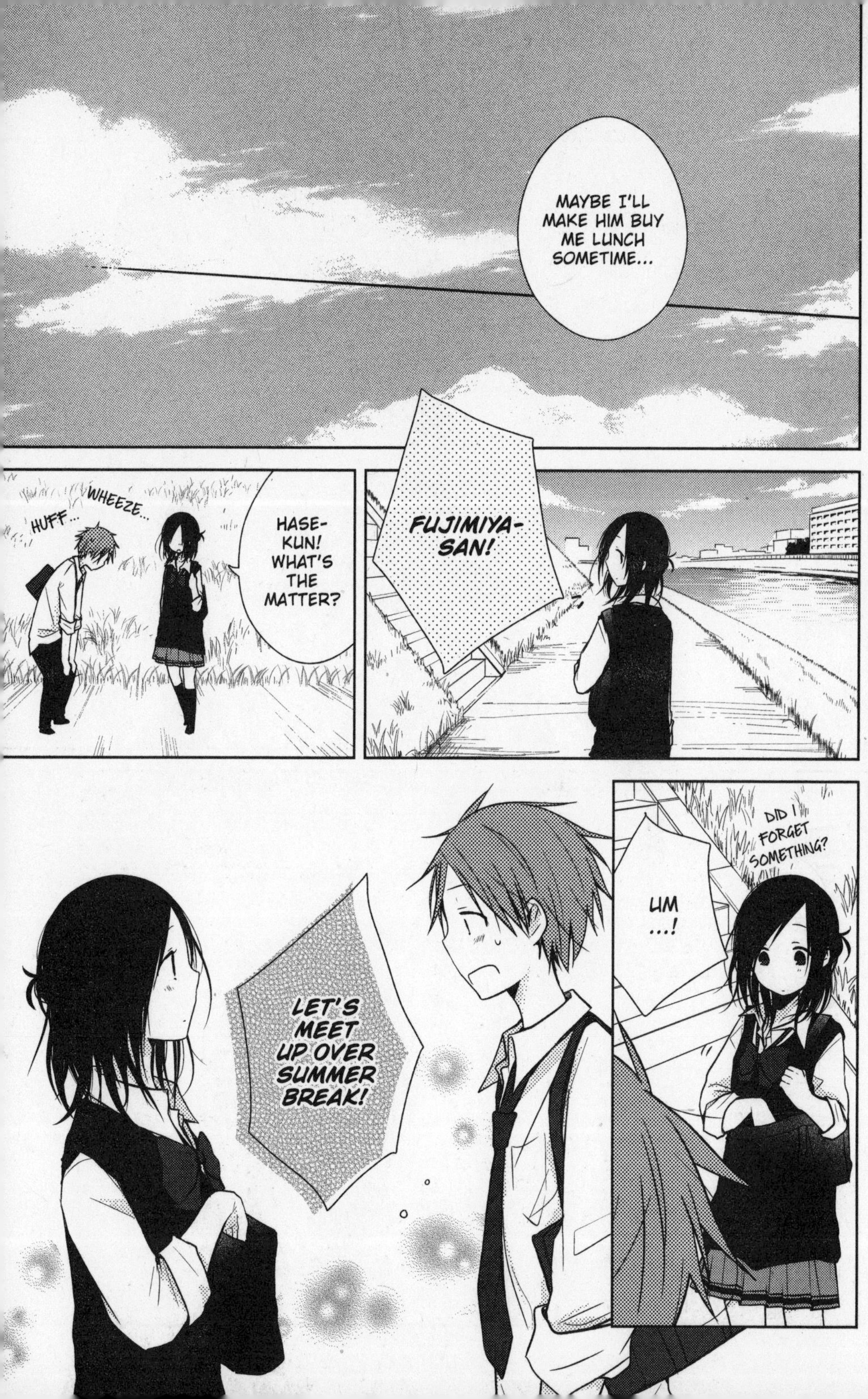
MAYBE I'LL MAKE HIM BUY ME LUNCH SOMETIME...
FUJIMIYA-SAN!
WHEEZE...
HUFF...
HASE-KUN! WHAT'S THE MATTER?
DID I FORGET SOMETHING?
UM ...!
LET'S MEET UP OVER SUMMER BREAK!

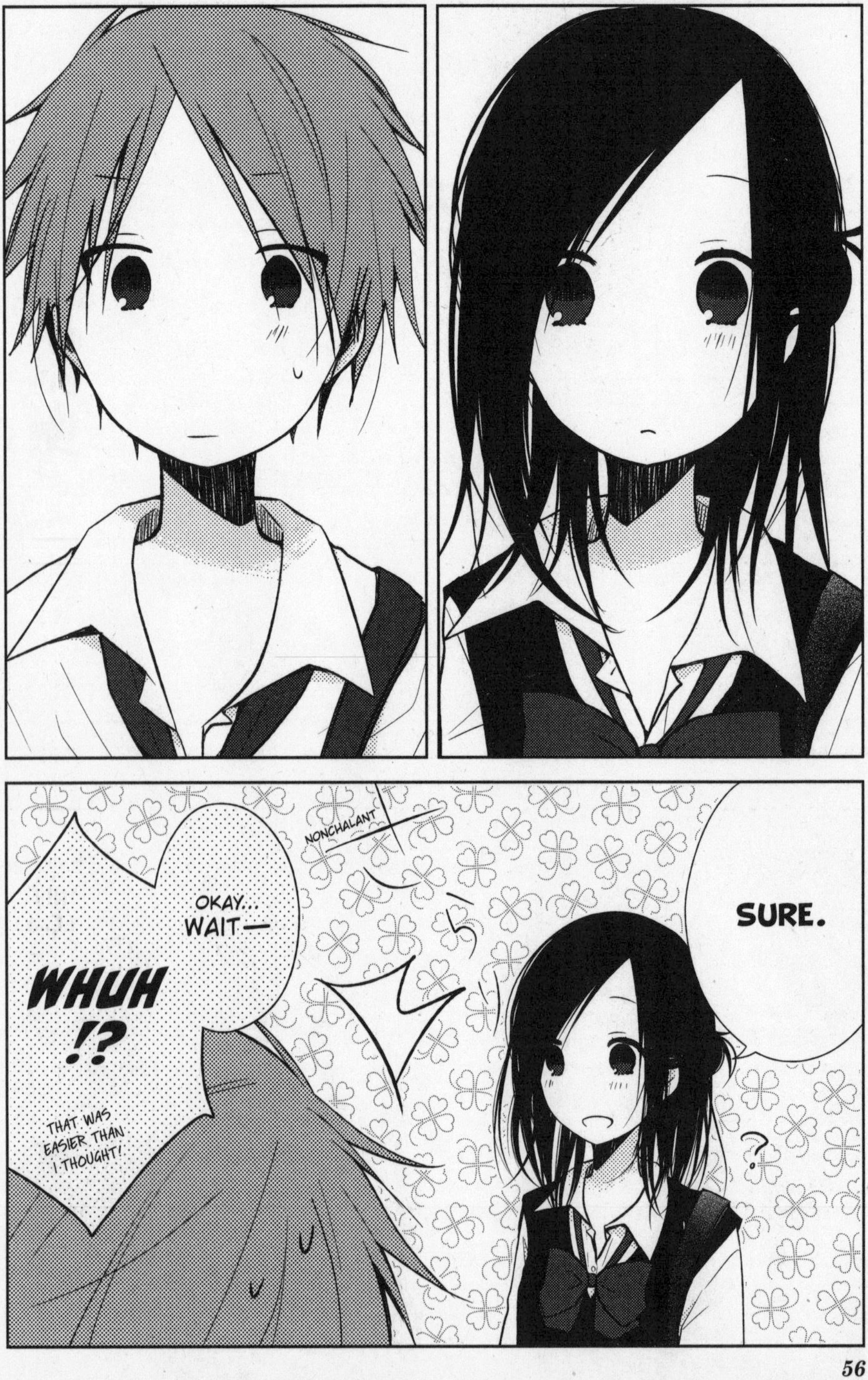
SURE.
NONCHALANT
OKAY... WAIT—
WHUH !?
THAT WAS EASIER THAN I THOUGHT!

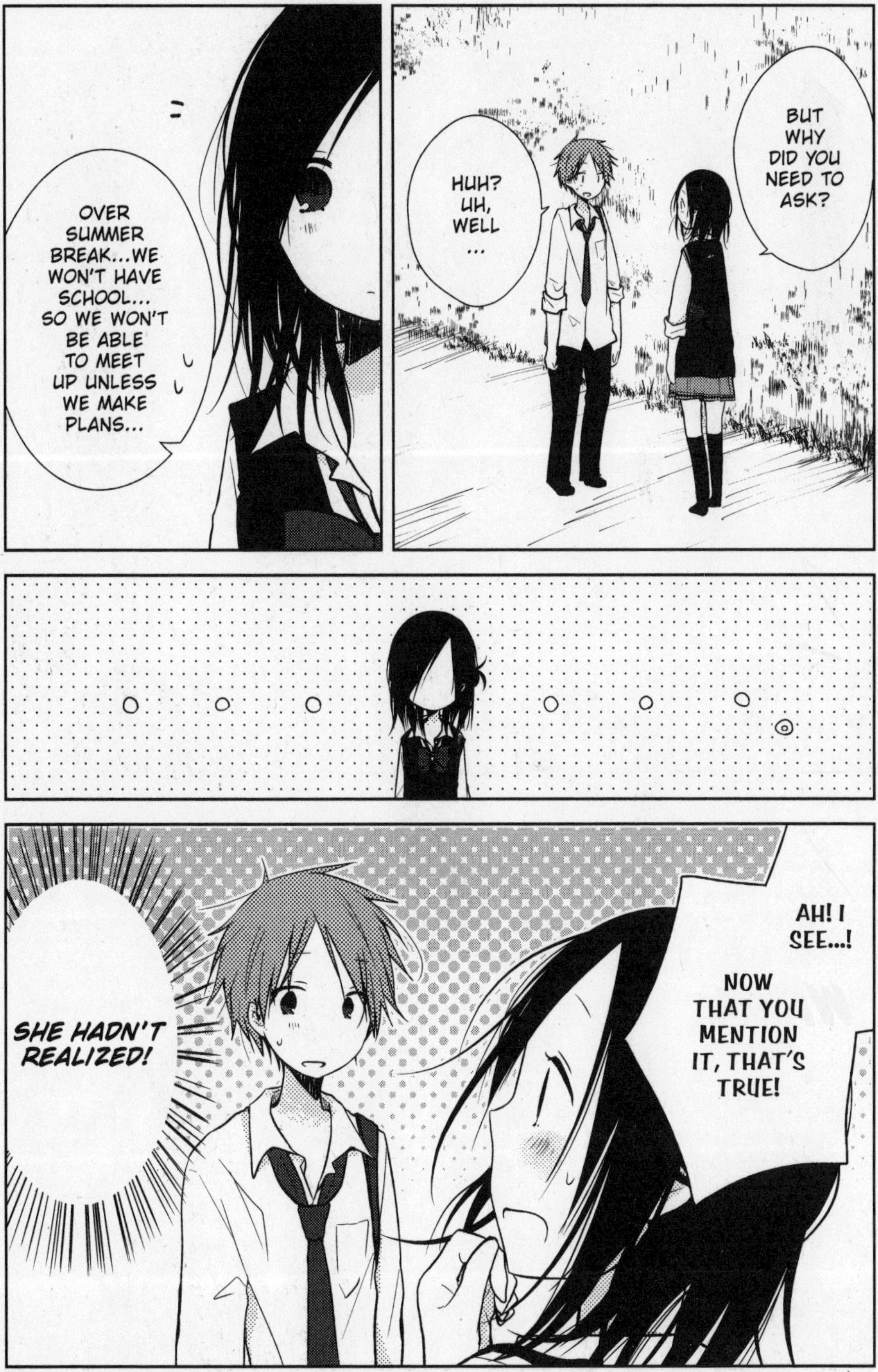
BUT WHY DID YOU NEED TO ASK?
HUH? UH, WELL ...
OVER SUMMER BREAK...WE WON'T HAVE SCHOOL... SO WE WON'T BE ABLE TO MEET UP UNLESS WE MAKE PLANS...
AH! I SEE...!
NOW THAT YOU MENTION IT, THAT'S TRUE!
SHE HADN'T REALIZED!

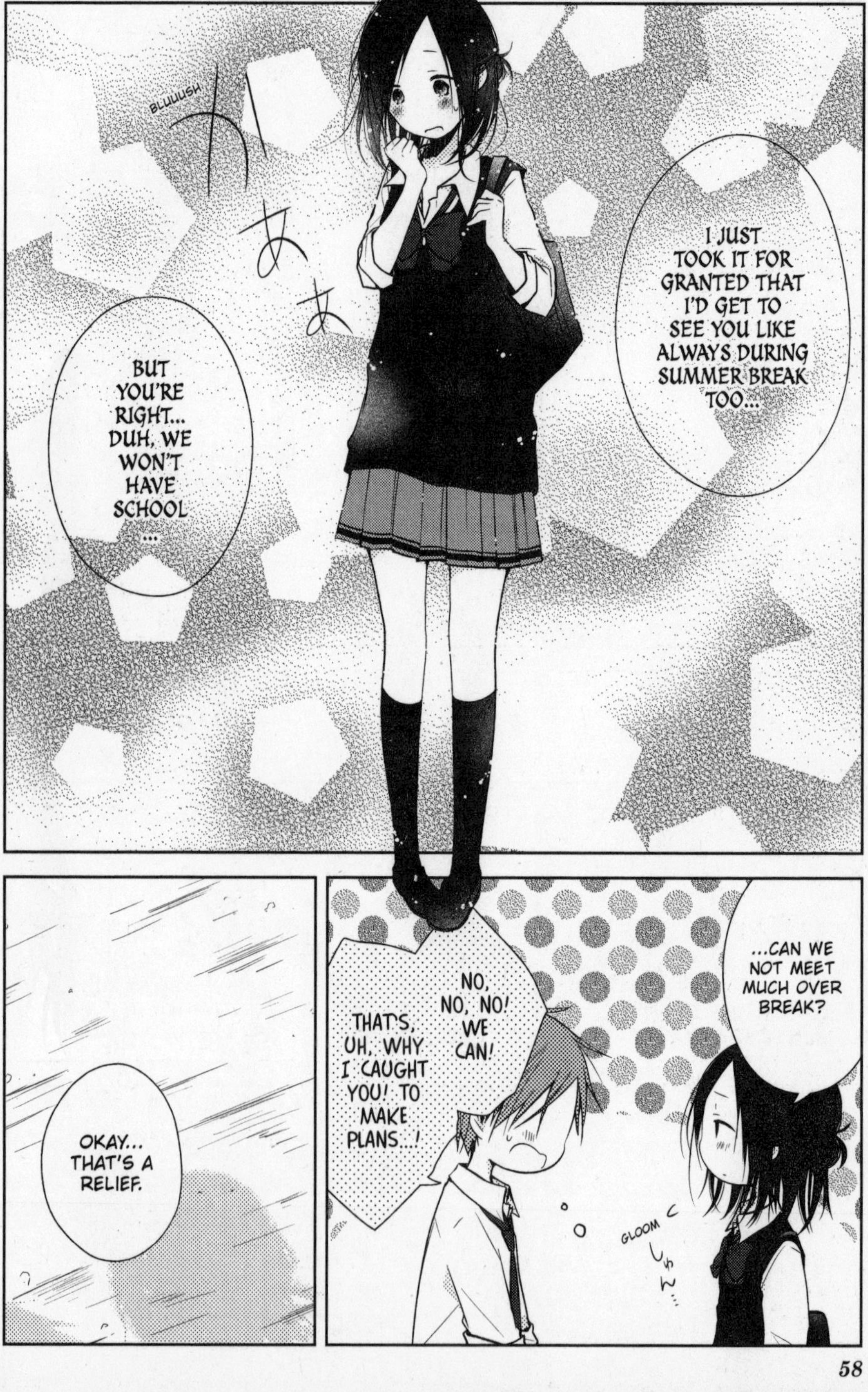
I JUST TOOK IT FOR GRANTED THAT I'D GET TO SEE YOU LIKE ALWAYS DURING SUMMER BREAK TOO...
BLUUUSH
BUT YOU'RE RIGHT... DUH, WE WON'T HAVE SCHOOL...
...CAN WE NOT MEET MUCH OVER BREAK?
NO, NO, NO! WE CAN!
THAT'S, UH, WHY I CAUGHT YOU! TO MAKE PLANS...!
GLOOM
OKAY... THAT'S A RELIEF.

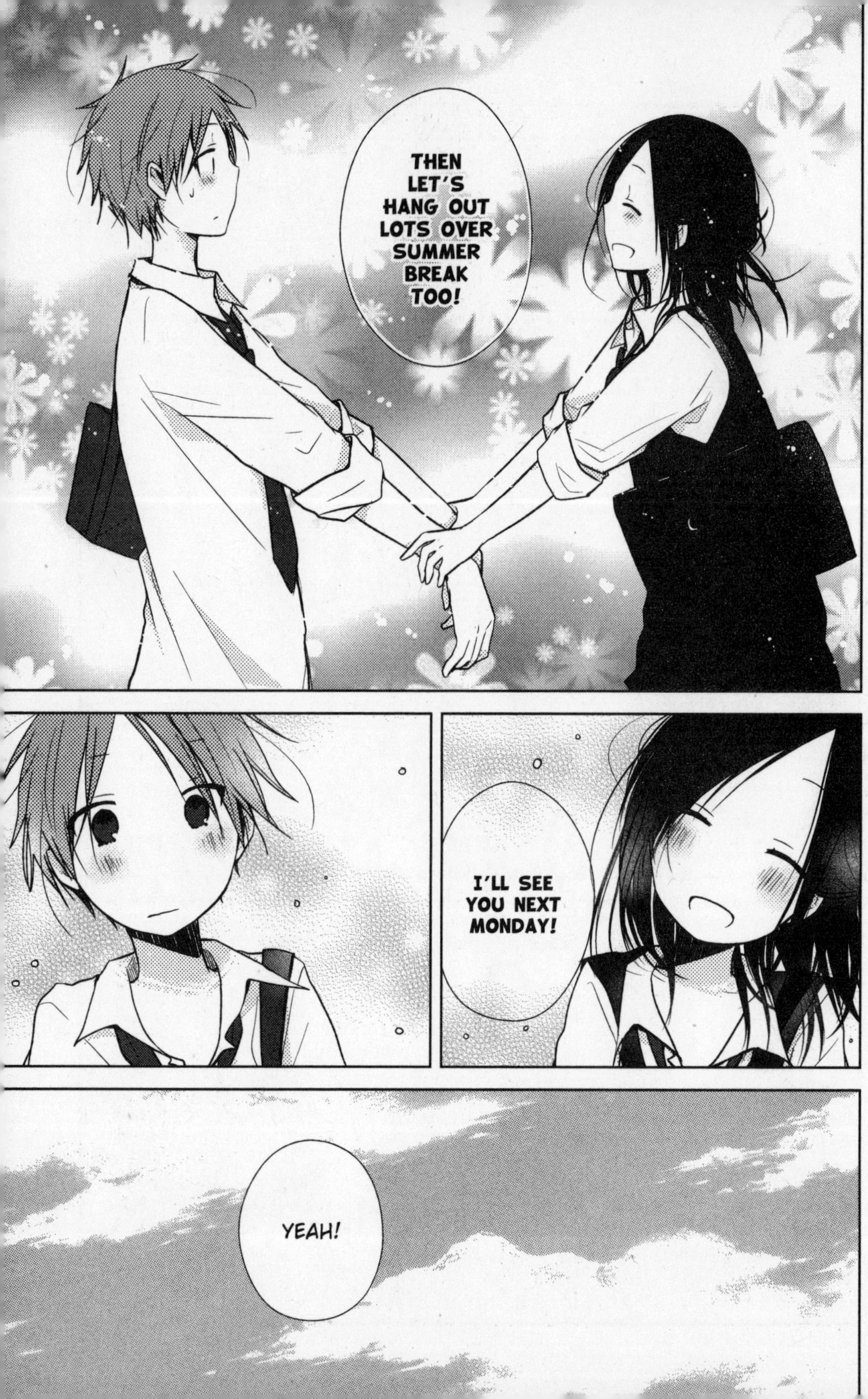
THEN LET'S HANG OUT LOTS OVER SUMMER BREAK TOO!
I'LL SEE YOU NEXT MONDAY!
YEAH!

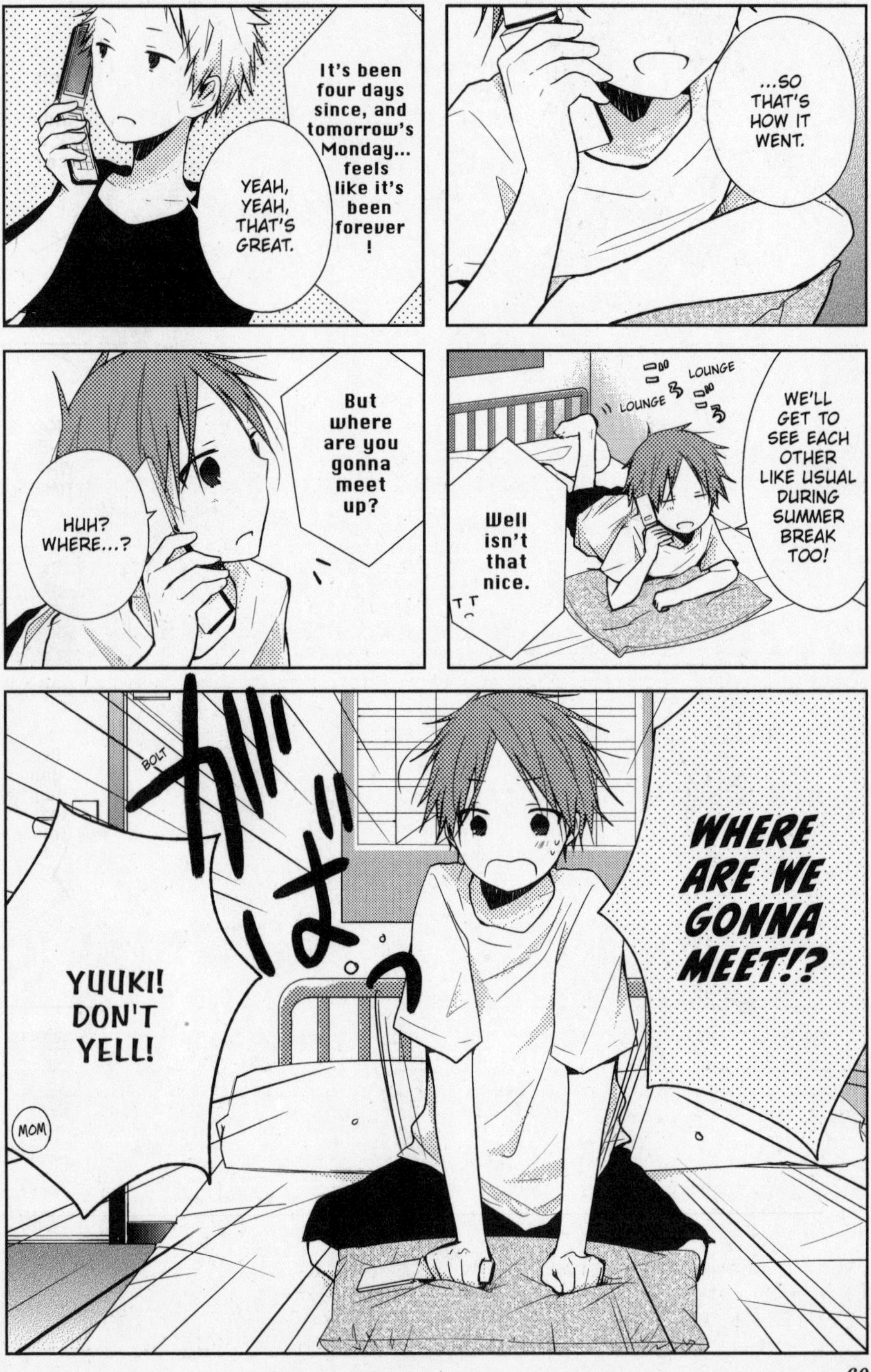
...SO THAT'S HOW IT WENT.
It's been four days since, and tomorrow's Monday... feels like it's been forever!
YEAH, YEAH, THAT'S GREAT.
LOUNGE
LOUNGE
WE'LL GET TO SEE EACH OTHER LIKE USUAL DURING SUMMER BREAK TOO!
Well isn't that nice.
But where are you gonna meet up?
HUH? WHERE...?
WHERE ARE WE GONNA MEET!?
BOLT
YUUKI! DON'T YELL!
MOM

FORGOT ABOUT THAT

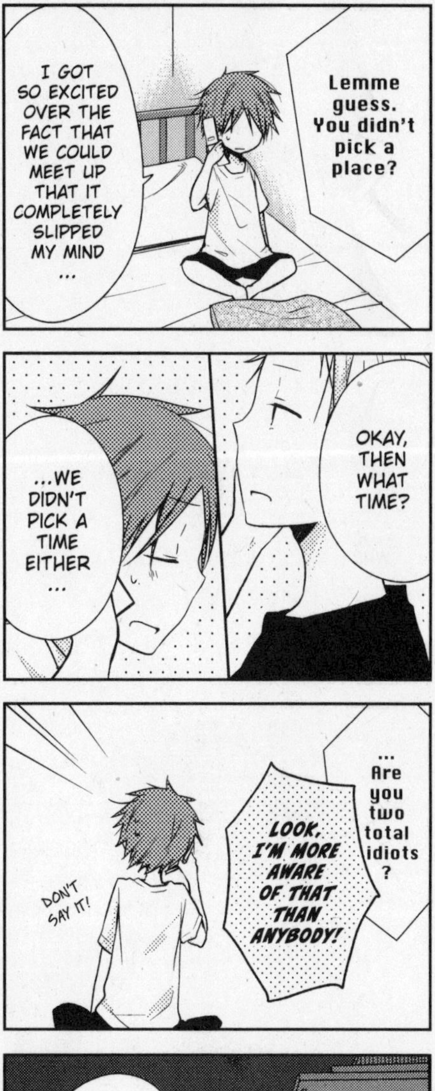
Lemme guess. You didn't pick a place?
I GOT SO EXCITED OVER THE FACT THAT WE COULD MEET UP THAT IT COMPLETELY SLIPPED MY MIND ...
OKAY, THEN WHAT TIME?
...WE DIDN'T PICK A TIME EITHER ...
... Are you two total idiots ?
LOOK, I'M MORE AWARE OF THAT THAN ANYBODY!
DON'T SAY IT!
FOR NOW, I GUESS THE PLAN IS TO GO TO HER HOUSE IN THE MORNING...

THAT KIND OF TWIST

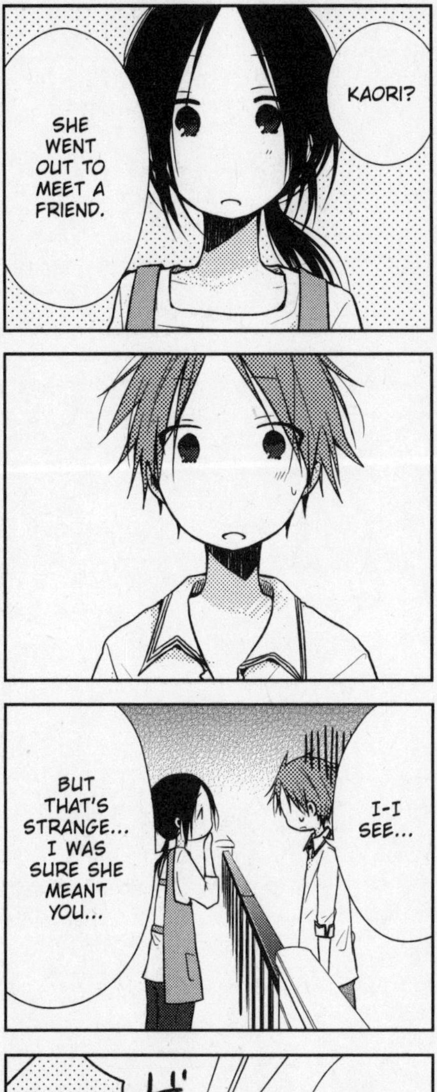
KAORI?
SHE WENT OUT TO MEET A FRIEND.
I-I SEE...
BUT THAT'S STRANGE... I WAS SURE SHE MEANT YOU...
WHAT HAPPENED? DID YOU MISS EACH OTHER? I QUITE LIKE THOSE SORTS OF TWISTS.
どき どき
BADUM BADUM
だっ
DASH
THANK YOU, MA'AM! SORRY FOR BOTHERING YOU!

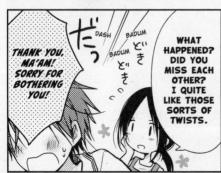

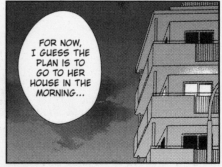

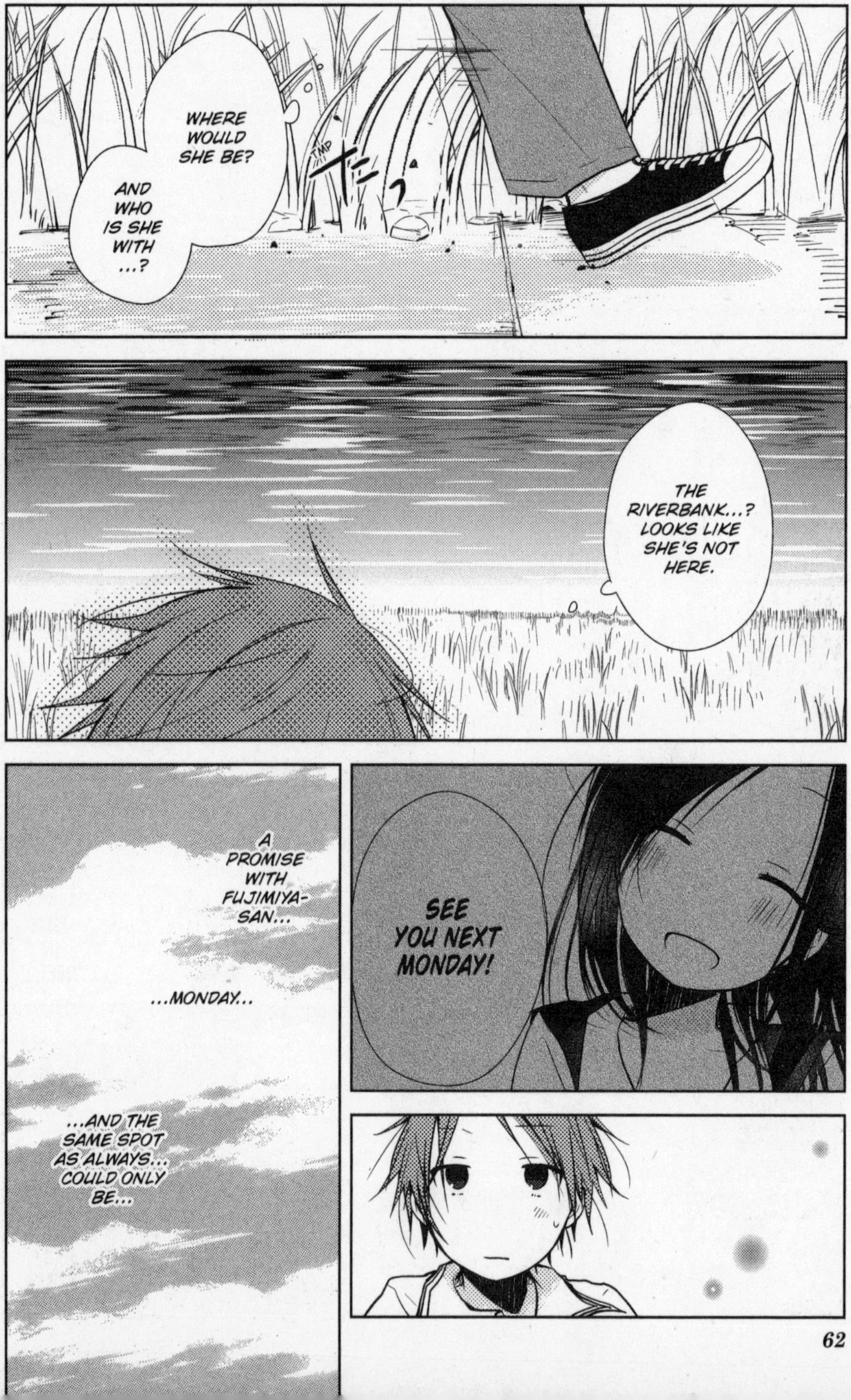
WHERE WOULD SHE BE?
AND WHO IS SHE WITH ...?
TMP
THE RIVERBANK...? LOOKS LIKE SHE'S NOT HERE.
SEE YOU NEXT MONDAY!
A PROMISE WITH FUJIMIYA-SAN...
...MONDAY...
...AND THE SAME SPOT AS ALWAYS... COULD ONLY BE...

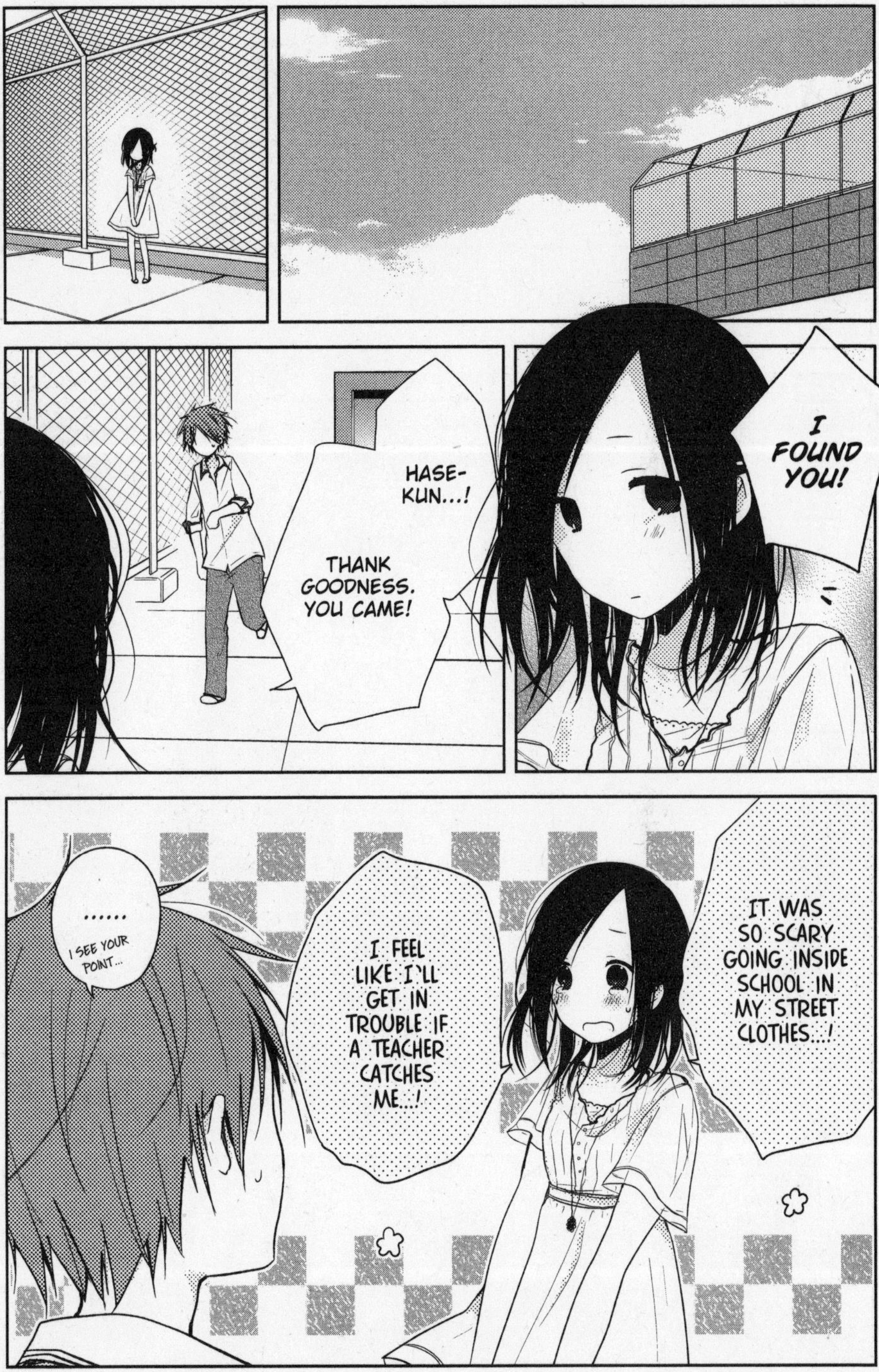
I FOUND YOU!
HASE-KUN...!
THANK GOODNESS. YOU CAME!
IT WAS SO SCARY GOING INSIDE SCHOOL IN MY STREET CLOTHES...!
I FEEL LIKE I'LL GET IN TROUBLE IF A TEACHER CATCHES ME...!
......
I SEE YOUR POINT...

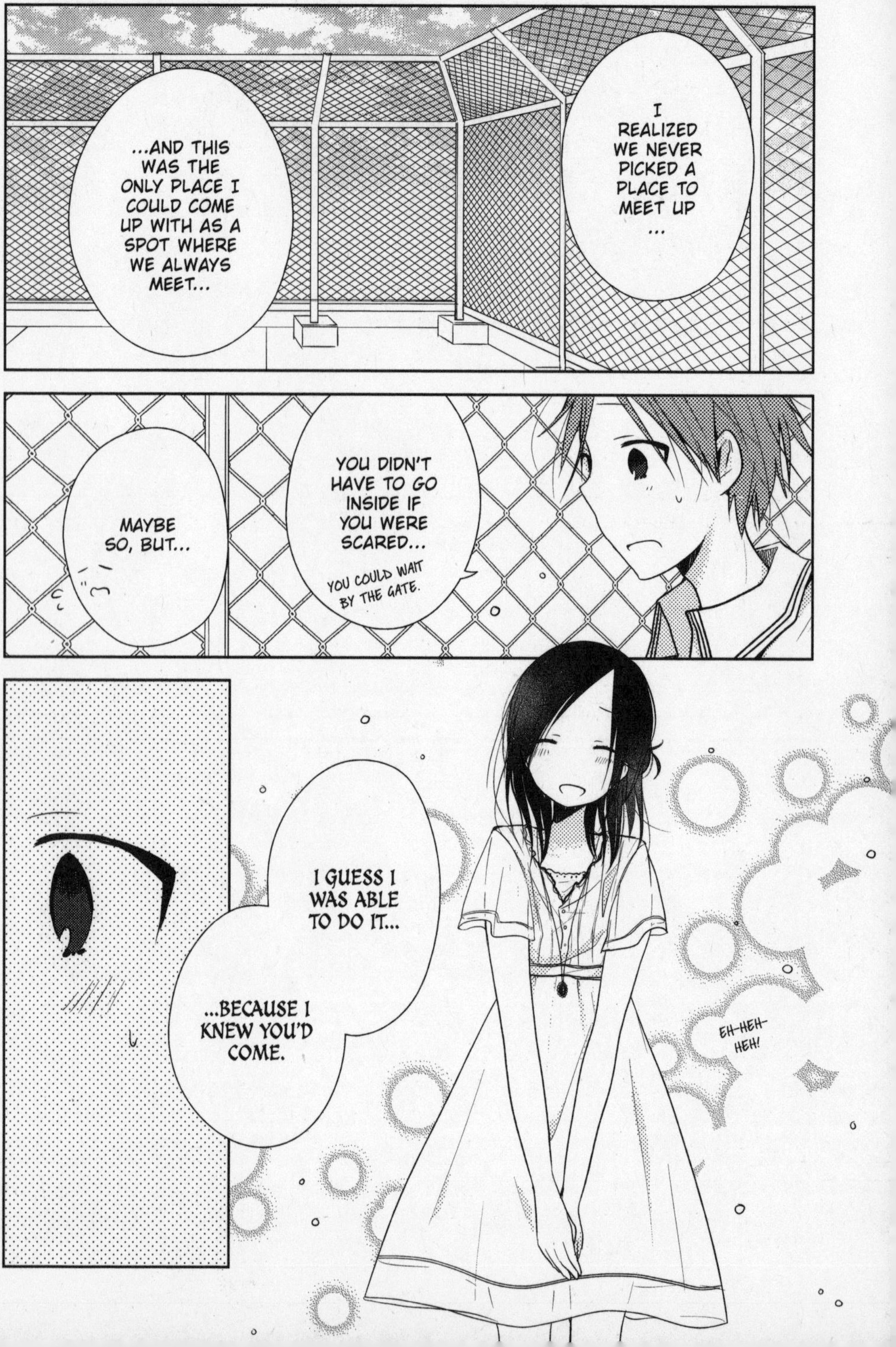
I REALIZED WE NEVER PICKED A PLACE TO MEET UP...
...AND THIS WAS THE ONLY PLACE I COULD COME UP WITH AS A SPOT WHERE WE ALWAYS MEET...
YOU DIDN'T HAVE TO GO INSIDE IF YOU WERE SCARED...
YOU COULD WAIT BY THE GATE.
MAYBE SO, BUT...
I GUESS I WAS ABLE TO DO IT...
...BECAUSE I KNEW YOU'D COME.
EH-HEH-HEH!

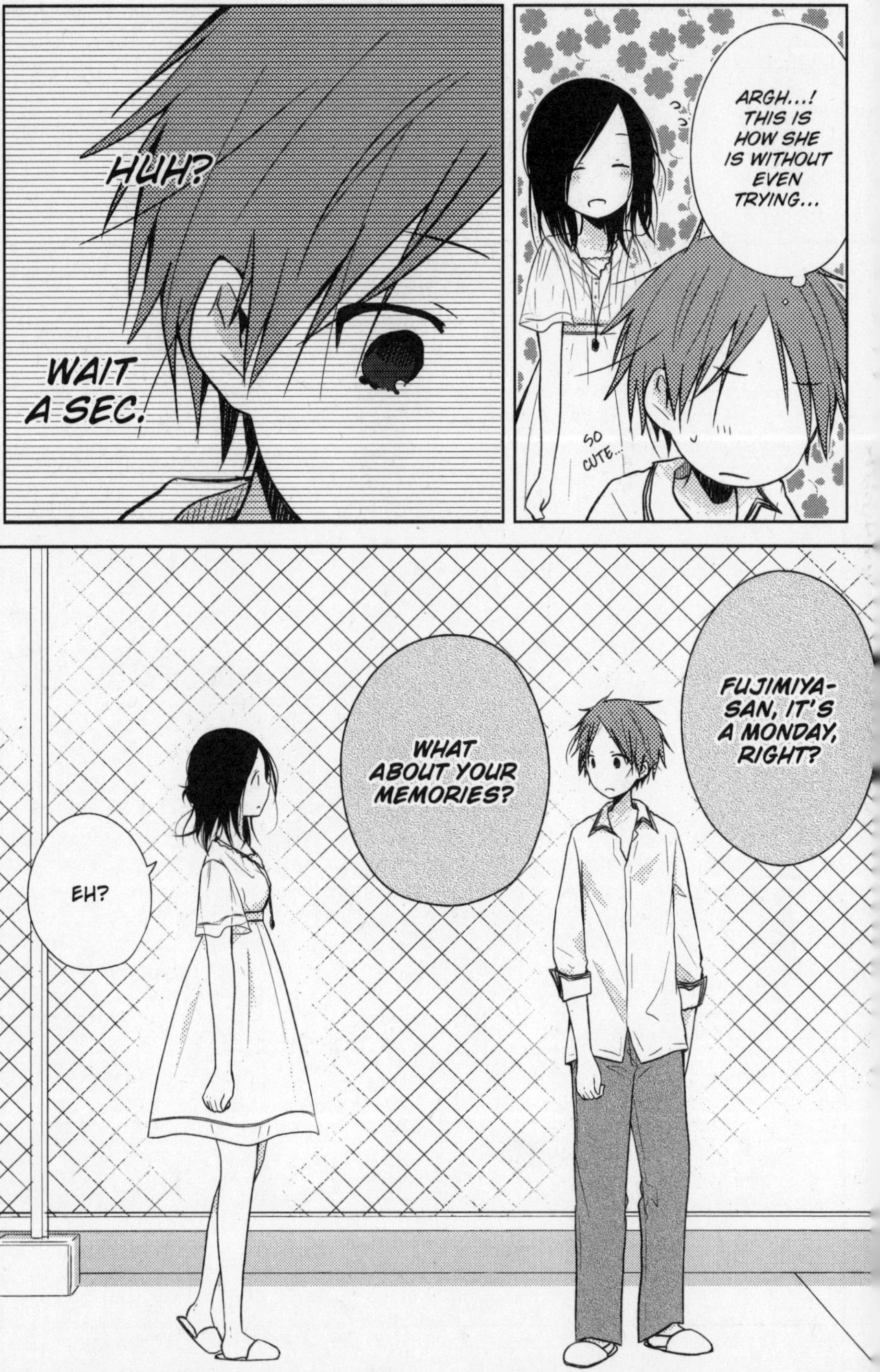
ARGH...! THIS IS HOW SHE IS WITHOUT EVEN TRYING...
SO CUTE...
HUH?
WAIT A SEC.
FUJIMIYA-SAN, IT'S A MONDAY, RIGHT?
WHAT ABOUT YOUR MEMORIES?
EH?

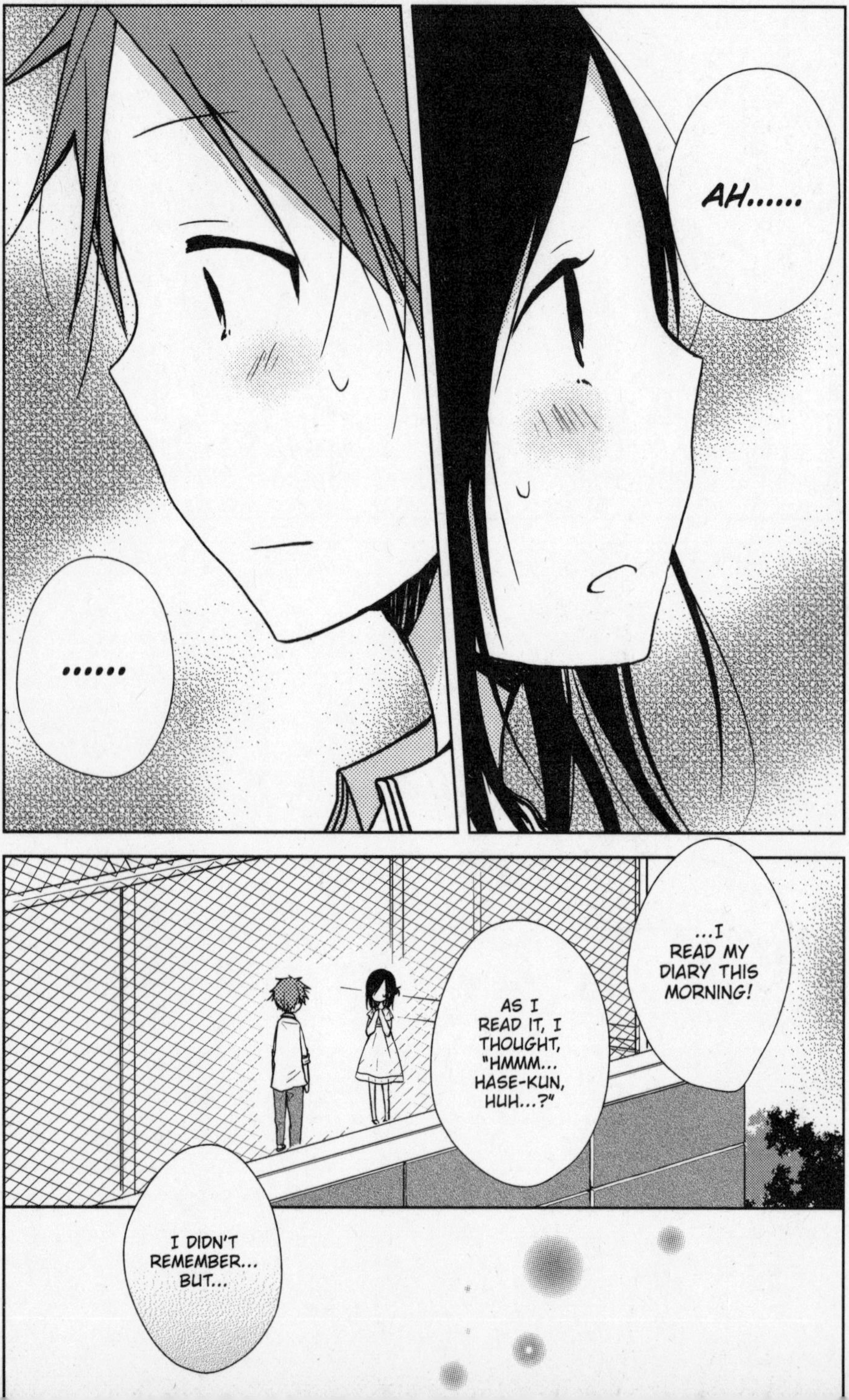
AH......
......
...I READ MY DIARY THIS MORNING!
AS I READ IT, I THOUGHT, "HMMM... HASE-KUN, HUH...?"
I DIDN'T REMEMBER... BUT...

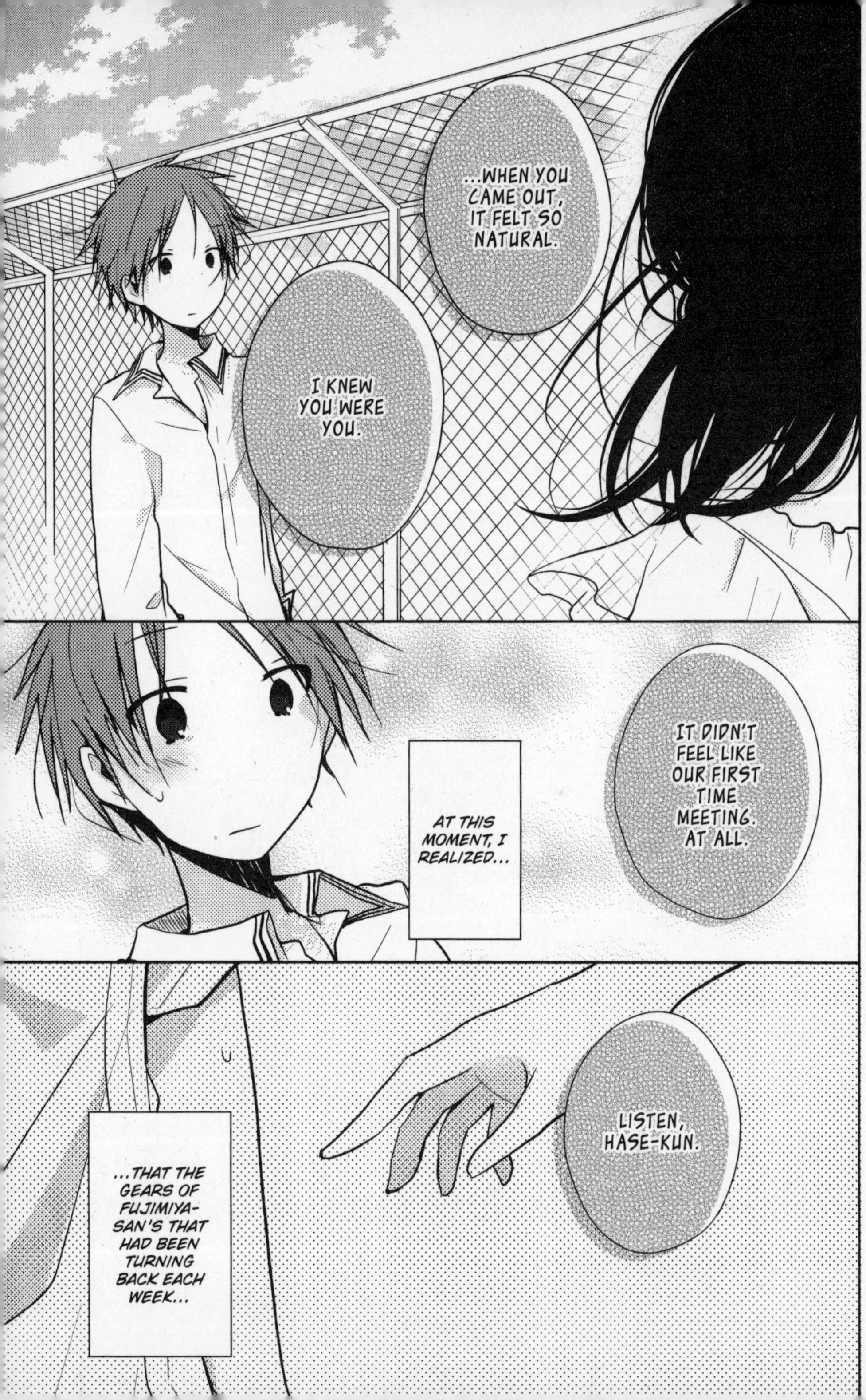
...WHEN YOU CAME OUT, IT FELT SO NATURAL.
I KNEW YOU WERE YOU.
IT DIDN'T FEEL LIKE OUR FIRST TIME MEETING. AT ALL.
AT THIS MOMENT, I REALIZED...
LISTEN, HASE-KUN.
...THAT THE GEARS OF FUJIMIYA-SAN'S THAT HAD BEEN TURNING BACK EACH WEEK...

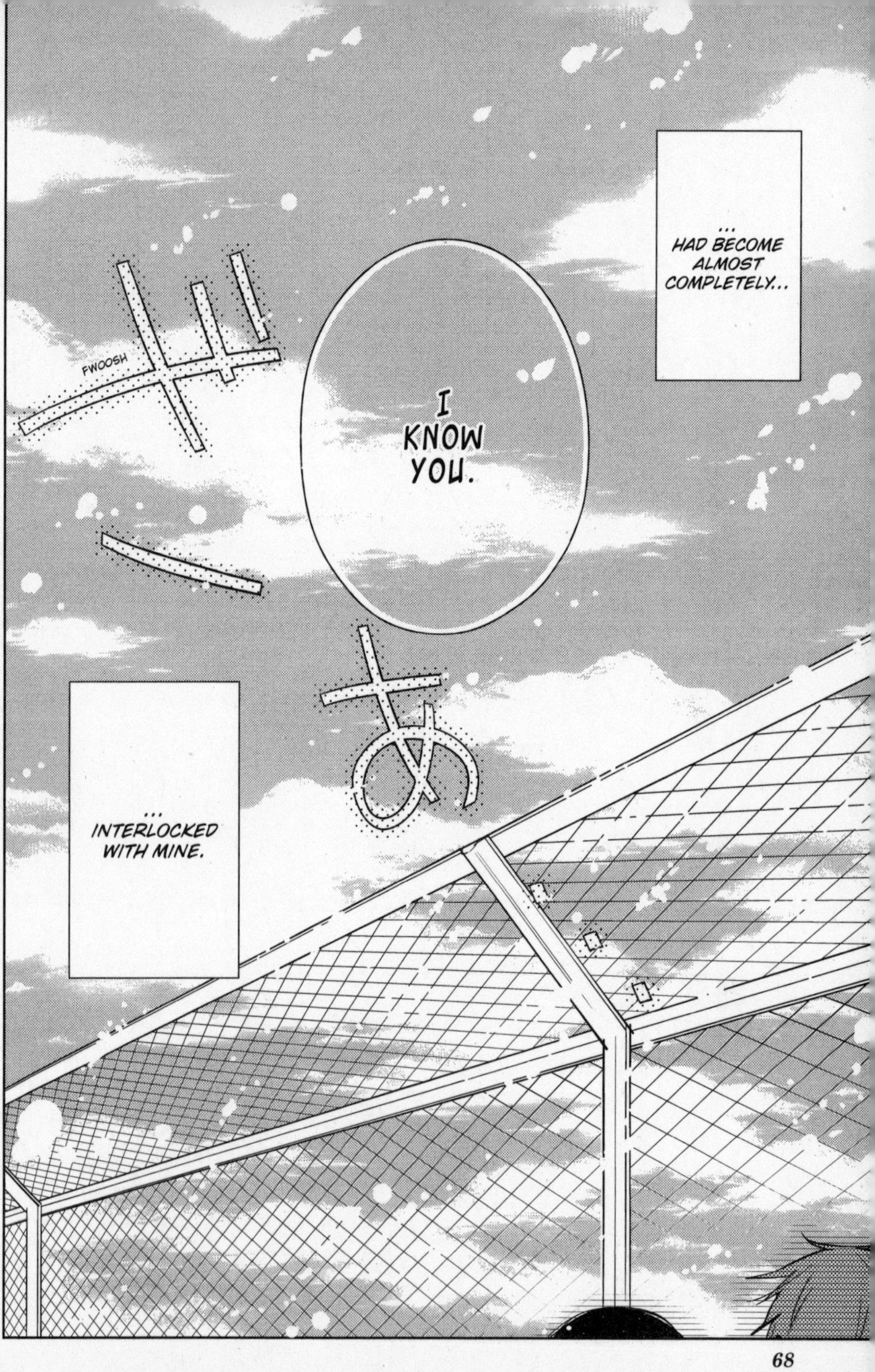
...HAD BECOME ALMOST COMPLETELY...
I KNOW YOU.
FWOOSH
...INTERLOCKED WITH MINE.

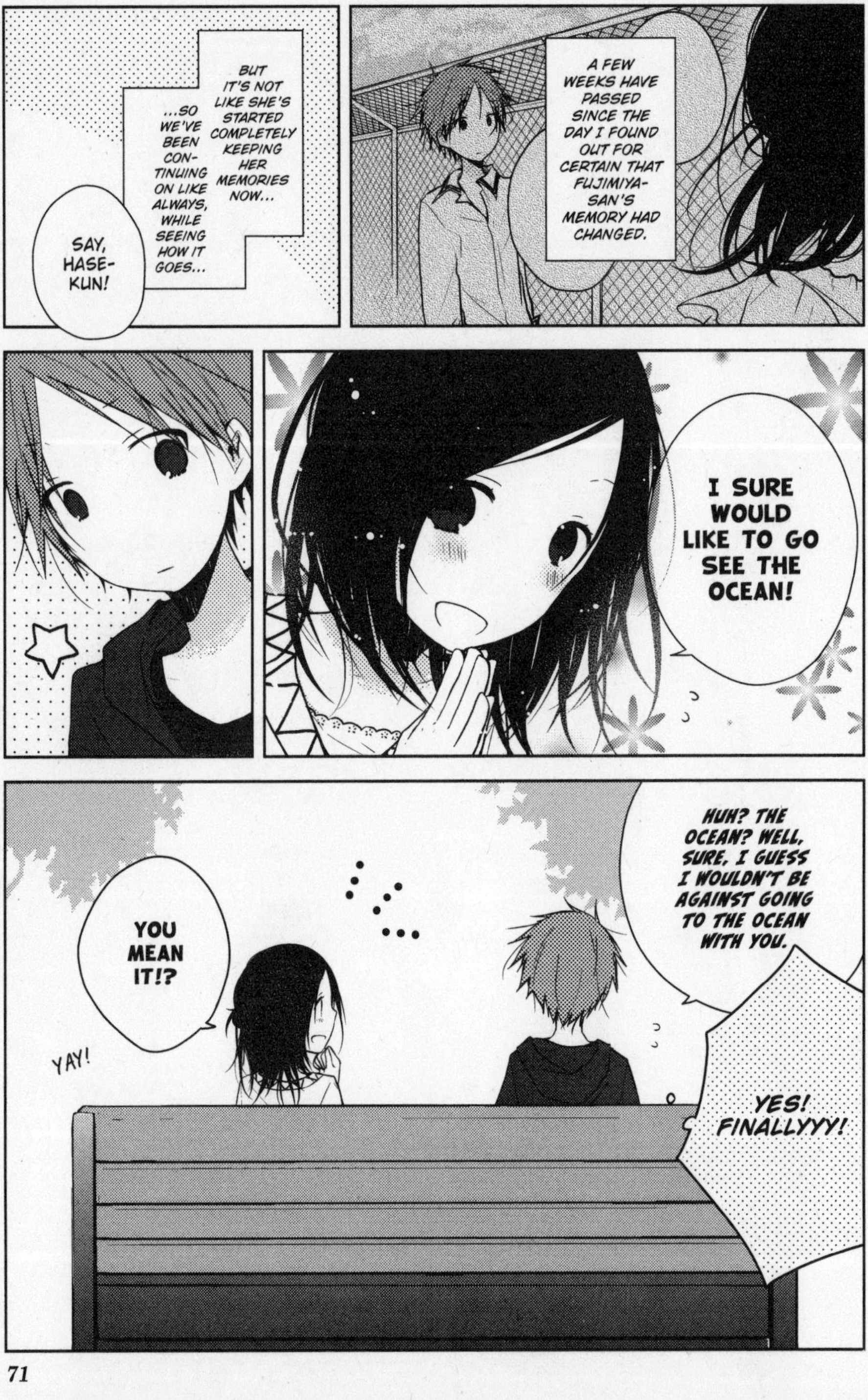
A FEW WEEKS HAVE PASSED SINCE THE DAY I FOUND OUT FOR CERTAIN THAT FUJIMIYA-SAN'S MEMORY HAD CHANGED.
BUT IT'S NOT LIKE SHE'S STARTED COMPLETELY KEEPING HER MEMORIES NOW...
...SO WE'VE BEEN CONTINUING ON LIKE ALWAYS, WHILE SEEING HOW IT GOES...
SAY, HASE-KUN!
I SURE WOULD LIKE TO GO SEE THE OCEAN!
HUH? THE OCEAN? WELL, SURE, I GUESS I WOULDN'T BE AGAINST GOING TO THE OCEAN WITH YOU.
YES! FINALLYYY!
YOU MEAN IT!?
YAY!

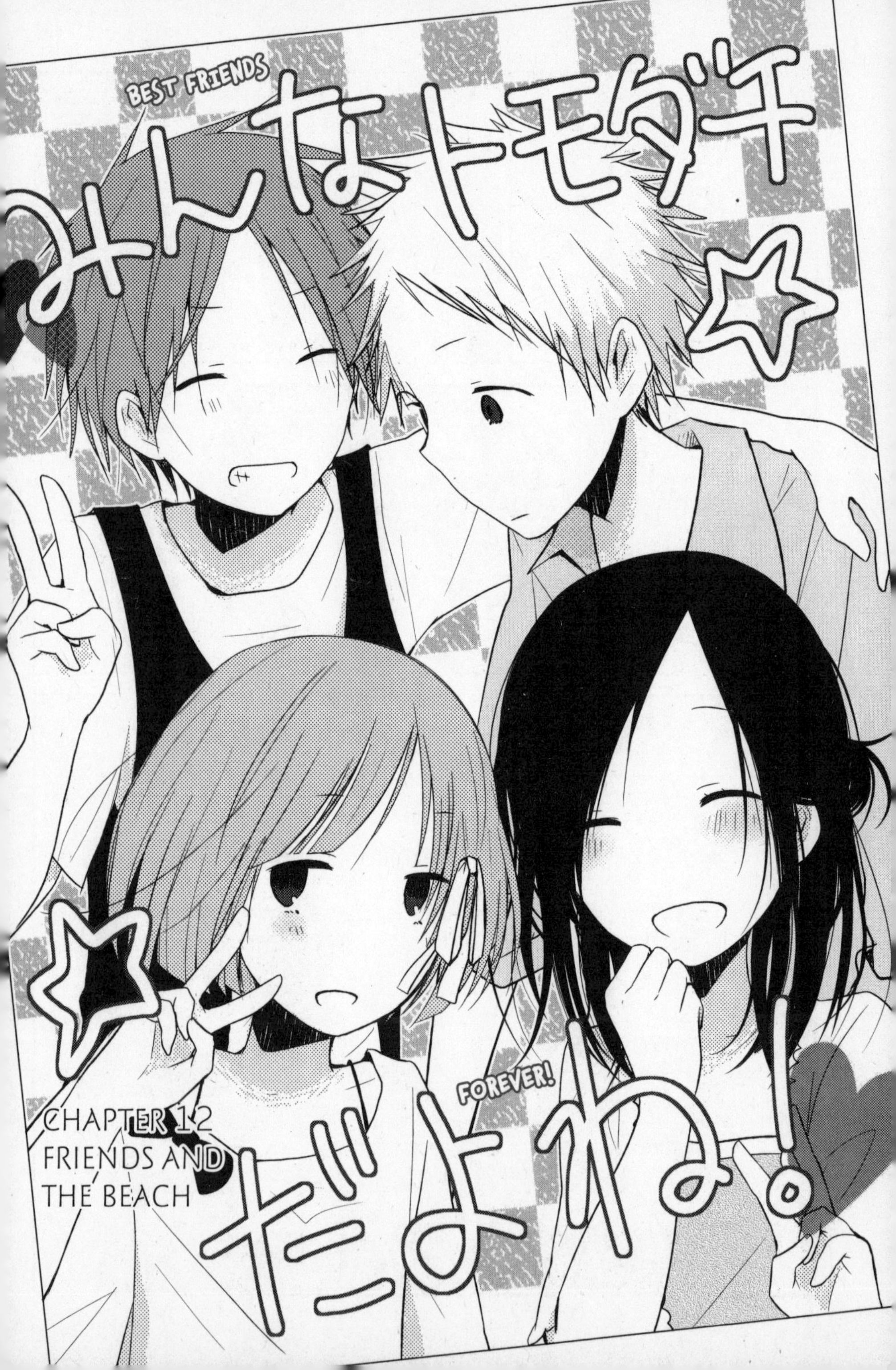
BEST FRIENDS
みんなトモダチ
FOREVER!
CHAPTER 12
FRIENDS AND
THE BEACH

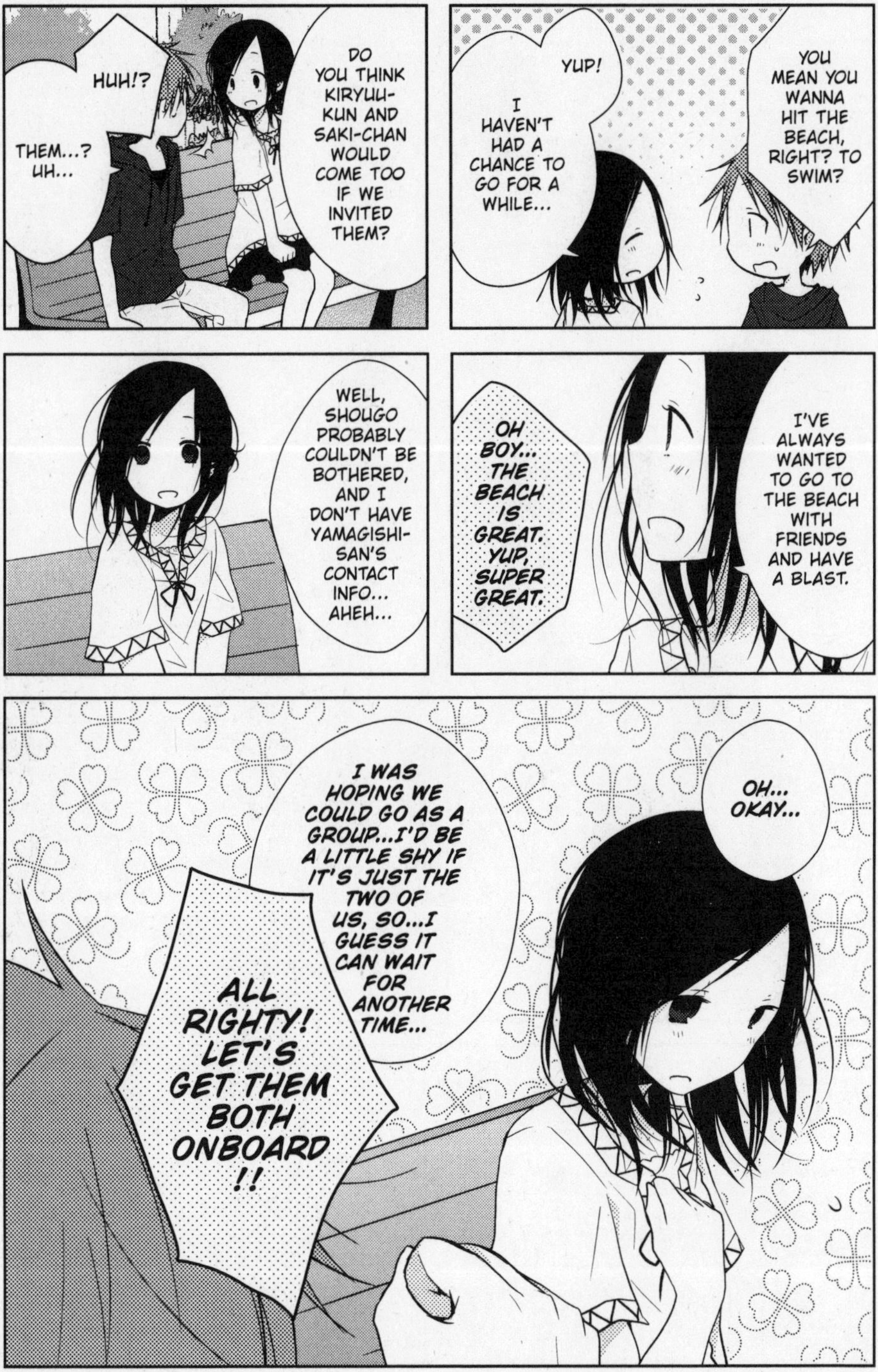
YOU MEAN YOU WANNA HIT THE BEACH, RIGHT? TO SWIM?
YUP!
I HAVEN'T HAD A CHANCE TO GO FOR A WHILE...
DO YOU THINK KIRYUU-KUN AND SAKI-CHAN WOULD COME TOO IF WE INVITED THEM?
HUH!?
THEM...? UH...
I'VE ALWAYS WANTED TO GO TO THE BEACH WITH FRIENDS AND HAVE A BLAST.
OH BOY... THE BEACH IS GREAT. YUP, SUPER GREAT.
WELL, SHOUGO PROBABLY COULDN'T BE BOTHERED, AND I DON'T HAVE YAMAGISHI-SAN'S CONTACT INFO... AHEH...
OH... OKAY...
I WAS HOPING WE COULD GO AS A GROUP...I'D BE A LITTLE SHY IF IT'S JUST THE TWO OF US, SO...I GUESS IT CAN WAIT FOR ANOTHER TIME...
ALL RIGHTY! LET'S GET THEM BOTH ONBOARD!!

SUMMER BREAK EVENTS

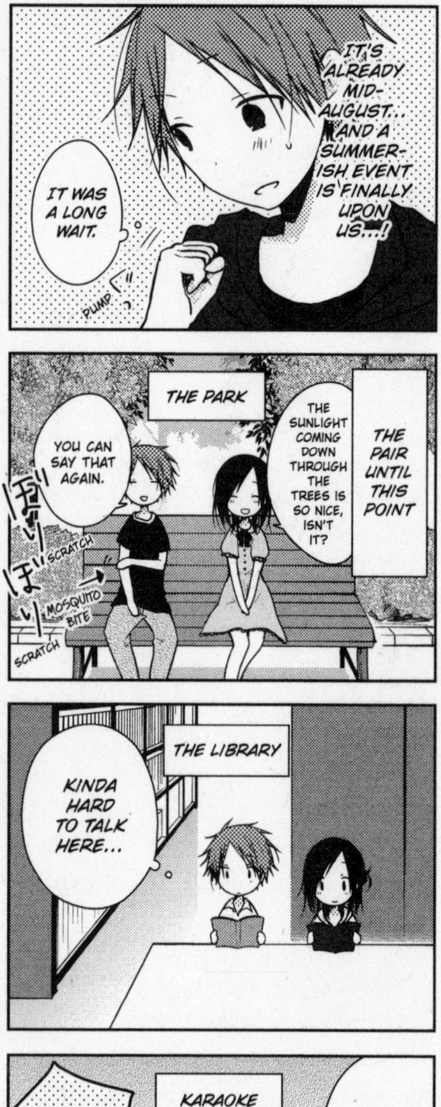
IT'S ALREADY MID-AUGUST... AND A SUMMER-ISH EVENT IS FINALLY UPON US...!
IT WAS A LONG WAIT.
PUMP
THE PARK
THE PAIR UNTIL THIS POINT
THE SUNLIGHT COMING DOWN THROUGH THE TREES IS SO NICE, ISN'T IT?
YOU CAN SAY THAT AGAIN.
ぼりぼり
SCRATCH SCRATCH
MOSQUITO BITE
THE LIBRARY
KINDA HARD TO TALK HERE...
KARAOKE
I FOUND A TAMBOURINE!
LIKE I SAID BEFORE, WE DON'T NEED THAT!
LEAVE IT THERE!
しゃんしゃん
SHK SHK

BUG BITE

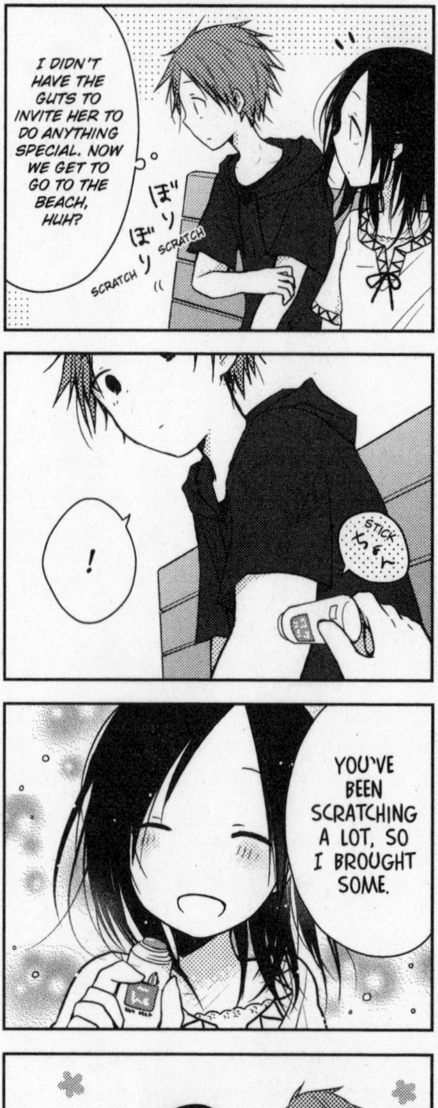
I DIDN'T HAVE THE GUTS TO INVITE HER TO DO ANYTHING SPECIAL. NOW WE GET TO GO TO THE BEACH, HUH?
ぼりぼり
SCRATCH SCRATCH
!
STICK
ちょん
YOU'VE BEEN SCRATCHING A LOT, SO I BROUGHT SOME.
ENJOYING YOUTH TO THE FULLEST
TWANG

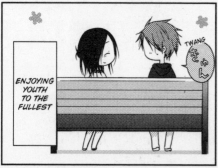

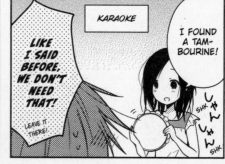

THAT TYPE OF GUY

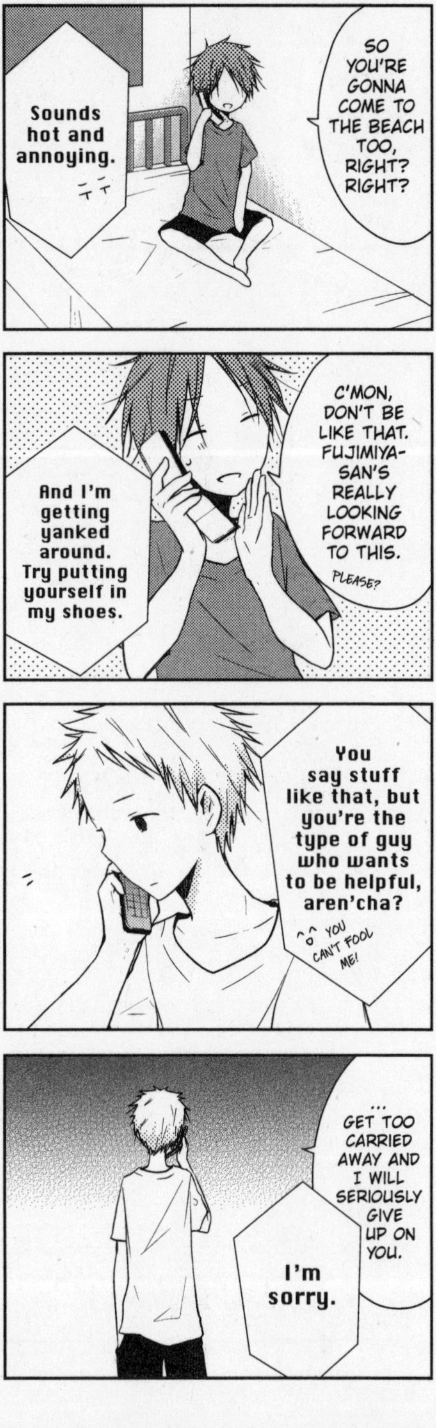
SO YOU'RE GONNA COME TO THE BEACH TOO, RIGHT? RIGHT?
Sounds hot and annoying.
C'MON, DON'T BE LIKE THAT. FUJIMIYA-SAN'S REALLY LOOKING FORWARD TO THIS.
PLEASE?
And I'm getting yanked around. Try putting yourself in my shoes.
You say stuff like that, but you're the type of guy who wants to be helpful, aren'cha?
^o^ YOU CAN'T FOOL ME!
... GET TOO CARRIED AWAY AND I WILL SERIOUSLY GIVE UP ON YOU.
I'm sorry.

HAND-OFF

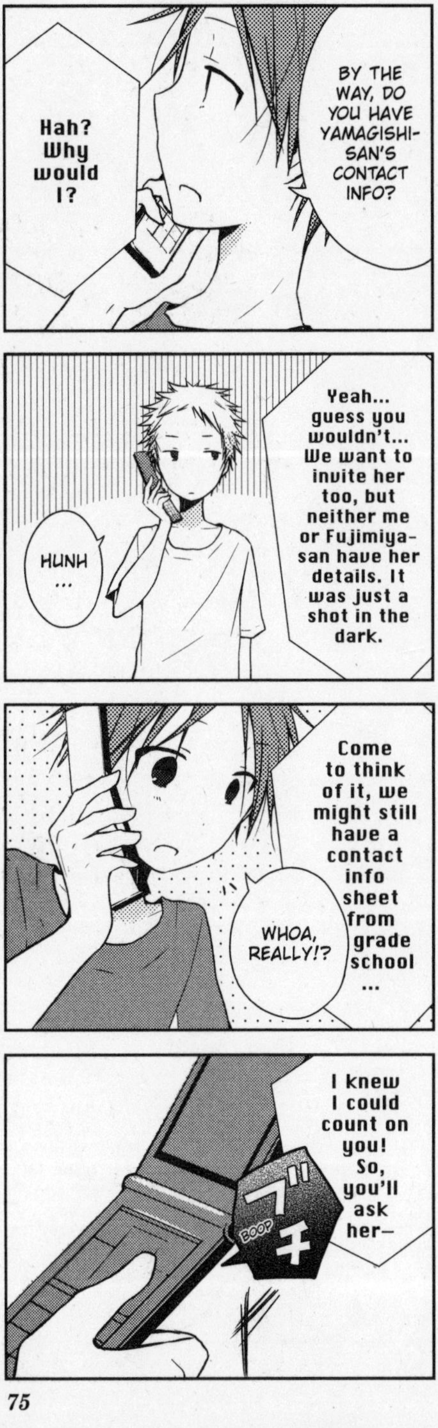
BY THE WAY, DO YOU HAVE YAMAGISHI-SAN'S CONTACT INFO?
Hah? Why would I?
Yeah... guess you wouldn't... We want to invite her too, but neither me or Fujimiya-san have her details. It was just a shot in the dark.
HUNH ...
Come to think of it, we might still have a contact info sheet from grade school ...
WHOA, REALLY!?
I knew I could count on you! So, you'll ask her—
ブチ
BOOP

RIGHT NUMBER

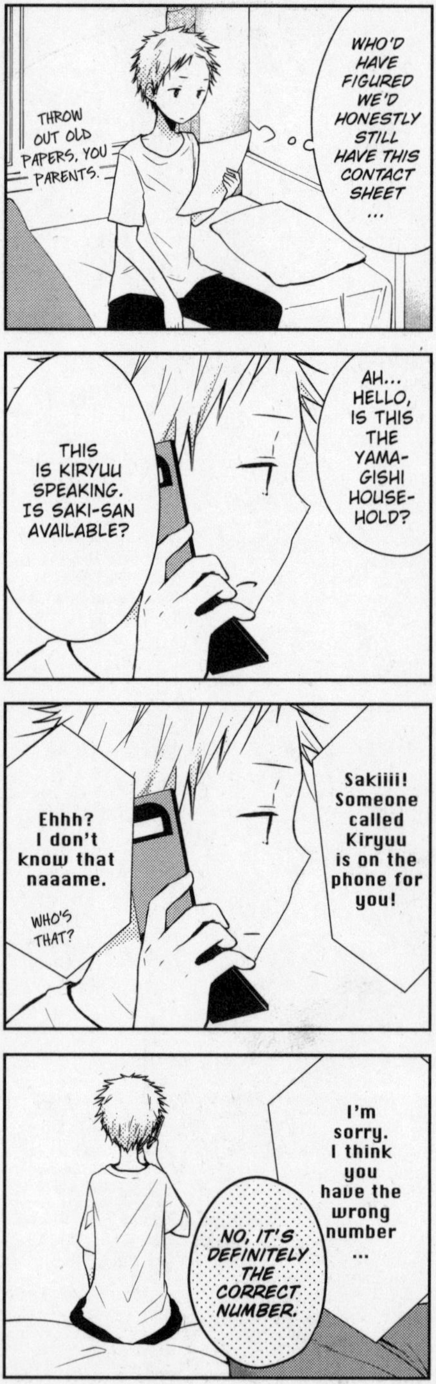
WHO'D HAVE FIGURED WE'D HONESTLY STILL HAVE THIS CONTACT SHEET ...
THROW OUT OLD PAPERS, YOU PARENTS.
AH... HELLO, IS THIS THE YAMAGISHI HOUSEHOLD?
THIS IS KIRYUU SPEAKING. IS SAKI-SAN AVAILABLE?
Sakiiii! Someone called Kiryuu is on the phone for you!
Ehhh? I don't know that naaame.
WHO'S THAT?
I'm sorry. I think you have the wrong number ...
NO, IT'S DEFINITELY THE CORRECT NUMBER.

FAVOR

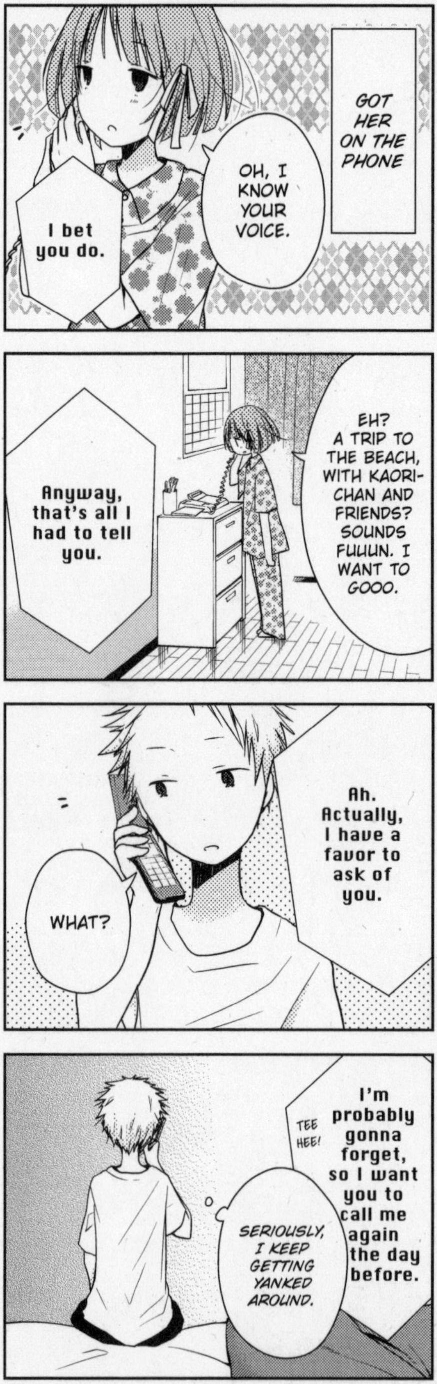
GOT HER ON THE PHONE
OH, I KNOW YOUR VOICE.
I bet you do.
EH? A TRIP TO THE BEACH, WITH KAORI-CHAN AND FRIENDS? SOUNDS FUUUN. I WANT TO GOOO.
Anyway, that's all I had to tell you.
Ah. Actually, I have a favor to ask of you.
WHAT?
I'm probably gonna forget, so I want you to call me again the day before.
TEE HEE!
SERIOUSLY, I KEEP GETTING YANKED AROUND.

RISKY

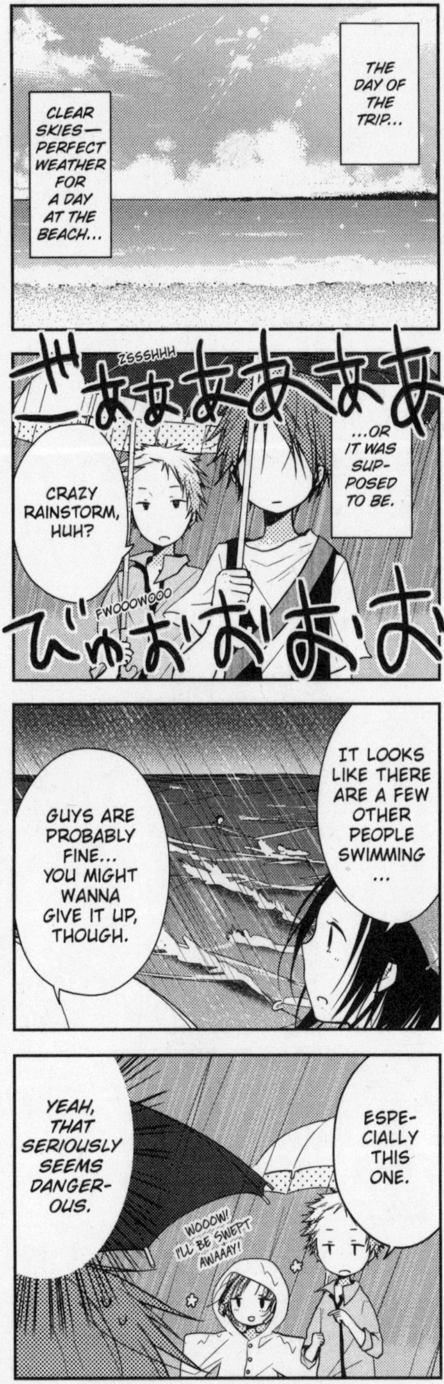
THE DAY OF THE TRIP...
CLEAR SKIES—PERFECT WEATHER FOR A DAY AT THE BEACH...
ZSSSHHH
...OR IT WAS SUPPOSED TO BE.
CRAZY RAINSTORM, HUH?
FWOOOWOOO
IT LOOKS LIKE THERE ARE A FEW OTHER PEOPLE SWIMMING...
GUYS ARE PROBABLY FINE... YOU MIGHT WANNA GIVE IT UP, THOUGH.
ESPE-CIALLY THIS ONE.
YEAH, THAT SERIOUSLY SEEMS DANGER-OUS.
WOOOW! I'LL BE SWEPT AWAAAY!

WHAT MATTERS MOST

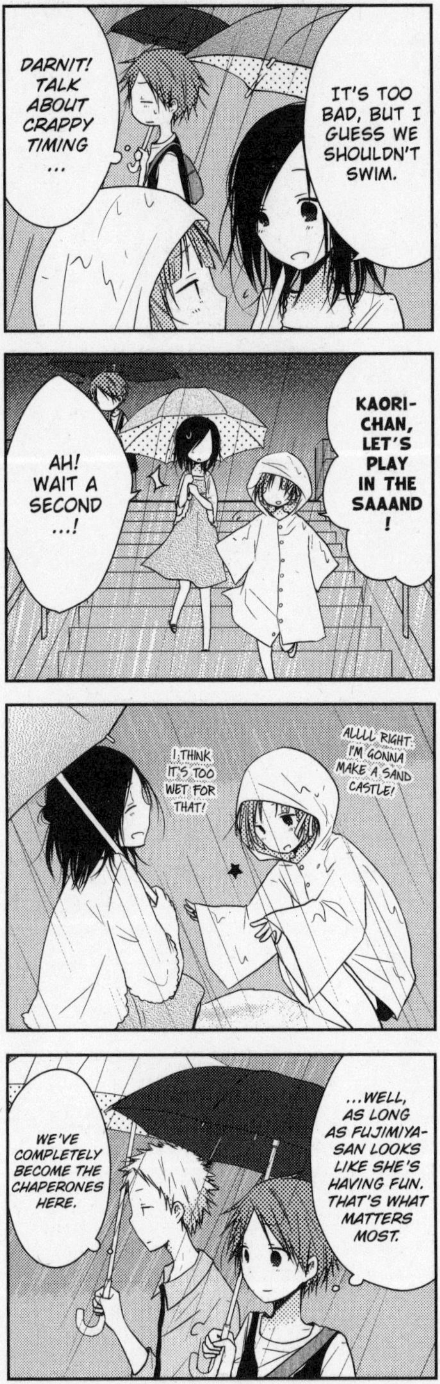
IT'S TOO BAD, BUT I GUESS WE SHOULDN'T SWIM.
DARNIT! TALK ABOUT CRAPPY TIMING...
KAORI-CHAN, LET'S PLAY IN THE SAAAND!
AH! WAIT A SECOND...!
ALLLL RIGHT. I'M GONNA MAKE A SAND CASTLE!
I THINK IT'S TOO WET FOR THAT!
...WELL, AS LONG AS FUJIMIYA-SAN LOOKS LIKE SHE'S HAVING FUN. THAT'S WHAT MATTERS MOST.
WE'VE COMPLETELY BECOME THE CHAPERONES HERE.

BEACH BALL

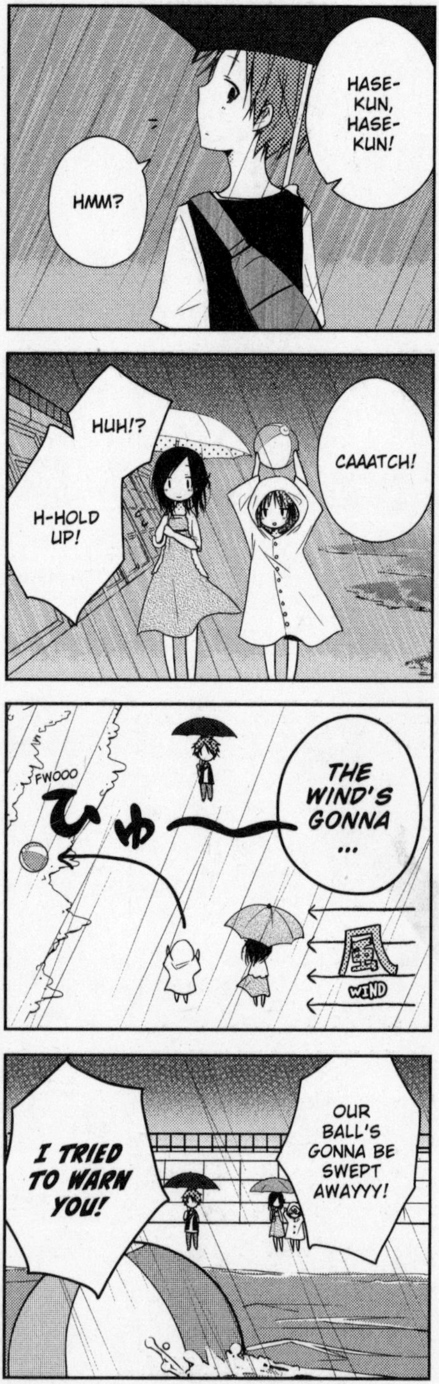
HASE-KUN, HASE-KUN!
HMM?
CAAATCH!
HUH!?
H-HOLD UP!
THE WIND'S GONNA ...
FWOOO
WIND
OUR BALL'S GONNA BE SWEPT AWAYYY!
I TRIED TO WARN YOU!

HOW TO PASS

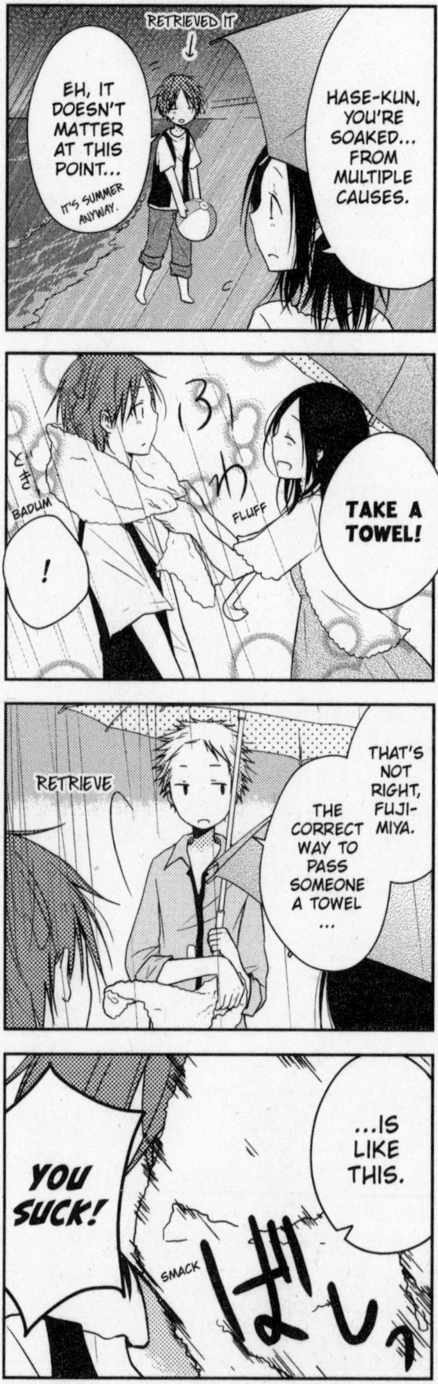
HASE-KUN, YOU'RE SOAKED... FROM MULTIPLE CAUSES.
RETRIEVED IT
EH, IT DOESN'T MATTER AT THIS POINT...
IT'S SUMMER ANYWAY.
TAKE A TOWEL!
FLUFF
BADUM
!
THAT'S NOT RIGHT, FUJI-MIYA.
THE CORRECT WAY TO PASS SOMEONE A TOWEL ...
RETRIEVE
...IS LIKE THIS.
SMACK
YOU SUCK!

ARCADE

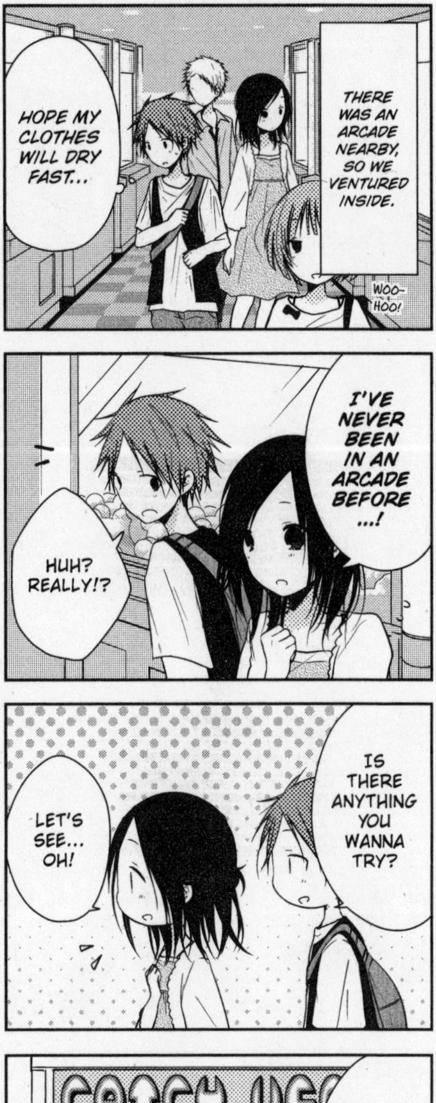
THERE WAS AN ARCADE NEARBY, SO WE VENTURED INSIDE.
HOPE MY CLOTHES WILL DRY FAST...
WOO-HOO!
I'VE NEVER BEEN IN AN ARCADE BEFORE ...!
HUH? REALLY!?
IS THERE ANYTHING YOU WANNA TRY?
LET'S SEE... OH!
I'D LIKE TO SEE SOMEONE PLAYING THIS.
URK ...!

CRANE GAME

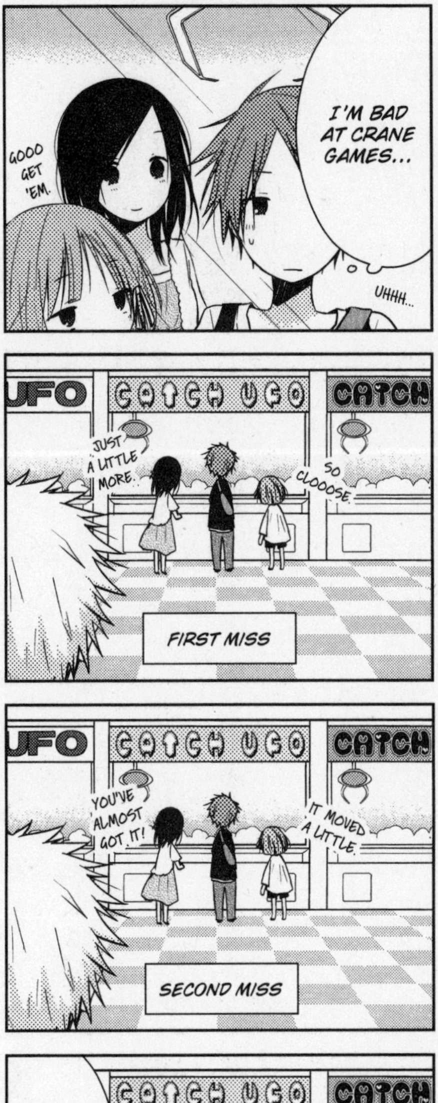
I'M BAD AT CRANE GAMES...
UHHH...
GOOO GET 'EM.
UFO
CATCH UFO
CATCH
SO CLOOOSE.
JUST A LITTLE MORE.
FIRST MISS
UFO
CATCH UFO
CATCH
IT MOVED A LITTLE.
YOU'VE ALMOST GOT IT!
SECOND MISS
CATCH UFO
CATCH
AWWW.
HMMM.
HE DOESN'T KNOW WHEN TO QUIT...
FIFTH MISS

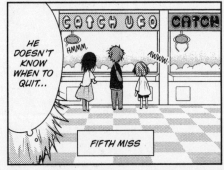

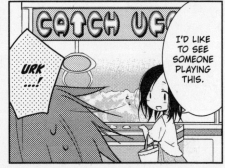

LUCK IS ON HIS SIDE

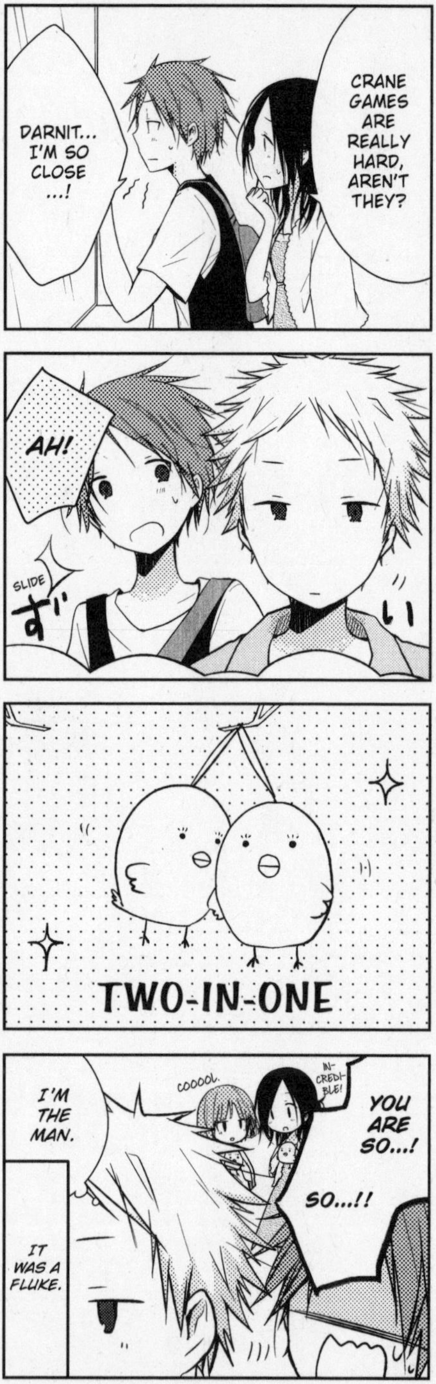
CRANE GAMES ARE REALLY HARD, AREN'T THEY?
DARNIT... I'M SO CLOSE ...!
AH!
SLIDE
TWO-IN-ONE
IN-CREDIBLE!
YOU ARE SO...!
COOOOL.
I'M THE MAN.
SO...!!
IT WAS A FLUKE.

THE FOUR OF US

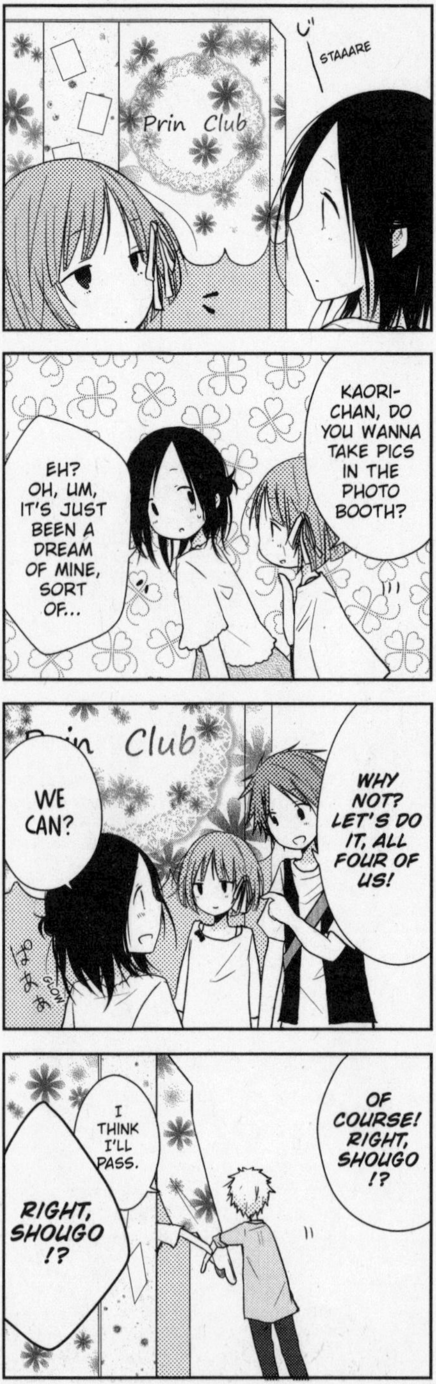
STAAARE
Prin Club
KAORI-CHAN, DO YOU WANNA TAKE PICS IN THE PHOTO BOOTH?
EH? OH, UM, IT'S JUST BEEN A DREAM OF MINE, SORT OF...
Prin Club
WHY NOT? LET'S DO IT, ALL FOUR OF US!
WE CAN?
GLOW
OF COURSE! RIGHT, SHOUGO !?
I THINK I'LL PASS.
RIGHT, SHOUGO !?

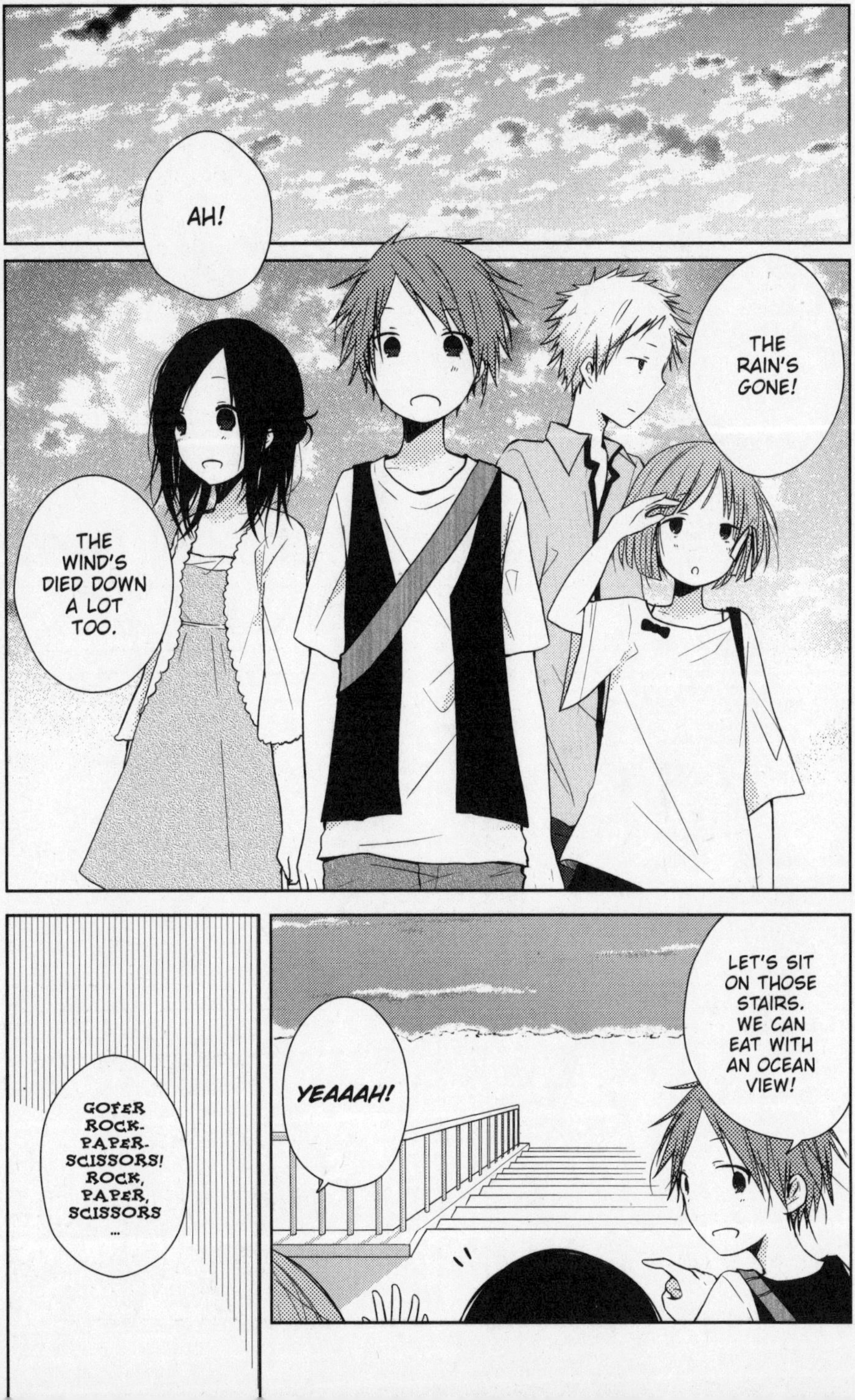
AH!
THE RAIN'S GONE!
THE WIND'S DIED DOWN A LOT TOO.
LET'S SIT ON THOSE STAIRS. WE CAN EAT WITH AN OCEAN VIEW!
YEAAAH!
GOFER ROCK-PAPER-SCISSORS! ROCK, PAPER, SCISSORS ...

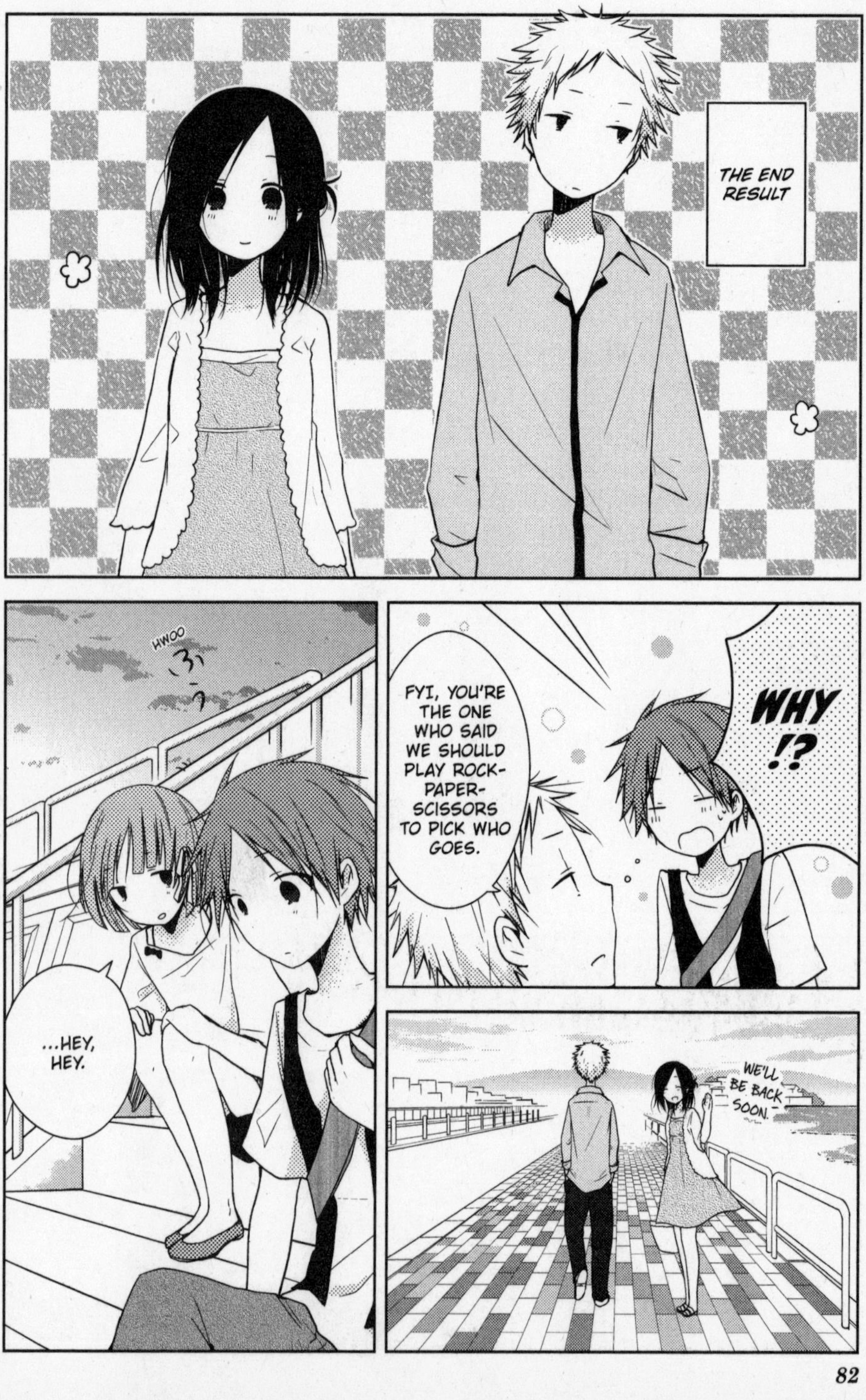
THE END RESULT
WHY !?
FYI, YOU'RE THE ONE WHO SAID WE SHOULD PLAY ROCK-PAPER-SCISSORS TO PICK WHO GOES.
WE'LL BE BACK SOON.
HWOO
...HEY, HEY.

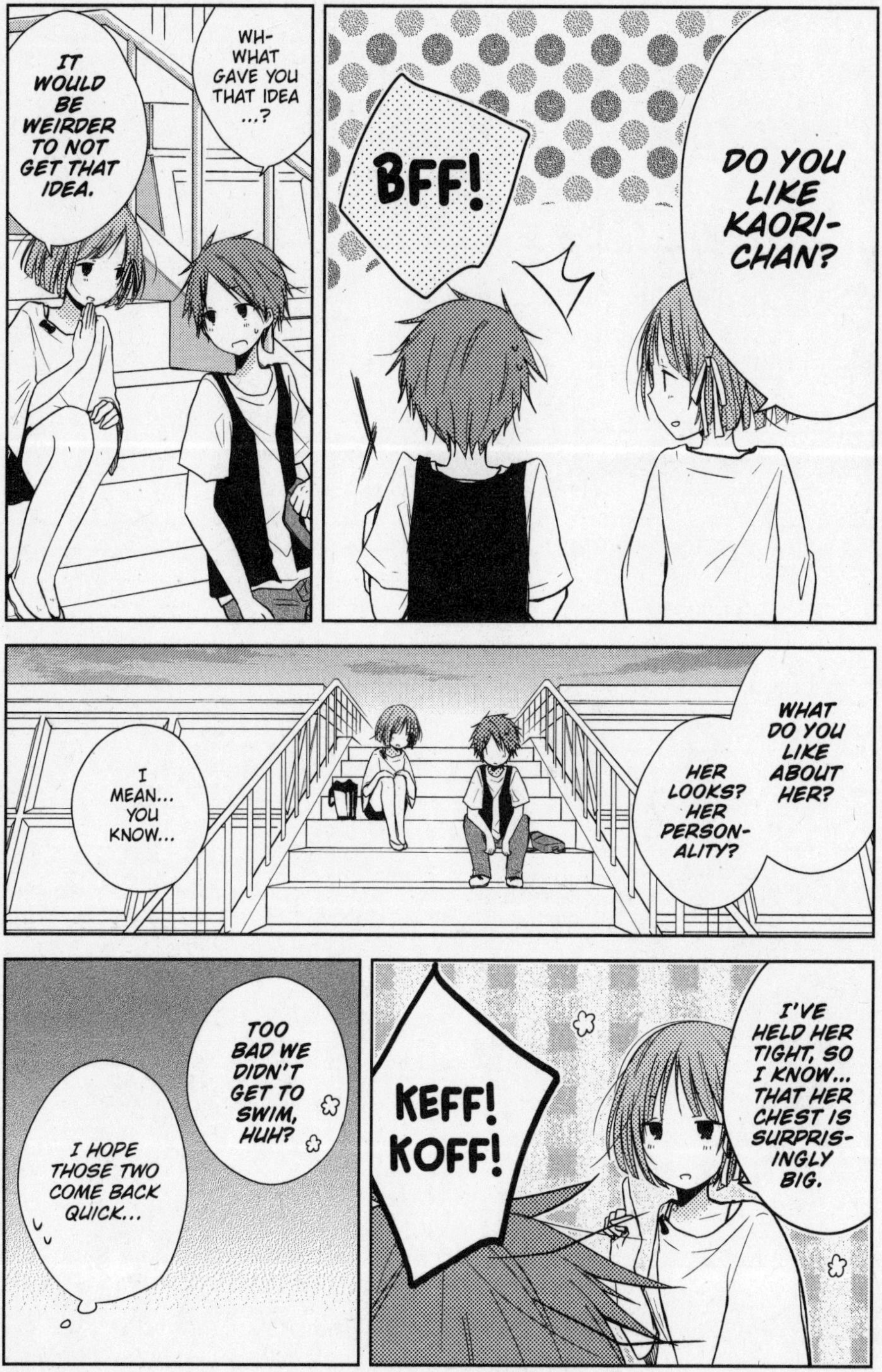
DO YOU LIKE KAORI-CHAN?
BFF!
WH-WHAT GAVE YOU THAT IDEA ...?
IT WOULD BE WEIRDER TO NOT GET THAT IDEA.
WHAT DO YOU LIKE ABOUT HER?
HER LOOKS? HER PERSONALITY?
I MEAN... YOU KNOW...
I'VE HELD HER TIGHT, SO I KNOW... THAT HER CHEST IS SURPRISINGLY BIG.
KEFF! KOFF!
TOO BAD WE DIDN'T GET TO SWIM, HUH?
I HOPE THOSE TWO COME BACK QUICK...

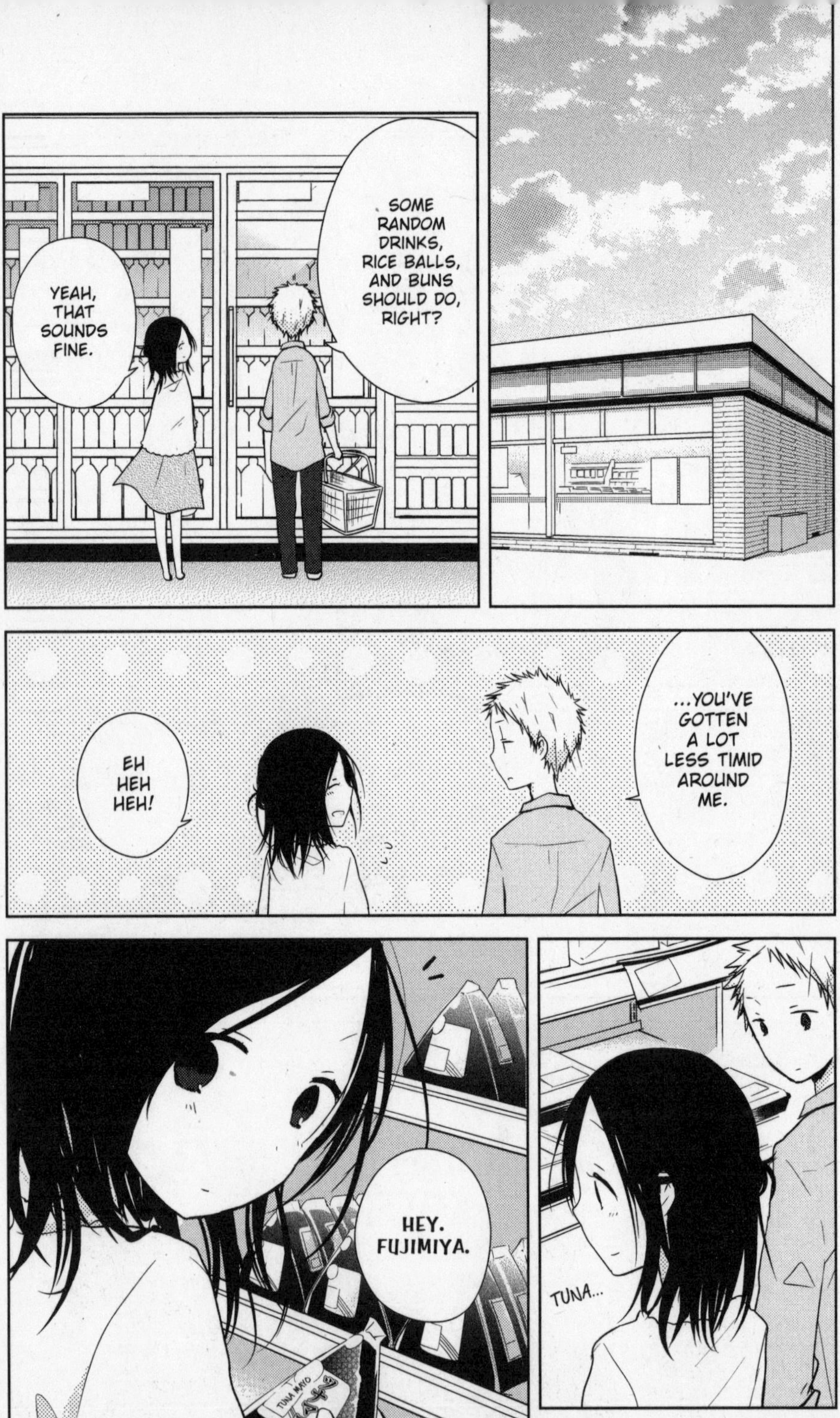
SOME RANDOM DRINKS, RICE BALLS, AND BUNS SHOULD DO, RIGHT?
YEAH, THAT SOUNDS FINE.
...YOU'VE GOTTEN A LOT LESS TIMID AROUND ME.
EH HEH HEH!
TUNA...
HEY. FUJIMIYA.
TUNA MAYO

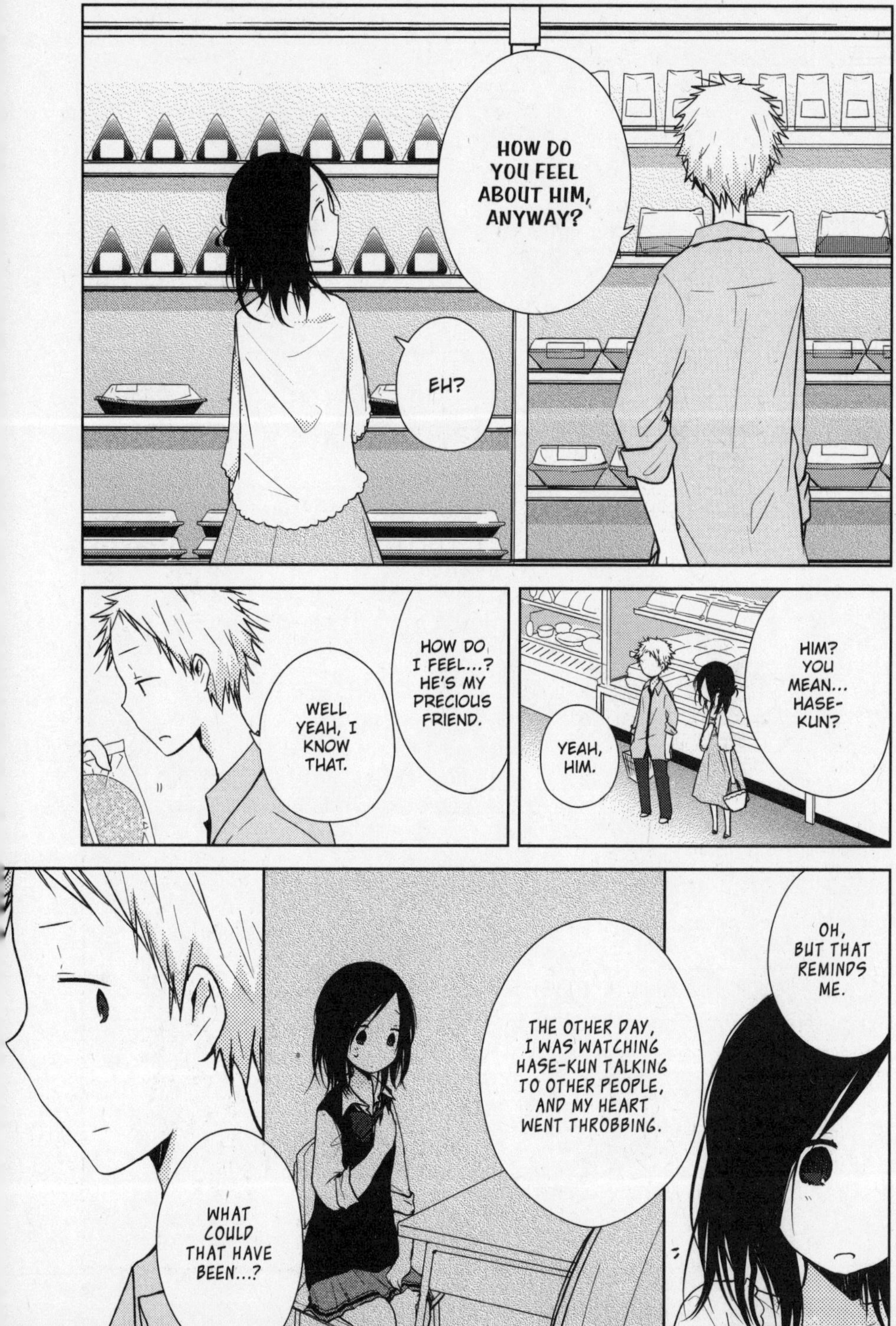
HOW DO YOU FEEL ABOUT HIM, ANYWAY?
EH?
HIM? YOU MEAN... HASE-KUN?
YEAH, HIM.
HOW DO I FEEL...? HE'S MY PRECIOUS FRIEND.
WELL YEAH, I KNOW THAT.
OH, BUT THAT REMINDS ME.
THE OTHER DAY, I WAS WATCHING HASE-KUN TALKING TO OTHER PEOPLE, AND MY HEART WENT THROBBING.
WHAT COULD THAT HAVE BEEN...?

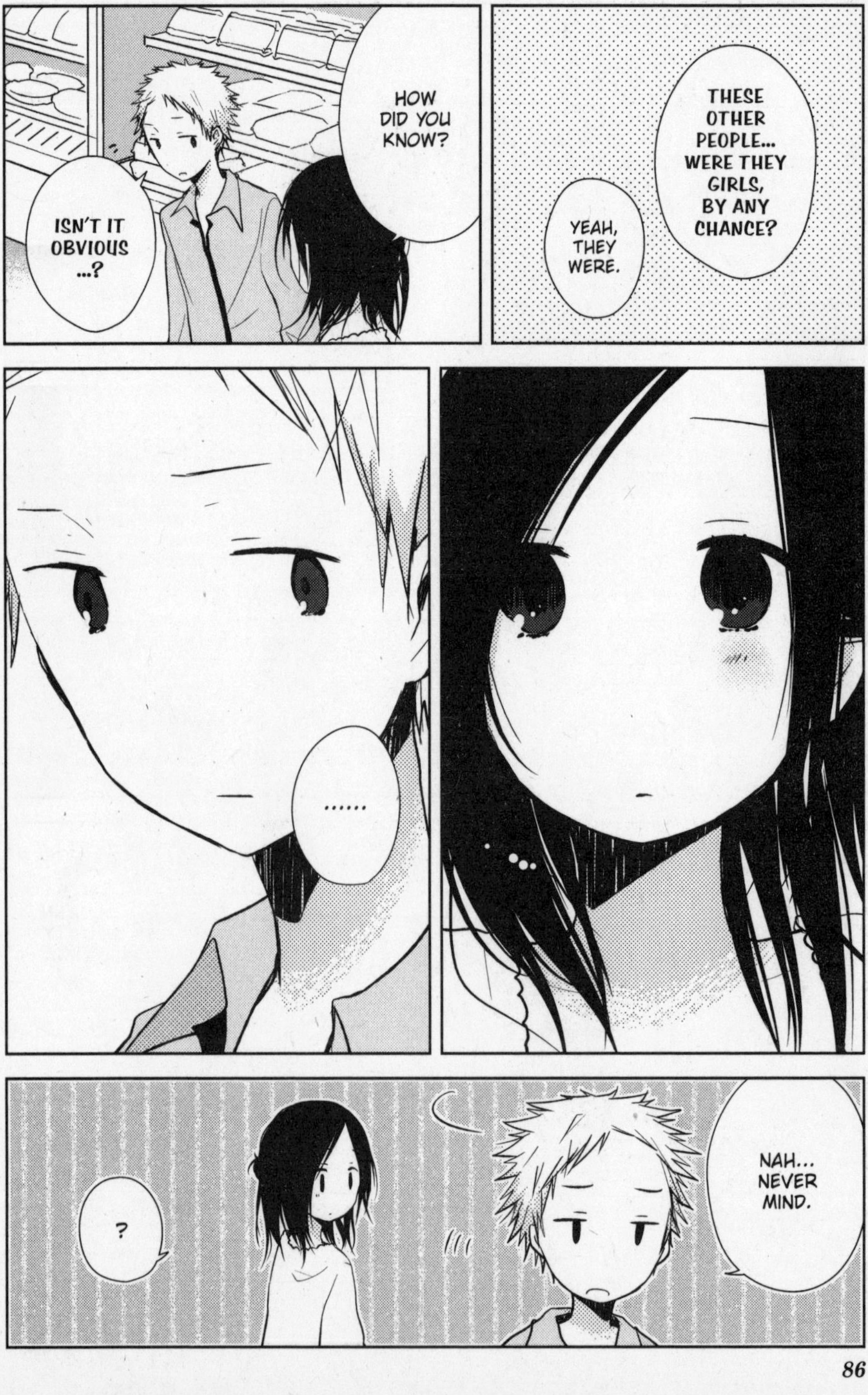
THESE OTHER PEOPLE... WERE THEY GIRLS, BY ANY CHANCE?
YEAH, THEY WERE.
HOW DID YOU KNOW?
ISN'T IT OBVIOUS ...?
......
NAH... NEVER MIND.
?

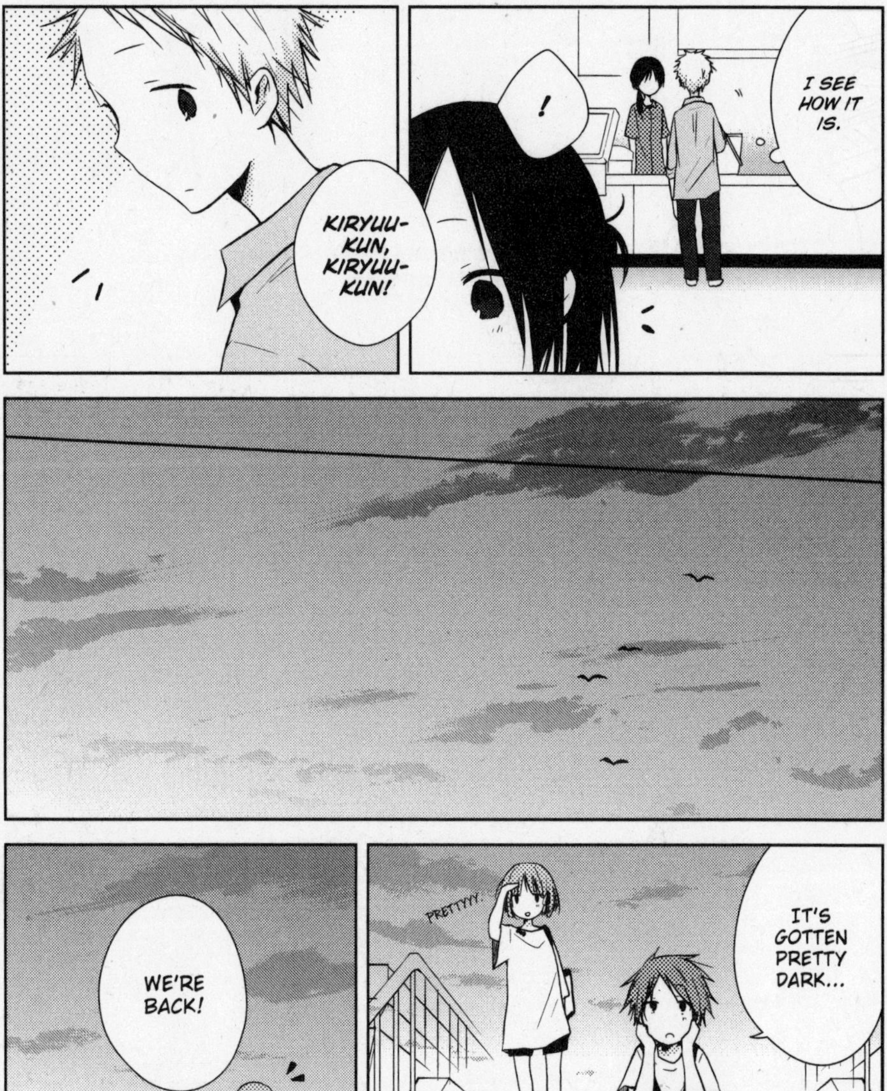
I SEE HOW IT IS.
!
KIRYUU-KUN, KIRYUU-KUN!
IT'S GOTTEN PRETTY DARK...
PRETTYYY.
WE'RE BACK!

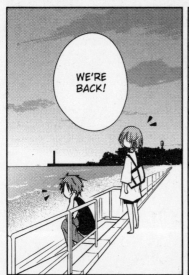

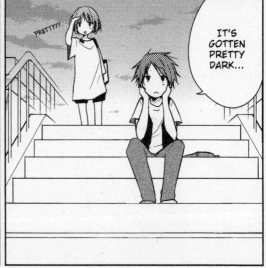

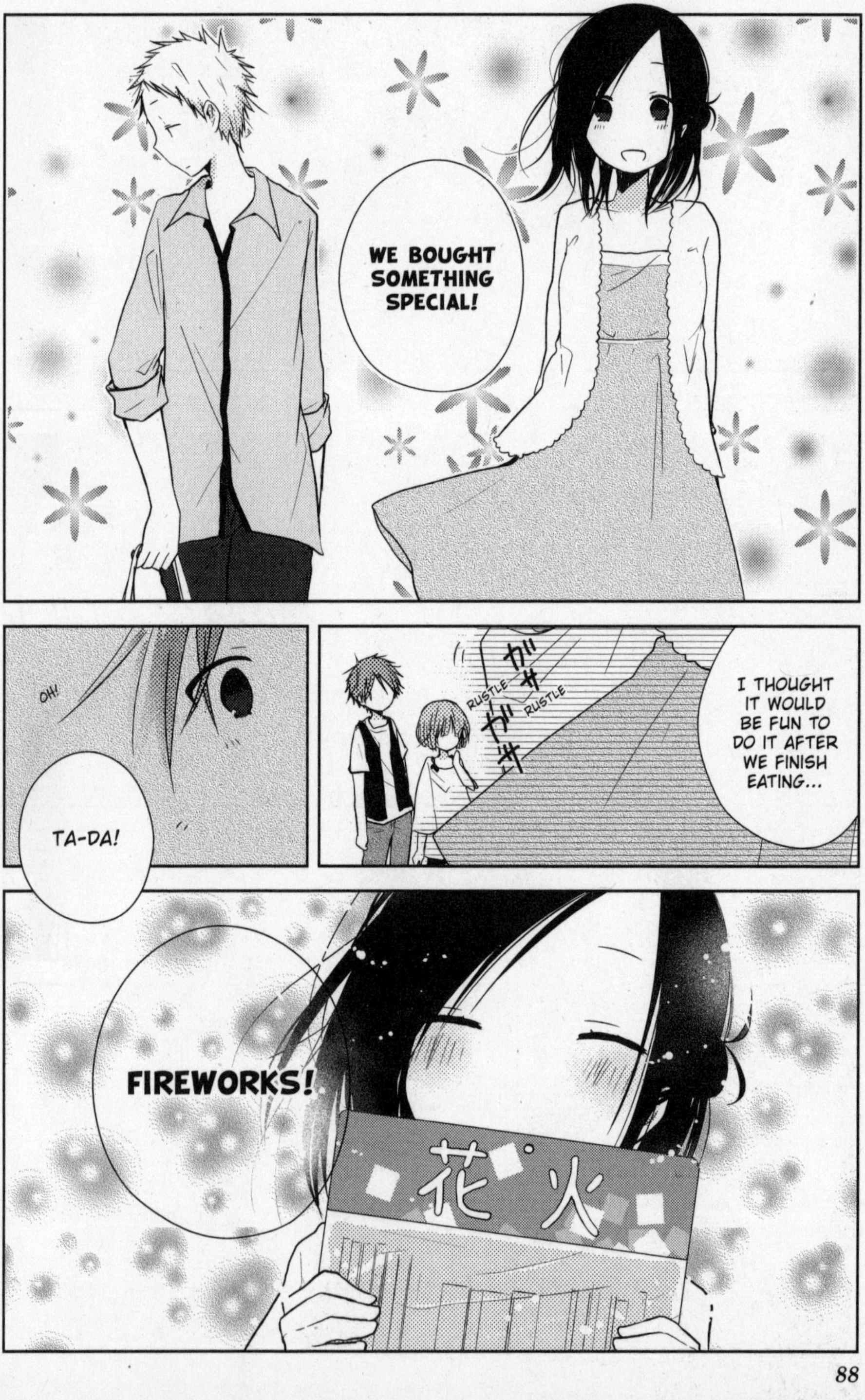
WE BOUGHT SOMETHING SPECIAL!
ガサ ガサ
RUSTLE RUSTLE
I THOUGHT IT WOULD BE FUN TO DO IT AFTER WE FINISH EATING...
OH!
TA-DA!
FIREWORKS!
花火

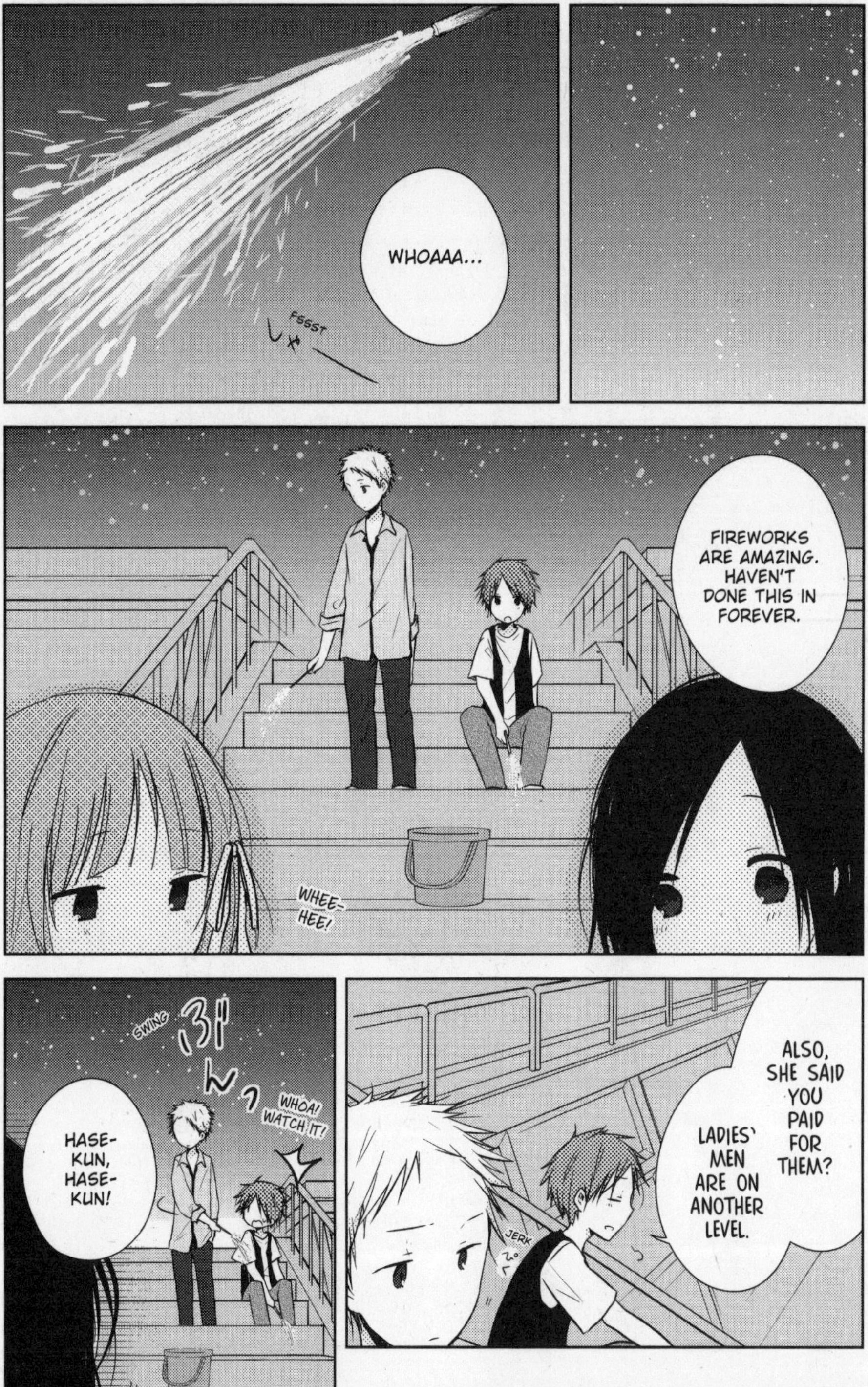
WHOAAA...
FSSST
FIREWORKS ARE AMAZING. HAVEN'T DONE THIS IN FOREVER.
WHEE-HEE!
ALSO, SHE SAID YOU PAID FOR THEM?
LADIES' MEN ARE ON ANOTHER LEVEL.
JERK
SWING
WHOA! WATCH IT!
HASE-KUN, HASE-KUN!

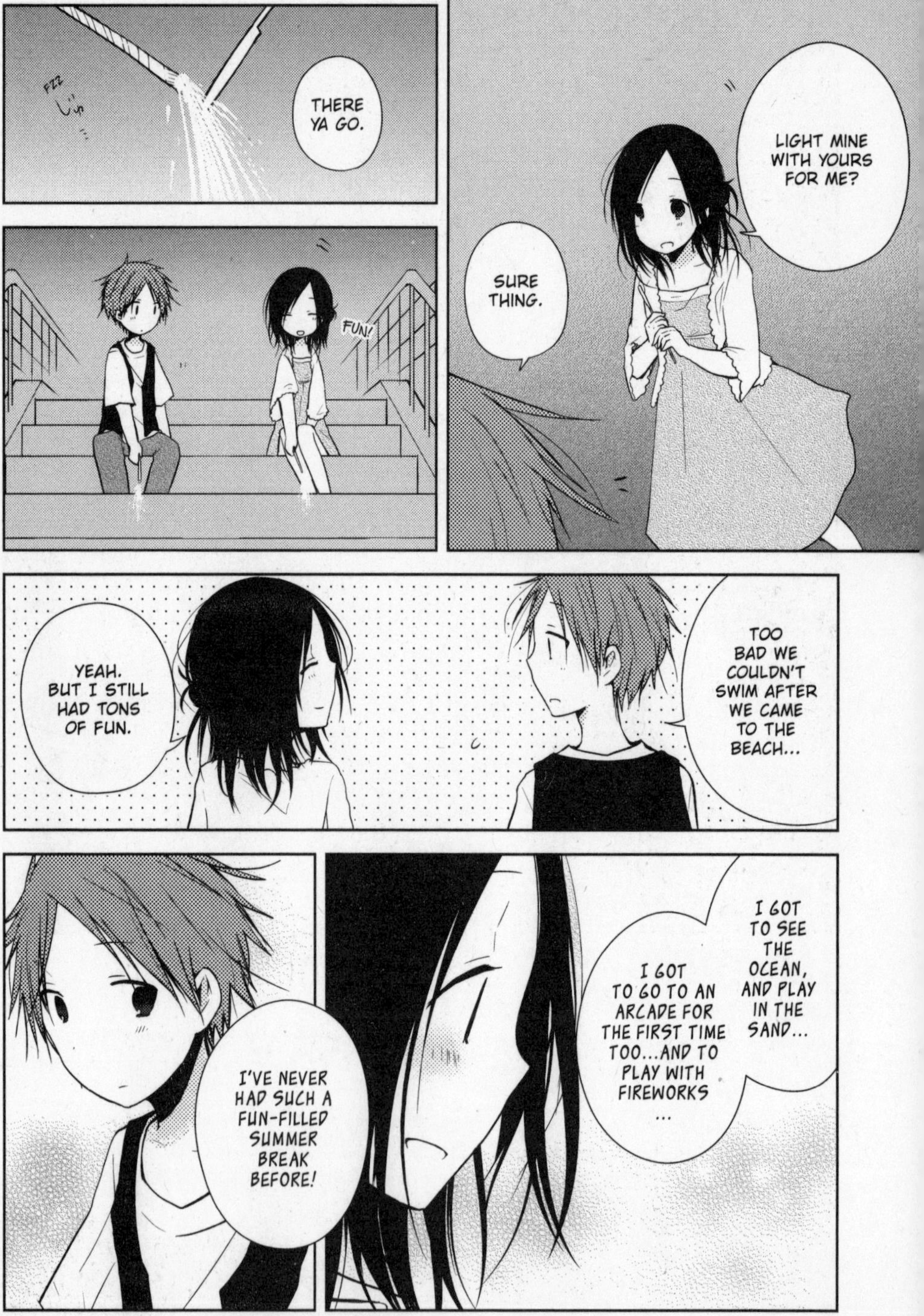
LIGHT MINE WITH YOURS FOR ME?
SURE THING.
THERE YA GO.
FZZ
FUN!
TOO BAD WE COULDN'T SWIM AFTER WE CAME TO THE BEACH...
YEAH. BUT I STILL HAD TONS OF FUN.
I GOT TO SEE THE OCEAN, AND PLAY IN THE SAND...
I GOT TO GO TO AN ARCADE FOR THE FIRST TIME TOO...AND TO PLAY WITH FIREWORKS...
I'VE NEVER HAD SUCH A FUN-FILLED SUMMER BREAK BEFORE!

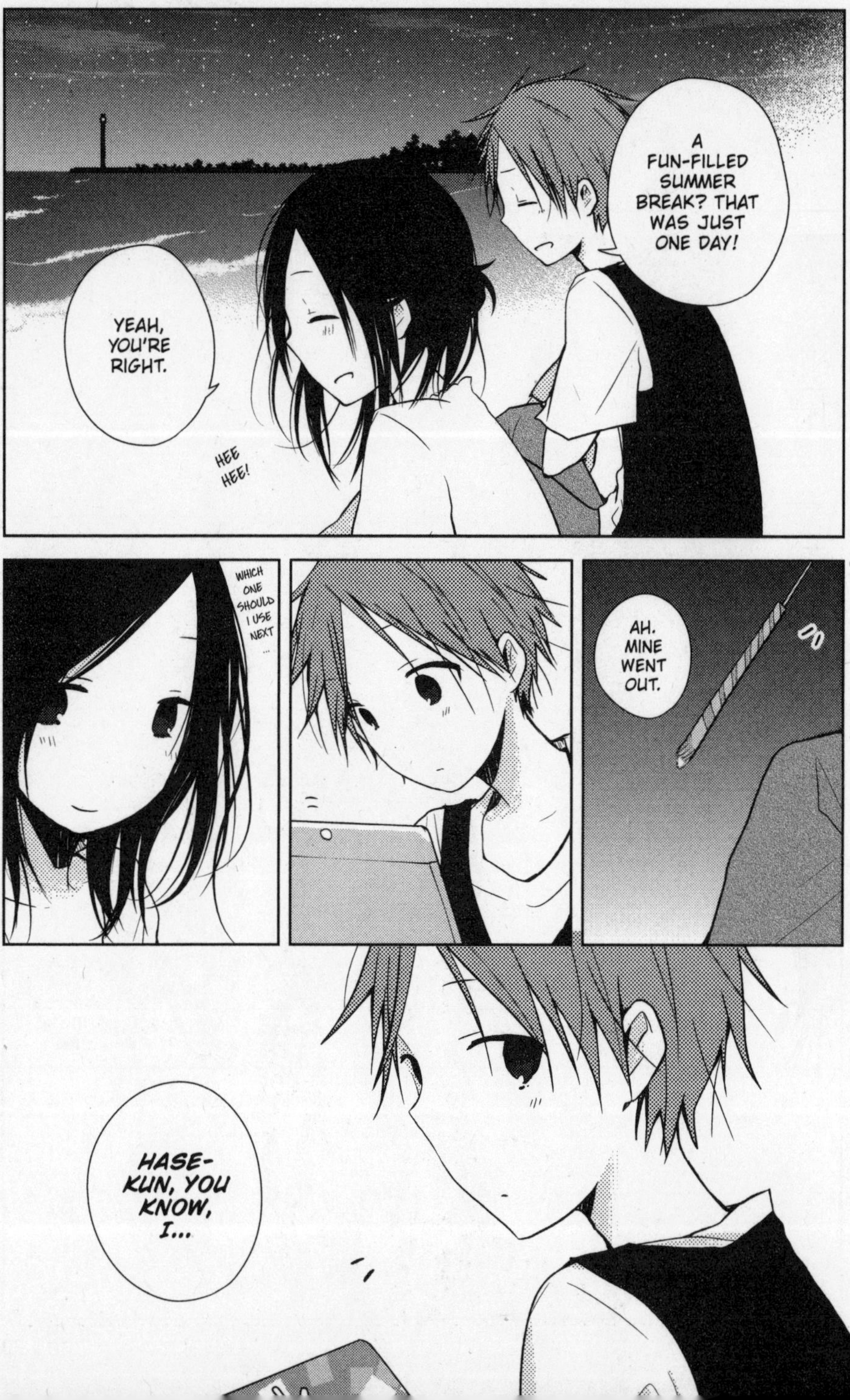
A FUN-FILLED SUMMER BREAK? THAT WAS JUST ONE DAY!
YEAH, YOU'RE RIGHT.
HEE HEE!
AH. MINE WENT OUT.
WHICH ONE SHOULD I USE NEXT...
HASE-KUN, YOU KNOW, I...

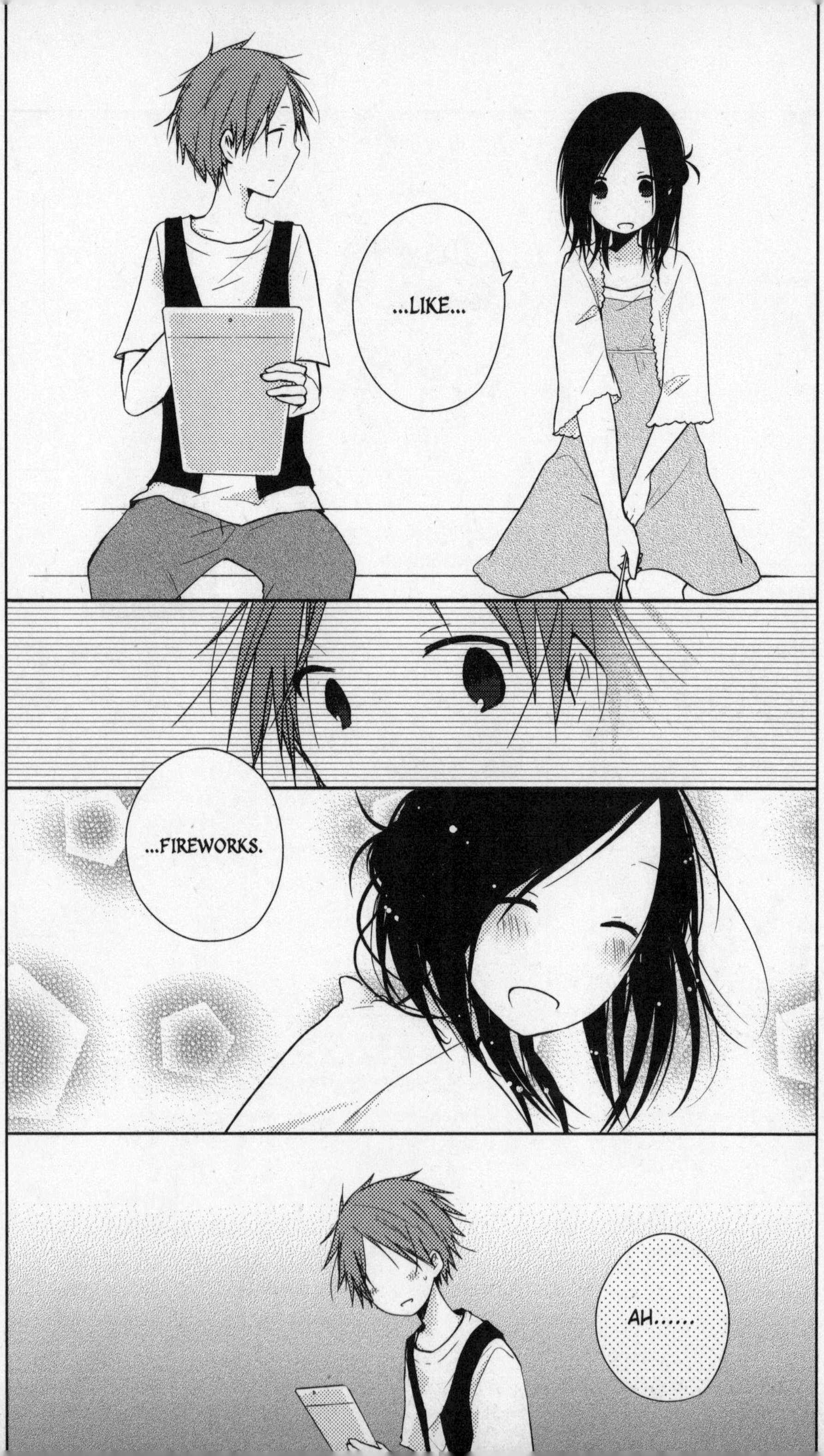
...LIKE...
...FIREWORKS.
AH......

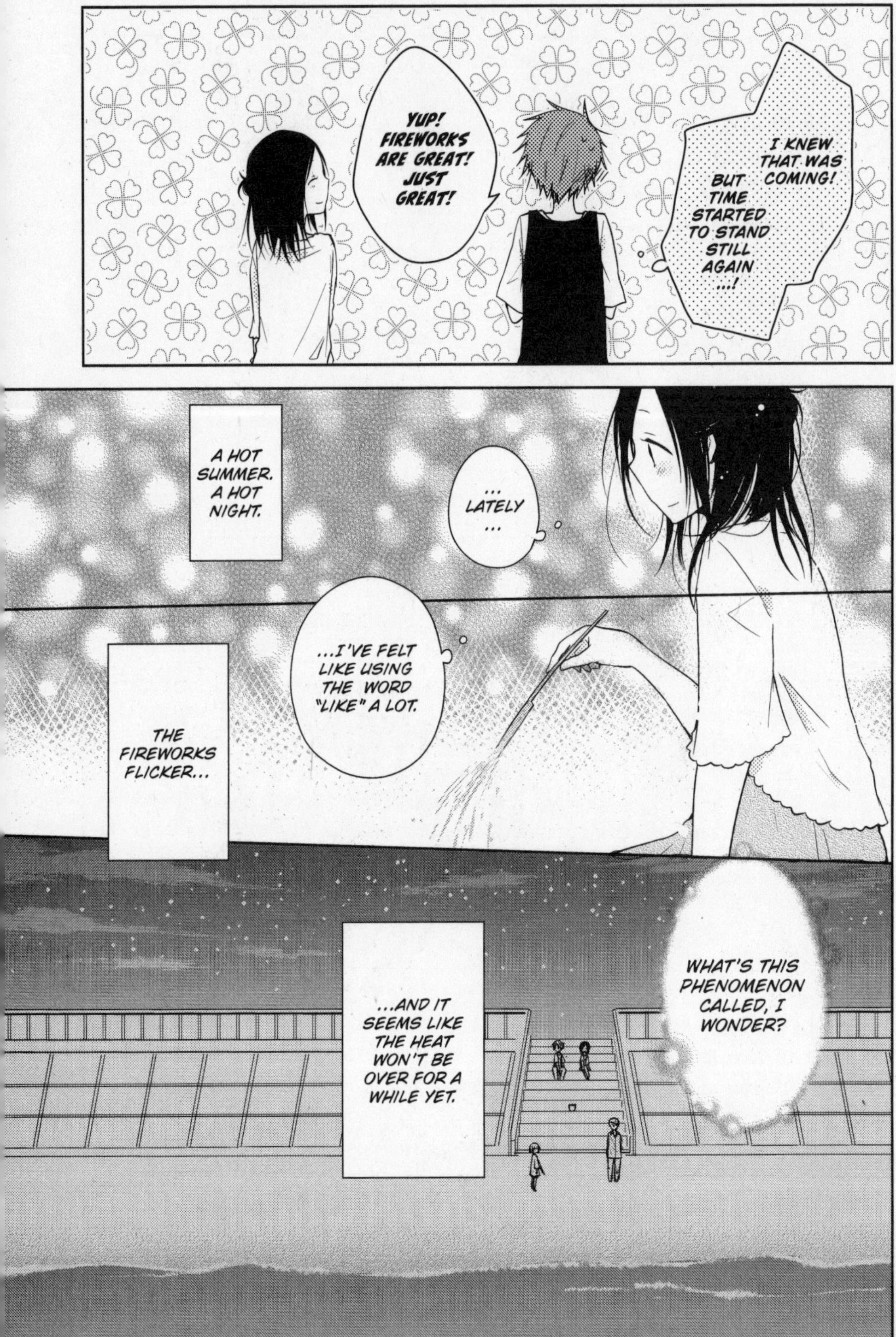
I KNEW THAT WAS COMING! BUT TIME STARTED TO STAND STILL AGAIN ...!
YUP! FIREWORKS ARE GREAT! JUST GREAT!
... LATELY ...
A HOT SUMMER. A HOT NIGHT.
...I'VE FELT LIKE USING THE WORD "LIKE" A LOT.
THE FIREWORKS FLICKER...
WHAT'S THIS PHENOMENON CALLED, I WONDER?
...AND IT SEEMS LIKE THE HEAT WON'T BE OVER FOR A WHILE YET.

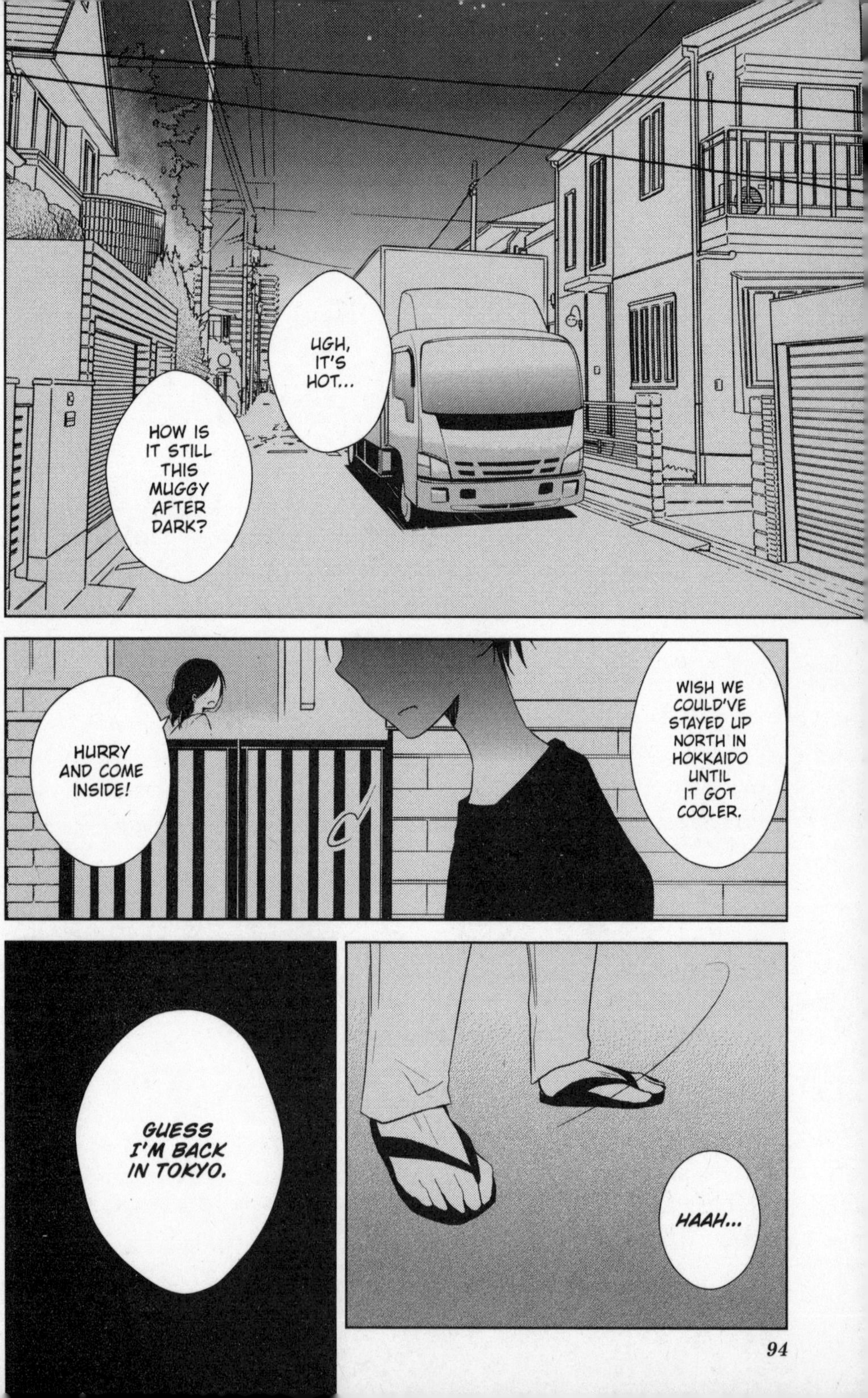
UGH, IT'S HOT...
HOW IS IT STILL THIS MUGGY AFTER DARK?
WISH WE COULD'VE STAYED UP NORTH IN HOKKAIDO UNTIL IT GOT COOLER.
HURRY AND COME INSIDE!
HAAH...
GUESS I'M BACK IN TOKYO.

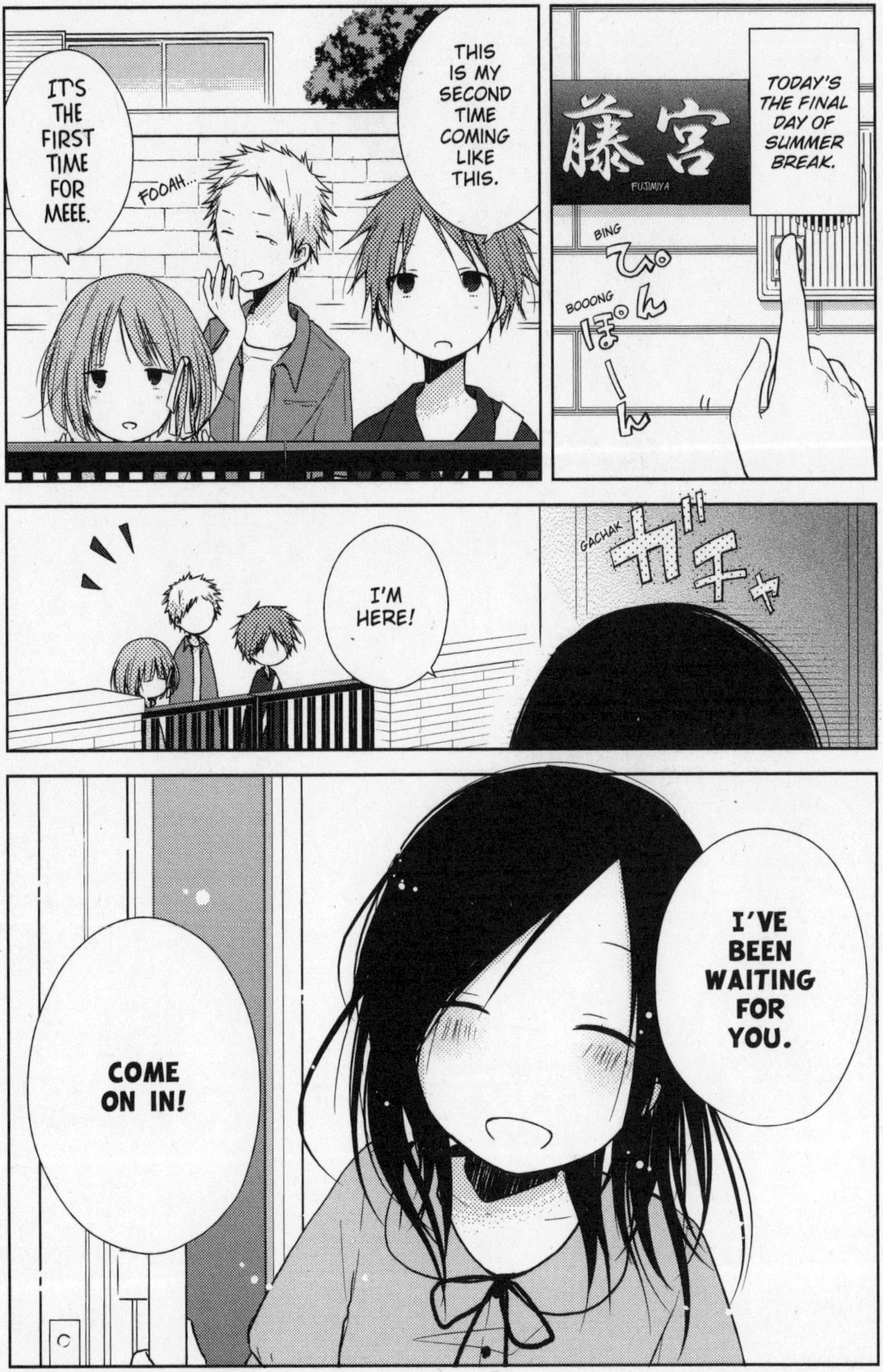
TODAY'S THE FINAL DAY OF SUMMER BREAK.
藤宮
FUJIMIYA
BING
ぴん
BOOONG
ぽーん
THIS IS MY SECOND TIME COMING LIKE THIS.
FOOAH...
IT'S THE FIRST TIME FOR MEEE.
GACHAK
ガチャ
I'M HERE!
I'VE BEEN WAITING FOR YOU.
COME ON IN!

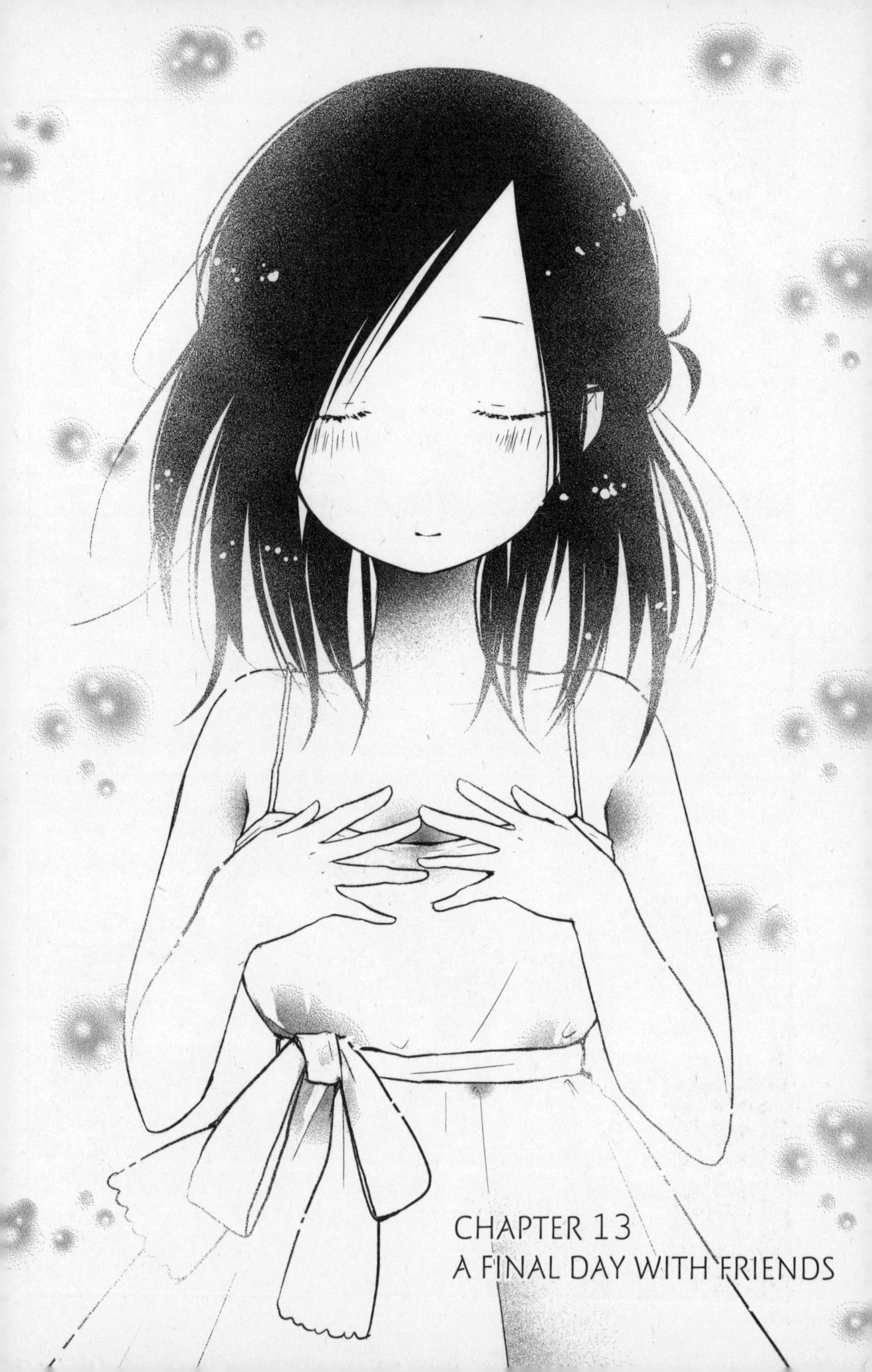
CHAPTER 13
A FINAL DAY WITH FRIENDS

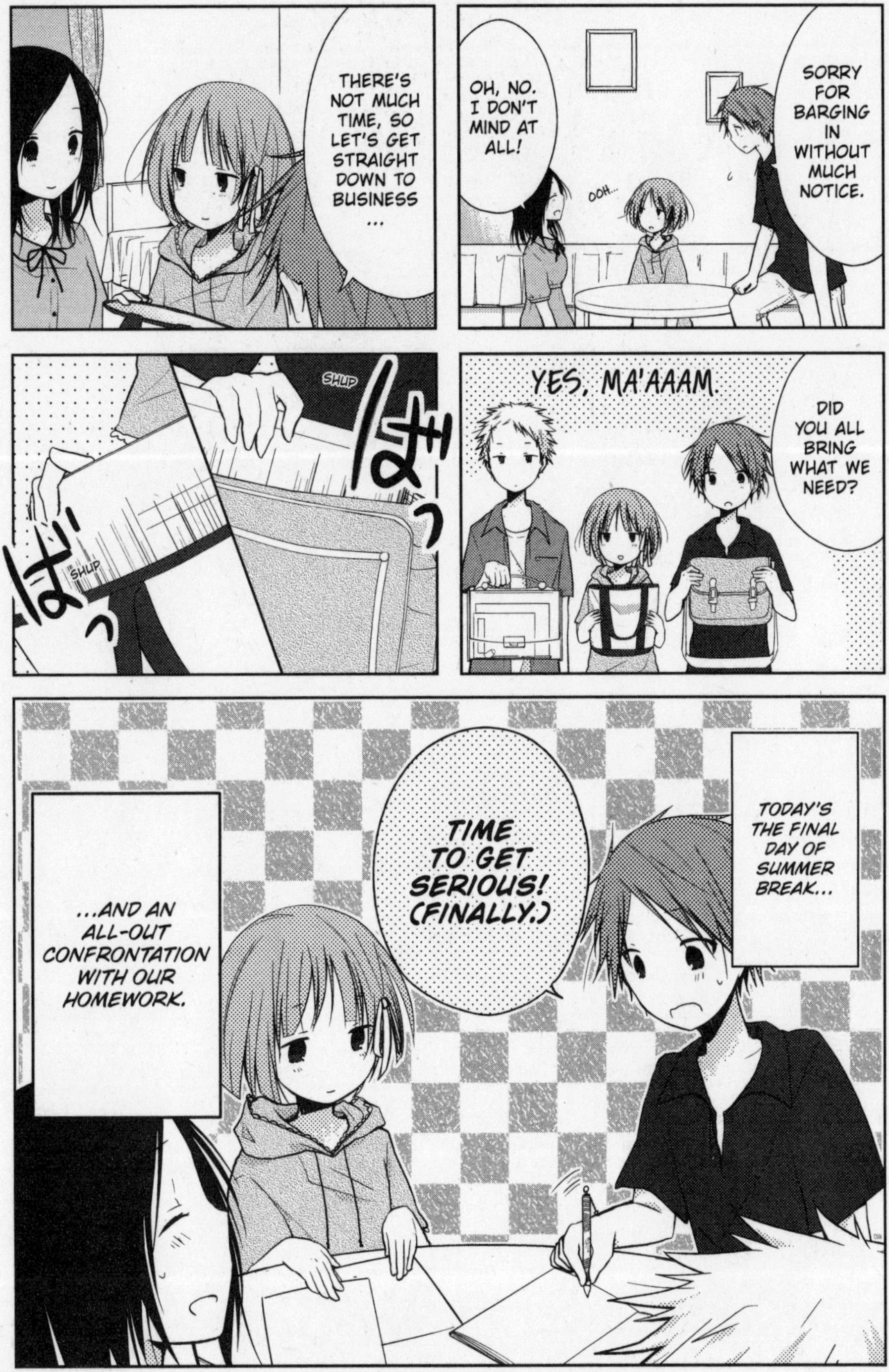
SORRY FOR BARGING IN WITHOUT MUCH NOTICE.
OOH...
OH, NO. I DON'T MIND AT ALL!
THERE'S NOT MUCH TIME, SO LET'S GET STRAIGHT DOWN TO BUSINESS ...
DID YOU ALL BRING WHAT WE NEED?
YES, MA'AAAM.
SHUP
ばっ
SHUP
ばっ
TODAY'S THE FINAL DAY OF SUMMER BREAK...
TIME TO GET SERIOUS! (FINALLY.)
...AND AN ALL-OUT CONFRONTATION WITH OUR HOMEWORK.

SUMMER HOMEWORK

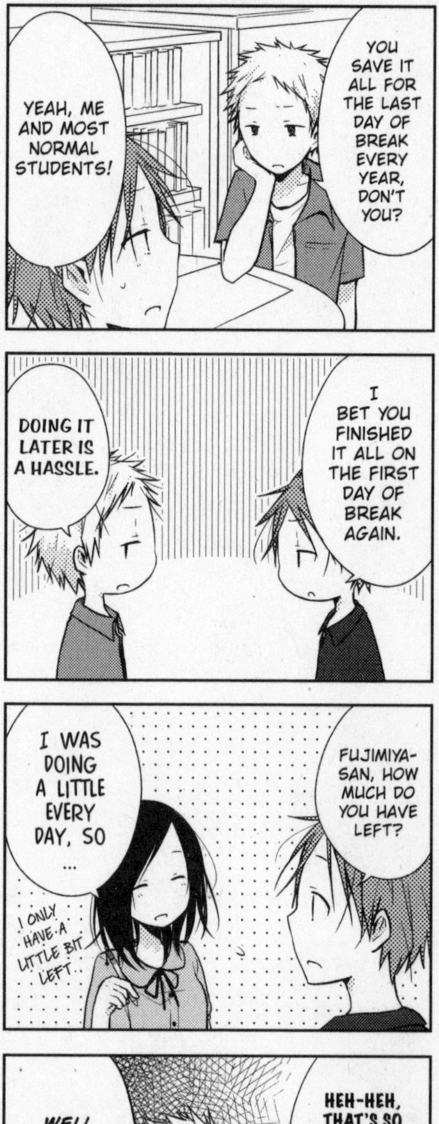
YOU SAVE IT ALL FOR THE LAST DAY OF BREAK EVERY YEAR, DON'T YOU?
YEAH, ME AND MOST NORMAL STUDENTS!
I BET YOU FINISHED IT ALL ON THE FIRST DAY OF BREAK AGAIN.
DOING IT LATER IS A HASSLE.
FUJIMIYA-SAN, HOW MUCH DO YOU HAVE LEFT?
I WAS DOING A LITTLE EVERY DAY, SO ...
I ONLY HAVE A LITTLE BIT LEFT
HEH-HEH, THAT'S SO YOU. I KNEW A GOOD STUDENT LIKE YOU WOULDN'T SAY ANYTHING NASTY.
WELL EXCUSE ME FOR BEING A NASTY, GOOD STUDENT.

SLIPPED MY MIND

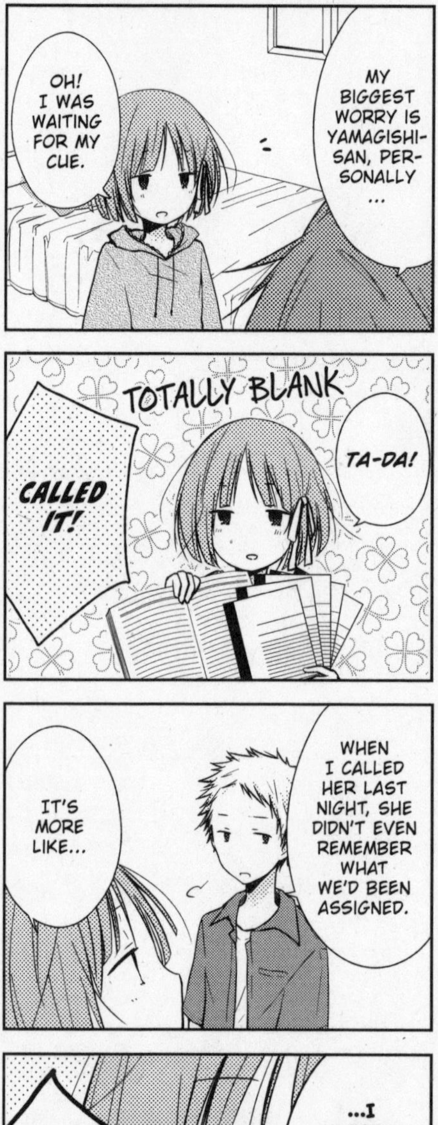
MY BIGGEST WORRY IS YAMAGISHI-SAN, PERSONALLY ...
OH! I WAS WAITING FOR MY CUE.
TA-DA!
TOTALLY BLANK
CALLED IT!
WHEN I CALLED HER LAST NIGHT, SHE DIDN'T EVEN REMEMBER WHAT WE'D BEEN ASSIGNED.
IT'S MORE LIKE...
...I FORGOT THE VERY FACT THAT SUMMER BREAK WAS ABOUT TO END.
YUP, THIS GIRL IS A TROUBLE MAGNET!
OOPSIES!

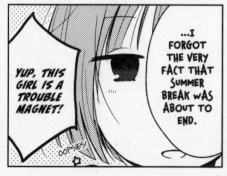

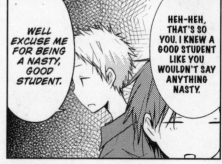

FRIENDS

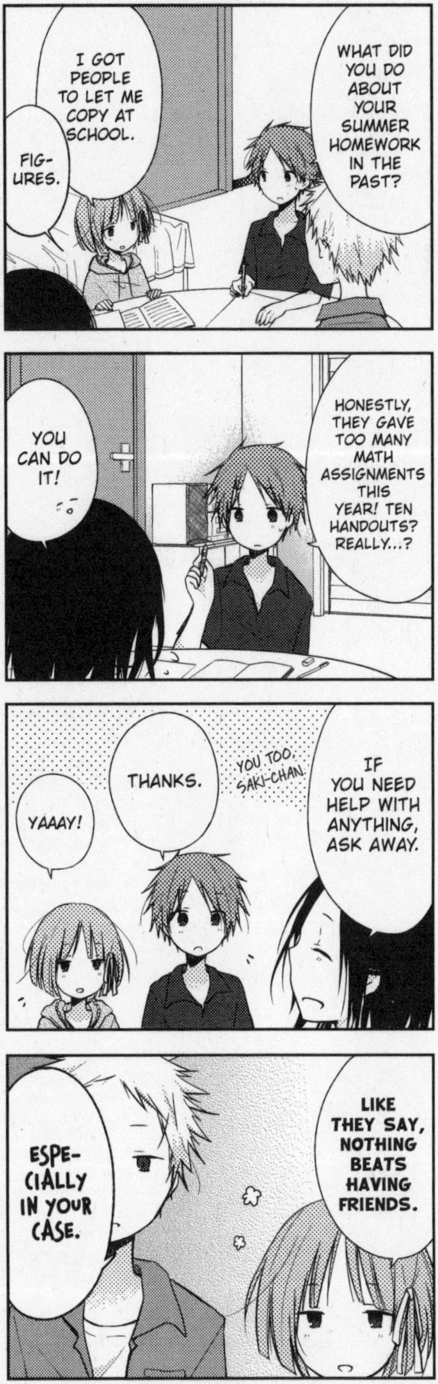
WHAT DID YOU DO ABOUT YOUR SUMMER HOMEWORK IN THE PAST?
I GOT PEOPLE TO LET ME COPY AT SCHOOL.
FIG-URES.
HONESTLY, THEY GAVE TOO MANY MATH ASSIGNMENTS THIS YEAR! TEN HANDOUTS? REALLY...?
YOU CAN DO IT!
IF YOU NEED HELP WITH ANYTHING, ASK AWAY.
YOU TOO, SAKI-CHAN.
THANKS.
YAAAY!
LIKE THEY SAY, NOTHING BEATS HAVING FRIENDS.
ESPE-CIALLY IN YOUR CASE.

COMPLETELY

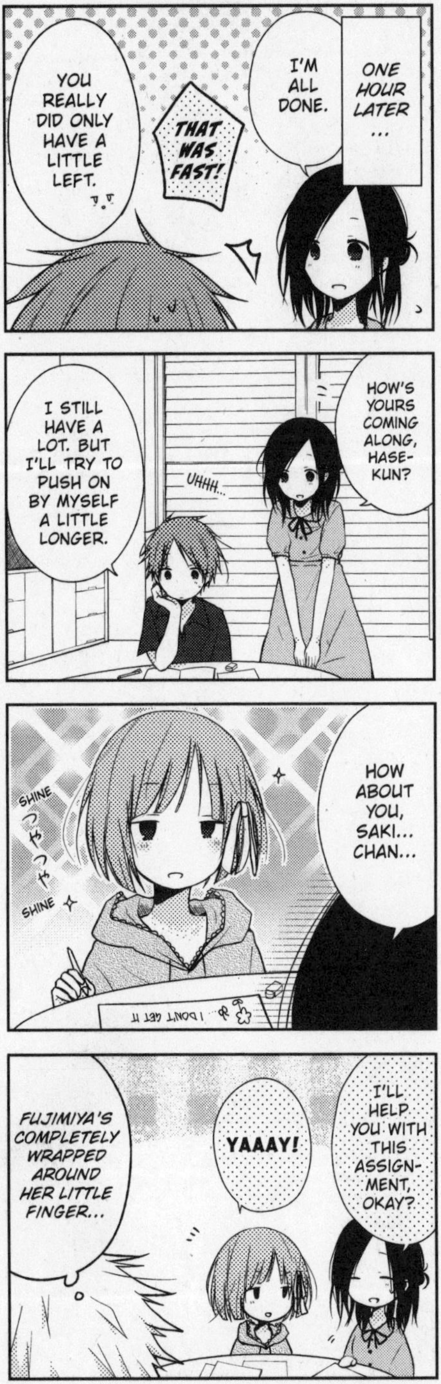
ONE HOUR LATER ...
I'M ALL DONE.
THAT WAS FAST!
YOU REALLY DID ONLY HAVE A LITTLE LEFT.
HOW'S YOURS COMING ALONG, HASE-KUN?
UHHH...
I STILL HAVE A LOT. BUT I'LL TRY TO PUSH ON BY MYSELF A LITTLE LONGER.
HOW ABOUT YOU, SAKI... CHAN...
SHINE
SHINE
I DON'T GET IT
I'LL HELP YOU WITH THIS ASSIGN-MENT, OKAY?
YAAAY!
FUJIMIYA'S COMPLETELY WRAPPED AROUND HER LITTLE FINGER...

YOUTHFUL

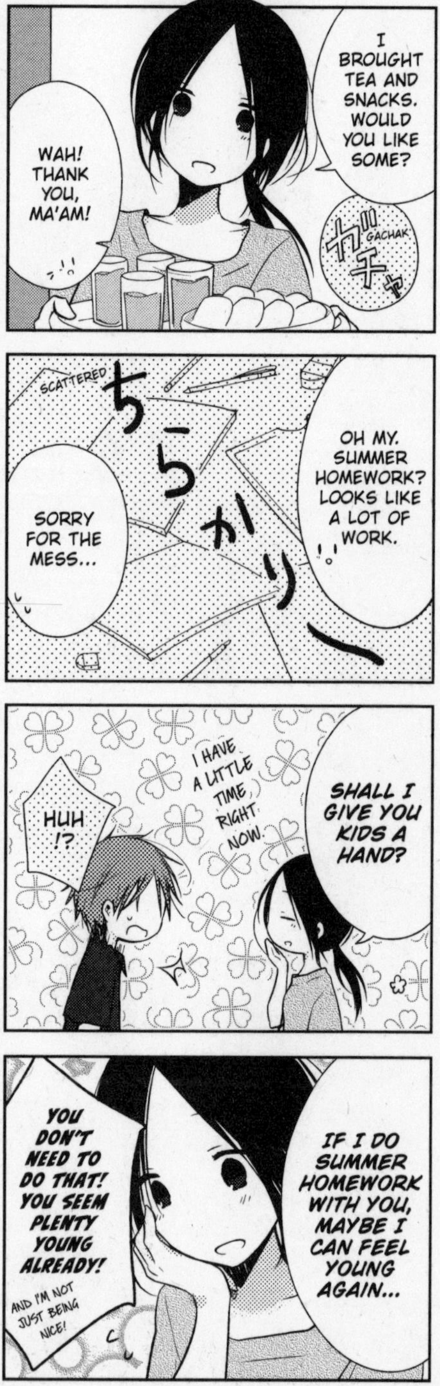
I BROUGHT TEA AND SNACKS. WOULD YOU LIKE SOME?
GACHAK
WAH! THANK YOU, MA'AM!
SCATTERED
OH MY. SUMMER HOMEWORK? LOOKS LIKE A LOT OF WORK.
SORRY FOR THE MESS...
SHALL I GIVE YOU KIDS A HAND?
I HAVE A LITTLE TIME RIGHT NOW.
HUH!?
IF I DO SUMMER HOMEWORK WITH YOU, MAYBE I CAN FEEL YOUNG AGAIN...
YOU DON'T NEED TO DO THAT! YOU SEEM PLENTY YOUNG ALREADY!
AND I'M NOT JUST BEING NICE!

COOPERATIVENESS

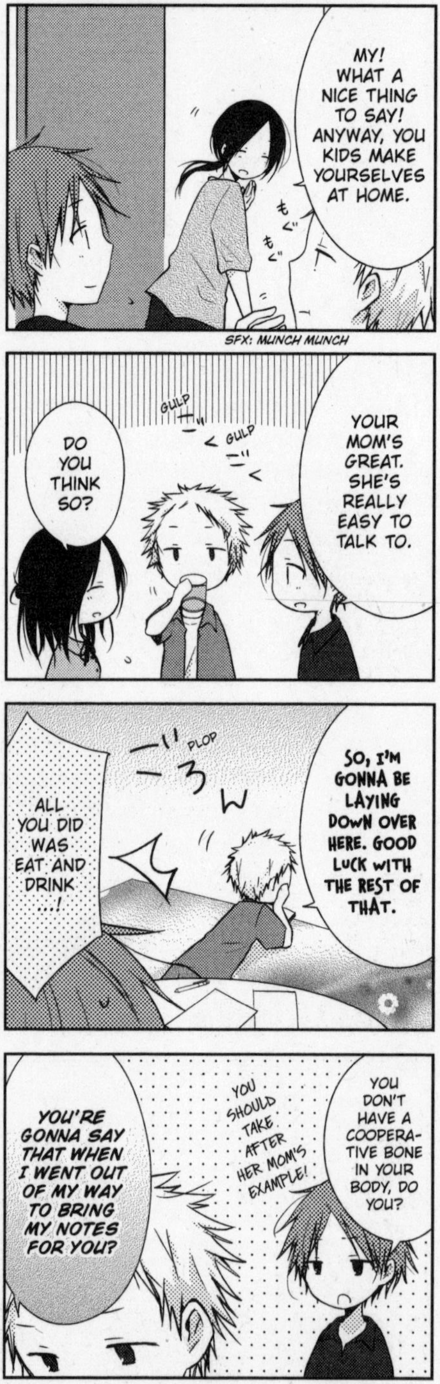
MY! WHAT A NICE THING TO SAY! ANYWAY, YOU KIDS MAKE YOURSELVES AT HOME.
SFX: MUNCH MUNCH
YOUR MOM'S GREAT. SHE'S REALLY EASY TO TALK TO.
GULP
GULP
DO YOU THINK SO?
SO, I'M GONNA BE LAYING DOWN OVER HERE. GOOD LUCK WITH THE REST OF THAT.
PLOP
ALL YOU DID WAS EAT AND DRINK ...!
YOU DON'T HAVE A COOPERATIVE BONE IN YOUR BODY, DO YOU?
YOU SHOULD TAKE AFTER HER MOM'S EXAMPLE!
YOU'RE GONNA SAY THAT WHEN I WENT OUT OF MY WAY TO BRING MY NOTES FOR YOU?

INTO THE PATTERN

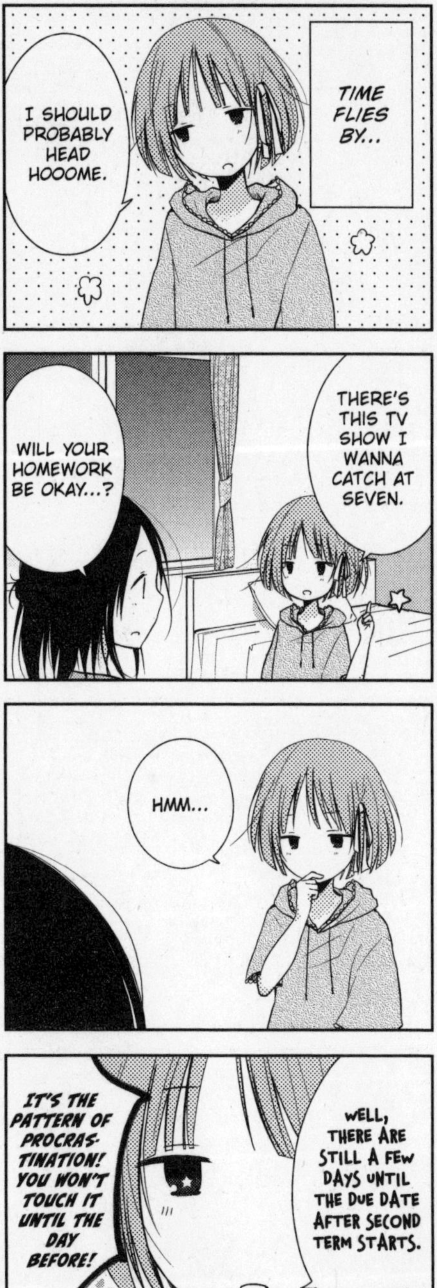
TIME FLIES BY...
I SHOULD PROBABLY HEAD HOOOME.
THERE'S THIS TV SHOW I WANNA CATCH AT SEVEN.
WILL YOUR HOMEWORK BE OKAY...?
HMM...
WELL, THERE ARE STILL A FEW DAYS UNTIL THE DUE DATE AFTER SECOND TERM STARTS.
IT'LL GET DONE.
IT'S THE PATTERN OF PROCRASTINATION! YOU WON'T TOUCH IT UNTIL THE DAY BEFORE!

OBLIVIOUS

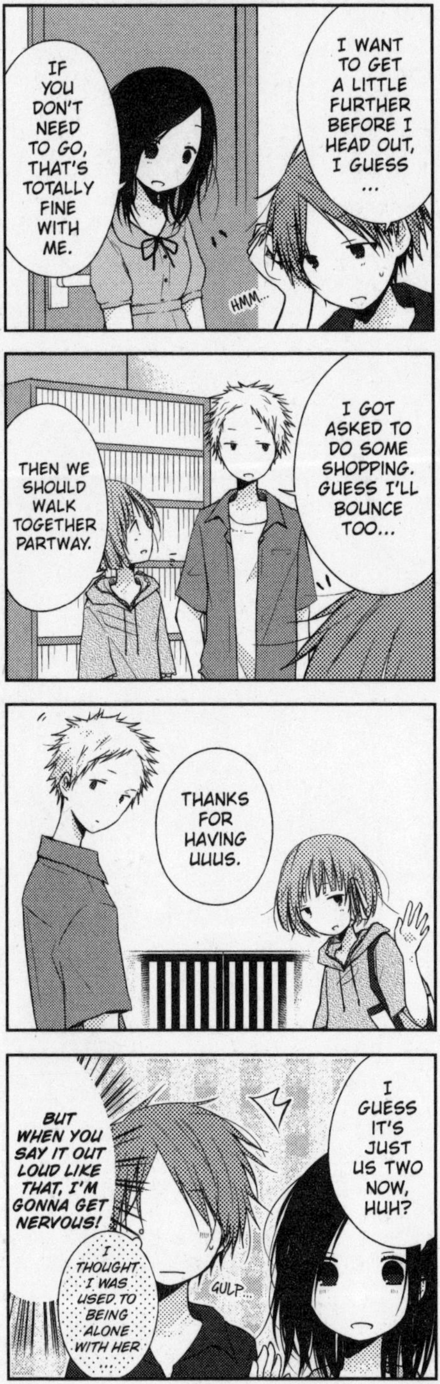
I WANT TO GET A LITTLE FURTHER BEFORE I HEAD OUT, I GUESS ...
HMM...
IF YOU DON'T NEED TO GO, THAT'S TOTALLY FINE WITH ME.
I GOT ASKED TO DO SOME SHOPPING. GUESS I'LL BOUNCE TOO...
THEN WE SHOULD WALK TOGETHER PARTWAY.
THANKS FOR HAVING UUUS.
I GUESS IT'S JUST US TWO NOW, HUH?
GULP...
BUT WHEN YOU SAY IT OUT LOUD LIKE THAT, I'M GONNA GET NERVOUS!
I THOUGHT I WAS USED TO BEING ALONE WITH HER

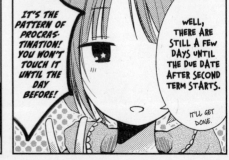

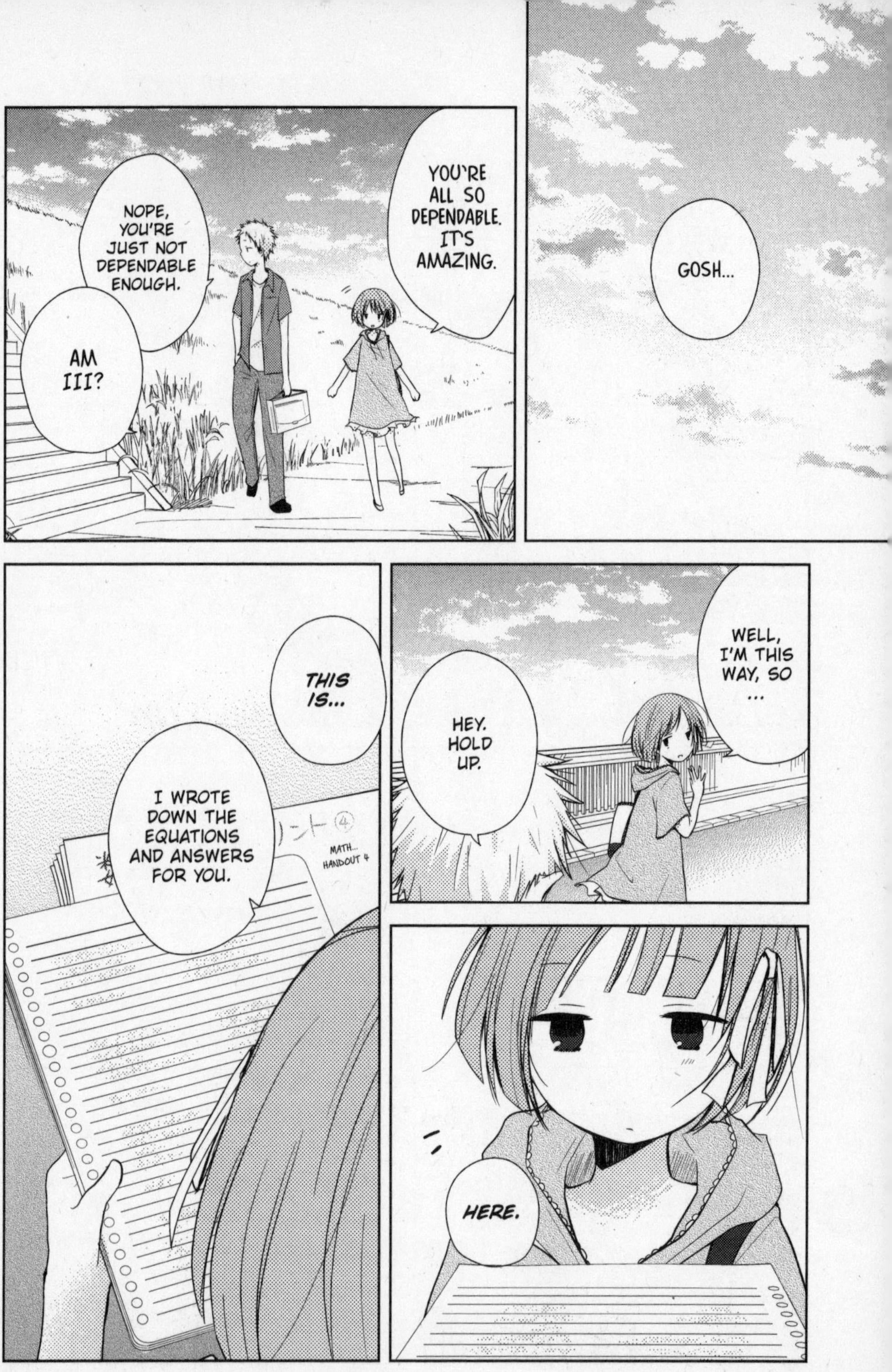
GOSH...
YOU'RE ALL SO DEPENDABLE. IT'S AMAZING.
NOPE, YOU'RE JUST NOT DEPENDABLE ENOUGH.
AM III?
WELL, I'M THIS WAY, SO ...
HEY. HOLD UP.
HERE.
THIS IS...
I WROTE DOWN THE EQUATIONS AND ANSWERS FOR YOU.
MATH... HANDOUT 4

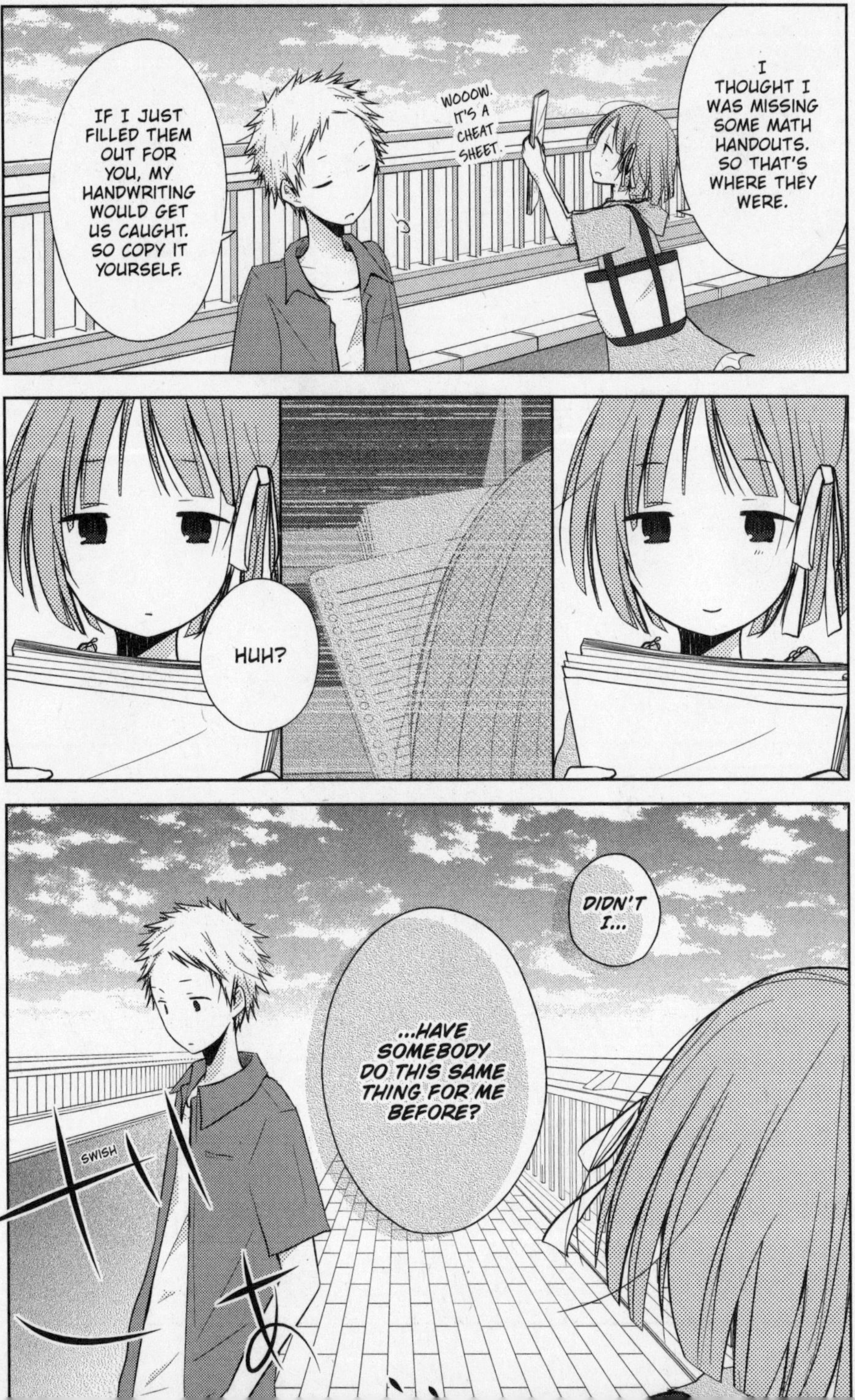
I THOUGHT I WAS MISSING SOME MATH HANDOUTS. SO THAT'S WHERE THEY WERE.
WOOOW. IT'S A CHEAT SHEET.
IF I JUST FILLED THEM OUT FOR YOU, MY HANDWRITING WOULD GET US CAUGHT. SO COPY IT YOURSELF.
HUH?
DIDN'T I...
...HAVE SOMEBODY DO THIS SAME THING FOR ME BEFORE?
SWISH

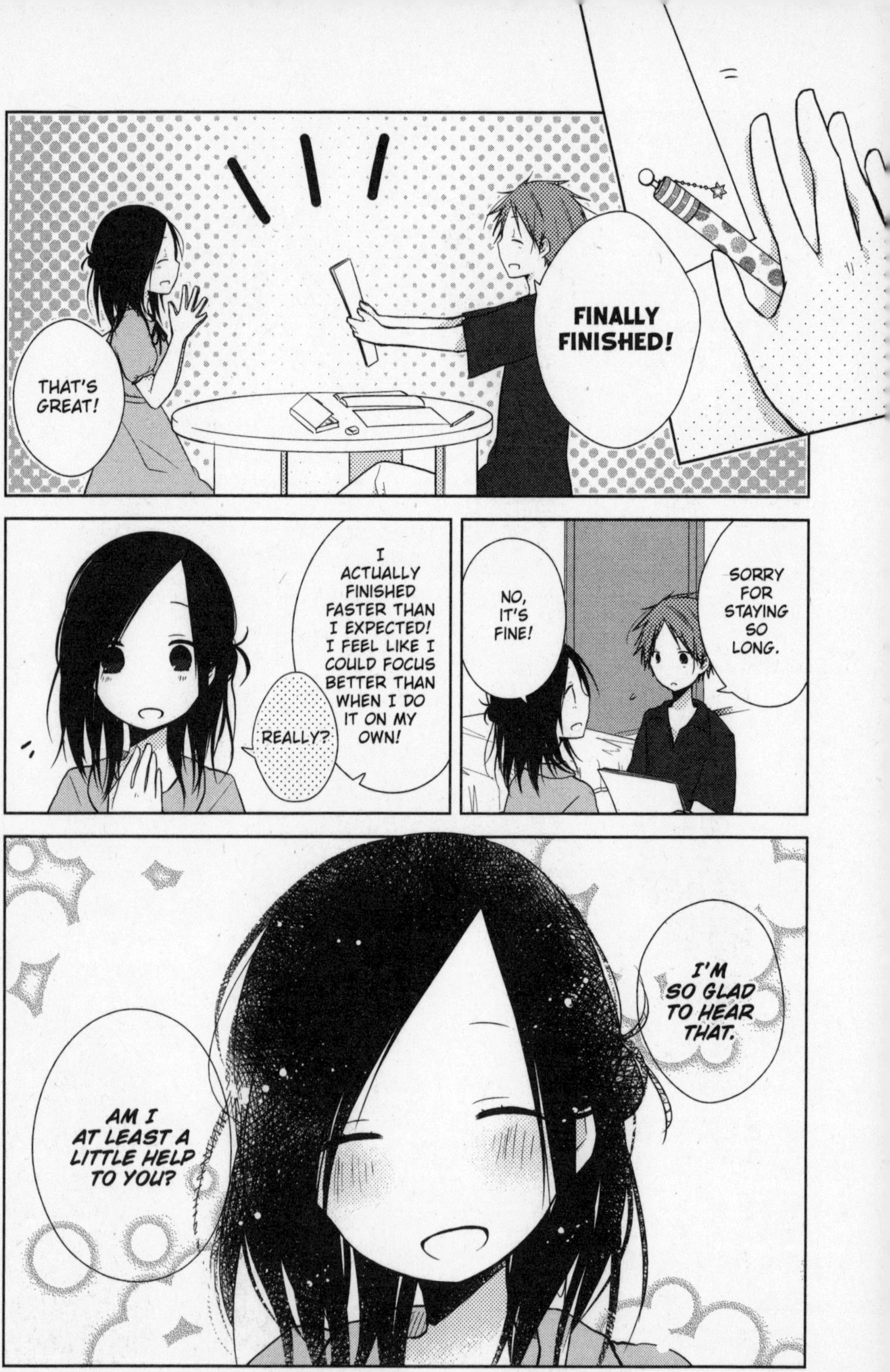
FINALLY FINISHED!
THAT'S GREAT!
SORRY FOR STAYING SO LONG.
NO, IT'S FINE!
I ACTUALLY FINISHED FASTER THAN I EXPECTED! I FEEL LIKE I COULD FOCUS BETTER THAN WHEN I DO IT ON MY OWN!
REALLY?
I'M SO GLAD TO HEAR THAT.
AM I AT LEAST A LITTLE HELP TO YOU?

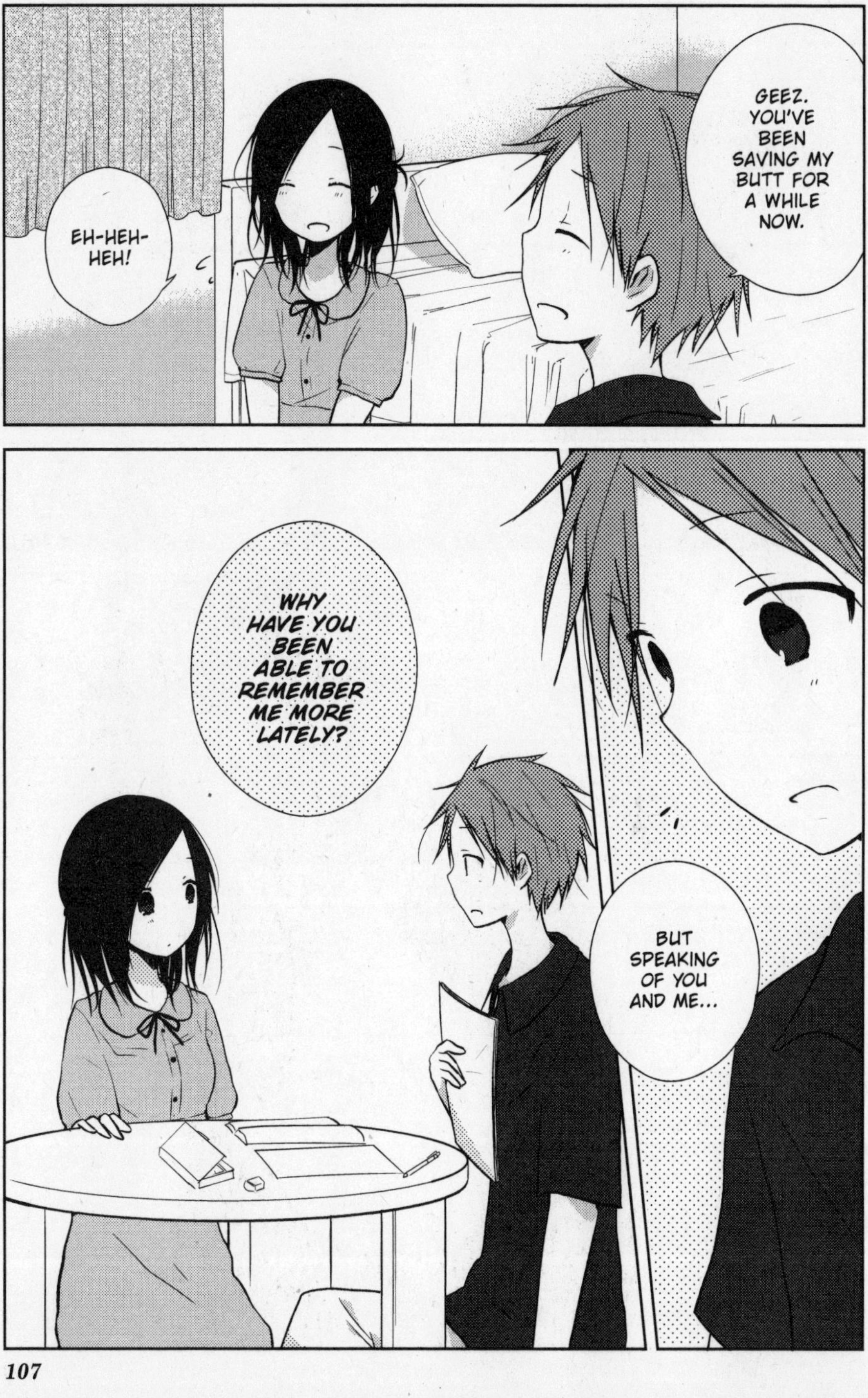
GEEZ. YOU'VE BEEN SAVING MY BUTT FOR A WHILE NOW.
EH-HEH-HEH!
BUT SPEAKING OF YOU AND ME...
WHY HAVE YOU BEEN ABLE TO REMEMBER ME MORE LATELY?

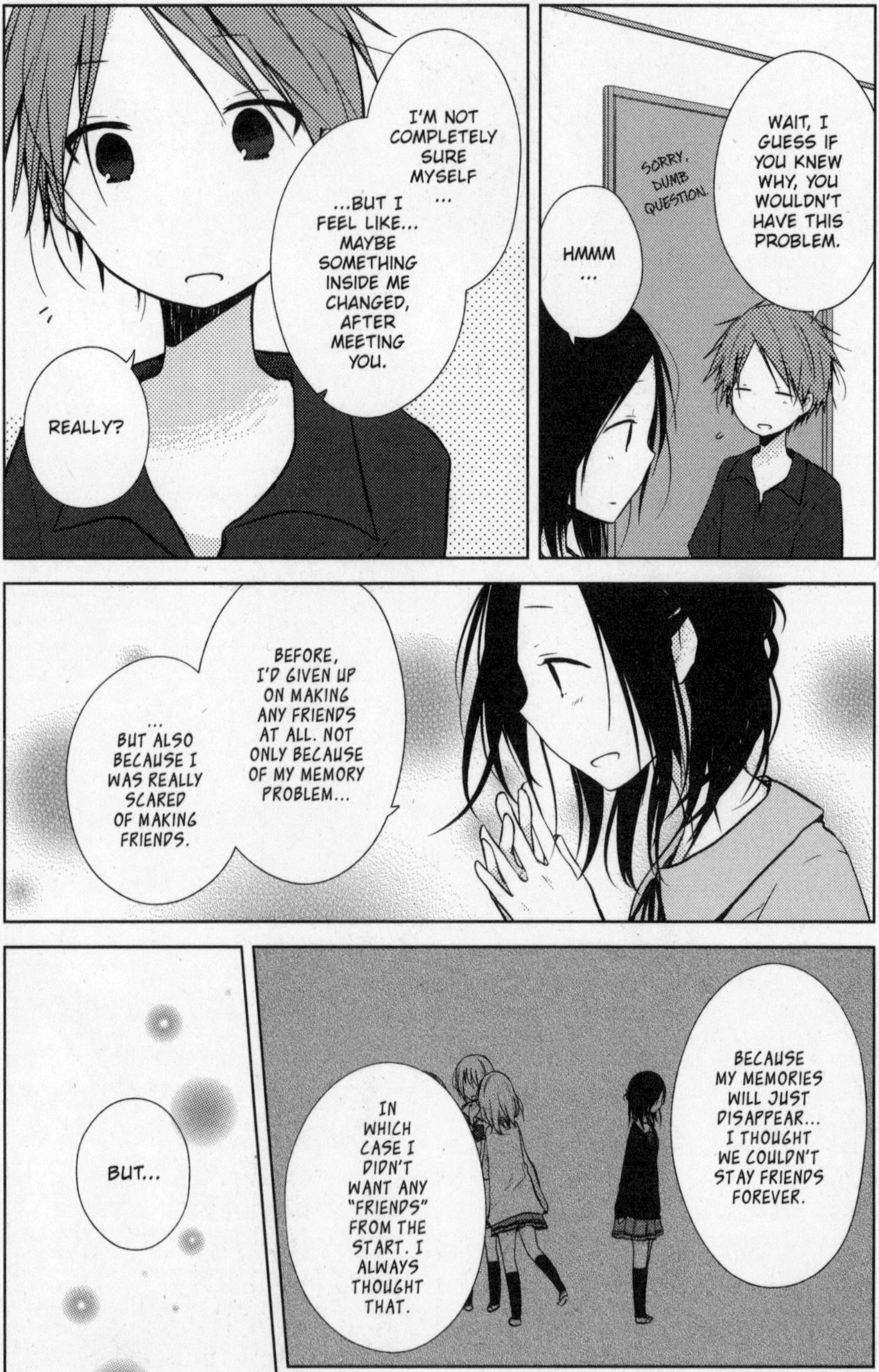
WAIT, I GUESS IF YOU KNEW WHY, YOU WOULDN'T HAVE THIS PROBLEM.
SORRY, DUMB QUESTION.
HMMM ...
I'M NOT COMPLETELY SURE MYSELF ...
...BUT I FEEL LIKE... MAYBE SOMETHING INSIDE ME CHANGED, AFTER MEETING YOU.
REALLY?
BEFORE, I'D GIVEN UP ON MAKING ANY FRIENDS AT ALL. NOT ONLY BECAUSE OF MY MEMORY PROBLEM...
... BUT ALSO BECAUSE I WAS REALLY SCARED OF MAKING FRIENDS.
BECAUSE MY MEMORIES WILL JUST DISAPPEAR... I THOUGHT WE COULDN'T STAY FRIENDS FOREVER.
IN WHICH CASE I DIDN'T WANT ANY "FRIENDS" FROM THE START. I ALWAYS THOUGHT THAT.
BUT...

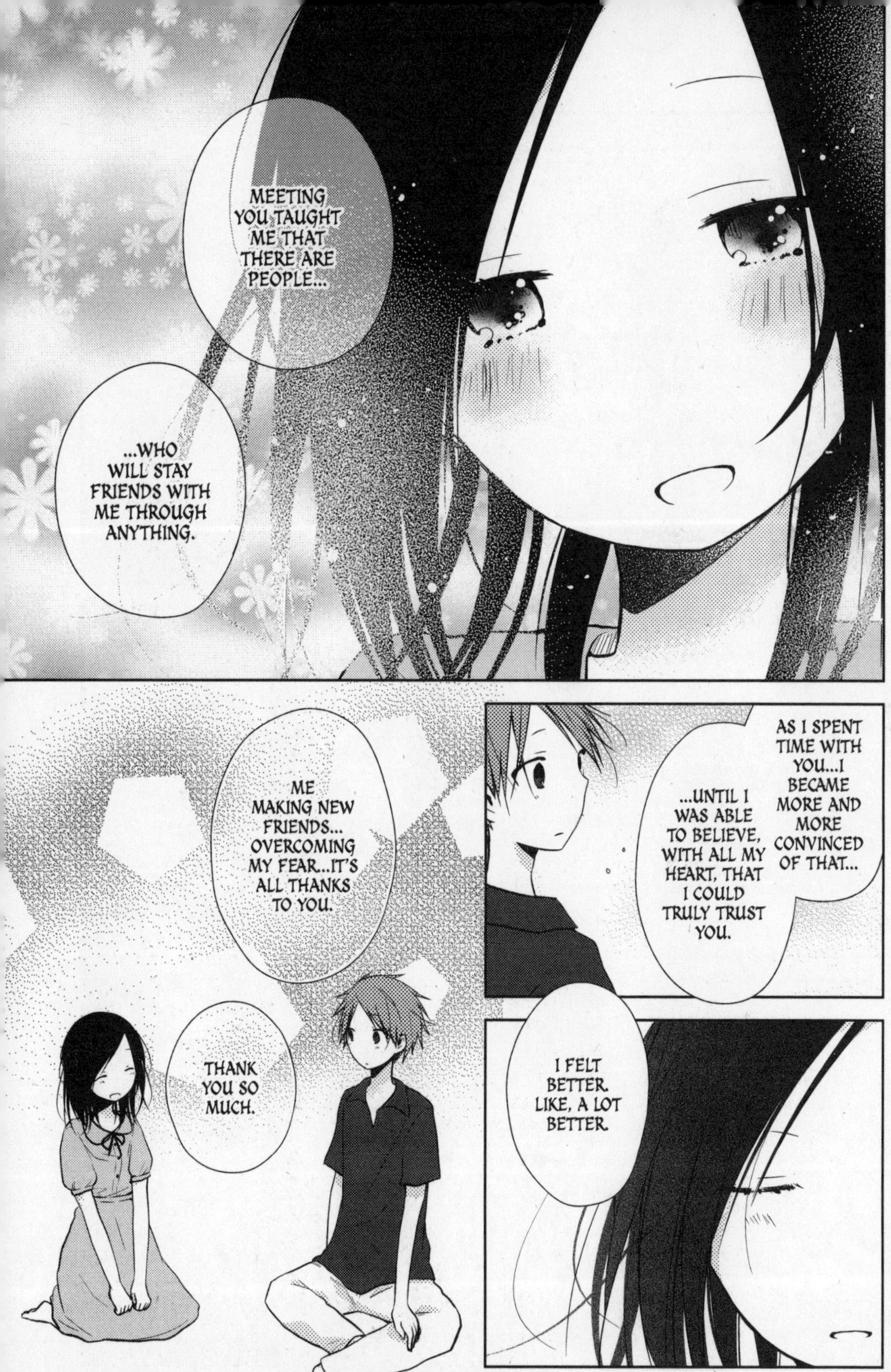
MEETING YOU TAUGHT ME THAT THERE ARE PEOPLE...
...WHO WILL STAY FRIENDS WITH ME THROUGH ANYTHING.
AS I SPENT TIME WITH YOU...I BECAME MORE AND MORE CONVINCED OF THAT...
...UNTIL I WAS ABLE TO BELIEVE, WITH ALL MY HEART, THAT I COULD TRULY TRUST YOU.
I FELT BETTER. LIKE, A LOT BETTER.
ME MAKING NEW FRIENDS... OVERCOMING MY FEAR...IT'S ALL THANKS TO YOU.
THANK YOU SO MUCH.

FUJIMIYA-SAN...

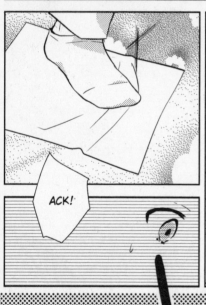

ACK!

HUH? OH GEEZ, IT'S TOO SUDDEN... I COULDN'T ...!

OH!

YOU WANT TO STAY FOR DINNER? I'LL ASK MOM IF THERE'S SOME FOR YOU TOO.

ずいたーん!

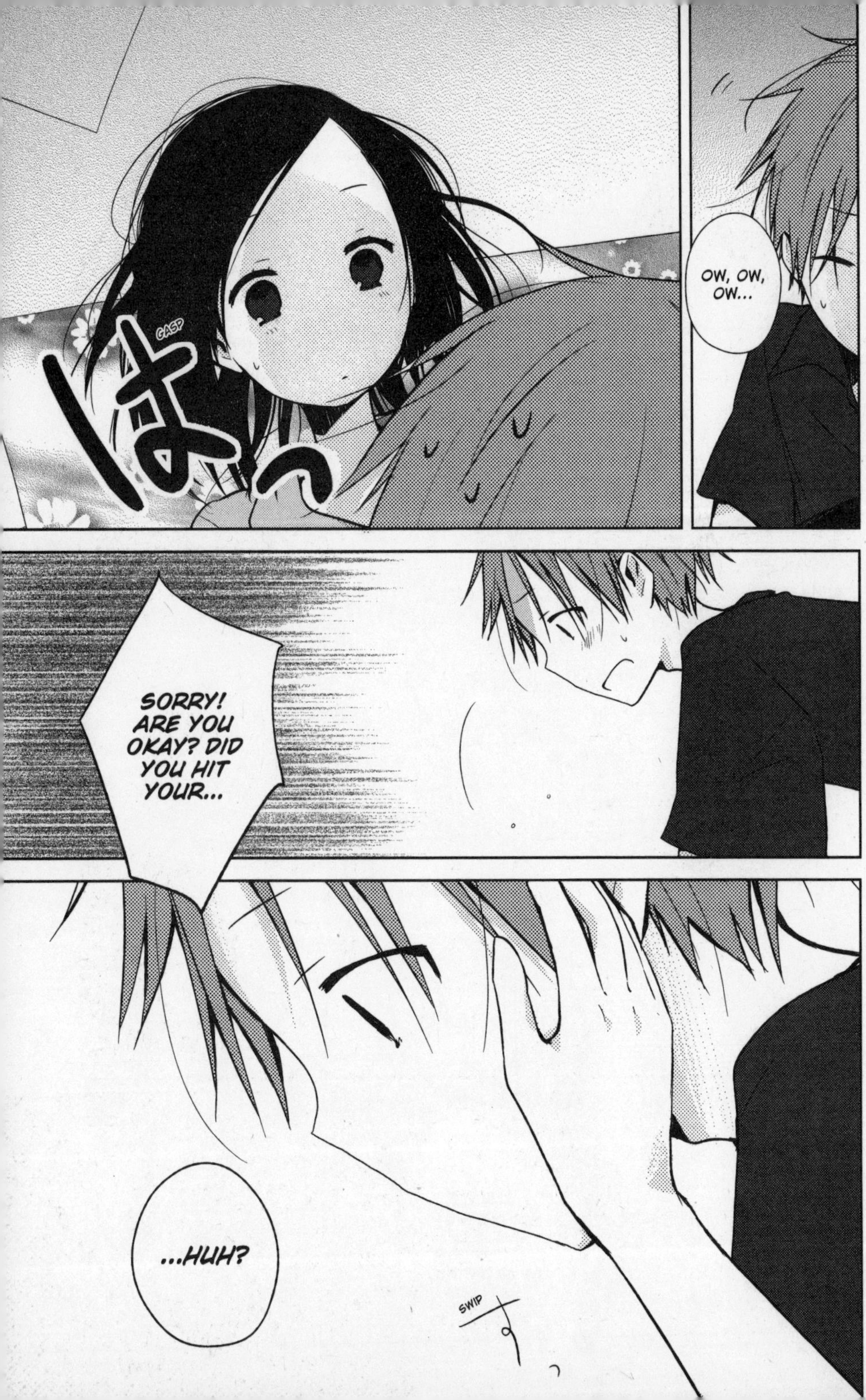
OW, OW, OW...
GASP
はっ
SORRY! ARE YOU OKAY? DID YOU HIT YOUR...
...HUH?
SWIP
す

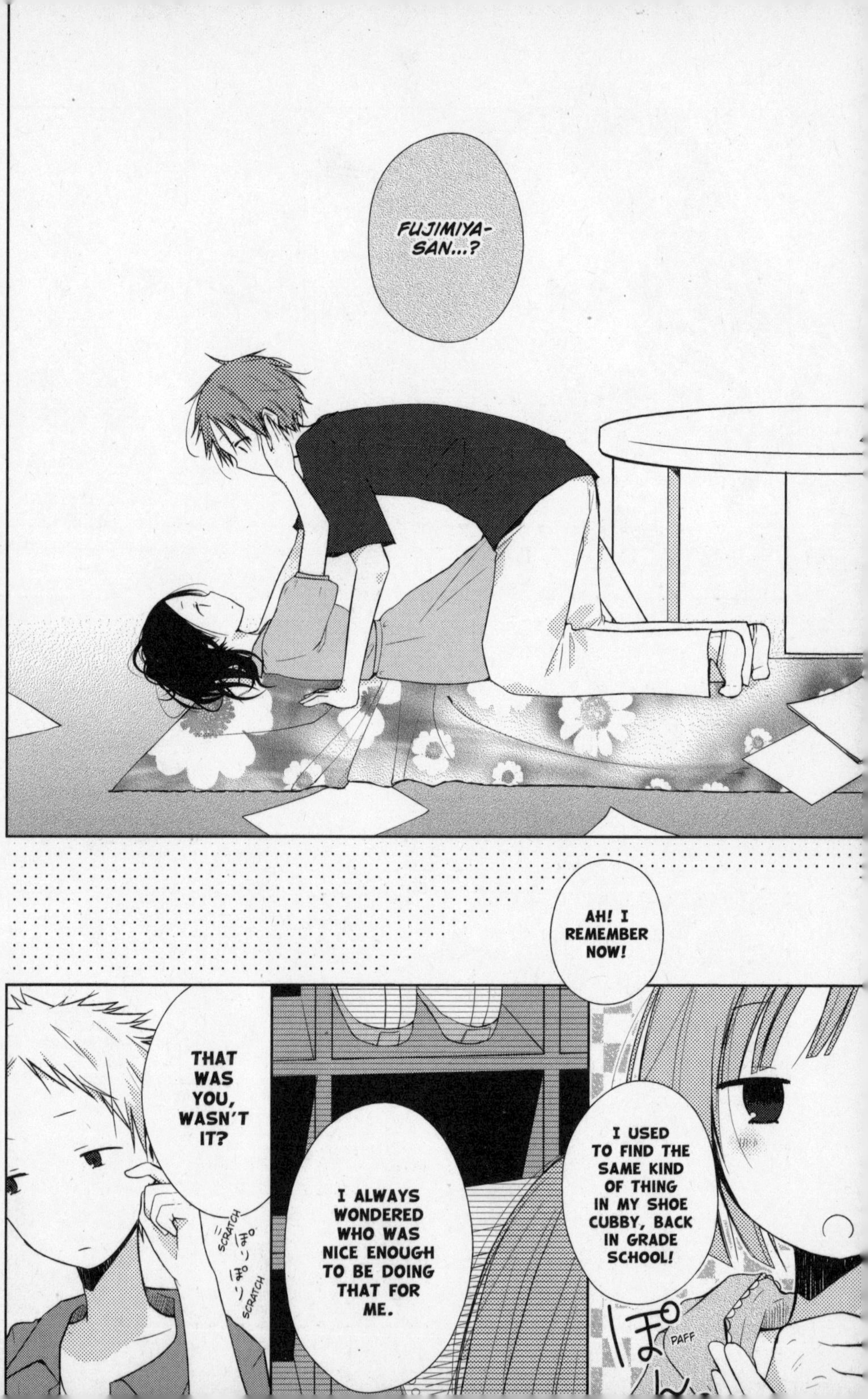
FUJIMIYA-SAN...?
AH! I REMEMBER NOW!
I USED TO FIND THE SAME KIND OF THING IN MY SHOE CUBBY, BACK IN GRADE SCHOOL!
PAFF
I ALWAYS WONDERED WHO WAS NICE ENOUGH TO BE DOING THAT FOR ME.
THAT WAS YOU, WASN'T IT?
SCRATCH
SCRATCH

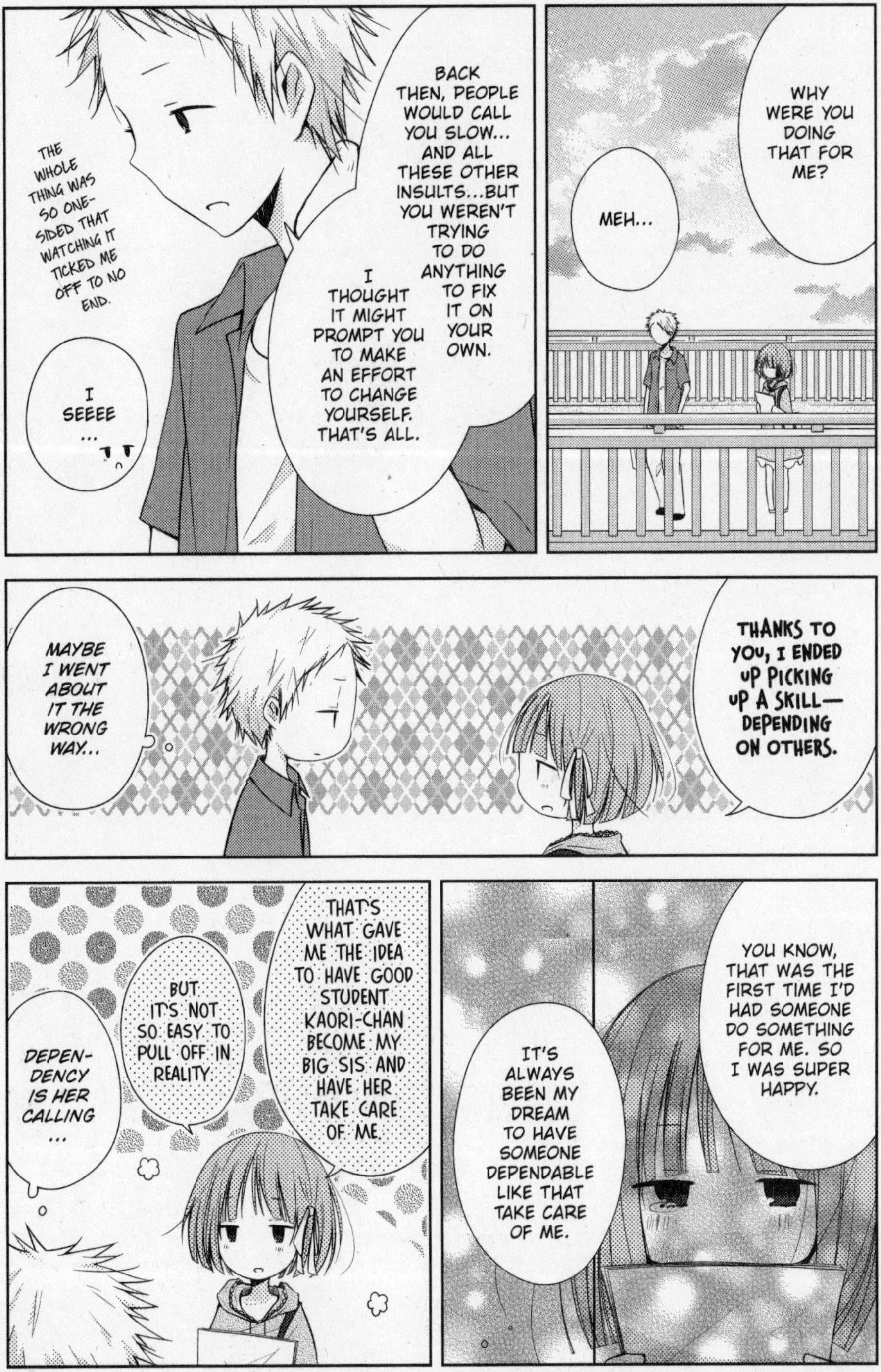
WHY WERE YOU DOING THAT FOR ME?
MEH...
BACK THEN, PEOPLE WOULD CALL YOU SLOW... AND ALL THESE OTHER INSULTS...BUT YOU WEREN'T TRYING TO DO ANYTHING TO FIX IT ON YOUR OWN.
I THOUGHT IT MIGHT PROMPT YOU TO MAKE AN EFFORT TO CHANGE YOURSELF. THAT'S ALL.
THE WHOLE THING WAS SO ONE-SIDED THAT WATCHING IT TICKED ME OFF TO NO END.
I SEEEE...
THANKS TO YOU, I ENDED UP PICKING UP A SKILL—DEPENDING ON OTHERS.
MAYBE I WENT ABOUT IT THE WRONG WAY...
YOU KNOW, THAT WAS THE FIRST TIME I'D HAD SOMEONE DO SOMETHING FOR ME. SO I WAS SUPER HAPPY.
IT'S ALWAYS BEEN MY DREAM TO HAVE SOMEONE DEPENDABLE LIKE THAT TAKE CARE OF ME.
THAT'S WHAT GAVE ME THE IDEA TO HAVE GOOD STUDENT KAORI-CHAN BECOME MY BIG SIS AND HAVE HER TAKE CARE OF ME.
BUT IT'S NOT SO EASY TO PULL OFF IN REALITY.
DEPENDENCY IS HER CALLING...

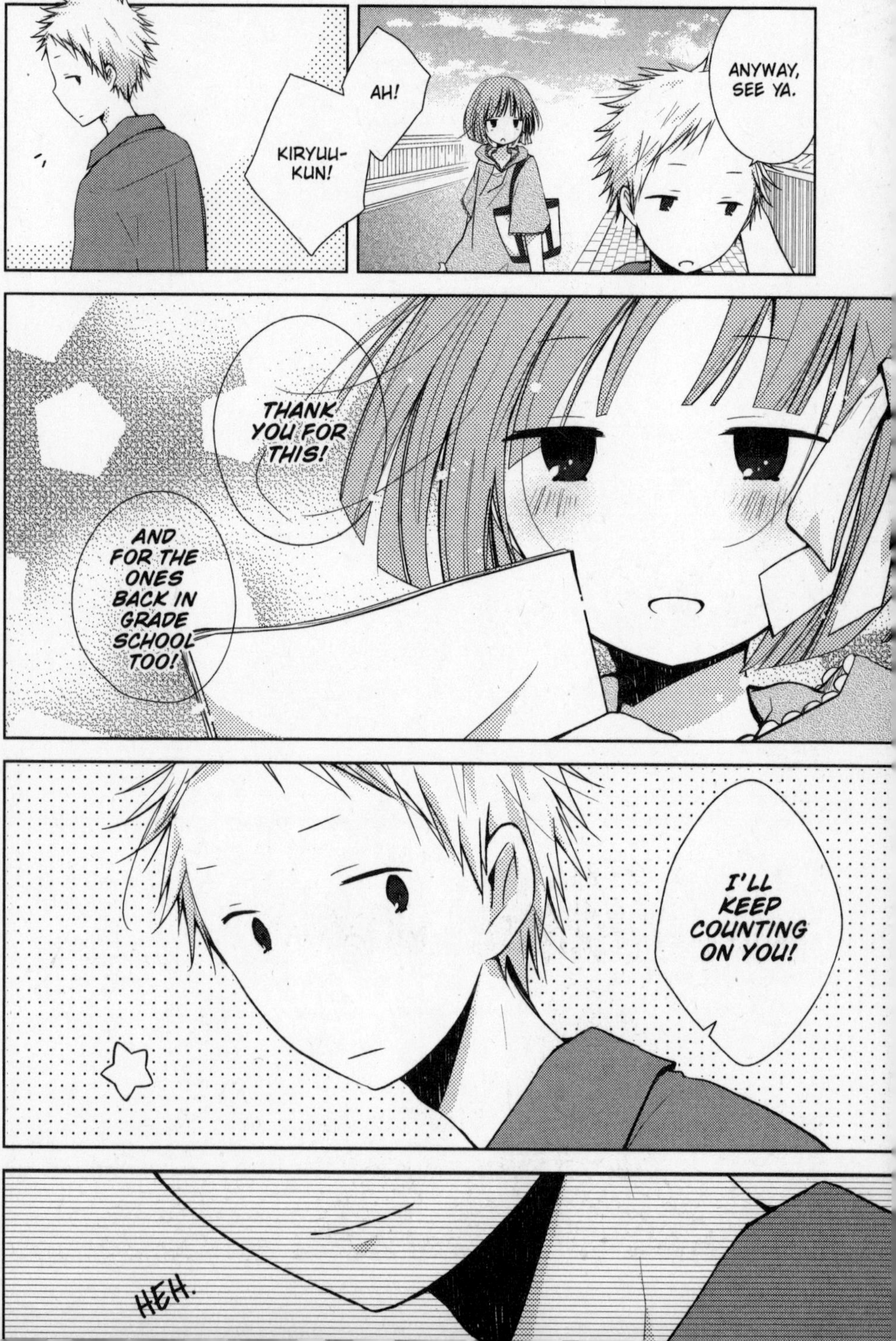
ANYWAY, SEE YA.
AH! KIRYUU-KUN!
THANK YOU FOR THIS!
AND FOR THE ONES BACK IN GRADE SCHOOL TOO!
I'LL KEEP COUNTING ON YOU!
HEH.

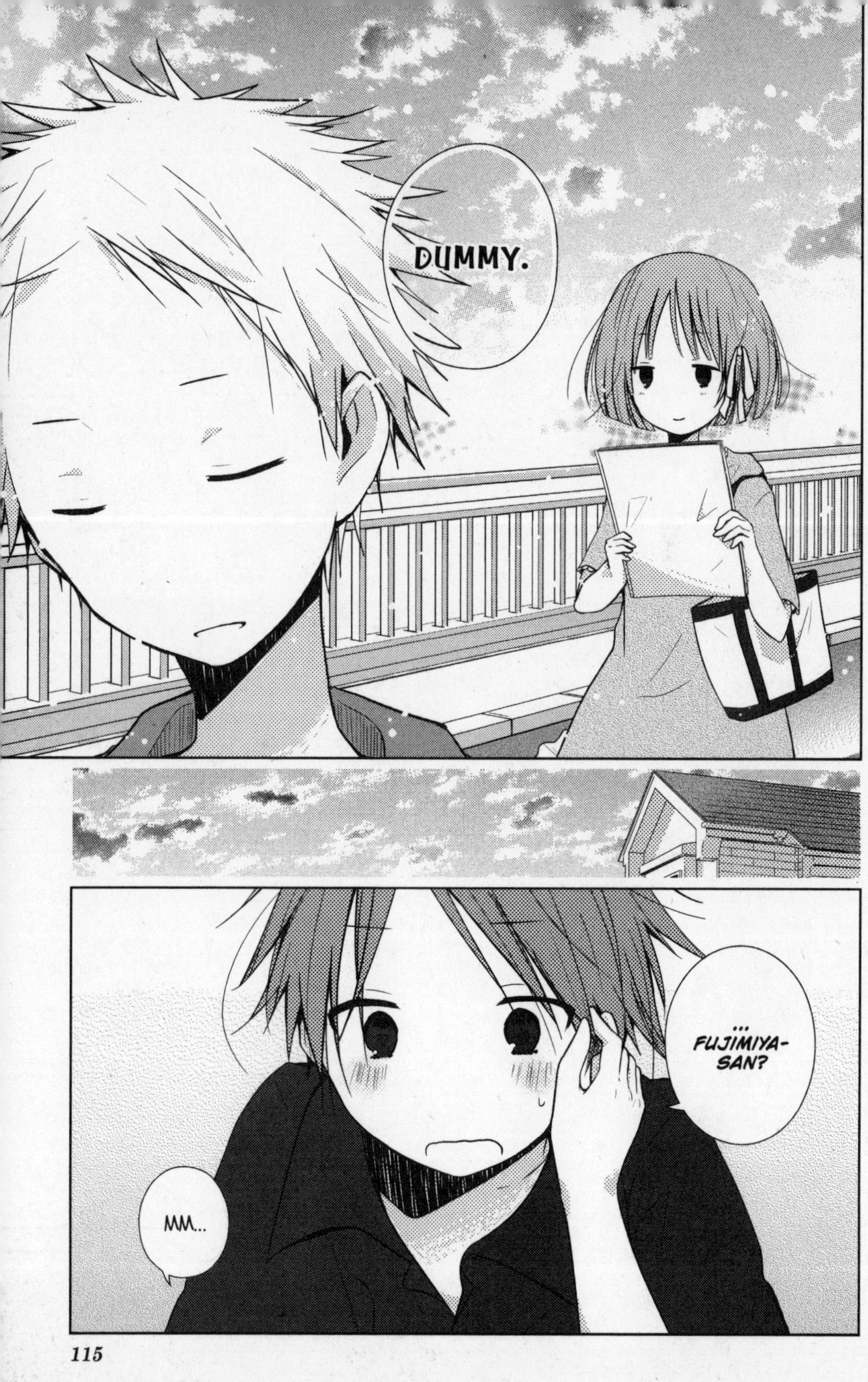
DUMMY.
...FUJIMIYA-SAN?
MM...

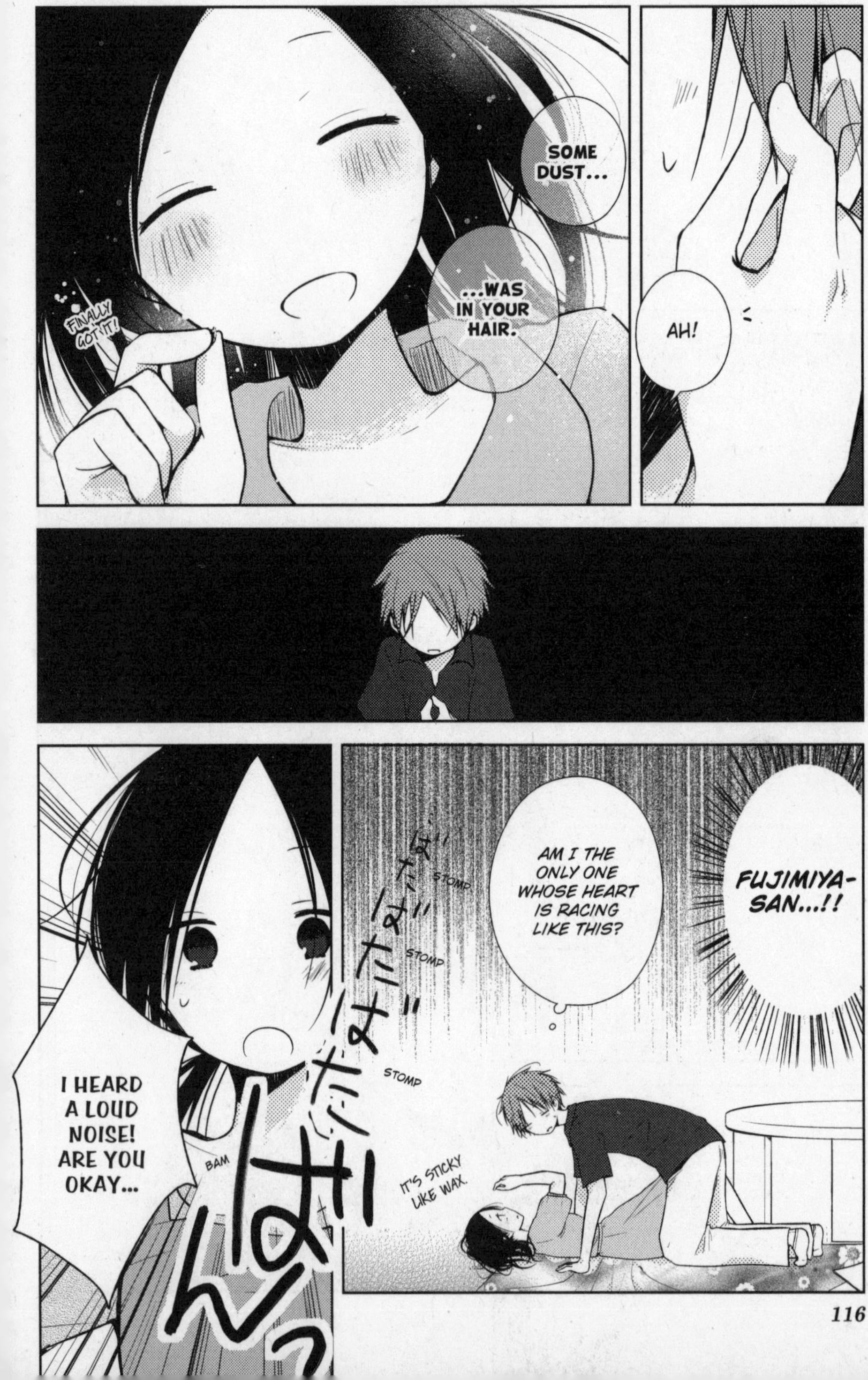
AH!
SOME DUST...
...WAS IN YOUR HAIR.
FINALLY GOT IT!
FUJIMIYA-SAN...!!
AM I THE ONLY ONE WHOSE HEART IS RACING LIKE THIS?
ばたばた
STOMP
STOMP
ばたばた
STOMP
IT'S STICKY LIKE WAX.
I HEARD A LOUD NOISE! ARE YOU OKAY...
ばんっ
BAM

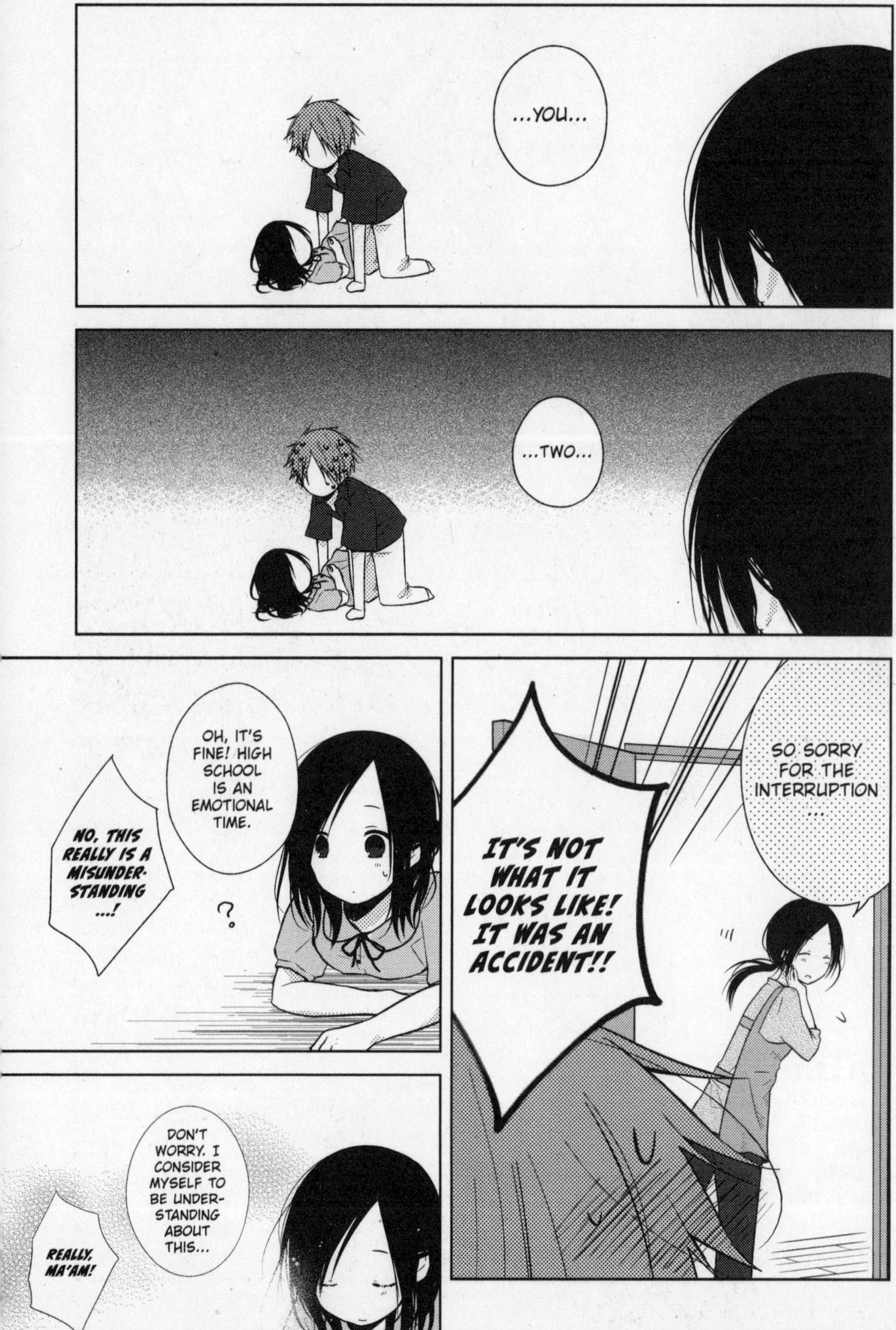
...YOU...
...TWO...
SO SORRY FOR THE INTERRUPTION...
IT'S NOT WHAT IT LOOKS LIKE! IT WAS AN ACCIDENT!!
OH, IT'S FINE! HIGH SCHOOL IS AN EMOTIONAL TIME.
NO, THIS REALLY IS A MISUNDER-STANDING...!
?
DON'T WORRY. I CONSIDER MYSELF TO BE UNDER-STANDING ABOUT THIS...
REALLY, MA'AM!

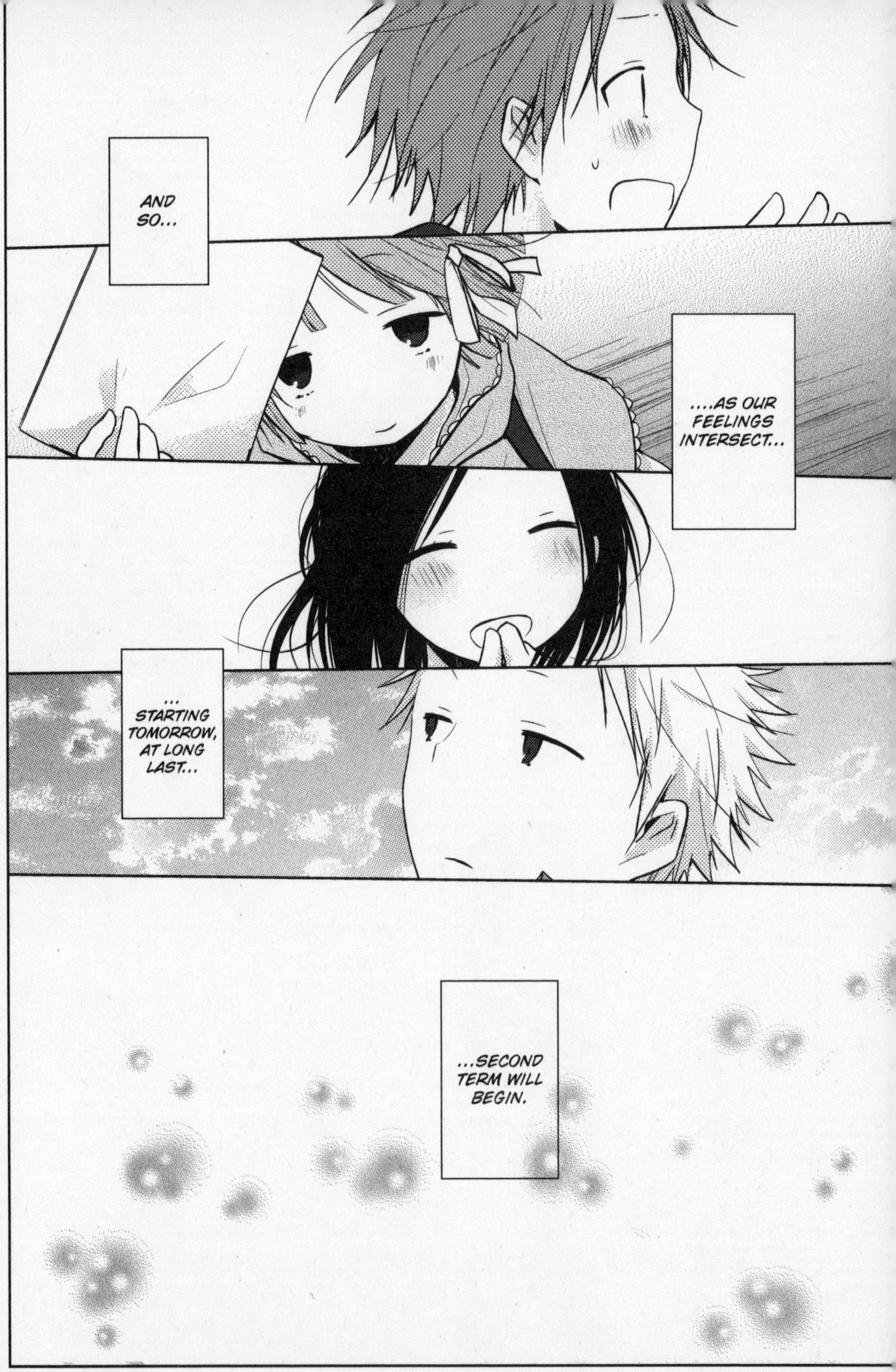
AND SO...
....AS OUR FEELINGS INTERSECT...
... STARTING TOMORROW, AT LONG LAST...
...SECOND TERM WILL BEGIN.

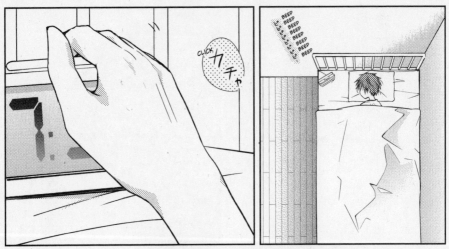

CLICK カチャ

BEEP BEEP BEEP BEEP BEEP BEEP BEEP

ALL RIGHT...

I MANAGED TO WAKE UP.

I'M OFF TO SCHOOL!

CHAPTER 14 LESS THAN FRIENDS

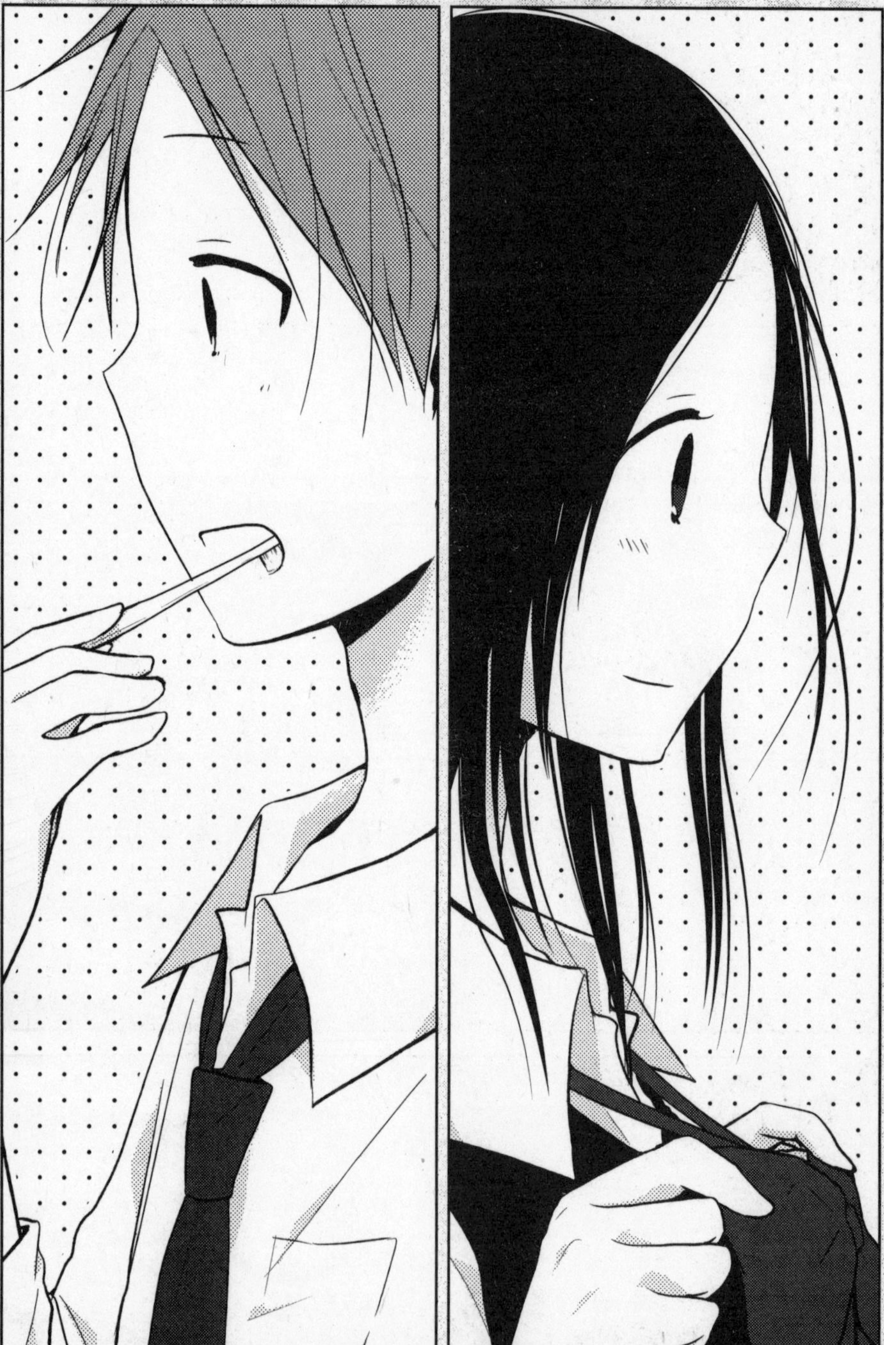

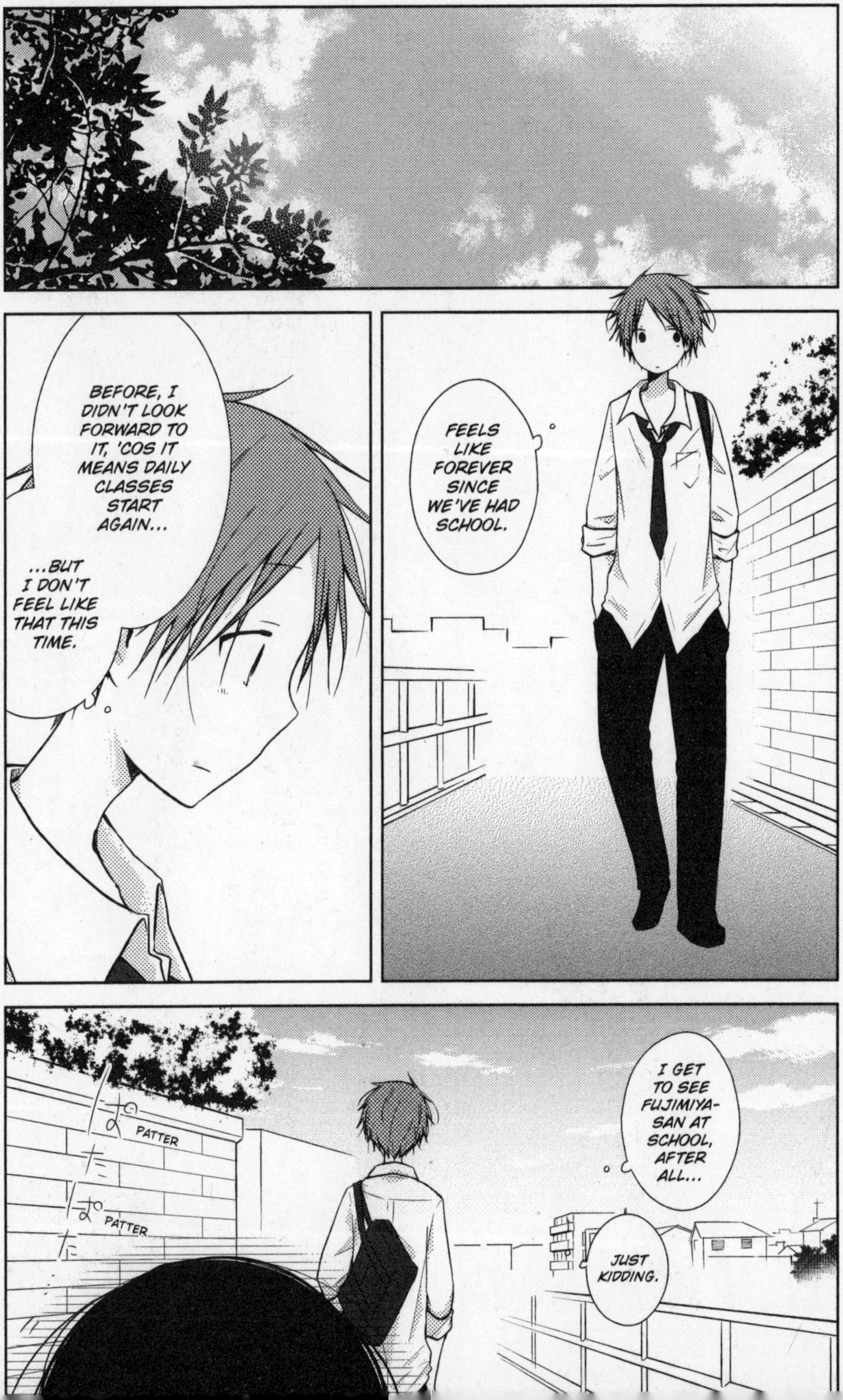
FEELS LIKE FOREVER SINCE WE'VE HAD SCHOOL.
BEFORE, I DIDN'T LOOK FORWARD TO IT, 'COS IT MEANS DAILY CLASSES START AGAIN...
...BUT I DON'T FEEL LIKE THAT THIS TIME.
I GET TO SEE FUJIMIYA-SAN AT SCHOOL, AFTER ALL...
JUST KIDDING.
ぱた PATTER
ぱた PATTER

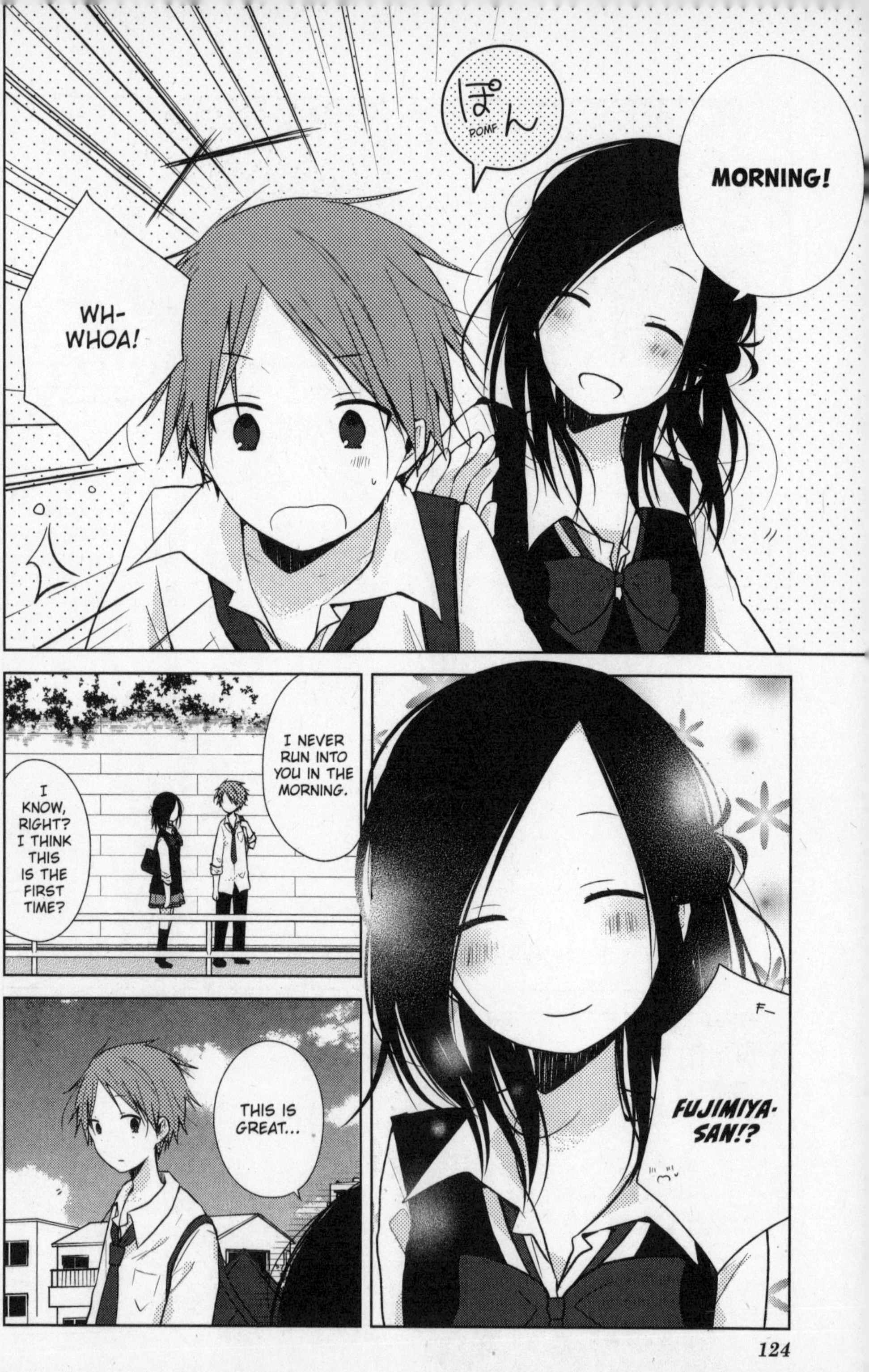
MORNING!
ぽん
POMF
WH-WHOA!
F–
FUJIMIYA-SAN!?
I NEVER RUN INTO YOU IN THE MORNING.
I KNOW, RIGHT? I THINK THIS IS THE FIRST TIME?
THIS IS GREAT...

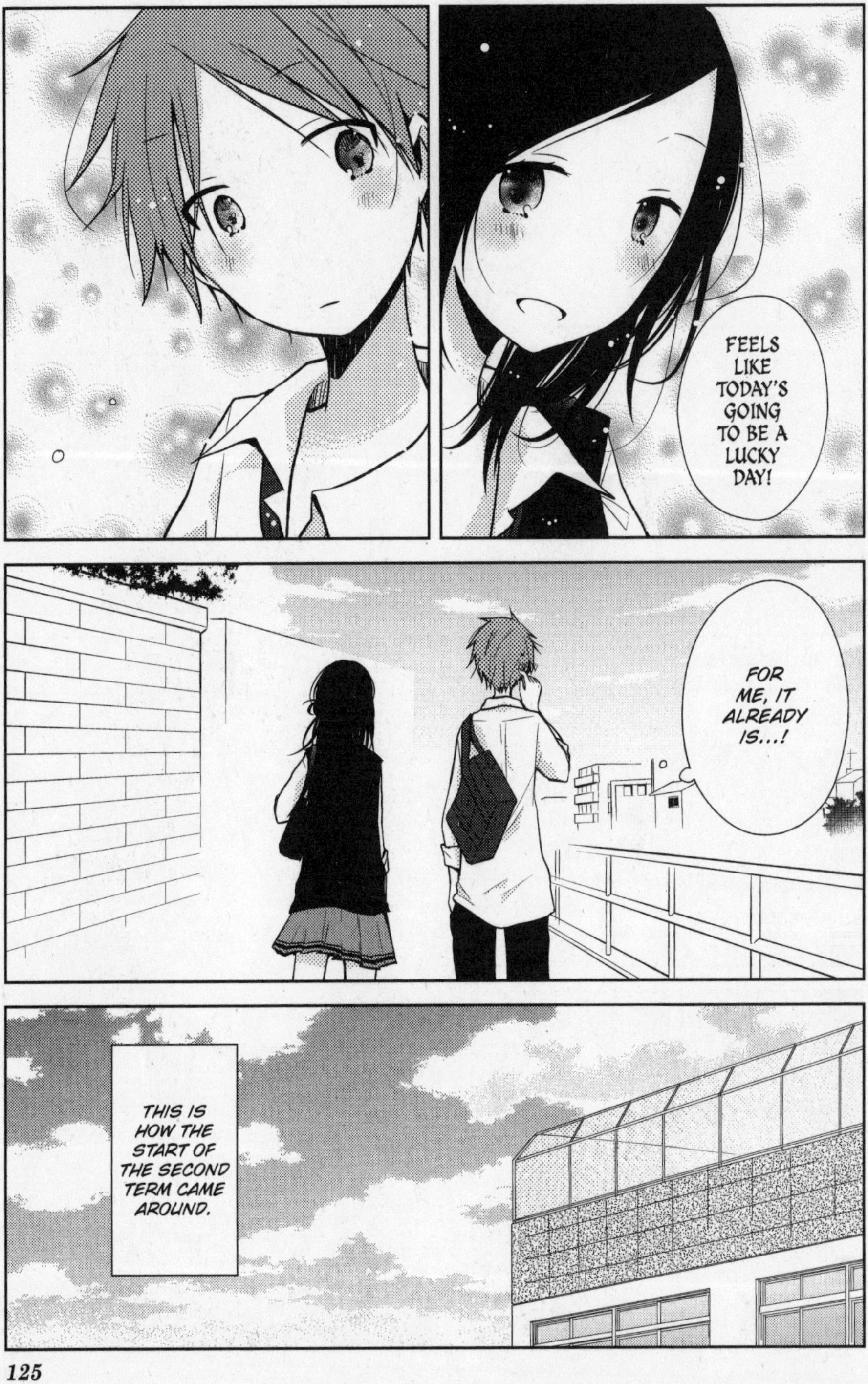
FEELS LIKE TODAY'S GOING TO BE A LUCKY DAY!
FOR ME, IT ALREADY IS...!
THIS IS HOW THE START OF THE SECOND TERM CAME AROUND.

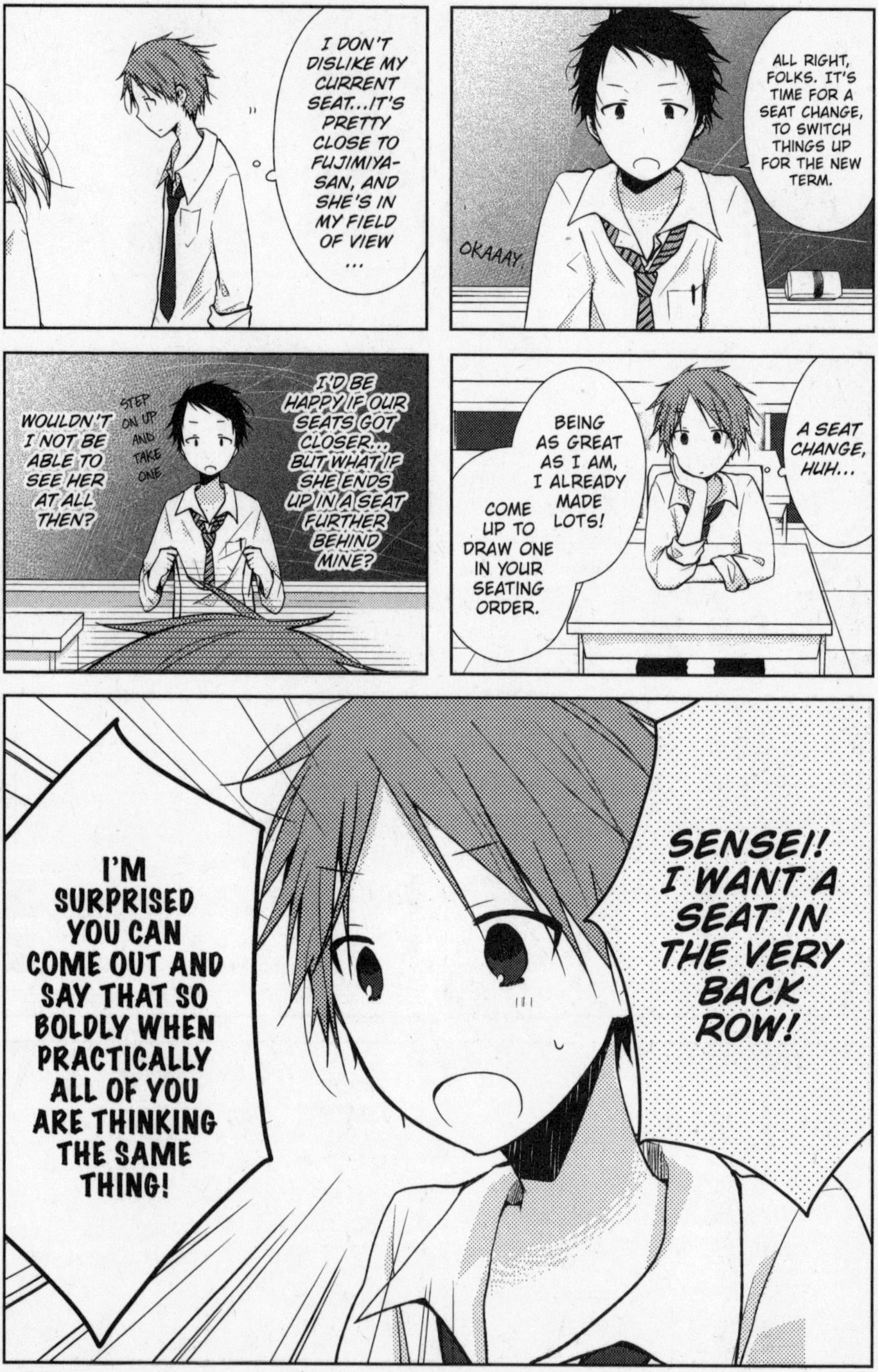
ALL RIGHT, FOLKS. IT'S TIME FOR A SEAT CHANGE, TO SWITCH THINGS UP FOR THE NEW TERM.
OKAAAY.
I DON'T DISLIKE MY CURRENT SEAT...IT'S PRETTY CLOSE TO FUJIMIYA-SAN, AND SHE'S IN MY FIELD OF VIEW ...
A SEAT CHANGE, HUH...
BEING AS GREAT AS I AM, I ALREADY MADE LOTS!
COME UP TO DRAW ONE IN YOUR SEATING ORDER.
I'D BE HAPPY IF OUR SEATS GOT CLOSER... BUT WHAT IF SHE ENDS UP IN A SEAT FURTHER BEHIND MINE?
STEP ON UP AND TAKE ONE
WOULDN'T I NOT BE ABLE TO SEE HER AT ALL THEN?
SENSEI! I WANT A SEAT IN THE VERY BACK ROW!
I'M SURPRISED YOU CAN COME OUT AND SAY THAT SO BOLDLY WHEN PRACTICALLY ALL OF YOU ARE THINKING THE SAME THING!

SEAT CHANGE

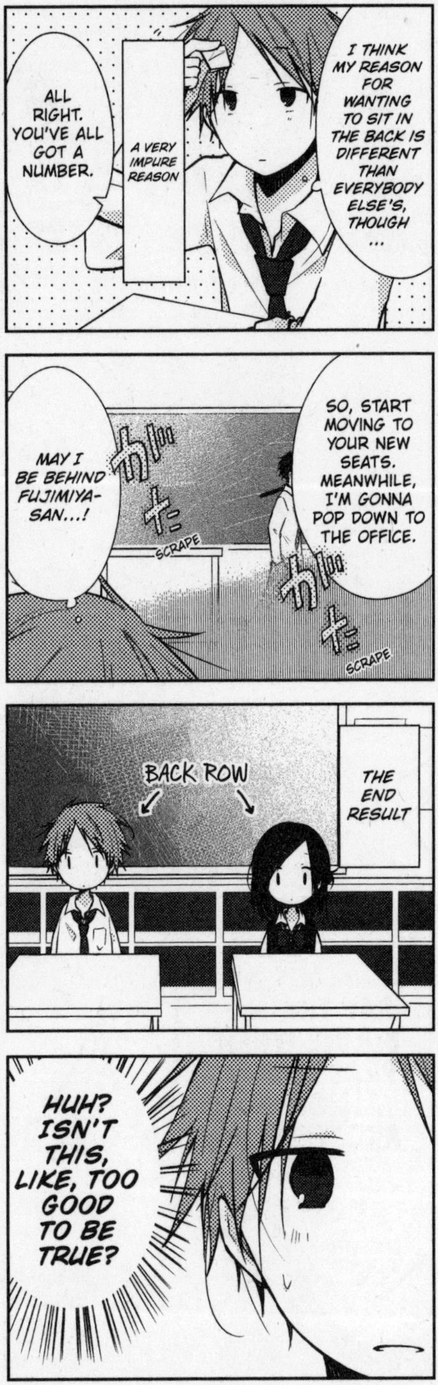
I THINK MY REASON FOR WANTING TO SIT IN THE BACK IS DIFFERENT THAN EVERYBODY ELSE'S, THOUGH ...
A VERY IMPURE REASON
ALL RIGHT. YOU'VE ALL GOT A NUMBER.
SO, START MOVING TO YOUR NEW SEATS. MEANWHILE, I'M GONNA POP DOWN TO THE OFFICE.
SCRAPE
SCRAPE
MAY I BE BEHIND FUJIMIYA-SAN...!
THE END RESULT
BACK ROW
HUH? ISN'T THIS, LIKE, TOO GOOD TO BE TRUE?

LUCKY

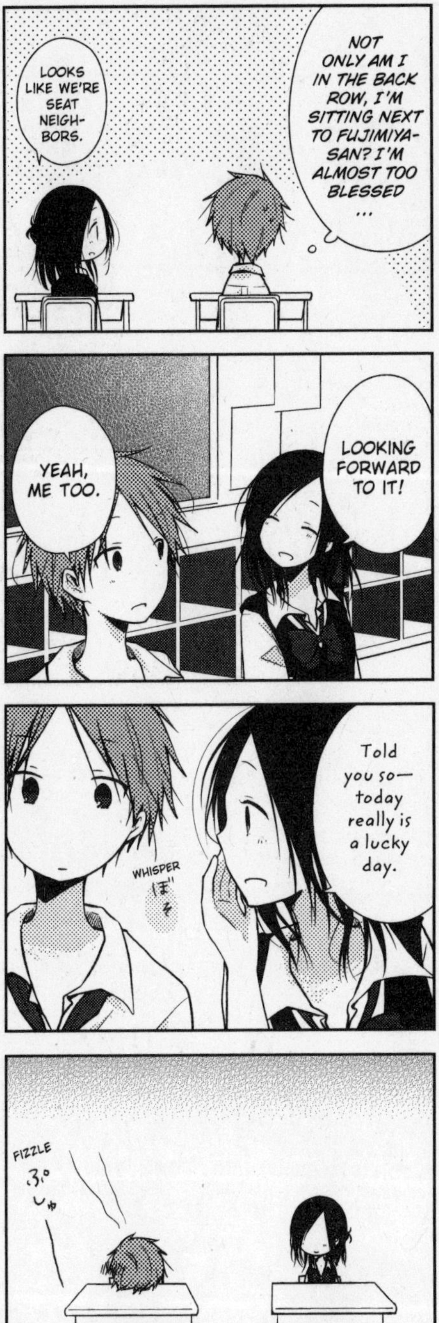
NOT ONLY AM I IN THE BACK ROW, I'M SITTING NEXT TO FUJIMIYA-SAN? I'M ALMOST TOO BLESSED ...
LOOKS LIKE WE'RE SEAT NEIGH-BORS.
LOOKING FORWARD TO IT!
YEAH, ME TOO.
Told you so— today really is a lucky day.
WHISPER
FIZZLE

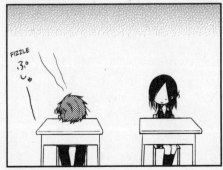

MY SEAT

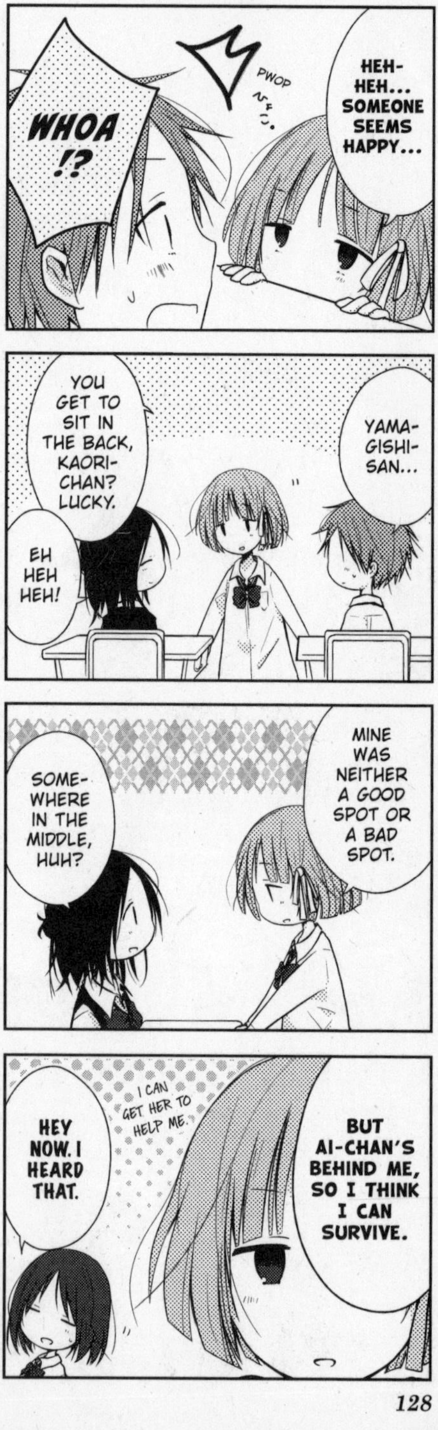
HEH-HEH... SOMEONE SEEMS HAPPY...
PWOP
WHOA!?
YAMA-GISHI-SAN...
YOU GET TO SIT IN THE BACK, KAORI-CHAN? LUCKY.
EH HEH HEH!
MINE WAS NEITHER A GOOD SPOT OR A BAD SPOT.
SOME-WHERE IN THE MIDDLE, HUH?
BUT AI-CHAN'S BEHIND ME, SO I THINK I CAN SURVIVE.
I CAN GET HER TO HELP ME.
HEY NOW. I HEARD THAT.

WITH A STRAIGHT FACE

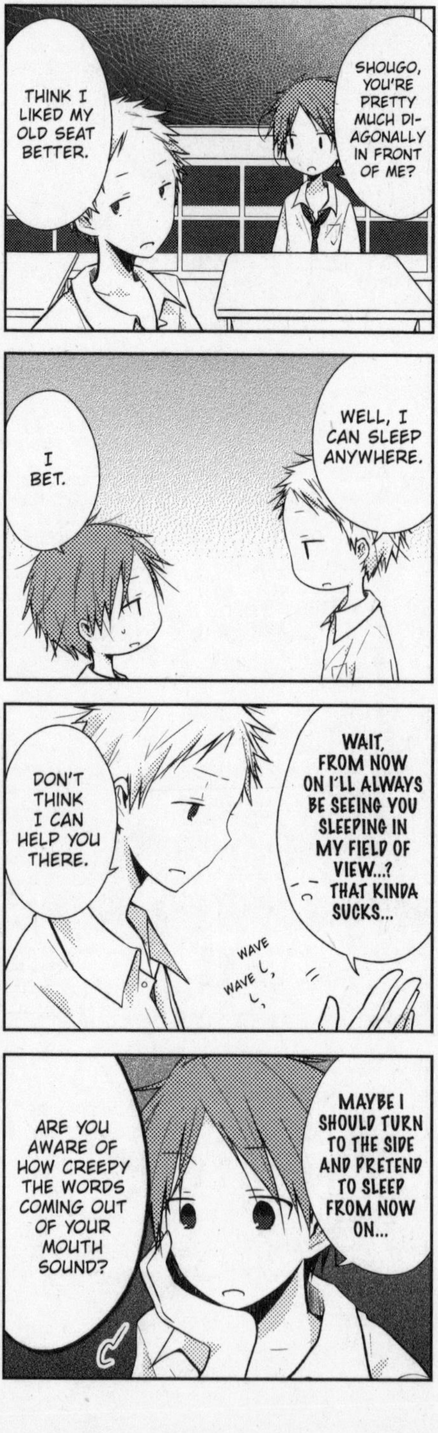
SHOUGO, YOU'RE PRETTY MUCH DI-AGONALLY IN FRONT OF ME?
THINK I LIKED MY OLD SEAT BETTER.
WELL, I CAN SLEEP ANYWHERE.
I BET.
WAIT, FROM NOW ON I'LL ALWAYS BE SEEING YOU SLEEPING IN MY FIELD OF VIEW...? THAT KINDA SUCKS...
WAVE WAVE
DON'T THINK I CAN HELP YOU THERE.
MAYBE I SHOULD TURN TO THE SIDE AND PRETEND TO SLEEP FROM NOW ON...
ARE YOU AWARE OF HOW CREEPY THE WORDS COMING OUT OF YOUR MOUTH SOUND?

HONEST PERSON

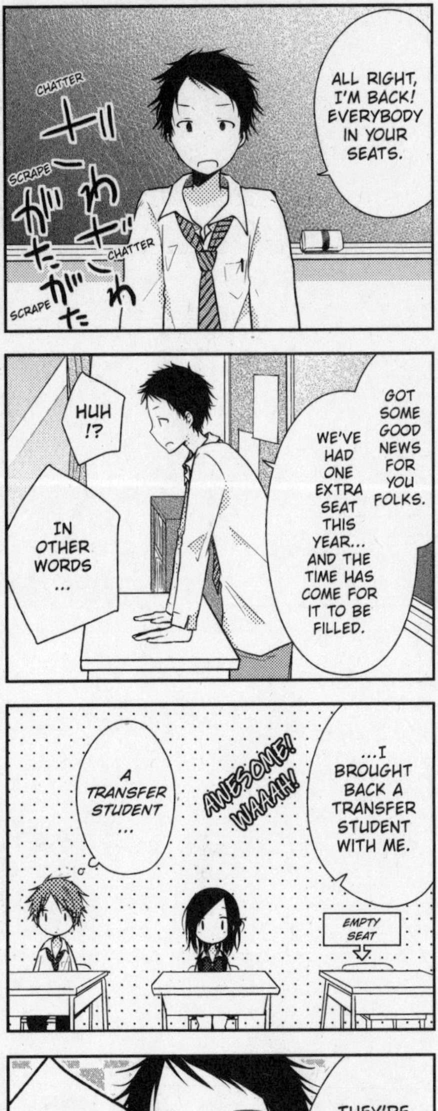
ALL RIGHT, I'M BACK! EVERYBODY IN YOUR SEATS.
CHATTER
SCRAPE
CHATTER
SCRAPE
GOT SOME GOOD NEWS FOR YOU FOLKS.
WE'VE HAD ONE EXTRA SEAT THIS YEAR... AND THE TIME HAS COME FOR IT TO BE FILLED.
HUH!?
IN OTHER WORDS...
...I BROUGHT BACK A TRANSFER STUDENT WITH ME.
AWESOME! WAAAH!
A TRANSFER STUDENT...
EMPTY SEAT
THEY'RE NOT MY FAVORITE KIND OF PERSON, BUT I WANT YOU GUYS TO BE NICE TO THEM.
UM, SENSEI, I DON'T THINK YOU SHOULD SAY THINGS LIKE THAT!

TRANSFER STUDENT

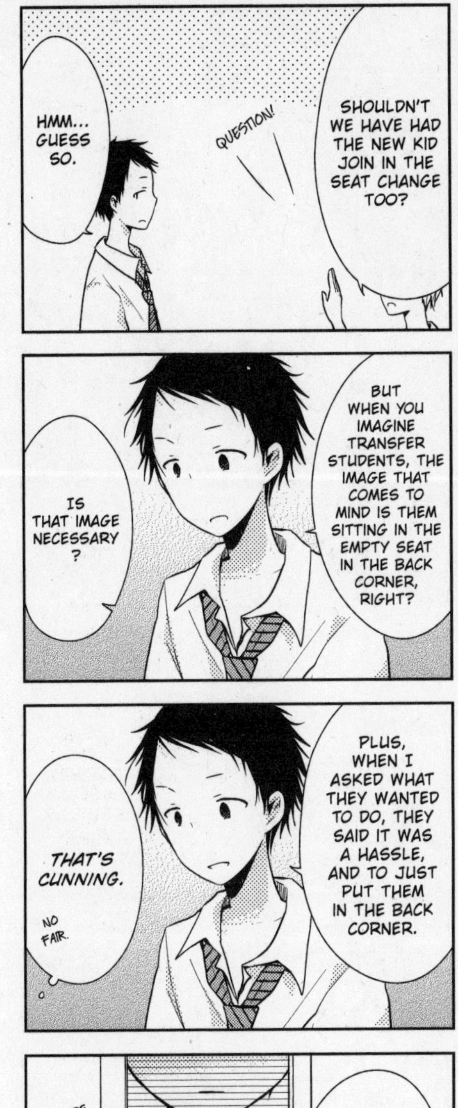
SHOULDN'T WE HAVE HAD THE NEW KID JOIN IN THE SEAT CHANGE TOO?
QUESTION!
HMM... GUESS SO.
BUT WHEN YOU IMAGINE TRANSFER STUDENTS, THE IMAGE THAT COMES TO MIND IS THEM SITTING IN THE EMPTY SEAT IN THE BACK CORNER, RIGHT?
IS THAT IMAGE NECESSARY?
PLUS, WHEN I ASKED WHAT THEY WANTED TO DO, THEY SAID IT WAS A HASSLE, AND TO JUST PUT THEM IN THE BACK CORNER.
THAT'S CUNNING.
NO FAIR.
NOW THAT I'VE FINISHED MY SPIEL... C'MON IN.
SLIDE

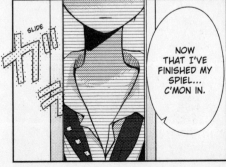

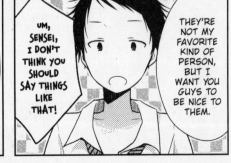

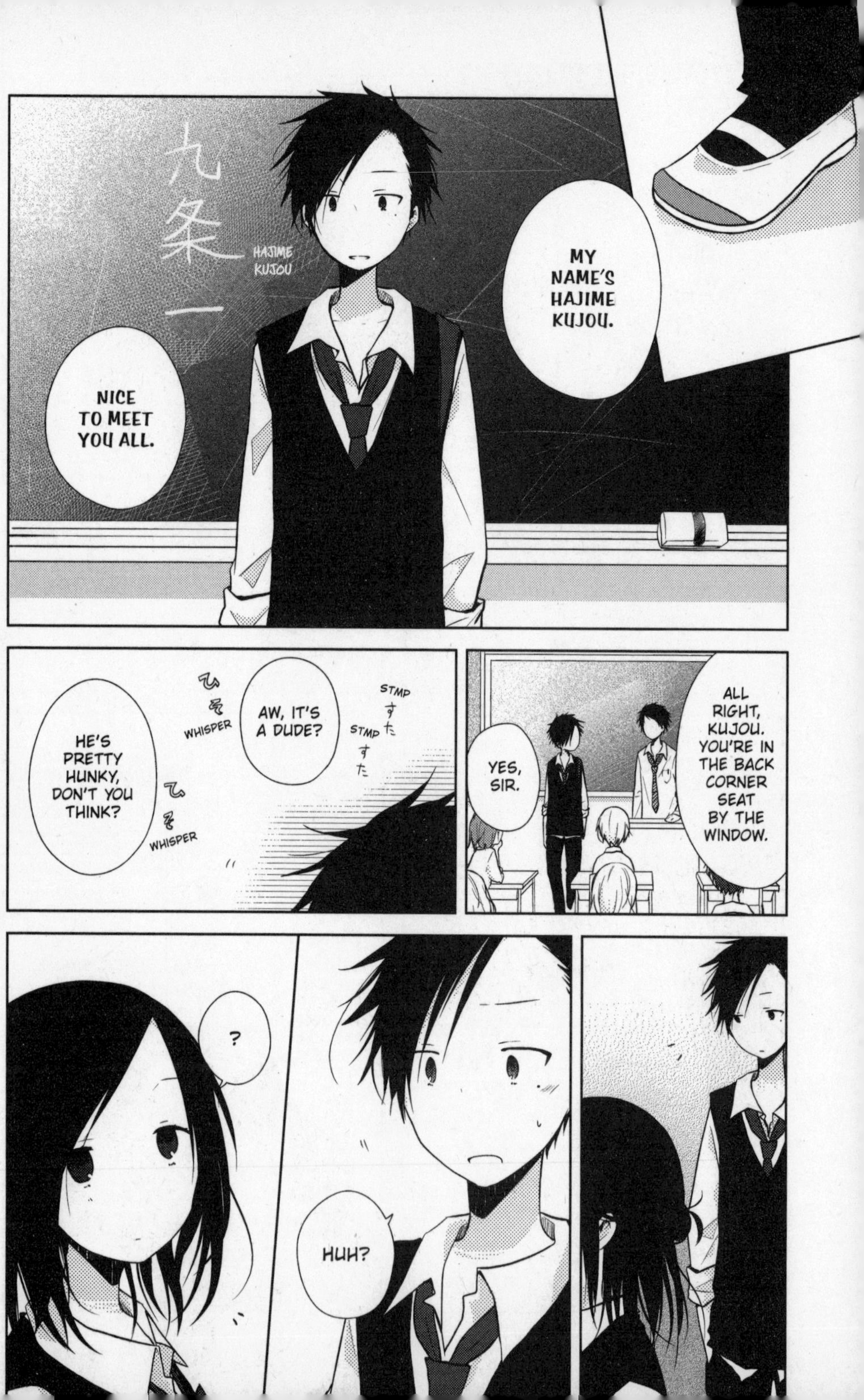
九条一
HAJIME KUJOU
MY NAME'S HAJIME KUJOU.
NICE TO MEET YOU ALL.
ALL RIGHT, KUJOU. YOU'RE IN THE BACK CORNER SEAT BY THE WINDOW.
YES, SIR.
STMP すた
STMP すた
AW, IT'S A DUDE?
ひそ WHISPER
HE'S PRETTY HUNKY, DON'T YOU THINK?
ひそ WHISPER
HUH?
?

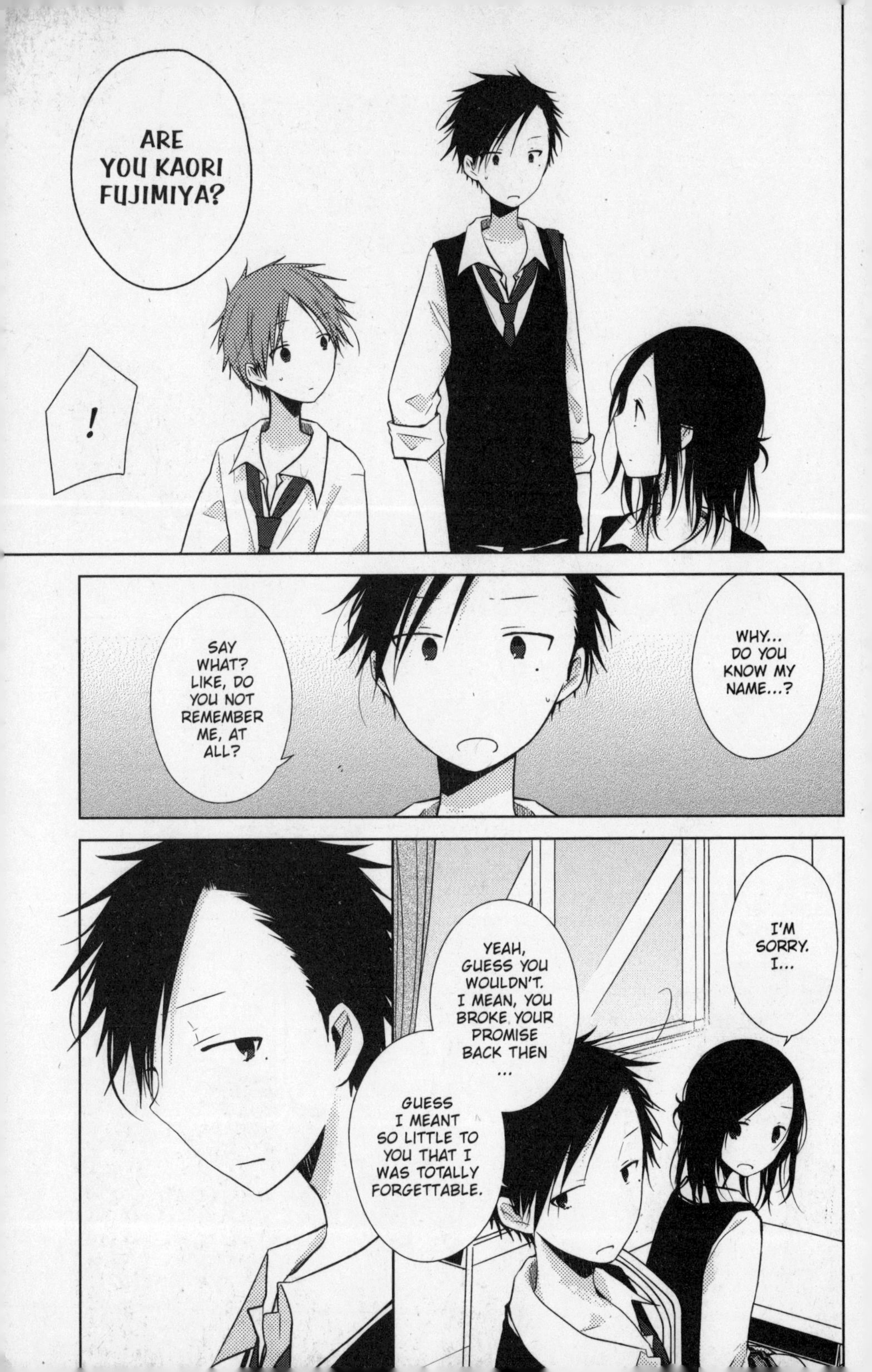
ARE YOU KAORI FUJIMIYA?
!
WHY... DO YOU KNOW MY NAME...?
SAY WHAT? LIKE, DO YOU NOT REMEMBER ME, AT ALL?
I'M SORRY. I...
YEAH, GUESS YOU WOULDN'T. I MEAN, YOU BROKE YOUR PROMISE BACK THEN ...
GUESS I MEANT SO LITTLE TO YOU THAT I WAS TOTALLY FORGETTABLE.

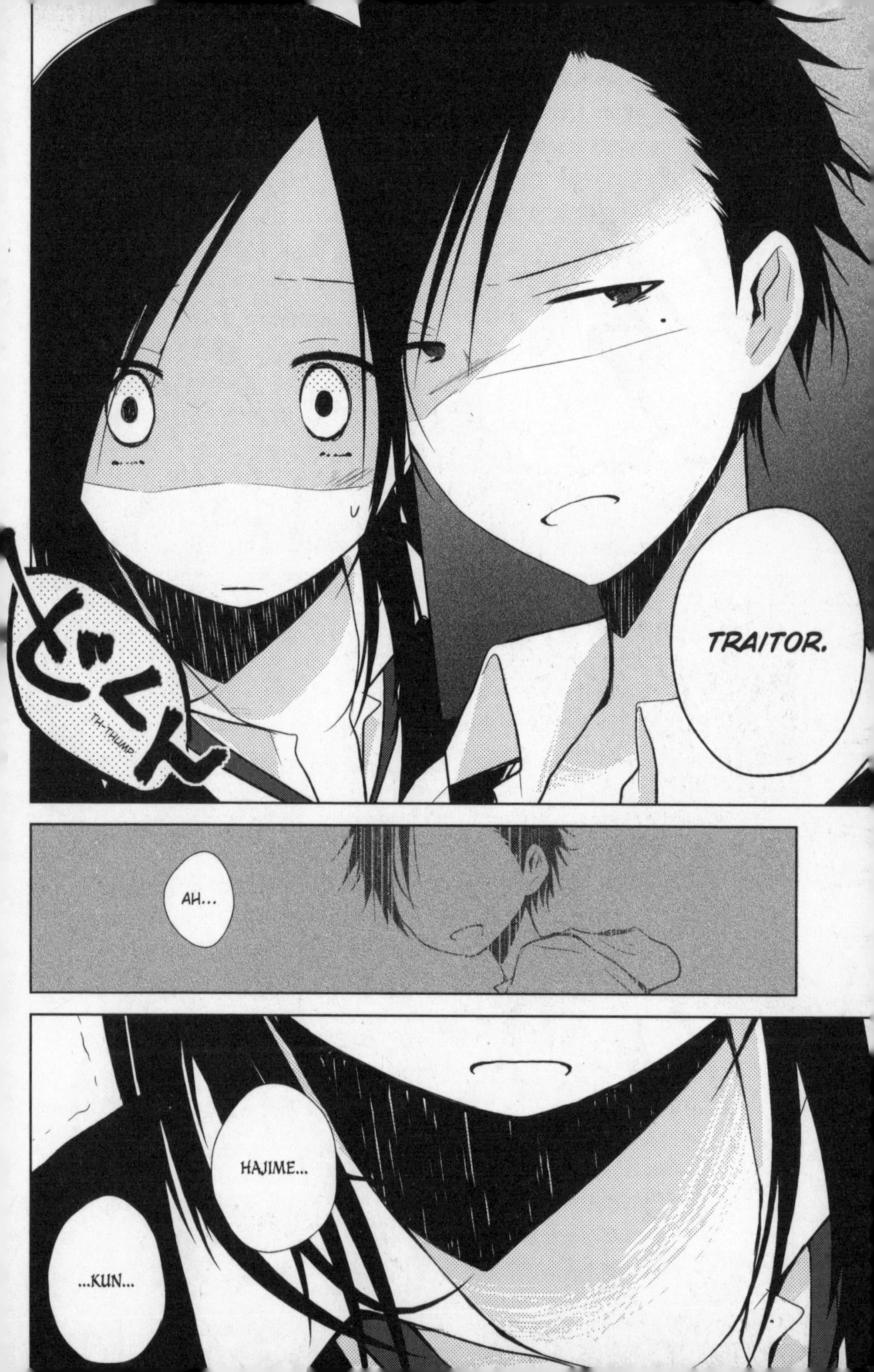
TRAITOR.
TH-THUMP
AH...
HAJIME...
...KUN...

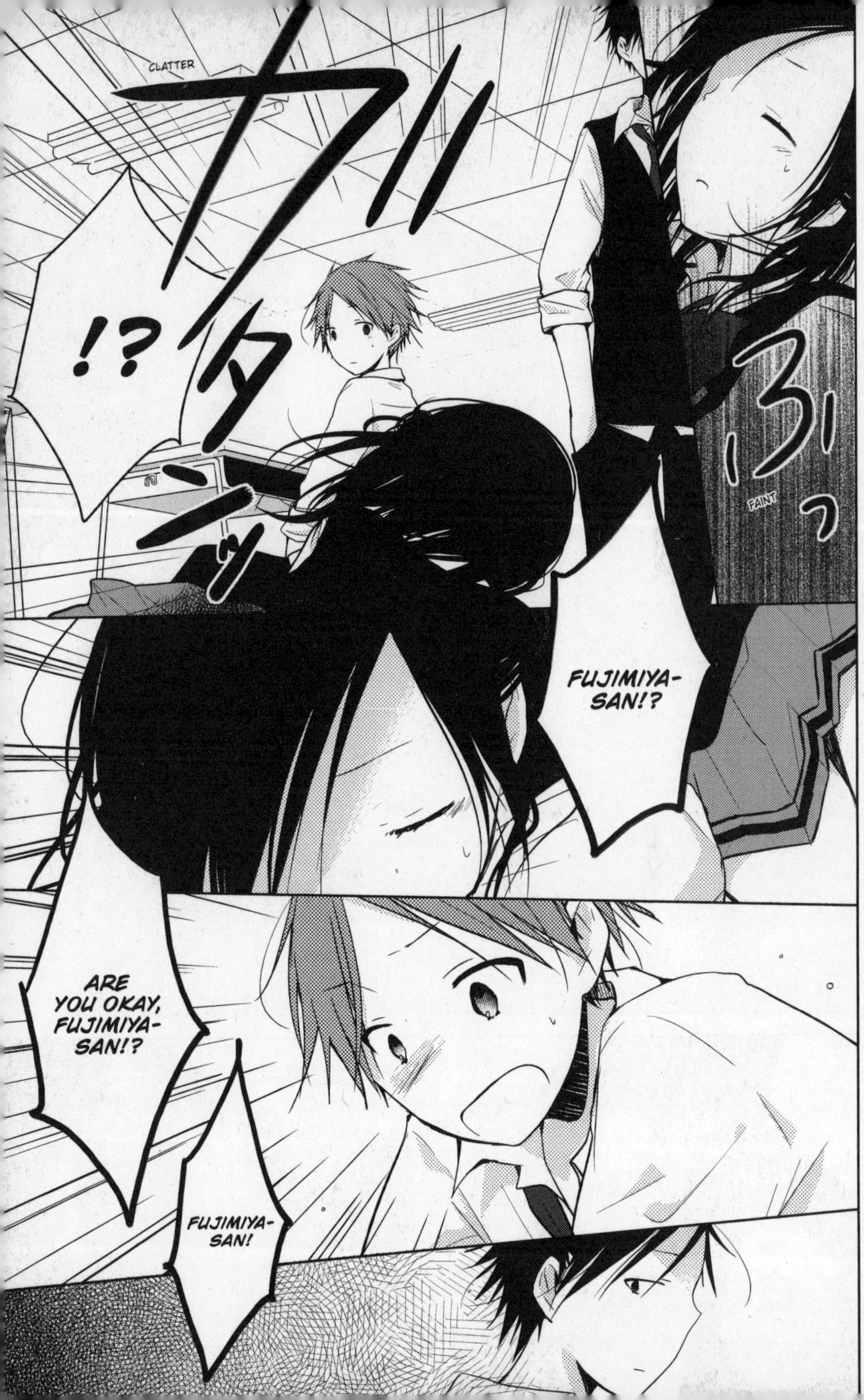
FAINT
CLATTER
!?
FUJIMIYA-SAN!?
ARE YOU OKAY, FUJIMIYA-SAN!?
FUJIMIYA-SAN!

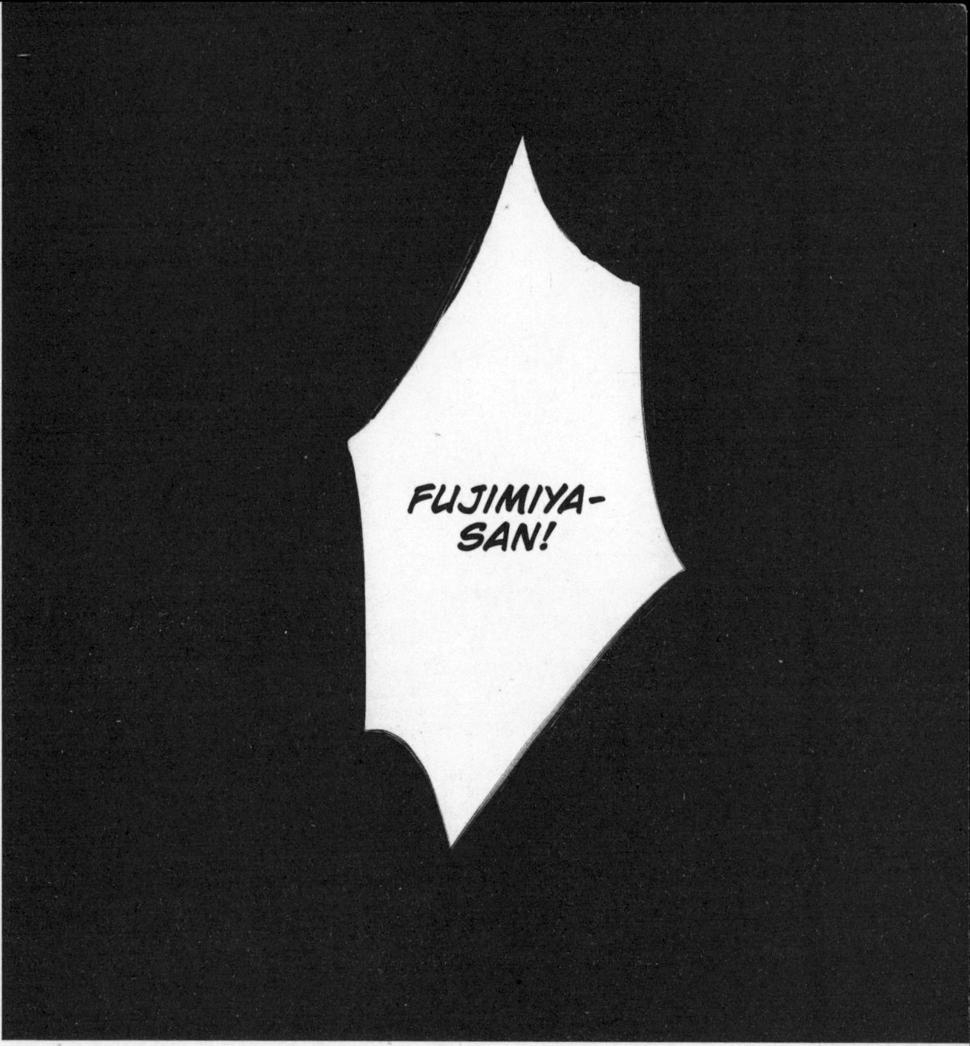
FUJIMIYA-SAN!

SIGN: NURSE

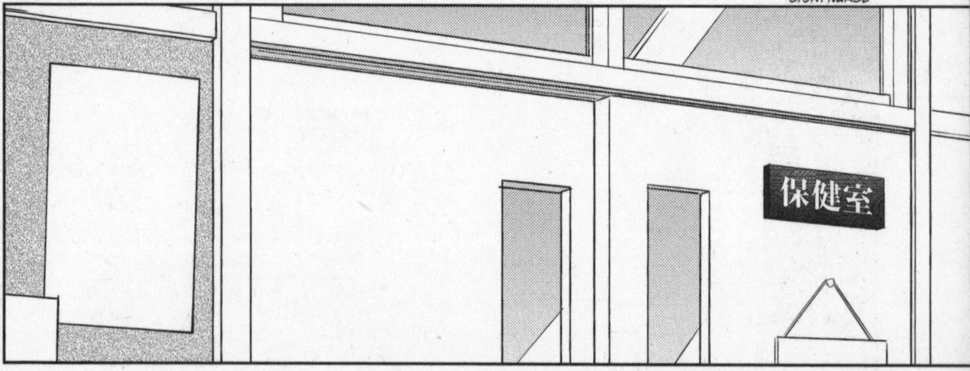
保健室

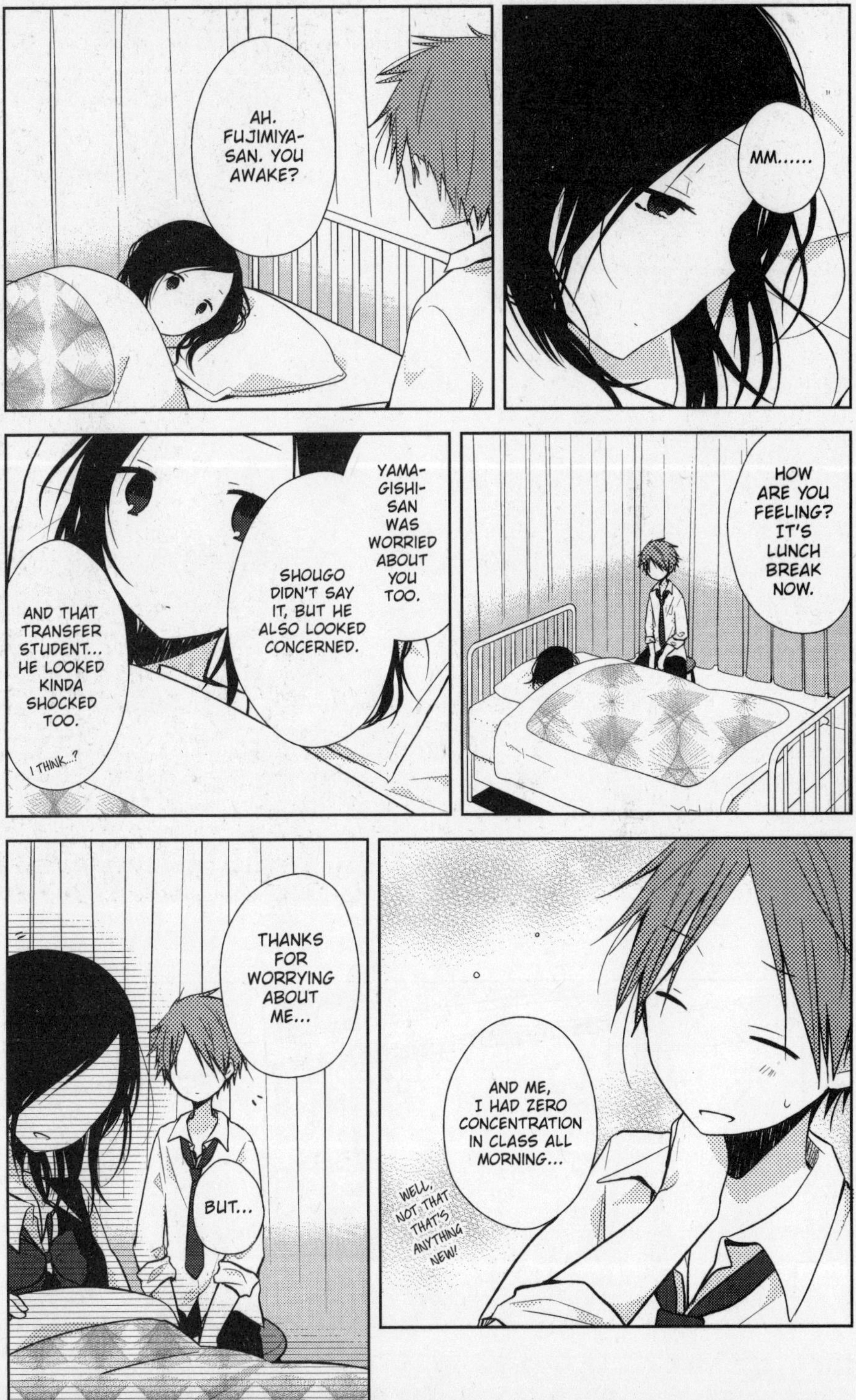
MM......
AH. FUJIMIYA-SAN. YOU AWAKE?
HOW ARE YOU FEELING? IT'S LUNCH BREAK NOW.
YAMA-GISHI-SAN WAS WORRIED ABOUT YOU TOO.
SHOUGO DIDN'T SAY IT, BUT HE ALSO LOOKED CONCERNED.
AND THAT TRANSFER STUDENT... HE LOOKED KINDA SHOCKED TOO.
I THINK...?
AND ME, I HAD ZERO CONCENTRATION IN CLASS ALL MORNING...
WELL, NOT THAT THAT'S ANYTHING NEW!
THANKS FOR WORRYING ABOUT ME...
BUT...

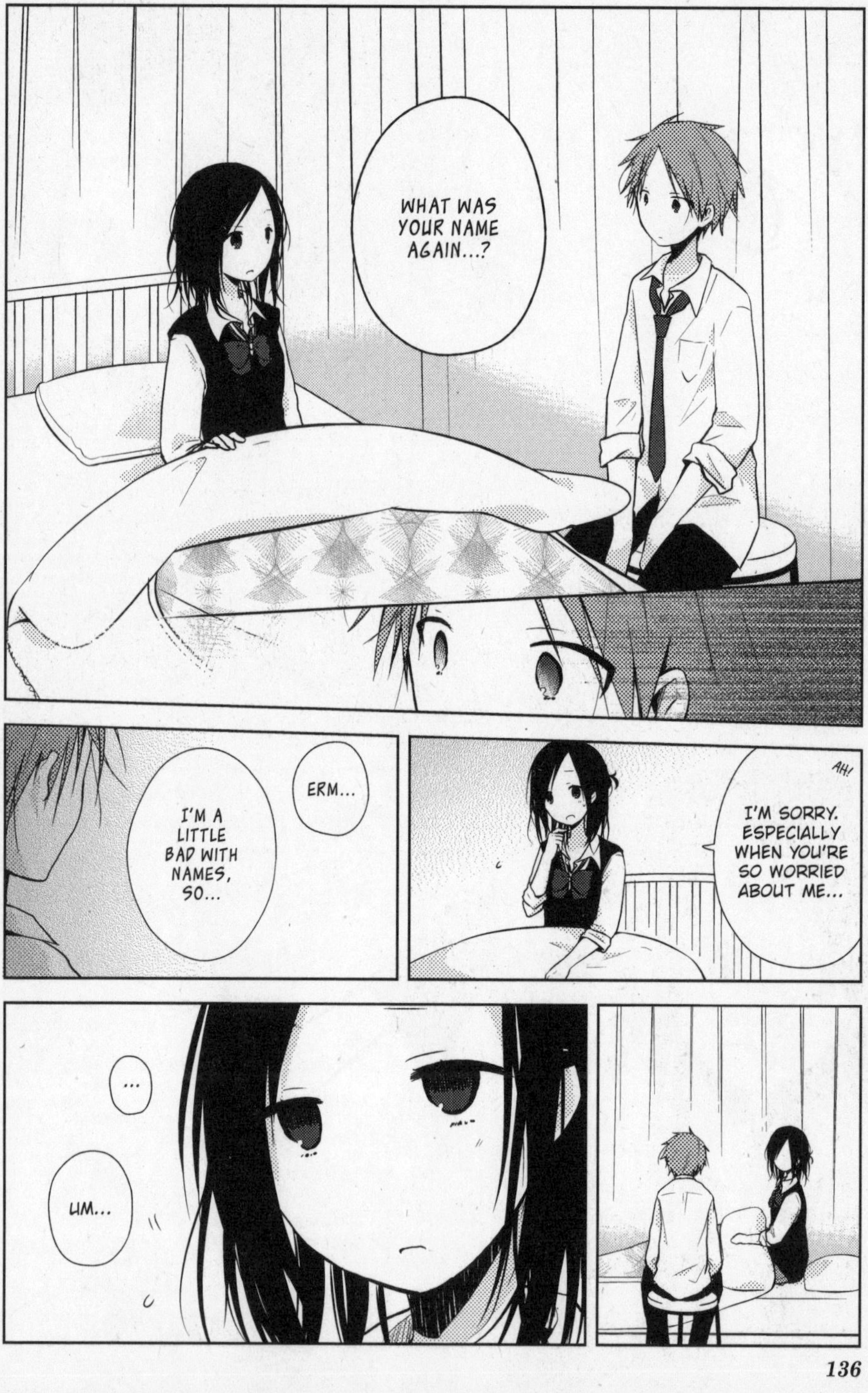
WHAT WAS YOUR NAME AGAIN...?
AH!
I'M SORRY. ESPECIALLY WHEN YOU'RE SO WORRIED ABOUT ME...
ERM...
I'M A LITTLE BAD WITH NAMES, SO...
...
UM...

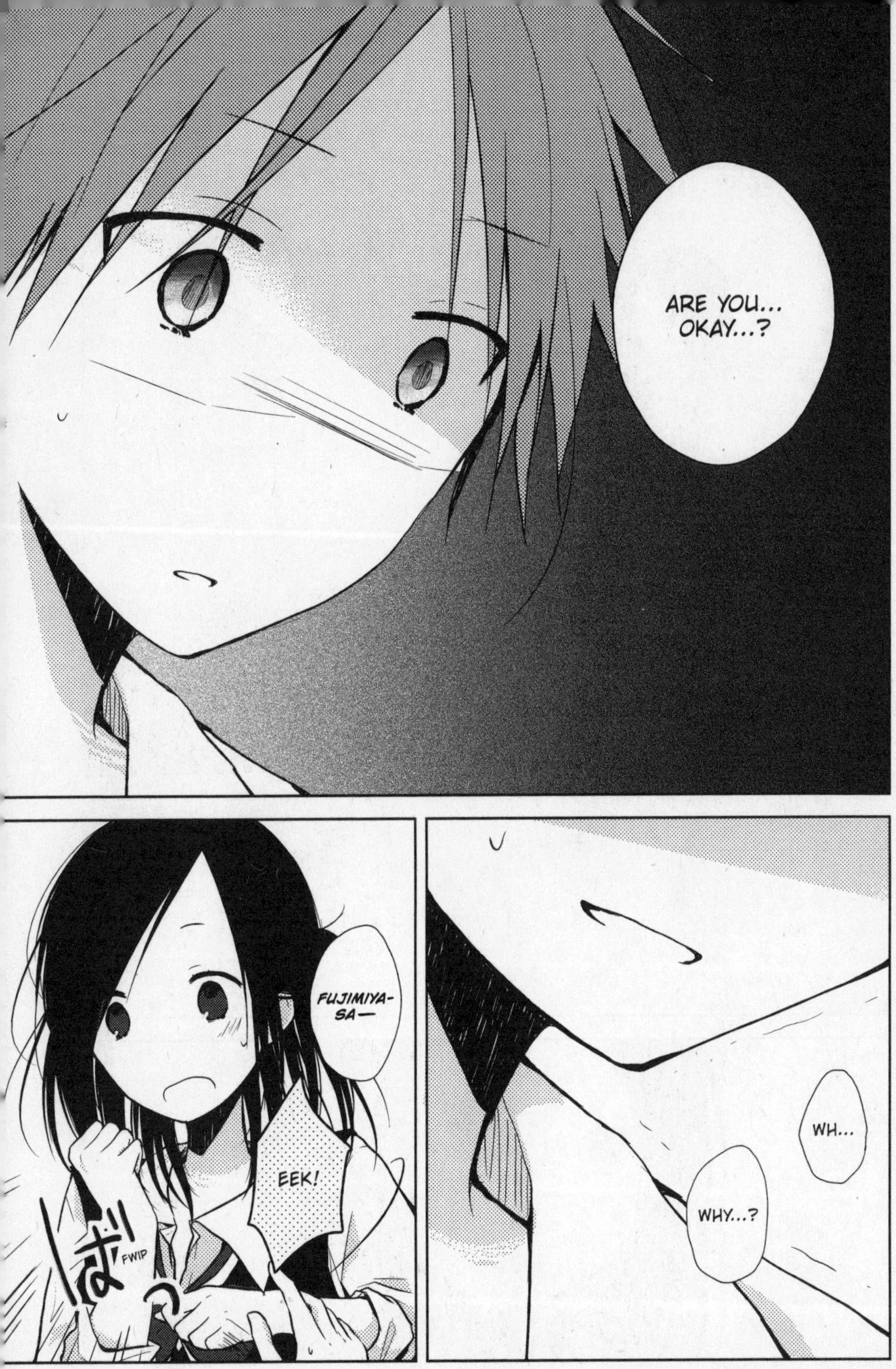
ARE YOU... OKAY...?
WH...
WHY...?
FUJIMIYA-SA—
EEK!
FWIP

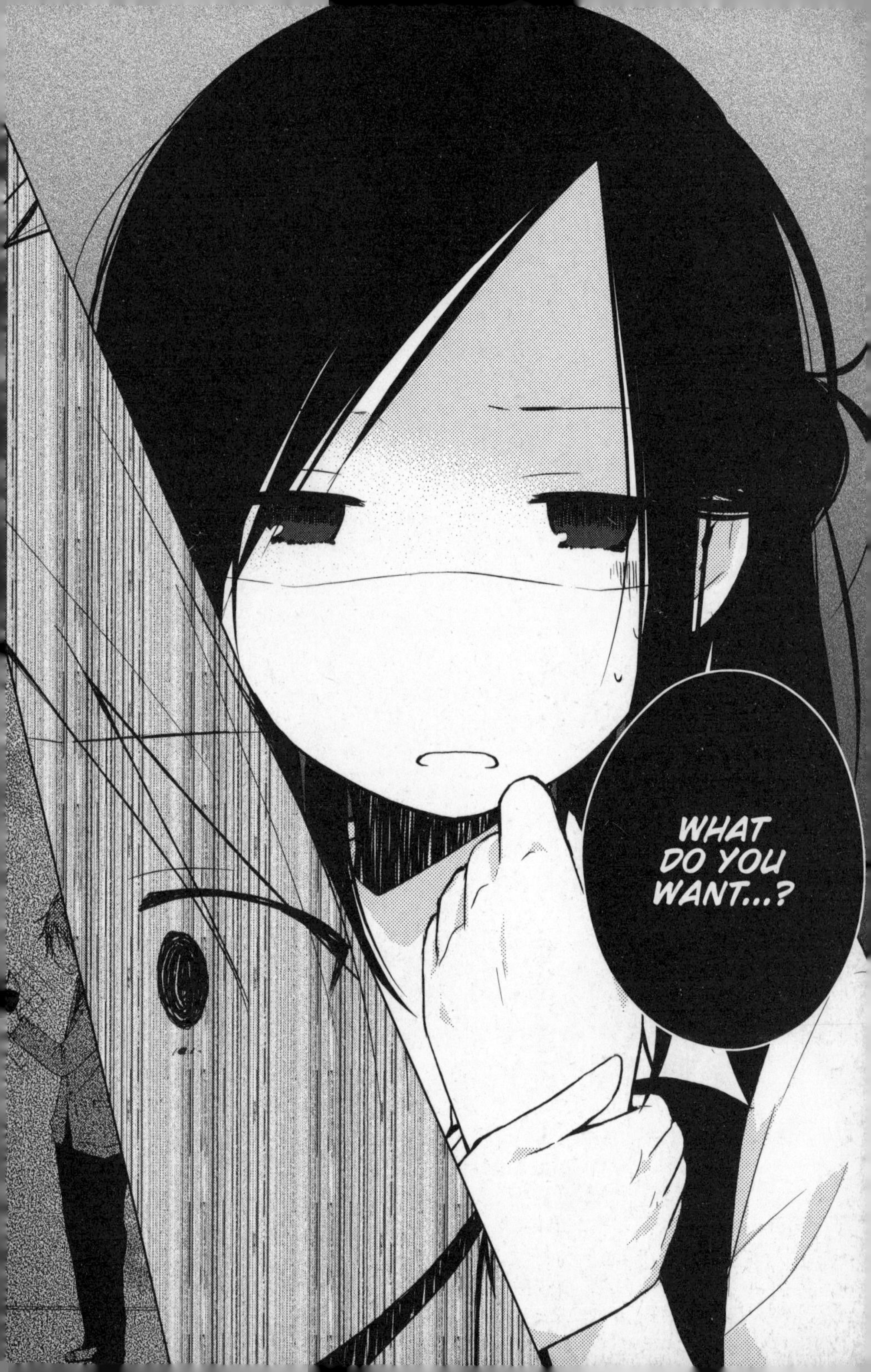
WHAT DO YOU WANT...?

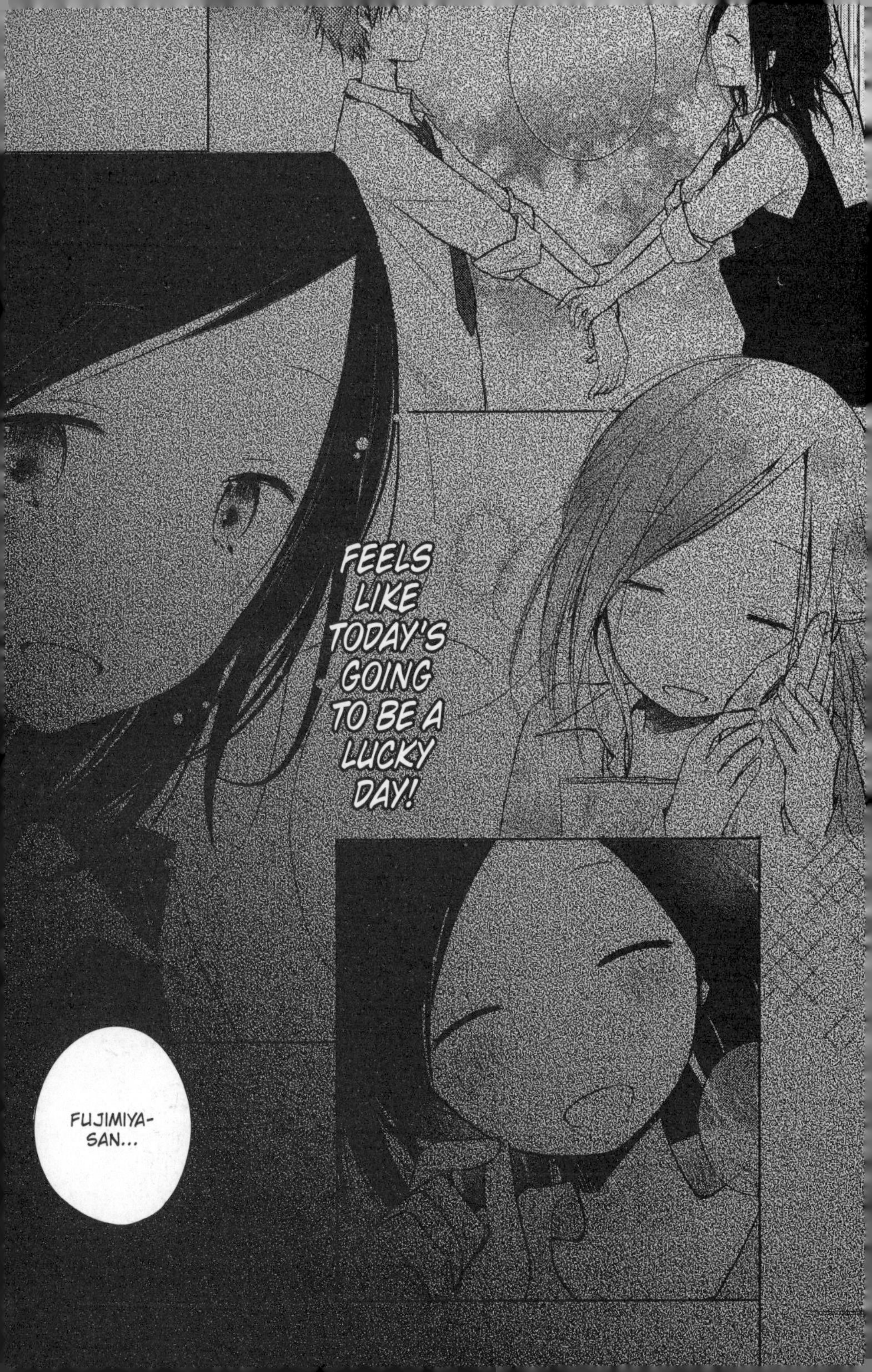
FEELS LIKE TODAY'S GOING TO BE A LUCKY DAY!
FUJIMIYA-SAN...

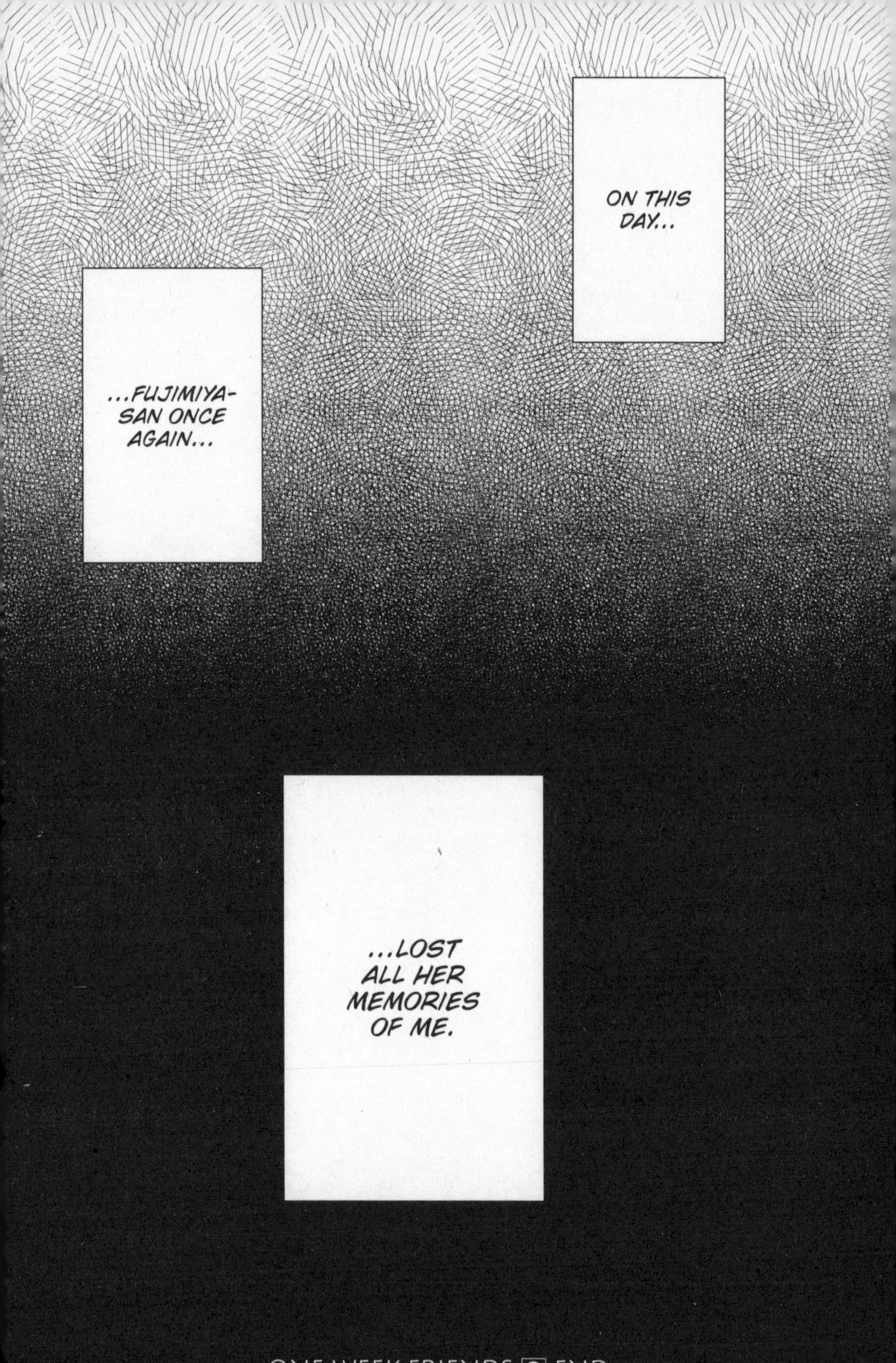
ON THIS DAY...
...FUJIMIYA-SAN ONCE AGAIN...
...LOST ALL HER MEMORIES OF ME.

ONE WEEK FRIENDS 3 END

TRANSLATION NOTES

COMMON HONORIFICS
No honorific: Indicates familiarity or closeness; if used without permission or reason, addressing someone in this manner would constitute an insult.
-san: The Japanese equivalent of Mr./Mrs./Miss. If a situation calls for politeness, this is the fail-safe honorific.
-kun: Used most often when referring to boys, this indicates affection or familiarity. Occasionally used by older men among their peers, but it may also be used by anyone referring to a person of lower standing.
-chan: An affectionate honorific indicating familiarity used mostly in reference to girls; also used in reference to cute persons or animals of either gender.
-sensei: A respectful term for teachers, artists, or high-level professionals.

nee: Japanese equivalent to "older sis."

nii: Japanese equivalent to "older bro."

PAGE 6
In Japan and other Asian countries, there's a superstition that **sneezing** means someone else is talking behind your back.

PAGE 47
In schools in Japan, spring break is the vacation between grade years, while **summer break** is the vacation between first term and second term.

PAGE 51
Izu Peninsula is a popular resort area. It's about one hundred kilometers away from Tokyo, where Kaori and friends live.

ONE
WEEK
FRIENDS

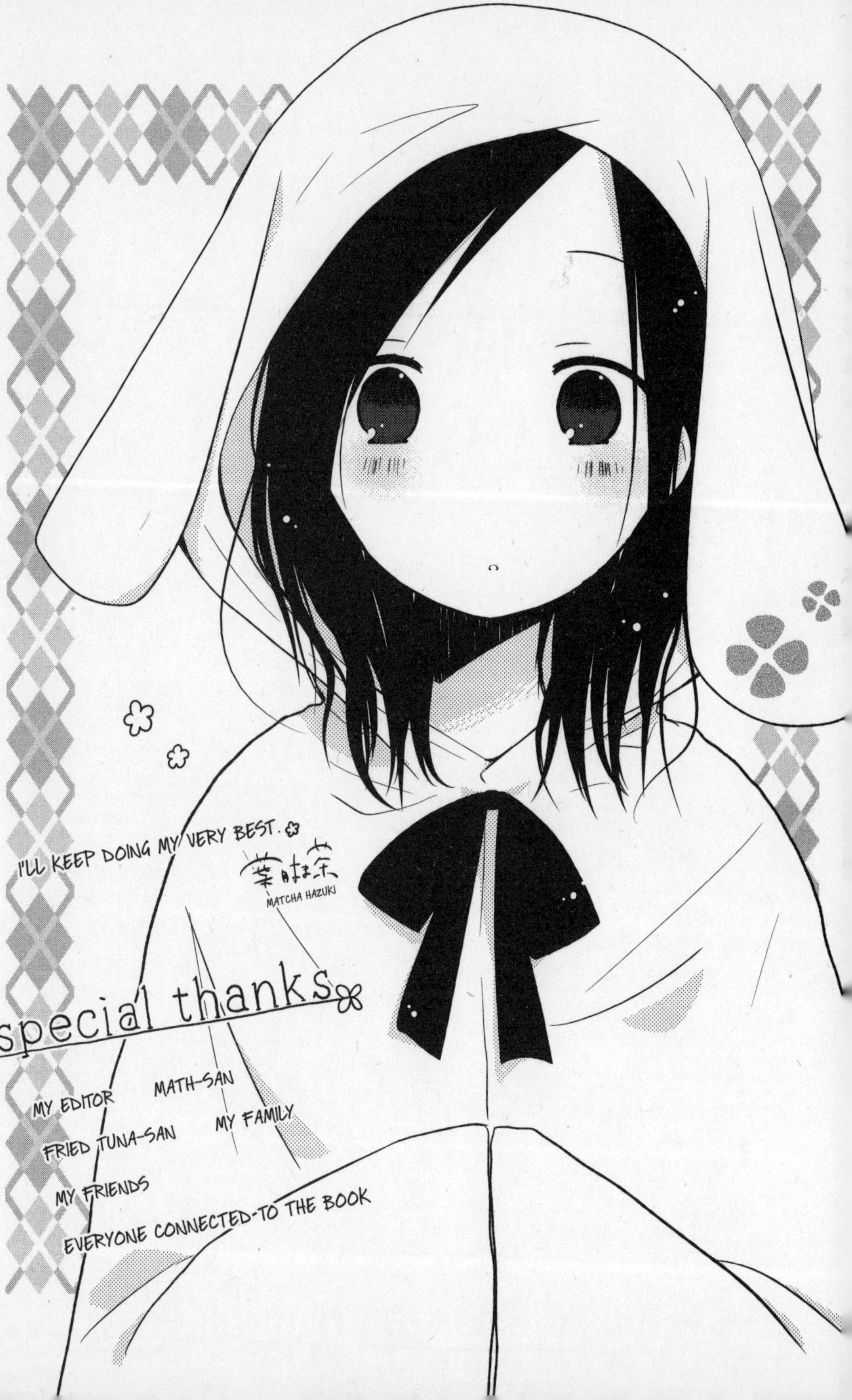
I'LL KEEP DOING MY VERY BEST.
MATCHA HAZUKI
special thanks
MY EDITOR
MATH-SAN
FRIED TUNA-SAN
MY FAMILY
MY FRIENDS
EVERYONE CONNECTED TO THE BOOK

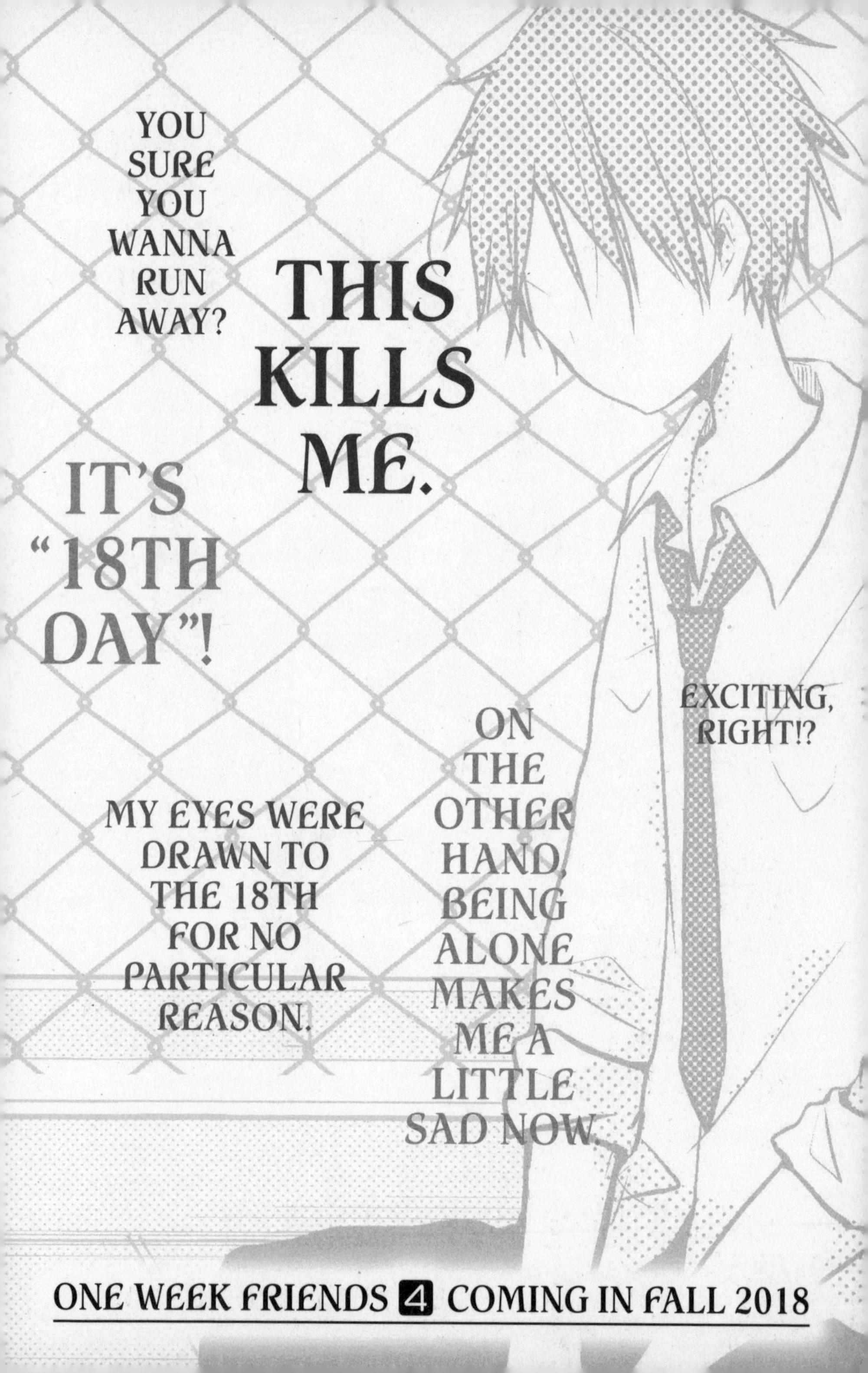
THIS KILLS ME.
YOU SURE YOU WANNA RUN AWAY?
IT'S "18TH DAY"!
EXCITING, RIGHT!?
ON THE OTHER HAND, BEING ALONE MAKES ME A LITTLE SAD NOW.
MY EYES WERE DRAWN TO THE 18TH FOR NO PARTICULAR REASON.
ONE WEEK FRIENDS 4 COMING IN FALL 2018

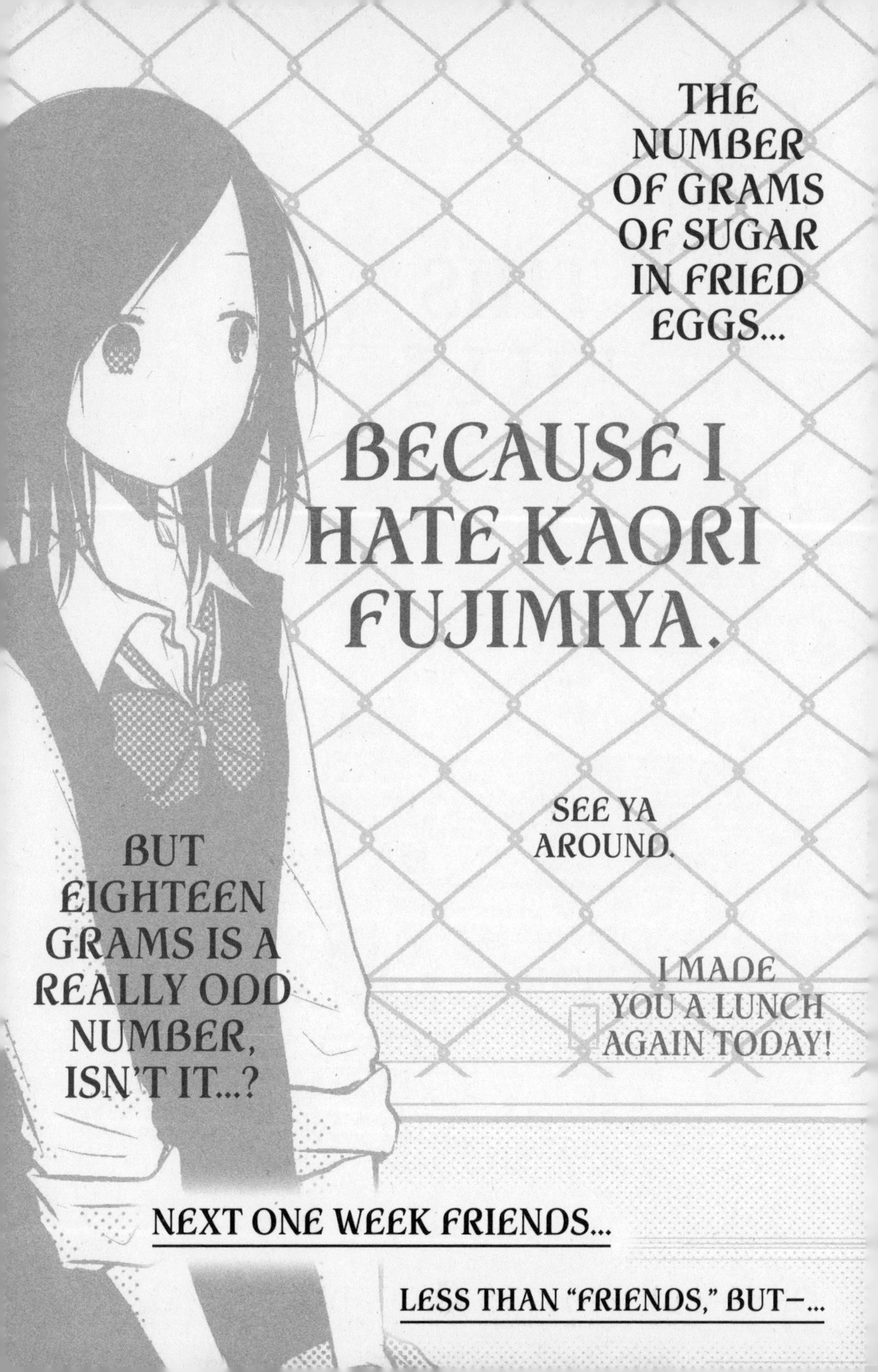
THE NUMBER OF GRAMS OF SUGAR IN FRIED EGGS...
BECAUSE I HATE KAORI FUJIMIYA.
SEE YA AROUND.
BUT EIGHTEEN GRAMS IS A REALLY ODD NUMBER, ISN'T IT...?
I MADE YOU A LUNCH AGAIN TODAY!
NEXT ONE WEEK FRIENDS...
LESS THAN "FRIENDS," BUT—...

ONE WEEK FRIENDS 3

MATCHA HAZUKI

Translation/Adaptation: Amanda Haley

Lettering: Bianca Pistillo

ONE WEEK FRIENDS Volume 3 ©2013 Matcha Hazuki/
SQUARE ENIX CO., LTD. First published in Japan in 2013 by SQUARE ENIX CO., LTD. English translation rights arranged with SQUARE ENIX CO., LTD. and Yen Press, LLC through Tuttle-Mori Agency, Inc.

English translation © 2018 by SQUARE ENIX CO., LTD.

Yen Press
1290 Avenue of the Americas
New York, NY 10104

Visit us at yenpress.com
facebook.com/yenpress
twitter.com/yenpress
yenpress.tumblr.com
instagram.com/yenpress

First Yen Press Edition: June 2018

Yen Press is an imprint of Yen Press, LLC.
The Yen Press name and logo are trademarks of Yen Press, LLC.

The publisher is not responsible for websites (or their content) that are not owned by the publisher.

Library of Congress Control Number: 2017954140

ISBNs: 978-0-316-44739-3 (paperback)
        978-0-316-44740-9 (ebook)

10 9 8 7 6 5 4 3 2 1

WOR

Printed in the United States of America